MAYHEM
ON THE DANUBE

A Novel by Robert Landori

authorHOUSE®

AuthorHouse™
1663 Liberty Drive
Bloomington, IN 47403
www.authorhouse.com
Phone: 1-800-839-8640

Published by AuthorHouse   01/30/2012

ISBN: 978-1-4685-4913-3 (sc)
ISBN: 978-1-4685-4912-6 (e)

Library of Congress Control Number: 2012901839

This book is dedicated to Susan, Keith, and Claire

To Hanley

My surprise mom.

Robert Camden

June 19/12

ACKNOWLEDGMENTS

This book's plot was inspired by Saddam Hussein and his incredibly dumb bluff about possessing Biological Weapons of Mass Destruction.

The idea of staging the action on the banks of the Danube belongs to Eva, the champion canoeist, who keeps her boats and oars in a lean-to next to a 52 foot storage container along the river.

Keith laboured hard at helping me retain my 'voice' and to keep the action flowing. He also ensured that I avoid redundancies, contradictions and circumlocutions in the story.

Sarah's wise advice kept me up-to-date on how the publishing industry was changing and, with it, the market for the propagation of the written word.

Alla patiently taught me the finer points of how to use a computer, thereby making it easier for me to write faster, more fluidly and better.

The dramatic cover – front and back – was created by Stuart Beckett, the well-known graphic designer for which I owe him my deepest appreciation.

And, of course, to all my friends and family, a big 'thank-you' for putting up with my temper tantrums.

This said, let me state clearly that I assume full responsibility for any and all shortcomings, errors and omissions in this work.

Montreal, February 15, 2012

MAYHEM ON THE DANUBE
CAST OF MAIN CHARACTERS

Jason MOSCOVITCH	a Canadian virologist
Amina DADAKNE	his secretary/assistant
Esad DELIC	his Bosnian partner
Robert LONSDALE	a CIA contract officer
Adys MARQUEZ	his companion
James MORTON	the CIA's Director of Counterterrorism
Klara MOSCOVITCH	Jason's mother
Roger SANDERS	her lover
Abel DRUSZA	a Director of the Hungarian State Property Agency
FRAKKOS	Lonsdale's driver/investigator
Zoltán HORVÁTH	a Budapest police Lieutenant
Thérèse LAPOINTE	the Canadian Consul in Budapest
Rezzah KHAMANI	an Iranian businessman living in Budapest
Milan JURIC	a Bosnian barge owner
Saif AL-ADEL	a member of Al Qaeda's Military Committee
Ali-Hassan AL-MAJID	Iraq's Minister of Industry a.k.a. "Chemical Ali"
Colonel Barzan HASSANI	AL-MAJID's right hand man

PREFACE

Colonel Barzan Hassani, Chemical Ali's right-hand man, resented the situation. He felt he was taking a risk for nothing.

Hassani's distant cousin and commander, President Saddam Hussein, had recently become deeply concerned about Iraq's position in the Middle East. Osama Bin Laden's emergence as an Islamic leader was a threat to Saddam's vision of himself as the man who would unite the Arab world. The success of the recent Al Qaeda major strike against the Great Satan, the destruction of the twin towers of the World Trade Center, had given a greater urgency to Saddam's need for a spectacular coup of his own, one that would again make him feared and respected.

To this end, he had asked his Minister of Industry, Ali Hassan Al Majid, otherwise known as Chemical Ali, to dispatch his best officer, Hassani, to meet with Bin Laden's representative in Cizre, one of the world's oldest cities. The purpose of the meeting was to negotiate the control of Arabia's chemical and biological warfare program and, most importantly, the acquisition of the latest Weapon of Mass Destruction, recently identified by agents of Al Qaeda.

Hence the need for Hassani to vist Cizre incognito. Located on the border between Turkey and Syria, about a hundred miles north of Mosul in Iraq, it was a convenient venue for a short, safe and stealthy meeting for Islamic supremacists.

Hassani, whose nickname was The Butcher, was not happy about attending. He had gassed thousands of people during the war between Iraq and the Kurds in 1988, and was reluctant to stick his neck in the noose by revisiting the scene of his crimes in an area where he was hated and feared.

However, Saddam wanted him to attend and Saddam's word was law.

Cizre's mayor was hosting the meeting because he could provide the security called for by the occasion. The town was in Kurdish-Turkey. Turkey was a member of NATO and NATO maintained a discrete electronic surveillance post just outside Cizre, manned by US Air Force military and 'technical' personnel.

Although those involved knew that the US would not pass up the opportunity to seize whomever they thought was of interest to them, the participants were not worried. The border with Syria lay literally five minutes away downriver and they had a speedboat standing by alongside the mayor's property.

The mayor's house, the most imposing residence in the town, was located on the Tigris River. Its garden, lush and cool, was a welcome oasis from the dust and heat in the street and the bone-dry environment of the quasi-desert some of his visitors had had to cross to meet face to face.

His guests did not really trust the mayor, but they were aware that he was a member of the PKK (the Kurdish independence movement) and forced to act with scrupulous impartiality. He had to remain on good terms with the competing factions in the area because nobody could foretell who would ultimately emerge as the supreme leader of the region.

"Then it is agreed," said the mayor and, with a flourish, poured what he hoped was the last cup of fragrant mint tea for each of his four guests, "that the kidnapping of the Canadian scientist will be coordinated by Al Qaeda's chief in Budapest, with whom I'll maintain continuous contact." He nodded to the visitor sitting opposite him who nodded back.

The others waited and said nothing.

The mayor was quick to correct his oversight. "Of course, I will keep in close touch with the rest of you too."

"How?"

"Via coded wireless messages, Colonel Hassani."

"Back and forth? That's too cumbersome and slow." Hassani was not happy.

"But safe—for all of us." This from the Al Qaedda representative.

The two other guests said nothing.

Exhausted, the mayor was glad to say good-by to his guests just after sunset. He had spent most of the day cunningly defending the interests of his own people in complex negotiations with these representatives of the wider Muslim world, a world divided into God knows how many ever-changing combinations of factions; the Shia and the Sunni, the Iraqis and the Iranians, the Jordanians and the Palestinians, Fatah and Hamas, the Pakistanis and the Afghanis, not to mention the Wahabi.

The list was endless and so were the permutations and combinations!

* * *

CHAPTER 1

Jason Moscovitch was having a wonderful dream.

On his way to the podium to accept the Nobel Prize for Virology, he acknowledged the thunderous applause that greeted him with an elegant wave of his hand. He glanced skyward to catch a glimpse of the jetfighters screaming overhead in his honor . . . and awoke with a start in his Budapest apartment on *Széchenyi* Street to the insistent, high-pitched buzzing of the front door telephone.

Cursing, he struggled into his dressing gown and padded to the foyer. "Who is it?" he croaked into the mouthpiece, incensed. Once again, some drunk must have picked *his* bell's button to push, forcing him from the comfort of his warm bed at two a.m. on a Sunday morning.

"It's Amina. I need to see you right away." His secretary, and lover when she felt like it, sounded agitated. "Open the door. It's urgent . . ."

He buzzed her in, unlatched the apartment door and headed for the bathroom where she joined him a couple of minutes later, out of breath, and disheveled from running up three flights of stairs. "Get dressed and come with me," she panted. "Don't ask questions. My car's downstairs. We'll talk on our way to the lab."

The word 'lab' did it for Moscovitch. Fearing the worst, he threw on some clothes, grabbed his special flashlight and rushed after Amina who was already halfway down the stairs.

"I was at the Nadasi Tavern around the corner," she explained as she piloted her Suzuki Swift 1000 through the deserted streets of the Hungarian capital at top speed, "and got involved with a couple of Iraqis, recent arrivals from Baghdad".

"I thought they were not supposed to leave their compound . . ."

"Don't interrupt. As I said, I got involved with these two—I'm sure you know what I mean." She gave Moscovitch a sideways glance and watched him pretend that he was not feeling jealous. Tall, with flashing dark eyes and a body that wouldn't quit, his secretary was a fabulous looking woman, exuding sex appeal.

"They were competing fiercely for the honor of seeing me home when this third guy appeared out of nowhere. He began to speak very softly in Arabic and never suspected that I would hear him or understand. He thought I was Italian." She swerved to avoid one of the many potholes that dotted *Nádor* Street and paused to catch her breath. Then she made a few neat maneuvers, at times sliding sideways on the road slick with rain until she hit one of the main thoroughfares, *Rákóczi* Boulevard.

"What's all this got to do with me?" Moscovitch didn't follow.

"The third man who seemed to be their boss wanted my two guys to help him drill the safe of a pharmaceutical company so they could steal some vaccine samples."

Jason Moscovitch felt as if an icy hand were reaching for his heart. He gulped and moistened his lips. "Did they mention the name of the company?"

"No, but one of them asked if I knew where *Zászló* Street was."

The twenty-nine-year old Moscovitch gagged. He was the Managing Director and Chief Scientific Officer of Phylaxos Pharmaceuticals, a company of which he owned a third. Fifteen per cent belonged jointly to the Hungarian Government and Moscovitch's working partner, Esad Delic, an Iraq-trained virologist. The rest was the property of a Japanese conglomerate.

Phylaxos had just submitted a patent application for an experimental vaccine against a new variety of Creutzfeldt-Jakob (human Mad Cow) disease. The new virus was highly contagious and invariably fatal, a new plague, easily turned into a means of mass destruction.

As long as no protection existed against nv.C-JD, no one dared to think of converting it into a weapon, but Moscovitch's preliminary discovery was about to change the rules. Those possessing the vaccine could declare open season with impunity on those who did not.

It had taken Moscovitch two years to produce a dozen test tubes of his discovery as seed stock for testing on humans. Some of these 'samples' were now in Phylaxos' built-in vault at the company's laboratory *on Zászló Street for God's sake. A*lthough the vault had two combination locks that needed to be operated in unison, its door was almost a hundred years old, and drillable.

"Were these guys still at Nadasi's when you left?"

Amina nodded as she watched the imposing building of the Eastern Railway Terminal flash by.

"We must get the samples to somewhere safe," Moscovitch insisted. "We can open the vault because you know the combination of the lower lock."

"So do others."

"But I'm the only one who knows the one for the lock on top. You think we have the time?"

"The men were going to be picked up by their leader at three."

Moscovitch glanced at his watch, then out the window. They were crossing the wide expanse of *Mexikói* Boulevard. "It's a quarter to and we're almost there. Ten minutes to open the vault and another ten to get away. We might or might not make it. Why don't we just call the police?"

"Because by the time they get their shit together it would be too late." Amina had seen the Budapest police at work. "They'd never send a patrol car unless a burglary was actually in progress and for sure not on the strength of a conversation overhead in a bar."

The Phylaxos laboratory was in the *Zugló*, a district of Budapest in which modestly priced residences alternated with buildings housing fair-sized industries.

Entrance to the complex was through a tall steel door for cars and trucks with a smaller entrance cut into it for pedestrians. Amina parked nearby and followed Moscovitch who unlocked the pedestrian access then stood aside for Amina to enter. In seconds they were in the company's third floor lab. Squeezing past the centrifuge and the fermenting vat, they raced along the equipment-laden tables to Moscovitch's corner office.

The scientist shone his flashlight's beam on the locks while first Amina then he, their fingers slippery with sweat, twirled the knobs, until they managed to open the vault door on their third try.

"I have to pee, I'm bursting," Amina said, making a face. "Don't forget to relock the vault door when you're done." She headed for the corridor.

Moscovitch entered the vault, turned on the light and, with a key hanging from a platinum chain around his neck, opened one of the ten steel drawers fitted into the left wall. He extracted a brown leather cigar case containing four vaccine-filled test tubes and clipped the special flashlight he had brought with him to the case.

He looked around for Amina then shut the vault's steel door, re-engaged the locking bars, and gave the combination locks a couple of twirls.

He was pocketing the cigar case when Amina reappeared in the doorway, smiling broadly.

"Look what I found." She brought her hand out from behind her back and pointed a large silencer-equipped automatic at Moscovitch's head. "Put the case on the worktable slowly." She was no longer smiling.

Momentarily stunned, Moscovitch managed to recover, and pressed the button on the flashlight twice in rapid succession, counted slowly to three and, taking his time, placed the case on the table.

Amina backed away from him. "Step away and turn your back to me." Paralyzed with fear, Moscovitch was unable to move. "I said, turn around," Amina commanded, the barrel of her pistol now pointing downward. "Move or I'll shoot you in the knee."

Something snapped inside Moscovitch's head. How could this be happening? Ever since beginning to work in Hungary in mid-2001, and especially since the events of 9/11, he had been fretting about what would happen if his vaccine were to fall into the wrong hands. He had, therefore, arranged for destroying the samples at a moment's notice through ultraviolet radiation, hence the special flashlight that he had designed himself. With the Hungarian government as co-owner of his company, he had felt that the security arrangements he had put in place were adequate, never expecting that Amina—lovely, loving, tender Amina—would be the one to betray him.

His partner Delic, the Iraqi-trained Bosnian, maybe, but not Amina!

Tears welled up in his eyes. "How could you?" he stammered, "after all we've done together; the confidences shared; the joint work, the lofty goals. Why?" he sobbed, realizing that, unless he acted decisively, he was a dead man. Feigning submission, he started to turn.

"You Jews are all the same," she spat at him. "Conceited and arrogant. Did you really believe that I worked like a dog for long hours and slept with you because of your ugly body? Or for the lousy wages you paid me? Did you think that Esad Delic, Islam's foremost virologist, agreed to play second fiddle to you as your junior partner because he was dazzled by your knowledge and talent?"

Pent up frustrations, fuelled by unrequited hatred caused her to lose control. She pulled the trigger. The bullet ricocheted off the metal table behind Moscovitch with a whining ping. The shot gave him an excuse to accelerate his turn. His left arm half-raised, he pivoted on his right heel and swept the lab reagent bottles off the table beside him. They crashed to the tile floor, splattering hydrochloric and sulfuric acids in Amina's direction.

She lost her balance as she stepped away to avoid being burned.

Moscovitch completed his turn then lunged at the woman. His right shoulder caught her in the gut and knocked the wind out of her. Hurt, she doubled over and dropped her weapon. As he bent down to pick it up, she kicked him in the face, breaking his nose. In spite of the blinding pain and the blood, Moscovitch kept groping for the gun, but she managed to kick it away. The weapon slid into the next aisle and they both scrambled after it. Moscovitch got there first and kneeled to retrieve it. She kicked him in the chest. He grabbed her leg and fell backwards. She tumbled forward and hit him in the nose with the palm of her outstretched hand.

Moscovitch fainted.

*   *   *

The cell phone on Esad Delic's hip began to vibrate. He lifted the instrument to his ear, depressing the 'SEND' button in the process.

"Yes?"

"Come fetch us. We're ready for Phase Two."

"On my way." Delic hung up and looked at his watch. Three-thirty a.m., fifteen minutes behind schedule.

He told his three companions in the SUV to wait and walked forward to the cab of the semi-trailer parked behind it. He stepped up to the driver's window and knocked. "Follow my car to the gate. When I open it, drive to Building B, it's on the right." He reached the main entrance, unlocked the heavy metal gate and, straining, pushed it back into the courtyard. He waved the semi-trailer and the SUV through.

The vehicles pulled up in front of Building B. The men knew exactly what to do. While Delic and Shabir, his second-in-command, went to Amina's assistance, the other four opened the rear of the specially constructed container behind the cab and winched down a double gangplank. Next, one of the men drove a forklift truck down the ramp and to the freight elevator entrance at the rear of Building B.

Delic found Amina standing guard over a semi-conscious Moscovitch sitting, back-to-wall on the floor, his face a puffed-up, bloody mess, his nose grotesquely distorted.

"I told you not to harm him," Delic remonstrated. "We need to get him to a doctor and quick. He's no use to us in the state he's in."

"It couldn't be helped," The woman shrugged coldly. "He resisted."

"Did you get the samples?"

Amina pointed at the cigar case on the worktable. Delic pocketed it, told Shabir to fetch the forklift and the rest of the men, then gave his wounded partner a glass of water and a couple of pills that Moscovitch mistook for extra-strength Tylenol caplets. Actually, they contained 50 milligrams of Demerol each.

"Sorry she became so physical with you," Delic apologized as he wiped Moscovitch's face with a wet cloth, "but she says you started

6

it. I'll get a doctor to set your nose as soon as possible, but I'm afraid this won't happen for a few hours, so let the painkillers do their work and try to rest."

Mercifully, the Demerol kicked in within minutes. It gave Moscovitch relief from pain and dulled his combativeness. This helped Amina to control him during the hour it took to transfer the essential equipment in the lab to the container downstairs and to place remote controlled phosphorous incendiary devices at strategic points of the facility.

At a quarter to five, the semi-trailer, carrying the drugged Moscovitch and enough equipment for a bare-bones mini lab, pulled out of the complex.

Sunday morning at five a.m. on the dot, Delic locked Building B's front door then had himself driven to the main entrance in the SUV. He got out, waved the SUV through, locked the gate, got into Amina's car and told her to drive him home.

At six thirty-seven on Monday morning, on her way to work, Amina detonated the incendiary devices by calling her office from a public telephone and dialing nine. The explosion and fire that followed gutted the lab.

CHAPTER 2

After toweling down, Robert Lonsdale carefully lowered his aching body into the deckchair and arranged his limbs in a way that would cause the least amount of discomfort. The bullet wound had healed, but the chipped bone was taking longer than expected to get better and the pain remained constant.

It was a pleasant, warm day and he luxuriated for a while in the late autumn sunshine, enjoying the tranquility of the deserted pool area. He was glad he had chosen not to stay at his business partner's house near the southern tip of Palm Beach where the comings and goings became unbearable at times. In contrast, his client's condo on Bradley Place in a luxury building with only two apartments on each of its four floors had been just what the doctor had ordered. There was peace here, and quiet, plenty of rest and an opportunity to exercise. His tender hip prevented jogging for the time being, but not swimming. Lonsdale was up to thirty laps per day in the heated pool.

His companion, Adys, appeared with two glasses of freshly squeezed grapefruit juice on a tray that also held slices of mango, flavored with lemon. She placed the refreshments on the table and sat down beside him. "How's the hip *querido?*"

He gave her his standard answer. "Sore, but getting better."

She knew he was lying, but pretended not to '*la vista gorda*', seeing but not seeing as the saying went in Cuba, the country of her birth.

They had only known each other for about a year, half of which they had spent living together in Washington. Falling head over heels for an exciting and sophisticated man with a dangerous job had been one thing, nursing him back to health after he had almost gotten killed while exercising his profession, another.

They were both still adjusting.

She didn't really mind because she had begun to understand how passionately her man felt about the Western concept that embraced the right of every person to life, liberty and the pursuit of happiness, safe from totalitarian rulers. Before she left Cuba she had experienced what the loss of these rights could mean in a country where the population lived under the yoke of a dictator. She also perceived clearly that life under the rule of Muslim tyrants practicing Sharia law would deny these rights universally, but especially to women.

"What time do you expect Jim Morton to show?"

Lonsdale glanced at his watch. "I'd guess around noon." He had a couple of hours left before having to come to a final decision.

Sensing his unease, she finished her drink then leaned over and kissed him on the lips. "Whatever you decide will be all right with me," she murmured, but her heart was aching. "I'll be here when you come back."

He squeezed her arm. "I know that."

She smiled and changed the subject. "What shall we offer our guest for lunch?"

"How about picking up some stone shell crabs while I make my Hungarian potato salad that he likes so much? Do we have a decent Chardonnay left to help wash it down?"

"*Si* on all counts."

"You mean the crabs and the wine, or did you have something more in mind?"

She blushed, miffed by his flippant way of dismissing her, and left him to fight his demons alone.

Robert Lonsdale's name, before his induction into the CIA's employee protection program, had been Bernard Lands. Half Austrian, half Hungarian, he had settled in Canada after knocking about for years in England and on the Continent while his parents searched for a place to start a new life after World War Two.

He had been a loner even before coming to Canada.

Drifting from boarding school to boarding school in a war-ravaged Europe is not conducive to making close friends. Since his family had been part Austrian, he had ended up more or less on the losing side after the war. Not the best of backgrounds for the only foreign-born pupil at an English public school, where his classmates believed that all Europeans were Nazis.

In Canada things had gone better and he would have enjoyed life at the university had he known how to make friends. Unfortunately, he had not. The British had drilled into him that showing emotion, showing ambition, and showing off were not 'proper form'. Since Lonsdale had been born a gregarious show-off, it had taken an immense effort to change into a person with the characteristics he perceived were expected of him: aloofness and arrogance. This, coupled with his sense of being a perennial outsider, made it difficult for him to build relationships.

He had continued to be a loner in Montreal as well and had compensated for his loneliness by consoling himself with the thought that he was superior to 'them'—meaning everybody else—and who needed 'them' anyway.

Not only had he studied hard, but he had also worked hard at making money since his expensive tastes had required extra cash beyond his modest allowance. He wangled a part-time clerical job at the university's teaching hospital, a job he held throughout his four undergraduate years, unaware that the hospital's psychiatric department derived some of its funding from the CIA.

The CIA makes a point of recruiting individuals with real or potential clout, political leaders, captains of industry, scholars, artists, scientists, since it is more difficult to recruit a successful, well-established personality than one on the way up. The Agency is forever scouting for 'comers'—men and women in communities outside the U.S. who show promise of becoming influential one day.

At the hospital, fate put Lonsdale in charge of accounting for special psychiatric funds and the CIA spotters had no choice but to look him over. The shrinks at Langley had a field day analyzing his

10

psychological profile and, having identified his principal weakness (he needed to feel that he belonged and that he was being appreciated), had turned him into a viable 'asset', an agent programmed to act with intelligent independence, yet with absolute loyalty.

Morton and Lonsdale had joined the CIA at roughly the same time. The middle son of a successful Boston liquor manufacturer, Morton had attended Exeter before going on to Harvard, graduating with a B.S. in applied psychology. Instead of becoming the head of PR at the family' liquor distribution firm, he had applied for work in the Office of Personnel at the CIA. Kennedy's message about doing something for America had resonated with Morton. He believed that people in advantaged positions owed a debt to the society that had allowed their families to prosper.

Morton had a very special talent, the uncanny ability to make men disclose their most selfish and basic motives. One way or another he would trick them into blurting out what they stood for, who they really were, in which direction their fondest aspirations lay. Once his prey revealed its inner self, Morton would manipulate his victim at will by using its own motives as the lever.

Such a gift was at a premium at Langley, Virginia.

As a result, Morton's advancement at The Agency had been rapid and his superiors, recognizing his talent, arranged for his transfer from an administrative job to one involving Operations. They made him a Controller in the Department of Special Personnel Relations.

SPR Controllers are trained to handle sensitive 'assets', men and women who cannot be fitted into The Agency's regular administrative hierarchy, who cannot report through normal channels, and on whom the CIA's hold is tenuous.

That is how Robert Lonsdale—a special asset working for The Agency under contract, but not directly employed by it, thereby maintaining the myth of plausible deniability—became associated with Jim Morton, first as his colleague then as his 'almost' friend. 'Almost', because, in their line of business, trust did not exist. Nor did true friendship, not even after three decades of working closely together.

Or did it?

"Morton is certainly playing up the friendship angle," Lonsdale mused as he struggled with the decision he knew he had to make soon. "And he *had* been a friend—at times." Lonsdale could picture the chaos in Morton's office on the day Mohammed Atta and his team flew their aircraft into the World Trade Center. As Director of The Agency's Counter-terrorism Division, Morton must have known that, ultimately, the finger of blame would point at him for the CIA's failure to warn the U.S. about the impending attack. Yet, in spite of the tremendous pressure, he had found time on that fateful day in September to mount a rescue operation to save Lonsdale's life.

"Of course, he did have an ulterior motive." Lonsdale was playing devil's advocate. "He wanted to lay his hands on the cell phones our team had captured from the terrorists after we had chased them down in the Caribbean Sea the day the Twin Towers collapsed. Still and all, how can you refuse a person who saved your life?"

He finished his drink and got up, then picked up the tray with the glasses and headed for the elevators.

CHAPTER 3

A tired-looking Morton turned up at noon, bearing extravagant gifts, a bottle of Chateau Beauregard Pomerol for Lonsdale and an exquisite box of Belgian chocolates for his companion.

While Morton changed into casual clothes, Adys prepared a couple of large Mojitos that she placed on the table between two reclining chairs on the shady side of the terrace overlooking the pool. "Why don't the two of you have a drink while I get lunch ready," she suggested, sensing the tension between the men. "It'll help you relax." Grateful for the attempt at making him feel at home, Morton sat down with a sigh and took a generous gulp of his drink.

"How are you bearing up, sport?" he enquired with forced joviality from behind very dark sunglasses.

"I'm pretty well recovered physically, except for the chipped hip-bone which needs a couple more weeks' rest, or so the doctors say."

"We don't have a couple more weeks." Morton's brusque statement jolted Lonsdale, but he said nothing. The best way to deal with his ex-boss was to outwait him.

"It's been about three weeks since Moscovitch disappeared and the Hungarian police are none the wiser." This direct approach was a surprise. Morton's usual speech pattern of circumlocution was absent. "We're afraid some very bad people are forcing him to reproduce the vaccine samples which we suspect were destroyed when Moscovitch's laboratory went up in flames."

"Suspect?"

Morton had no time to waste. "Stop pretending you don't remember," he snapped. "I last saw you soon after Moscovitch's lab burned down. Since then the Hungarians have determined that, although the facility was gutted by the flames, there is evidence of some key equipment having been removed before the fire . . ." He sounded exasperated.

"What about the samples? Why would whoever had set the fire not have removed them as well?"

"We think Moscovitch had them in or near his steel desk. The forensic people found test tube remains, but the vaccine had evaporated in the intense heat . . ."

"No way of reconstituting it?"

Morton shook his head. "Absolutely none."

"What you're telling me then is that the bad guys got away with some equipment and perhaps some lab notes, plus Moscovitch, who you believe is now hard at work reinventing what he had invented before."

"That's it in a nutshell."

"How about our side? Are we working on the vaccine too?"

"The people in Budapest are in the process of rebuilding what's been destroyed, but they are still looking for a virologist with enough state-of-the-art knowledge to carry on the research."

"How about Esad Delic, Moscovitch's partner?" Lonsdale interrupted. He had met the Canadian Moscovitch in Budapest a year previously while searching for the vanished CEO of Plasmalab, the blood company for which Moscovitch had worked in Toronto before moving to Hungary. "Delic is an Iraqi-trained Bosnian whom Moscovitch held in high esteem. Couldn't stop bragging about him."

"After the fire Delic hung around for a few days then left for Baghdad. He said he'd return as soon as Phylaxos' lab was operational again."

"Have your guys interviewed him?"

"No Robert, we have not. I want *you* to do that for us."

Lonsdale let out a short laugh that sounded more like a bark. "Is that all you want me to do? Go to Baghdad and just interview Delic?" He recognized the thin end of a wedge when he saw it.

Morton took off his glasses and Lonsdale looked away. His erstwhile colleague's sunken, bloodshot eyes were lusterless . . . his will to go on seemingly no longer there. The man's face seemed to have shrunk; he appeared beaten—at least ten years older than his age.

'Is he ill?' Lonsdale wondered. 'Nah,' he dismissed the idea. 'He would've told me.' They were close, weren't they?

Morton continued. "I've hardly slept since 9/11 and can't keep my food down. I'm past caring about what's going to happen to me, but I'm worried sick about a biological attack on the U.S. by Al-Qaeda or Saddam Hussein or some other Muslim fanatic. Not by way of bugs spread through bombarding us with Anthrax-loaded shells or other types of harmful bacteria. That way we'd at least know we've been attacked. What I dread," he blurted, "is some insidious form of sneak attack, say a dose of nv.C-JD virus propagated through tainted blood-based glue used in surgery by doctors unaware of what they were doing. Nothing would be further from their minds than suspecting that their supplies were contaminated."

Morton shuddered. "This is just one of the many horror scenarios that keep me awake at night, but one I know I could defend against if you helped me."

"Meaning?"

"I want you back. I very much *need* you back at The Agency's Counter-terrorism Division as my Deputy *pro tem*."

"*Pro tem*? For how long?"

"Minimum six months, maximum a year."

"And what do I tell Gal, my business partner?"

In spite of having prepared himself for a proposition, Morton's answer unsettled Lonsdale. "We'll make it worth his while as well. Rather than paying you a salary we'll retain your firm as full time consultants at your regular rates plus bonus."

"Has the DCI agreed to this?"

"Yes." Morton handed Lonsdale an envelope, from which he extracted a single handwritten page on which the Director of Central

Intelligence's unmistakable cursive calligraphy confirmed everything Morton had said.

Lonsdale felt trapped.

Four years previously, after almost three decades of loyal service, he had decided to retire from The Agency in which he had served, first as an idealistic, somewhat naïve, but versatile field agent, then, as a hardened, cynical, embittered senior operative, having somehow survived years of double-dealing and treachery and the death of his wife. 'Survived' was perhaps, an exaggeration. Although he was alive and in good physical condition for his age the state of his mental health was iffy. The years of stress, insecurity and aloneness imposed on him by his responsibilities had altered his psyche.

Before the death of his wife, who perished in an Agency-inspired operation that had gone desperately wrong and for which Lonsdale still blamed himself thirty years later, he had been gregarious and action-driven. A hard-living raconteur with a busy social life that served to conceal his real activities, he had developed a profile perhaps too high for a man in his profession. All that changed after he lost his wife. He became reclusive, introspective—and even better at his job which was to coordinate counter-terrorist activity worldwide from a secret location in Bethesda, near Washington.

Then, in the mid-nineties, with Milosevic making mischief in Belgrade, the West had become nervous about what was happening in the Balkans. NATO became involved and the US, NATO's principal member, had insisted on direct access to the Alliance's intelligence harvest. It wanted one of its own as NATO's Director of Intelligence. But, to remove the incumbent, General Richter, would have upset the Germans and this the U.S. did not wish to do.

The next best solution had been to get an American appointed as Richter's Chief of Staff. This had meant finding a multilingual, senior intelligence manager with field experience, superior language skills and familiarity with Europe's ways.

The computers at Langley and at the NSA had done their dance and had come up with Lonsdale, multilingual, born in Europe, naturalized Canadian, granted U.S. citizenship upon placement in the CIA's employee protection program, an excellent program administrator with remarkable successes to his credit.

He was senior enough to hold down the job, but not so senior as to make General Richter feel threatened. In the late stages of his career with The Agency and not in line for further promotion, Lonsdale had been at a dead end. He had jumped at the opportunity, moved to Brussels, but had kept his apartment in Washington, and focused his energies on monitoring the un-monitorable, the mood of the Balkans.

Richter and Lonsdale found they could work well together and did so for three years. Then Lonsdale became eligible for a six-month leave of absence that he decided to take.

He never returned to NATO. At the end of his leave, he went 'civilian', going into partnership with Reuven Gal, a Mossad-trained security specialist working out of Palm Beach in Florida.

Their first case involved an industrial accident at Plasmalab, a blood-products company in Toronto, where, due to a manufacturing oversight, blood-based surgical glue became contaminated with the nv.C-J virus—human Mad Cow disease.

The accident resulted in the death of hundreds of surgical patients and the closing of Plasmalab. This prompted its Acting Chief Scientific Officer, Jason Moscovitch, to move, to Hungary to continue the search for a vaccine against the deadly disease there.

"Lunch is served."

Adys was calling them from the spacious dinette off the kitchen where she wanted to serve an informal meal at which she intended to be present. Never again would she miss an opportunity to protect her man against himself.

"Stone shell crabs and potato salad!" Morton's bad mood evaporated as soon as he spotted his favorite food. "Next you're going to tell me you've made Zabaglione for desert."

Adys laughed. "You must have taken a peek inside the fridge." She poured the wine while they put on their aprons. Eating crabs with rock-hard shells is a messy undertaking.

Although she liked Morton she didn't quite trust him. He was too Anglo-Saxon for her—too smooth, too devoid of warmth.

Adys Marquez and her twin sister, Gina, were born in Santiago de Cuba, the island's capital during Spanish colonial days. Before escaping to the States, their father had owned a successful 'cram' academy and the family resided in a huge edifice, a palace, housing not only their private quarters, but the school as well.

Theirs was a joyful, comfortable, middle-class household. Cousins, uncles and aunts living in the immediate vicinity stopped by often; very seldom did less than a dozen people turn up at meal times.

Life was good.

This being said, not all was sunshine and laughter in the Cuba of the forties and early fifties. Prostitution and drug dealing were rampant, government officials were self-serving and there was no medical help for the poor. Twenty-five per cent of the population was illiterate because public schooling was available only in the towns and cities. Those in the villages and on the farms—the *campesinos*—were condemned to living in ignorance, neglect and abject poverty.

When Fidel Castro started his campaign against the tyrant Batista, most *Santiagueros,* merchants, professionals, students and teachers, enthusiastically endorsed his fight against the all-pervasive corruption that characterized the regime.

After the triumph of the Revolution, the Marquez sisters volunteered to teach the *campesinos* to read and write. For this, they were rewarded with jobs in Fidel's government despite their having been '*gusanos*', worms—members of the middle class.

For a while, the Revolution continued to live up to its noble ideals and the *Fidelistas* enjoyed enormous popular support. Then the Americans attempted to re-impose their will and Castro turned to Russia for help. The US response isolated the island and the economic situation deteriorated. Assistance from the Soviet Union was insufficient to counteract the effects of the blockade completely.

The economy collapsed, Cuba became a vassal of the USSR and civil liberties were sharply curtailed, especially those of the middle class.

Deeply disillusioned, Adys and her family decided to leave.

The harassment began as soon as they declared their intention to emigrate. By the time the Marquez finally received permission to exit Cuba two years later everything they had owned had been taken from them. They arrived in Florida penniless, obliged to take on the most menial jobs to get by while learning the American way.

Industrious, they all did well.

Adys landed the prestigious job of Managing Director of the *Repertorio Español*, a well-known Spanish-language theatre group in New York. Gina became a bank manager in West Palm Beach and started dating Reuven Gal. One day Gina brought Adys along to a party that Gal was throwing at which she met Lonsdale.

It was love at first sight.

"Jim wants me back at The Agency *pro tem*." Lonsdale said to Adys. "I told him I'll do nothing without consulting you."

"How long is *pro tem*?"

"Six months . . ."

"And after?"

"Back to the salt mines with Reuven Gal."

"Would it involve field work?"

"I'd have to spend some time in Europe, yes."

"But you are not healed yet."

"Jim says this thing can't wait."

"*Querido*, I've told you that whatever you decide is all right with me. I'm just worried about your physical well-being. Although you tried to hide it this morning, I saw how much your hip was still hurting."

"Not that much."

Adys left the table, visibly upset. She knew her man was proud, but found it difficult to put up with his bravado. Publicly, she would remonstrate only mildly, but, within, she was aching to tell Morton, supposedly Lonsdale's close friend, about the physical pain Lonsdale had to endure as he healed, and the psychological impact his last mission had had on him.

He would awake night after night, screaming, sweating, and trembling, haunted by recurring nightmares that he would never describe to her. She'd comfort him as best she could, but feared that another traumatic assignment would push him over the edge.

She, too, began to feel psychologically stressed, and started to worry about their life together. Very much in love with him she felt threatened by his devotion to his job—or was it *jobs*? Was he really interested in making a go of his partnership with Gal, or was he just marking time, waiting for The Agency to come begging him to return to the fold. And if he did go back, what would become of their love for each-other in the pressure-cooker that she imagined a senior bureaucrat and his wife had to cope with in Washington: close scrutiny of everything they did, suspicion because she was not born American, funny looks because her English was not colloquial enough, her Latina accent?

She was well past fifty, old enough to know that, eventually, Lonsdale's interest in her physical attributes was bound to fade. What would happen if, during one of his assignments, he met a younger, more interesting, more attractive, woman? Would he drop her and renege on his promise to look after her for the rest of her life? She had only her sister for family in the US, and few American friends. Would she have the strength to start over again?

She needed security and craved tranquility—and wanted a companion who would provide a safe haven for her. Was he ready and stable enough to settle down?

She wasn't sure.

But she loved him so . . . and life with him was exciting, interesting and opulent.

Lonsdale, sensing what Adys was thinking, made up his mind. "Jim I'm not going to sacrifice my chances of happiness with Adys for The Agency. I owe you my life and I know it. You're in trouble and I'll help you, but my conditions must be clearly understood. I'll try to find Moscovitch for you, but if, by the end of three months I have not succeeded, I'm coming home and quitting forever." He held out his hand.

Morton nodded. "Three months it is."

"Do I have your word as a friend?"

"You do."

They shook hands.

"I appreciate the handshake and your word, but we both know that your hold on your job is not as firm as before." Lonsdale looked his friend squarely in the eyes. "Even so, I wouldn't insist, but there are other people involved. Adys and Reuven Gal, to mention just two."

Morton caught on right away. "I suppose you want a written contract."

"You've got it. I want what we call a temporary contract officer's agreement through my firm, with you named as my Control so I report to you directly and to no one else."

"That can be arranged."

"Do it then Jim, and make sure I don't find myself back on the payroll again."

Lonsdale and Adys returned to Washington the next day.

During the flight home, they had their first serious argument.

"What happens if three months is not enough to complete the mission?"

"I'll quit and come home," he answered.

'You really believe they'll let you do that?"

"I'll have Jim's and his boss's written promise."

She looked at him and he saw incredulity in her eyes. "Do you really believe The Agency will honor its commitment?"

"I do."

"Well, I don't." Her eyes were beginning to tear up. "I've seen how hard it is to oppose powerful government agencies."

"Not in a free society." Then Lonsdale realized he was sounding smug and burst out laughing.

She looked at him sadly. "You're naive, *querido*, you're incredibly naive."

He tried to object, but she wouldn't listen.

When they got to their apartment, she relented and allowed him to prepare a peace offering: a late lunch of *spaghetti alla crema di scampi,* one of his special creations, a dish that called for *Prosecco* wine, and plenty of it.

They drank a bottle each—definitely a liquid lunch.

The wine made them mellow and forgiving and they made up by making love.

Lonsdale then spent forty-eight hours with Morton on the Moscovitch file and on completing the paperwork relating to his contract.

He was on a plane to Budapest via Montreal by the end of the week.

CHAPTER 4

Of the five attendees at the Cizre Conference (as the meeting became known subsequently), only two really appreciated the supreme importance of kidnapping and holding the Canadian scientist. They were Essan Delic, the Bosnian biologist, because, as the Canadian's business partner, he had seen the WMD´s effects on mice, and Hassani, The Butcher, because he had taken the samples Delic had provided and had applied them to humans.

The Butcher was typical of the younger men who surrounded Saddam Hussein. He was born into a prominent Tikriti family that was a member of the Al-Bu Nasir, the Dictator's, tribe. Educated in England, a privilege granted him by his uncle and mentor, Ali Hassan Al Majid, he was ready to do whatever it took to become a member of Saddam's inner circle.

The Butcher imitated Saddam shamelessly. He worshiped his mother, idolized his children and abused his wife. Chemical Ali considered him his younger *alter ego*.

A year before the fall of the Twin Towers, The Butcher, acting on direct orders from his immediate boss and uncle, had arranged for the building of a hermetically sealable, secret laboratory near the town of Najaf, about one hundred and thirty kilometers south of Baghdad. The building was finished in record time because the equipment and facilities of the single storey structure were relatively

22

standard: an air-conditioned, covered doughnut about two hundred feet in diameter. The 'hole' in the doughnut housed a small operating theater, a fully equipped industrial kitchen, and whatever else was required to operate a forty-two-seat restaurant efficiently 24/7.

The doughnut itself contained eight hermetically sealed '*Tomns*'— equally divided sections. Six of these, each contained six trapezoidal-shaped, twelve-by-fifteen-foot bedrooms with *en-suite* bathrooms, and a very large living-dining area contiguous with the doughnut's core. The walls common with the core were made of one-way mirror glass. This allowed those working in the core to monitor what was going on inside the doughnut.

Tomns A, B, C, D, E and F had hermetically sealed individual heating and air conditioning units on the roof. *Tomn* G housed the staff's sleeping quarters, and *Tomn* H the general access to the facility.

All disposable items inside the doughnut were made of plastic or cloth (trays, glasses, knives, forks, plates, linens, etc.) and, once used, were 'flushed down' through a sealed chute in each *Tomn* that led down to a highly efficient, powerful high-temperature vaporizing unit in the basement.

It had taken five months to construct, equip, test and staff the facility. Once the construction phase of the project was completed, Hassani, The Butcher, an exceptionally ruthless and cruel man, well trained in brutality by his superior, did the rounds of Iraq's prisons that housed inmates hostile to the Bathist regime.

He carefully selected twenty-four male and twelve female guinea pigs, ranging in age between eighteen and sixty, and installed four men and two women in each of *Tomns* A to F.

On Day One of the experimental phase, Patient 1, a man, had his tonsils removed; Patient 2, also a man, had the top of his left index finger amputated; and Patient 3, a woman, had her left ear removed.

Surgical glue, infected with the newest version of the nv.Creutzfeldt- Jakob disease virus was used in all three operations.

This First Trio of patients was then returned to *Tomn* A where it took up residence with Patients 4, 5, and 6, (the Second Trio), and settled down to a comfortable existence with good food and TV and Video entertainment.

Two weeks after their operations, members of the First Trio began to complain about recurring dizziness. A fortnight later, they began to vomit sporadically and, by the end of the sixth week after their operations they were dramatically weak and dehydrated—*in extremis*. All three died during Week Seven, in spite of the desperate efforts of the Second Trio's members who tried to help them as best they could.

Members of the Second Trio, infected by members of the First Trio in Week Four, were transferred to *Tomn* B in Week Five where they infected members of the Third Trio (Patients 7, 8, and 9). After going through periods of dizziness in Weeks Six and Seven, members of the Second Trio died in Week Ten.

Before dying, members of the Second Trio infected members of the Third Trio, and so it went until members of the Fourth Trio (Patients 10, 11, and 12) finally died in Week Fourteen.

Six weeks later, though, The Butcher became aware of a strange phenomenon. Members of the Sixth Trio (Patients 16, 17 and 18) failed to infect members of the Seventh Trio (Patients 19, 20 and 21) and by the time it was the Eighth Trio's turn to go through the process, none of the patients involved became infected or died.

The Butcher continued the experiment until Week Twenty Four, at the end of which he shut down the facility without warning, sealed it and gassed everyone remaining alive inside.

This included most of the staff.

Those employees who did survive, simply because they had the good fortune of not being on duty the day the facility was sealed, were so afraid of retribution that they absolutely refused ever to talk about Hassani's experimental project.

The Butcher, of course, considered the operation a great success. It had proved to him that the infected glue did, indeed, have the potential of a highly successful, relatively cheap and simple-to-produce WMD. It was unfortunately not air-borne, but propagated by close human contact. Once unleashed it would kill hundreds of thousands of people *unless checked by an effective vaccine.*

And therein lay the rub. Nobody knew how to manufacture the damned vaccine except perhaps a Canadian scientist who, in addition to being an infidel was, to boot, a Jew.

After analyzing the results of his experiment and having participated in the Cizre Conference, Hassani concluded that Al Qaeda did not possess the technology to mass-manufacture the glue, but Iraq and Iran did.

On the other hand, Iraq and Iran did not have the capability of clandestinely introducing the glue into infidel hospitals worldwide, but Al Qaeda did.

But Iraq could not allow Al Qaeda to have unfettered sole possession of the new WMD because, in such a situation, Al Qaeda might very well attempt to go into partnership with Sunni Iraq's traditional enemy, Shia Iran, rather than Iraq,

To overcome this problem Hassani proposed to manufacture the new WMD outside Iraq, preferably in small mobile laboratories such as barges and large trucks, to allow Iraq the option of credible deniability in case it were accused by the West of crimes against humanity.

Colonel Hassani's final and most important conclusion was that, in the interest of brotherly, and safe, cooperation between the parties concerned, it was essential to kidnap the Jewish scientist within the framework of an Al Qaeda-Iraq combined operation before the Americans realized how important the scientist really was.

CHAPTER 5

After almost three weeks of drug induced semi-conciousness, Moscovitch was getting desperate. He knew no more than he did the night they had snatched him. He was not even sure about the weeks because they fed him at irregular intervals and kept him sedated.

He remembered being dragged downstairs and placed on a cot in the container of a semi-trailer parked in the yard of the Phylaxos complex. Next, Delic had given him some pills and he had fallen asleep. He had still been in the same semi-trailer when he had awoken, or so it had seemed to him then. He had no way of knowing whether it was night or day. There were no windows and his watch was gone.

Still too drugged to panic, he had surveyed his surroundings in considerable discomfort through swollen eyes. His body was aching all over and his nose throbbed with dull persistence, still broken despite Delic' promise to have a doctor set it.

Nausea had kept overcoming him every time he had tried to get up, so he had given up and had gone to sleep again.

The next time he had awoken, he had found a tracksuit, some underwear, a tuna salad sandwich and a glass of milk next to his cot. Hungry, but rested and clearheaded except for his nose which continued to throb dully, he had devoured the snack and had set about exploring his surroundings;

His "home" appeared to be a fifty-three foot insulated air conditioned transport container. Half the floor space was taken up by a steel cot, a desk, and a chair. A treadmill stood in front of a TV set on top of a cabinet that housed a video cassette player. An old reclining armchair faced the cot.

The other half accommodated a small chemical laboratory: a metal worktable with its own sink, a small fridge, a mini-centrifuge and a fermenting machine with growth medium in it under the worktable. Above, neatly arranged in wooden racks, were the essential laboratory glassware and Bunsen burners needed for conducting research.

A high-powered microscope and a box of slides completed the equipment list.

His personal notes and a few reference books were on a shelf protruding from the wall above his cot.

A shower/toilet combination installed in the corner furthest from the cot served as a secondary source of water and waste disposal. Mercifully, there was also a gas water heater, so he could wash in comfort.

A double row of neon lights suspended from the ceiling illuminated the space. Moscovitch searched for a switch and, finding none, concluded that the lights, the heating and the air conditioning were controlled from outside.

Access to his cramped quarters was through a door without handles in the center of one of the walls, securely locked and quite immovable. Curiously enough, there was a similar door through the opposite wall, but this had a handle.

Moscovitch tried to move it but found that it was jammed into a locked position by means of a large mortise lock.

A TV camera, bolted to the ceiling above the shower and protected by what looked like a bulletproof glass box, monitored what was going on inside.

Its red light kept blinking,

The container in which he found himself was not the one into which they had dragged him the night he had been abducted.

Moscovitch took a shower and reviewed his situation. From his surroundings, he deduced that he was in no imminent physical danger. His captors obviously wanted him to pursue his search for the nv.C-JD vaccine, more so since, by now they must have found out that the vaccine prototypes they thought they had obtained were nothing but a neutral liquid. That they expected to hold him for weeks, perhaps even months, was also evident. Why else would they have gone to the trouble of creating such an elaborate set-up . . . relatively comfortable living quarters and a fully equipped mini bio-lab.

Time was on his side.

He was washing the set of underwear he had been wearing when the door swung inward and a tall woman with Slavic features and jet-black hair entered. She was wearing running shoes and a tracksuit similar to his. She closed the door behind her quickly, but not before Moscovitch caught a glimpse of the outside: it was either dawn or dusk.

With the automatic in one of her hands she waved Moscovitch toward his bed. With the other, she gestured that he attach himself to the cot with the handcuffs dangling from the head bar. Moscovitch obliged and the woman left.

She returned after a short while carrying a steaming three-deck lunch pail that she placed on one of the worktables. She took a sheet of paper and a videocassette from her pocket, placed them at the foot of Moscovitch's bed, then drew her pistol from her waistband and motioned Moscovitch to read the typewritten note.

> *"The woman assigned to look after you does not understand any language you speak. Cooperate with her. Your life depends on it. You will be given good food two times a day. When the lights are switched off, go to bed and rest because you are expected to work hard on your project which is to perfect the vaccine you are developing against nv.C-JD.*
>
> *The door with the handle on it leads into a minilab where you will find a hermetic suit for conducting experiments that may expose you to contamination. The key to the lock will be given to you when you are ready to start working in earnest.*
>
> *Keep your quarters clean and tidy. Wash up after every meal and put the clean lunch pail next to the door when you are finished with it.*
>
> *Do your laundry regularly.*

Your TV is for watching videocassettes, not programs.
Follow the woman's instructions and do not try to get smart.
If you do, she will not hesitate to shoot you.
The woman will get you whatever REASONABLE *requirements*
you may have relating to your work. Write her a note about what
you need and give it to her when she serves you a meal.

The note was not signed.

Moscovitch looked up and the woman threw the key to the handcuffs on the bed then signaled Moscovitch to free himself and place the key back from where he had picked it up.

Then she left.

Moscovitch ate his meal: an excellent cauliflower soup, a delicious helping of chicken paprika with gnocchi, and apple strudel for desert. Bread, butter and a piece of cheese, a satchel of instant coffee and a couple of small containers of milk rounded out the meal. The printed material on the milk container said 'TEJ'—milk in Hungarian.

After washing the dishes and placing them near the door as instructed, Moscovitch used one of the lab beakers for making instant coffee then sank into his recliner to drink it and to contemplate his new circumstances.

He re-read the note very carefully. The language, though grammatically correct in idiomatic English, seemed simplistic. He suspected that his partner Delic had written it.

He could not help reflect on how much his jailer resembled Amina. Were they sisters, or cousins, may be? 'Don't think about the bitch' he admonished himself. 'Had you not become besotted with her you wouldn't have let your guard down and you wouldn't be in the shit you're in now.'

"Keep your pecker out of the payroll," his mother used to tell him when, on occasion, he'd bring a co-worker home on weekends. As usual, he had not listened.

Jason Moscovitch was no innocent virgin; on the contrary, his richly deserved nickname had been 'Stud' at the University of Toronto, where he had played basketball.

Well-proportioned and darkly handsome at six foot four, with catlike reflexes and the graceful movements of a natural athlete, Moscovitch was acknowledged as being an outstanding basketball player, *and* a 'brain'. A Ph.D. in virological biochemistry, he had, at age twenty-six, already been, for eighteen months, the Chief Scientific Officer of Plasmalab, the Toronto-based manufacturer of surgical glue made from bovine blood.

The job had become his when a careless supervisor 'overcooked' a batch of the glue thereby creating a new form of human Mad Cow (Creutzfeldt-Jakob) disease. Some of the batch had found its way into the operating theatres of dozens of hospitals around the world and had killed over a hundred people. Plasmalab's stock had tanked, but not before those in the know—the company's Chief Scientific Officer and its Chief Executive—had managed to 'short' Plasmalab's shares, thereby making millions.

The CSO, Dr. Keller, had done his best to mitigate the effects of the accident. He had hired Moscovitch (at that time a graduate student) to lead a crash program aimed at finding an antidote. Keller had also tried to alert the authorities to the danger of an epidemic, but the CEO, Michael Martin, fighting for time, had wanted to engineer a cover-up. To stop Keller from blowing the whistle Martin had poisoned Keller then attempted to disappear, but was caught, imprisoned and was being held for trial.

*　　*　　*

From the very start, two things had bothered Moscovitch about his work at Plasmalab: one, Dr. Keller never provided him with a formal letter of employment, and two, he paid cash for the services rendered by the graduate student.

"Let's keep the paperwork to a minimum," the CSO had said. "Doing things my way," he had added, "is more advantageous for you from an income tax point of view."

Moscovitch had readily acquiesced. He hated paying taxes.

After a while the young man had begun to suspect that the work he was doing for Dr. Keller was 'extracuricular', using company facilities on a discovery of his own which he had no intention of turning over to Plasmalab even though he was legally bound to do so as an officer of a listed company.

Why else, he had asked himself, did his boss insist that Moscovitch use the lab only in the evenings, after all the other employees had left?

Though Moscovitch was just starting his career, he was not naïve, and did not wish to jeopardize his reputation. A political animal, he always made sure his backside was covered and, whenever possible, he took the easy way out. Rather than confronting Dr. Keller, he sent a letter to Michael Martin requesting that Plasmalab's CEO confirm his awareness of the project on which Dr. Keller insisted Moscovitch work in such isolation.

Moscovitch got back from his winter vacation the day the police found Dr. Keller's lifeless, poisoned body in his Palm Beach apartment. The prime suspect in the case, Martin, had disappeared.

Having gotten five by putting two and two together, Moscovitch deduced that the death of his boss and the disappearance of Martin were part of a sinister Mafia plot to take over the company.

This frightened him, but he still needed money, so agreed to soldier on at the Board's request as Acting Chief Scientific Officer until a suitable replacement for Keller could be found.

Then the overcooking accident was uncovered and Moscovitch concluded, this time correctly, that only three people had been in a position to know about this unfortunate event the previous September: Keller, Martin and he.

The implications were clear. Though Moscovitch was innocent, neither Martin nor Keller was around to exonerate him. Prudence dictated that he distance himself from the situation. He packed up his notes and samples and left Canada, not without an ulterior motive, of course.

While working on his own during Dr. Keller's frequent absences, Moscovitch had found a way of at least directing, if not destroying, the prions that transmitted bovine spongiform encephalopathy—BSE—Mad Cow disease. He foresaw that this technique would have an enormous impact on the veterinarian pharmaceutical industry worldwide and intended to profit from it if he could.

During his search for a country where he could set up shop on the cheap and be assured of competent professional help he discovered that Hungary had been producing effective blood-based vaccines for prophylaxis in cattle for over a century. Hungary was far from Canada; was not yet a member of the European Union and therefore not subject to reciprocal Western copyright infringement agreements. The country's economic climate, solidly embracing entrepreneurial principles, rewarded North American-trained scientists with generous participation packages in exchange for knowhow. Budapest was a civilized city in which a dollar stretched far, and where Food and Drug Administration regulations did not apply.

What better place than Hungary, then, to start a modest manufacturing operation for producing a new, untested, vaccine with considerable potential for eradicating mad cow disease, both in humans and in animals?

He had yet another reason to make Hungary the location where he would live and work for the time being. His grandmother had been Hungarian-born and had taught him rudimentary 'kitchen' Hungarian while he was a little boy.

Moscovitch was about to get out of his recliner when all the lights went out. He had no choice so he went to bed, but couldn't fall asleep. Anxiety was gnawing at his innards. "Weeks have passed since you grabbed me," he shouted into the darkness, "but I'm not giving up, so go fuck yourselves."

This made him feel better and his ability to reason returned. He was still sure that, eventually, the authorities would find him, or, perhaps, that his captors would release him for ransom. After all, his skills were in high demand of late and he was sure his mother could find any number of sources of money to fund his freedom.

Seeking reassurance, he began to debate the issue with himself. Were his captors not doing their best to make him feel physically comfortable? Were they not showing signs of willingness to negotiate?

He finally fell asleep, emotionally exhausted.

Twenty-five days after his capture Moscovitch asked his keeper for his watch back. The woman returned it with a note urging him to start working on his vaccine again. It ended with: "*We have yet to figure out how you neutralized the vaccine samples. No matter—we do know the product's basic formula. Therefore, the best way forward for all of us (and by this we mean 'all mankind') would be to save precious time by working in parallel so as to develop, as quickly as possible, a viable, safe, and tested life-saving vaccine.*"

Moscovitch was elated. He was sure his captors would start negotiating soon and thanked his lucky stars for having had the foresight not to share with Delic the formula for the catalyst that was essential for replicating his vaccine.

So the next day he sent a message to his captors in which he confirmed his willingness to cooperate as long as the conditions under which he was to work were acceptable to him. He also asked for the key to the lock securing the door handle of the mini-lab and began work on setting up a functioning laboratory 'just to have something to do.' That night, as a reward, the woman brought him a heavily lined, tan raincoat and then, having hand-cuffed him, let him out into the fresh air, but not before tying him to an eighteen-foot steel hawser, one end of which was fastened to his handcuffs, the other to a steel ring soldered to the outside of the container, dead center above the door.

Moscovitch took great gulps of the cool fall air as he paced back and forth in the limited space defined by the length of the hawser. He looked for clues to his whereabouts and found that his 'prison' was, as he had guessed, a fifty-three foot semi-trailer placed on cinder blocks. The structure seemed to have some permanence to it. Cinder block steps, cemented together, led up to the door.

His semi-trailer stood between two other semis that looked exactly like the one he occupied. All had electric wiring leading to them. Though he couldn't see it, he supposed that insulated plumbing installed in the spaces beneath the structures connected them to water and sewage facilities.

Presumably, his keeper lived in one of the other semis, alone or not, he couldn't tell. He guessed the third container was for storage.

A nine-foot long wooden wall, about eight feet high, stretched from each semi-trailer to the one next to it thereby making it impossible for Moscovitch to see what lay on the other side of this obstacle that was over a hundred and fifty feet long.

Very bright crime lights on top of eighteen-foot steel poles placed in front of each trailer on the side away from the scientist illuminated the compound. When he tried to look beyond them, they blinded him and he could not discern the sky above.

A road, about fifteen feet wide and originating somewhere in the darkness outside his field of vision, ran parallel to the line of semis and curved away to his left. As for the terrain, the entire area stood on a reinforced concrete apron.

The air was damp and smelled of oil.

After half an hour the woman reappeared seemingly from nowhere and, carefully keeping her distance, and after unlocking his "tether", motioned Moscovitch back into his abode with a wave of her pistol.

The fresh air had done Moscovitch good. He slept soundly and long. When he awoke, he found his breakfast of eggs and trimmings augmented by the Toronto Globe and Mail. He devoured the daily while wolfing down his meal then reread the entire paper line by line. Its date gave him a bit of a shock: it seemed he had underestimated the length of his captivity by at least four days.

During the week, sustained by good food, buoyed by nightly walks and the occasional copy of his hometown paper, and motivated by the hope that his captors would open negotiations soon, he worked hard at fixing up his lab and coaxing the growth material to mature.

As the days wore on, though, Moscovitch's self-confidence began to ebb. Deeply affected by the isolation in which he lived, he gradually lost the ability to focus on his work and became less and less able to deal with the daily disappointment of not hearing from his captors.

At the end of four weeks, Moscovitch caved in. He began to send daily messages to his tormentors, first demanding a meeting and, as time passed, begging for one since the uncertainty of his situation was driving him crazy.

CHAPTER 6

The aircraft banked to the left as it approached *Ferihegy*, Budapest's International Airport. Following the captain's suggestion Lonsdale glanced down at the newly built terminal. Not just another building he said to himself, but a symbol of progress. A member of NATO, Hungary was about to join the European Union, having converted its state-planned economy in ten short years to an efficiently operating market-driven one.

Budapest, created by Royal Decree in 1873, is a beautiful city that boasts a number of World Heritage Sites, including some Roman ruins just to the north of it at Aquincum, from where the Romans governed their province of Pannonia.

Lonsdale was through customs and immigration in no time and headed for the nearest taxi.

"Where to?" The driver, having caught a glimpse of the KLM Frequent Flyer tag on his luggage and judging him to be North American by the cut of his clothes, addressed Lonsdale in English.

"To the *Béke* Hotel," Lonsdale replied.

"You mean the Radisson."

"Is that what they call it now?" Lonsdale asked. *Béke* in Hungarian meant 'peace'. It had also been the name of a political party during the 'transition period', the time it took to retire Janos Kadar's Communist government.

The driver did not reply. He knew the *Béke*, definitely not a first-class hotel.

'Must be a traveling salesman from America working for a small company in the States and on a tight budget,' he concluded as he sped along *Üllői* Boulevard then swung over to the *Teréz* Ring where he deposited Lonsdale in front of a 1900's building that had definitely seen better days.

Lonsnsdale paid his chauffeur, tipping him frugally.

"Don't worry," said the driver, unable to resist giving his passenger a shot, Hungarian style, "you won't starve to death. The *Béke* serves a nice buffet breakfast for their guests on a budget."

Lonsdale debated giving the man a tart reply, but thought better of it. His efforts to appear to be no more than a mid-level executive were paying off.

He had flown to Budapest from Toronto in coach-class and planned to interview people working in the trenches: police officers, employees of Phylaxos, government officials, who, he figured, would relate better to a plodder than to a flashy, high-ranking representative of The Agency.

It was well past eleven by the time he got himself sorted out because, initially, the receptionist couldn't "find" his reservation until Lonsdale tipped him to look for it more thoroughly.

After a fast shower he went for a short walk along the Ring toward the Danube, past the monstrous shopping center the Trizec Group had built on top of the huge excavation site it had created next to the Western Railway Station. Although the sun was shining brightly, there was no warmth in the air and Lonsdale got tired of dodging pushy pedestrians hell-bent on spending, spending, spending.

Starting to feel the cold, he retraced his steps and climbed the stairs to the hotel's dining-room on the mezzanine, all mirrors and mahogany. Very Art Deco. Very late 1920's. He felt his stomach growl with hunger, no doubt stimulated by the familiar rich smell of Hungarian cuisine.

He suddenly realized that he still missed his mother's cooking.

"How is the stuffed pepper dish?" he asked the waiter in English. "Do you make it with sweet tomato sauce?"

"Yes, Hungarian style."

"With boiled potatoes?"

The man turned up his nose. "Of course. What else?"

"Can I have a glass of the house red?"

"The Villányi or the Kékfrankos?"

"Which one is lighter?"

"The Kékfrankos of course." Another twitch of the nose.

Lonsdale kept a straight face. He knew all about stuffed peppers Hungarian-style. His mother used to make them for him when he was a little boy. As an adult living in North America, he'd invariably order the item if the restaurant he happened to be in had it on the menu, though he knew in advance that, unless made from tomato paste imported from Hungary, the sauce would not have the sweet, rich taste of his mother's cooking.

Or, was it just his imagination?

Memories of his youth began to crowd in as he waited for his food to arrive. 'Must be jet lag and the surroundings,' he thought. He tried to ignore them but they kept coming at him.

Sitting at his mother's feet in the drawing room, after school, and watching her as she worked on a decorative rug, the brilliant sunshine streaming through the windows and thousands of dust particles glittering like microscopic stars suspended in the rich, thick, almost palpable, ray of light.

Carefree and laughing, joyfully riding his bicycle back and forth on the street where they lived, showing off in front of his father who was running after him as fast as he could.

Performing an act of great bravery: swimming across a branch of the Danube with his Dad at the age of eleven.

Wonderful memories.

But there were bitter ones too:

The invasion by the Germans and the death of his Jewish classmates at the hand of the Nazis in '44,

The heart-wrenching departure from Hungary of his family, 'forever', chased away by the Communists.

That had been hard to take and had probably been the main reason for his going to work for The Agency.

*   *   *

The stuffed peppers had been excellent and the Kékfrankos mellow. Lonsdale mopped up with a piece of delicious, soft, white bread and ordered dessert, chestnut cream with whipped cream and chocolate sauce, and a thimbleful of rum in it, of course, to give it kick.

He signed his bill, put on his hat and coat and turned right after emerging from the hotel's main entrance into the cold.

Although it was barely mid-afternoon, dusk was already approaching. Budapest is at the easternmost edge of the wide Central European time zone stretching from Poland in the east to France in the west. There was still enough light by which to check for pursuit, but there seemed to be none. To make sure, Lonsdale ducked into the shopping center he had passed earlier in the day for a few evasive maneuvers, but, as far as he could tell, nobody was following him. He was "black".

He doubled back to the Western railway Station, located number 2024 in the row of lockers provided for the convenience of the public, opened it with the key he had been given in Washington and removed its content—his 'kit'. He returned to his room where he checked the contents of the small, especially constructed metal suitcase. An H&K automatic with silencer, four spare clips of ammunition, a portable GPS system, a multiple homing device to track vehicles remotely, night vision goggles, plastic restraining strips to be used as handcuffs and an encrypting cellular telephone with charger made up the inventory. Fitted into the inside cover there was also a specially designed plastic dagger in a sheath that he could fasten to his left forearm under his shirt.

He chuckled to himself as he locked the case and put it in the cupboard.

The dagger was one of his little inventions. It had a very thin metal rod embedded along its middle that protruded ever so slightly at the dagger's tip in the form of a sharp, stainless steel needle, thereby converting a harmless-looking toy made out of hard plastic into a portable, easily concealable and lethal weapon.

*   *   *

Before leaving for Europe Lonsdale had been careful to build his 'legend'. His passport said he was Bernard Kane, private investigator from Canada, born and residing in Montreal.

Having rented a full service office in the Place Ville Marie Complex, and having coached the secretary on duty about what to say when the phone rang ('Mr Kane is in Europe on business and will be back next week.') Lonsdale had visited Moscovitch's widowed mother in Outremont, on the edge of a district Montrealers call Mile End, an area that, together with Le Plateau, had become gentrified and fashionable of late.

Mrs. Moscovitch lived in the upper half of a duplex on Durocher Street.

After listening to her clatter down the narrow, inside staircase to answer the bell, Lonsdale had expected to meet an elderly widow, probably living on a modest pension and at a loss about how to deal with her son's disappearance.

He was in for a surprise.

Klara Moscovitch was a handsome woman of great composure and considerable beauty, much more so than her photograph reflected in the file Lonsdale had seen in Washington.

She had greeted him without preamble. "I presume you are Mr. Kane, the private investigator the Department of External Affairs has suggested I engage to look for my son. Come in and please follow me upstairs."

Lonsdale had nodded, hung up his coat in the corridor-vestibule, and stepped into a large, airy space encompassing living area and study that occupied the full width of the apartment. To the left, a large glass door, through which one could see across the wide street, led to a long balcony. Sunlight streaming through the generous window lit up this part of the living space. To his right he saw, and smelled, that Mrs. Moscovitch was preparing espresso coffee in a modern, well-equipped kitchen glistening with copper and aluminum utensils above the sink opposite the food preparation island.

He suspected that to the left of the kitchen there was a dining area with an internal 'gallery', or balcony, overlooking a courtyard,

39

and beyond that, a couple of bedrooms and a bathroom, the typical layout of the Montreal version of a New York 'brownstone'.

Two large skylights above the dining and living areas made the walls of the apartment, painted in the warm colors of Provence—golden yellow and pale blue—glow exquisitely in the October sunshine. Obviously, Mrs. Moscovitch had spent a considerable amount of money on renovating and decorating the place.

And on the artwork on the walls.

Three signed prints from the Marina Picasso collection, an original Braque, two beautifully executed life size torsos, one male the other female, by an artist whose name Lonsdale did not recognize, and a very rare Bateman print called 'Midnight—Black Wolf".

Sitting in a comfortable armchair across the coffee table from his host, Lonsdale had gratefully accepted the espresso offered and had helped himself to a touch of warm milk and sugar.

"The government is doing whatever it can to locate your son, but you must understand these things take time." He had looked the woman squarely in the eyes and had made himself sound encouraging. "As soon as the Department hears from the Hungarian authorities who, by the way, are being very cooperative I'm told, Mr. Yves Arsenault, who is in charge of your son's file, will get in touch with you and give you an update."

She met his gaze without flinching. "If that's the case, what, may I ask, are you doing here?" Her response had a sting, sufficiently sharp to jolt Lonsdale's gray matter into creative thinking mode. This was no ordinary woman, no helpless widow, nor a person with whom to trifle.

He made a mental note. Klara Moscovitch could prove to be a useful ally down the road.

"I'm here to help find your son, but before I go into details I would like to know a little more about you and your family."

"Have they not given you the file to read?"

"As a matter of fact, no. They just gave me a summary." He had grinned at her conspiratorially. "You see, I only consult with the Department; I don't work for it. They use me to help out when things are beginning to drag and a more informal approach is indicated."

Klara Moscovitch looked at her guest with renewed interest. There was something strangely fascinating about the man and his smile and his way of taking in everything at a glance. He seemed to be quick on the uptake.

Nor did he seem to have any difficulty making himself comfortable in her living space.

'Those gray-green eyes have a cruel streak in them' she cautioned herself, 'but they must be gorgeous when they looked at someone they loved'.

Mrs. Moscovitch was a very sensuous woman.

She erased the thoughts from her mind. 'Don't go there. This man is dangerous,' her logic warned. Yet she couldn't help checking his hands. No. He wasn't wearing a wedding band. 'Oh, those eyes …' She looked at him again and sensed the intellect behind his gaze, saw the telltale signs of suffering and deep-seated weariness in the face, and her heart went out to him in spite of herself.

'How old is he and where does he hail from?' she asked herself. 'Looks fifty because he seems to be very fit, but is probably older. Big nose, generous mouth, graying, but full head of hair.'

Aloud she said. "Are you telling me your people are beginning to think the pressure they are exerting through diplomatic channels is becoming counterproductive?"

'No slouch she' Lonsdale thought and began to see the woman in an entirely different light. "You may be right. In any event, tell me more about yourself."

CHAPTER 7

Novi Sad, Friday, October 12

The barge *Maria* was beating her way upstream on the Danube toward Budapest, a city she hoped to reach in about three days.

She was owned, like most river barges in the region, by a mom-and-pop outfit, with 'Mom' looking after the cooking and the paperwork and 'Pop' doing the piloting with the help of a couple of hired hands. Usually Mom and Pop lived on board, although in instances where the same owners operated more than one vessel they frequently used a converted container on the riverbank to serve as office and lodgings for the proprietor and his family.

The *Maria* was no exception. Owned by Milan Juric, a Bosnian Muslim, and his wife, Rada, her home base was on a spit of land alongside an inlet past the tip of the *Háros* peninsula south of the Hungarian capital. *Háros* was midway between Rotterdam, the northernmost point of the three thousand plus kilometer-long Trans European Waterway, and *Constanza* in Rumania, its southern terminal.

The Jurices had moved to Hungary during the 1999 NATO campaign against Serbia and bought the *Maria* for a song; her engine had seized and the river transportation business had gone to hell. With the purchase they also aquired a tugboat that came in handy when cargo was hard to find. The Danube had become un-navigable south of Novi Sad after NATO destroyed the seven bridges spanning the river in the area.

Juric was originally from Srebrenica where, during the height of the Balkan wars, the Orthodox Serbs, lead by Radovan Karadzic and Ratko Mladic, committed a series of atrocities against the Bosnian Muslims. Juric himself escaped death from starvation by the skin of his teeth when he managed to escape from Serbian detention with the help of a Turkish Red Crescent worker, who had taken pity on the emaciated man. Over several months she nursed him back to health and then married him.

Brutal captivity leaves an indelible mark on a man. Juric was no exception. He began thirsting for revenge obsessively, not only against the Serbs, but also against the West and NATO, for their failure to intervene to prevent the atrocities.

The consequences were predictable. His wife's friends put him in touch with the secular Turkish Pan-Islamic movement known as The Cause, a sort of Jihad, the purpose of which was revenge against the West through the creation of a very large group of secular Islamic countries modeled on Turkey. Though not a fanatic, Juric became an enthusiastic supporter of The Cause.

Al Qaeda's 'sleeper' members of The Cause had no difficulty recruiting Juric. They started by financing his business and then set him up to live an isolated way of life, well suited for the activities they had in mind for him. Soon, by virtue of their strategic location and occupation, the Jurices became one of Al Qaeda's most important Central European sleeper cells.

The *Maria* was a relatively modern, medium-sized, shallow draft barge, able to accommodate four standard uncoupled fifty-three foot semi trailers—twice two, side-by-side. Unfortunately, she was only a partial Ro-Ro (roll on, roll off) because she was too narrow. Thus, the semi-trailers had to be loaded onto her by backing the tractor-trailer combo onto the deck then detaching the tractor and repeating the operation for the next trailer.

Alternatively, she could also transport eight forty-foot standard containers (four in the hold and four on top), but Juric did not like to accept such a tall load because it partially obscured his view from the bridge. What's more, in a crosswind, the barge would crab, making her even more difficult to steer.

In the stern, on top of the bridge that took up the full thirty-odd foot beam of the vessel, the pilothouse accommodated the steering station, chart table and engine controls. On the main deck of the two-storey structure, there were two small cabins, a galley and a head.

The twin-diesel propulsion unit, situated below decks, was Juric's pride and joy; he had rebuilt the engines himself.

The vessel continued laboring upriver, its blunted bow slicing through the oil-tainted, dull-gray water. The wind from the west was noticeably strong, but she didn't crab; her heavy load kept her low in the water.

Juric sent one of his hired hands forward to look for hidden submerged obstacles then accelerated gradually. He carefully piloted his vessel through the narrow channel leading away from the gap which the Yugoslav authorities opened three times a week in the 'temporary' pontoon bridge across the river at Novi Sad to allow the convoys of barges lining both banks to resume their journey.

As always, the situation was chaotic, with vessels jockeying for position, gawking tourists and men seeking work or transportation milling about, and skippers arguing with the river police over the toll of 30 Euro cents per metric ton. Juric, of course, had welcomed the chaos. It had helped him the previous day to 'board' three extra hands without drawing attention to them.

These had flown in from Baghdad to Belgrade the day before: Barzan Hassani, better known as The Butcher, Esad Delic, a brilliant virologist working in Budapest, and Saif Al Adel, a member of Al Qaeda's consultation council and military committee.

In addition to Juric and his distinguished guests, there were six others on board. One was a specialized technician and five were guard/deckhands, all members of Saddam Hussein's State Security apparatus, sent to *Constanza*, the Rumanian port city, to provide the muscle in case of a 'mishap' during the loading of four specially designed semi-trailers, three of which bore the label 'agricultural machinery'. In reality, they contained equipment for mass-producing biological weapons of mass destruction and had originated in Iraq.

The fourth was a surgery/dormitory to accommodate two persons in luxury, or eight in lesser comfort.

To Juric, his passengers seemed to be strange bedfellows, brought together by the events of 9/11and the acceleration of change in the Middle East.

He, Delic and Al Adel represented Al Qaeda, the organization that had tumbled on to the existence of contaminated glue with the potential for becoming a WMD. However, Al Qaeda needed Iraq, represented by Hassani and the security men, to provide the facilities for the mass manufacture, packaging and distribution of this new WMD.

So far, so good: all those involved were Sunni!

How ironic then, Juric added to himself, that they should have to rely on a Jew to invent a vaccine to protect them from themselves!

*　　*　　*

As soon as the *Maria* cleared the bustle of local river traffic Juric yielded the helm to one of the security men and called his wife in Budapest.

"Rada, we just passed Novi Sad. Expect us around sundown a week from now. We have one more stop to make." He paused. "How is the extension working out?" They had recently acquired a third land-based container, which meant that they now had an office/ lodging type unit on both sides of the original unit—their 'home'.

"I check on it regularly. Seems OK as far as I can see."

"Everything is in order then."

"Yes, except that I miss you."

"Won't be long now." Juric hung up then sought out Hassani who was resting in the cabin opposite to Juric's.

"We're on our way again, Colonel and expect to arrive as scheduled."

Hassani grunted. He was not much for wasting words.

CHAPTER 8

Budapest, Friday, October 12

After an early breakfast, Lonsdale left the hotel, hailed a cab and told the driver to take him to the State Property Agency on *Pozsonyi* Street. Never having seen the building close up, it struck him how much the SPA's headquarters looked like a miniature copy of the CIA's main building at Langley, all aluminum, concrete and glass.

Logical. In its previous incarnation, the building had been the headquarters of Hungaluco, the state-owned aluminum conglomerate.

At the information desk, he found himself face to face with an attractive woman chatting on the phone in English.

"I'm anxious to contact a company called Phylaxos, I hope to do some export business with them" he told her after she had hung up.

"Please spell the name." He did so and gave her a wide smile. Within a minute, she had the information on her computer screen.

"What would you like to know?" Her strongly accented English was fluent.

"Who owns the company?"

"I am not allowed to give names, but I can tell this. Our government has five per cent interest in Phylaxos. The rest is private."

"Can you tell me who the Managing Director is, and where I can reach him?"

"His name is Jason Moscovitch, but I do not have a telephone number for him."

"And for the company?"

"No number for it either."

"Have you an address?"

She looked at him and he became flustered. She had the most incredibly blue eyes he had ever seen. "I do not have a number or an address," she said in pedantic, school-girl English, "because the company's office burned down and yet I do not have the new information." She sensed his discomfiture. "Is there anything else I can do for you?"

Lonsdale forced himself to concentrate, but the blazing blueness of her eyes was giving him trouble. He looked at her nameplate again and started afresh. "Mrs. Illman . . ."

"Please call me Eva." Startled, he pressed on. "Very well Eva, I need to contact the company, especially Mr. Moscovitch, as soon possible. Is there any way you can find a telephone number for him or maybe his assistant, or co-worker . . . ?" Of course, he already had the numbers, but he was hoping to manipulate her into suggesting he make an appointment with the person in charge of the Phylaxos file. That way, if she was ever asked to give details about her conversation with him, she would say he seemed to know almost nothing about the company, and certainly nothing about who was in charge of the file at the SPA.

"The best person to speak with, that is the man who is handling the file."

Bingo. "And who would that be?"

"His name is Abel Drusza and he is the Deputy Managing Director of the Medico-Pharmaceutical Division."

"Sounds like an important man . . ."

"He is, and he is very busy. If you want to see him, in advance you must make an appointment. You can't just go up like that . . ." she snapped her fingers.

"I don't really have much time. I've just arrived this morning and hope to return to Canada before the week end after next."

Eva looked at her calendar. "It's Friday, so that gives us only five business days."

Lonsdale bit his lower lip feigning great preoccupation. "You think . . . ," he began, but she cut him off.

"No. I don't think before the end of next week you can see him."

"But that's too long to wait." He tried to look forlorn and very disappointed.

"You must just have to visit us again after the holidays, in the New Year unless," she let her voice trail off. "Unless, perhaps, it's OK for you for me to do something . . ." Their eyes locked and she blushed. "Mr. Drusza's secretary is a good friend. I calling her and to try to squeeze an appointment for you on Monday. Is that all right?" Her eyes were boring into his.

"Monday would be fine."

She picked up the phone and he listened carefully to what she was saying in Hungarian. At first, the situation did not look good, but then Eva mentioned that Lonsdale was from Canada. That seemed to change things. He ended up with an appointment to see Drusza on Monday afternoon.

"I must warn you," Eva said after giving him the good news, "that, at moment's notice, appointments are subject to cancellation, so you leave me a number where I can telephone you."

He gave her his name, Kane, and told her he was staying at the *Béke*.

"Anyway," she continued, "my friend gave me contact number for Mr. Moscovitch's assistant, Miss Amina Dadakne. Call her. Mr. Moscovitch, we don't know where he is."

Lonsdale jotted down the number then turned to the woman. "How can I reciprocate?" he asked.

"Reciprocate? I do not understand the word."

She laughed after he had explained its meaning. "You owe me nothing. It's my job to welcome you in our country and to help you with horrible bureaucracy." She extended her hand and he shook it then took his leave.

"See you on Monday," she shouted after him, but, busy with his thoughts, he did not hear her.

CHAPTER 9

When Abel Drusza heard about it, he told his secretary to cancel the appointment with Kane, the Canadian, immediately and not to give out information to *anyone* about Phylaxos without first checking with him.

Born in the southern Hungarian city of Szeged to a Bosnian father and a Hungarian mother (who converted to Islam to please her husband), Abel Drusza was brought up a Muslim in the relative comfort of Sarajevo until 1989 when civil war broke out in the Balkans. Sixteen years old, he had been present at the abduction of his father by the Serbs to a concentration camp from which he never returned then had watched the rape and execution of his mother for being a turncoat, a Christian Hungarian woman who had sullied herself by marrying a Muslim.

The shock of losing his parents under such desperate circumstances had almost been more than Drusza could bear.

Raging against NATO for its hands-off attitude with regard to these atrocities, he became fanaticized and joined the secret supporters of Jihad to wage holy war against the West.

Somehow, he ended up in a refugee camp run by the Knights of Malta who sent him to West Germany where he graduated from Dresden University with a degree in Biology and another in Business Administration. Fluent in English, German, Hungarian and a number of Slavic languages, he returned to Hungary where, hiding his Muslim affiliations, he got a job at the State Property Agency. His timing was lucky. It took him less than five years to become Deputy Managing Director of the Medico-Pharmaceutical Division.

He was working hard to meet his boss' expectations and was struggling mightily when Jason Moscovitch landed in his office. The Canadian had brought with him two cases of contaminated surgical glue, thirty-six vials containing samples of his work relating to a potential vaccine against nv.C-JD, six hundred pages of lab notes, thirty thousand dollars (a loan from his mother) and a letter of introduction to Drusza from the Canadian Embassy's Commercial Counselor.

To Drusza, Moscovitch had been a Godsend, a means to justify the SPA plowing more money into Phylaxos Ltd., once the pride of Hungary's veterinarian pharmaceutical industry, but now teetering on the verge of bankruptcy. Drusza could not allow Phylaxos to go under. The company's international reputation demanded that the government keep it afloat somehow.

As a first step, Drusza appointed Moscovitch as Phylaxos' Chief Scientific Officer. Within a month Moscovitch reported that the company was beyond salvage, so Drusza sold Moscovitch Phylaxos' laboratory equipment and the right to use the name 'Phylaxos Veterinary Pharmaceuticals' for the tidy sum of one hundred thousand dollars.

But, Moscovitch didn't have that kind of money.

Sensing an opportunity to further his cause, Drusza called a fellow Bosnian Muslim, Esad Delic, his roommate at Dresden University who, after graduating with a Ph.D. in Virology had gone to Pakistan first, to be indoctrinated and trained by Al Qaeda, and then to Iraq to learn how to manufacture biological weapons for Sadam Hussein.

Delic was quick to realize that nv.Creutzfeldt-Jakob disease was a potentially very powerful biological weapon of mass destruction. He did not hesitate and immediately asked Al Qaeda to put up the seventy-odd thousand dollars to buy part of Phylaxos.

In exchange for thirty thousand dollars, plus the work he had done to date, Moscovitch received eighty per cent of the new company. Delic got twenty per cent for his money in spite of having tried hard to hold out for a fifty-fifty partnership and a job as Moscovitch's assistant, but Moscovitch was not about to give half of the technology away for a paltry seventy thousand. Nonetheless, Moscovitch did hire Delic, which was all the 'in' the Bosnian had really wanted.

Next, again with Drusza's help, Moscovitch sold ten percentage points of his Phylaxos holdings to Investments Hungary for six monthly payments of ten thousand dollars, sufficient to cover the fledgling company's overhead for half a year.

For five months Moscovitch and Delic worked twelve-hour days, seven days a week, perfecting a technique to direct prions, the propagators of Creutzfeldt-Jakob disease. This enabled them to produce a number of nv.C-JD variants, including one that was transmissible via air-born microorganisms and very contagious. It would spread through humankind like wildfire unless a vaccine were found to check its progress.

At first, the method of fabricating the vaccine kept eluding Moscovitch. This frustrated Delic's plan. He could not risk getting rid of the scientist by killing him or buying him out before the Canadian produced the antidote that Al Qaeda needed to protect the lives of the True Believers while the infidel died of nv.C-JD like flies in autumn.

Then the company ran out of money and Delic was forced to stand by idly (since Al Qaeda was not willing to put up more money) while Moscovitch sold fifty percentage points of the company to a Japanese conglomerate to keep Phylaxos afloat.

By the time, just before 9/11, Moscovitch stumbled onto the complicated methodology of producing an untested version of the vaccine, Drusza had become a full-fledged member of Al Qaeda. His job gave him ideal cover for clandestine dealings and highly placed contacts, freedom to travel and excellent geographical location. He was powerful enough to lay his hands on the money needed to buy Moscovitch out.

Too late. The Japanese had gotten there first.

So, Drusza and Delic had to resort to stealing the vaccine samples, an operation that they planned together, with Drusza providing the impeccable alibi for Delic as to his whereabouts on the night he and his team snatched Moscovitch.

When Delic had phoned Drusza from Baghdad a few days later to advise that the vials he had taken from Moscovitch had turned out to contain a neutral liquid, Drusza had gone ballistic. He had screamed at Delic and called him an incompetent fool for allowing his partner, with whom he had shared a lab on a daily basis for six months, to outfox him so completely.

Cursing and swearing was obviously of no help. Drusza was forced to admit that the kidnapping had been a total disaster.

The only way of salvaging the situation was to create conditions tempting enough for the Canadian to 'rediscover' and perfect the vaccine while working under Jihadist control.

Drusza had been around scientists long enough to realize that they were not particularly malleable, and that money was not always enough to force a man of Moscovitch's caliber to work while a virtual prisoner, no matter how gilded the cage in which he would be kept.

But he had to try!

He had racked his brains feverishly for a way to provide Moscovitch with lots of money and an outstanding opportunity to cover himself with glory through international recognition.

For obvious reasons Al Qaida could not be part of the solution, but Iraq could!

Off he had gone, therefore, to see Hassani in Baghdad to explain what he had in mind. In turn, The Butcher had taken Delic and Drusza to Saddam.

The dictator had loved his idea.

He had agreed on the spot to support the scheme with money and know-how because it fitted perfectly into his plans for expanding the Iraqi chemical and biological warfare capability.

As Drusza was leaving the meeting, the Dictator had looked at him hard with shrewd, merciless eyes. "Now that you have Saddam's financial support and the source of the principal raw material you need, is there any other major problem that remains to be solved?" he had asked.

"The problem of how to motivate the Canadian to work whole heartedly while a prisoner of ours, without thinking up plans for escaping from us."

"Then you think money and glory might not be enough?"

Drusza had cursed himself for having expressed his reservations, but he had wanted to have an escape hatch in case the project failed. Saddam was notorious for his vengefulness.

He had gulped, and had answered with great honesty: "They might not be, your Exalted Excellency."

Saddam had frowned, and Drusza had felt his heart constrict. His entire existence was hanging in the balance.

"This scientist is a Jew, is he not?"

"Yes, your Exalted Excellency."

"The Jews are a sentimental people. Is his mother alive?"

Drusza had looked at Delic who had nodded.

"She is, your Exalted Excellency."

"Well then," Saddam had said with a knowing smile. "Kidnap her too, and bring her to Baghdad. We'll keep her here for as long as we need the services of her son. I'm sure that will make him cooperate with enthusiasm."

Drusza had returned to Budapest and had set to work feverishly on the physical arrangements that needed to be in place by mid-October for his plans to succeed. He wisely left the planning and execution of Klara Moscovitch's kidnappings to a joint Al Qaeda/Iraqi task force headed by Hassani.

The last thing he needed now was interference from a bumbling Canadian private investigator hired by Moscovitch's mother to find her son.

CHAPTER 10

Budapest, Saturday, October 13

Half way through his daily routine of twenty-five push-ups, the telephone rang in Lonsdale's hotel room. Cursing, he rolled over gingerly, protecting his wounded hip that still hurt, and went to answer it.

"Mr. Kane I'm downstairs at reception. I have to see you." It was Eva Illman, the information clerk from the SPA. "I did something yesterday I should not have done and I will get in trouble if my mistake I don't correct."

Lonsdale checked his watch. Ten past seven.

"Meet me in the dining-room in five minutes." He hung up, put on a T-shirt, pulled a sweater over it, slipped into his jeans and joggers and headed for the door.

After helping themselves from the buffet, they sat down at a corner table. Lonsdale ordered two *cafés au lait*.

"Yesterday I told you about Amina, Mr. Moscovitch's assistant," Eva began, "and from my friend I got you her phone number. My friend Ilona is Mr. Drusza's secretary. I have to now ask you to not call Amina because if you do, lots of trouble will come to Ilona."

"Why . . .?"

"When my friend told Mr. Drusza that she had made an appointment for you on Monday . . ."

"After the week end . . ."

Eva nodded. ". . . for Monday, he became very angry and told her to cancel it. She will be calling you soon, before noon anyway. We close at that time Saturday", she added. "Ilona said he was so angry that she did not tell him about giving to me Amina's phone number. So, you see, you must not call her."

Lonsdale's mind was racing. For his cover as a private investigator to remain intact, he needed to show that he had obtained Amina's particulars locally. The main purpose of his visit to the SPA the previous day had been to establish a provable local source of information. To achieve this objective, he now had to pretend that he was taking the woman into his confidence.

"Look Eva," he said with a sheepish grin, "I find myself between a rock and a hard place."

The woman was puzzled. "I do not know that saying."

"Well then, let me explain. As you know, Mr. Moscovitch has disappeared and his mother hired me to find him. She doesn't have a lot of money and cannot afford to send me back here again to look for her son."

"That's the rock."

"Right. The hard place is that I always try to give my clients value for their money. I don't want to go home without really, *really* having done everything possible to find out *something* for her." He ate the food remaining on his plate. "Is there any way you can arrange for me to meet Amina without getting Ilona into trouble, without my having to call Amina?"

Eva hesitated. "There is perhaps something that could be done . . . Amina comes every Monday at ten to Mr. Drusza's office to see what is developing in Phylaxos file and picking up her paycheck."

"How come?"

"Mr. Delic, Amina's boss, has gone back to Iraq to wait there for the Phylaxos laboratory to be rebuilt. Amina, she is looking after . . . how you say . . . coordinating," she had finally found the word, "that's it, coordinating, the rebuilding and she reports on this to Mr. Drusza on Monday and Thursday mornings about what happened the previous days. On Mondays she also comes down to see me and I give to her her paycheck."

Lonsdale pretended to think for a moment then made a show of catching on. "So you want me to be in the lobby of the SPA on Monday around eleven-thirty to watch Amina pick up her check and then follow her home." Lonsdale made himself sound simplistic, inexperienced.

"Something like that. And you have to find a clever way of starting to speak with Amina, but you must be careful. She is very intelligent and very suspicious of strangers."

"Then it would, perhaps, be better if I did not speak with her at all."

Eva looked relieved. "That would be the best Mr. Kane. That way I would be not in trouble. OK?"

Lonsdale gave her his best smile. "Don't worry. I'll call Mr. Moscovitch's mother in Canada. I'm sure she has Amina's number." He hoped she would remember his remark, thereby maintaining the fiction that he had known very little about the Moscovitch file prior to arriving in Budapest.

After lunch, Lonsdale, special 'kit' in hand, crossed the Danube to *Óbuda*, a district of Budapest. He wanted to have a look at the area where Amina lived.

Her apartment on *Kis Korona* Street was in a so-called panel-house, built in the 'glorious' years of goulash communism during which the central government erected blocks upon blocks of ugly apartment structures made of large, grey prefabricated panels.

The complex consisted of four massive eight-storey buildings arranged around a park with a public telephone booth at each corner. As far as Lonsdale could judge from a cursory examination of the tenants' list, Amina's sixth floor apartment faced outward, and overlooked a row of low rise housing with a so-called cultural center at its end. This is where, during the years of socialist rule, comrades were encouraged to confess their shortcomings, criticize and, at times, denounce their neighbors and exhort each other to work harder for the good of the proletariat.

It took Lonsdale a quarter hour to circumnavigate the complex on foot during which he managed to identify Amina's red Suzuki with the help of the license plate number Morton's people had given him. The little car, parked next to the cultural center, was at a spot Lonsdale was sure the woman could see from her apartment. This meant that, if he wanted to attach a tracking device to it, he would have to return after dark.

A cab to *Galamb* Street in the city's center got him to Avis where he rented an Opel Kadet under the name of Philip Johnston (one of three aliases he could back up with suitable documentation). After locking his 'kit' in the trunk, he drove to the Intercontinental Hotel four blocks away where he arranged a week's inside parking for the car. Then he walked over to the Kempinski and asked the doorman to locate a limousine driver named Frakkos who, he had been told by Morton's people, was attached to the hotel. When the man appeared, Lonsdale explained in a voice loud enough for all to hear that his friends in Dallas had raved about Frakkos' prowess as a driver and tourist guide. He finished by retaining Frakkos as his chauffeur for a week.

After dinner, Lonsdale drove to *Kis Korona* Street. The Suzuki was still there. He drew up next to it and, on the pretext of cleaning his car's ashtray, leaned over and stuck the transmitting part of the tracking device from his kit under Amina's vehicle, making sure its powerful magnets held fast.

At ten pm, Lonsdale met Frakkos in an *Óbuda* greasy spoon, a stone's throw from Amina's apartment, gave him half a dozen photos of the woman, and a two thousand dollar cash advance. He instructed Frakkos to initiate round the clock surveillance of her immediately.

He also gave Frakkos the receiving unit of the tracking device he had planted under Amina's car.

Frakkos, a highly entrepreneurial Hungarian who, with his wife, ran a private detective agency on the side that concentrated on marital infidelity cases involving foreign, preferably Western, nationals. He derived his leads from contacts with guests of 'his' hotel.

It had not taken long for the CIA to become aware of his extracurricular activities.

"Hire three top notch men with cars, experienced in shadowing people," he instructed the driver.

"Shadowing?" Frakkos' English was fluent, but limited.

Although Lonsdale could have communicated with him in Hungarian, he preferred not to, for the time being.

"Shadowing means to follow people," he explained patiently. "Watch her, but don't frighten her. Try to get away without being spotted."

"And if she notices, yes?"

"She'll probably think you're the police."

"You mean trouble with the police also, yes? Not only with the wife of her lover?" Frakkos was curious. Lonsdale did not reply.

"What time do you think she'll go to work?"

"I have no idea."

"She's in the apartment, yes?"

"Her car's there." Lonsdale answered. "But let's make sure." He dialed the woman's telephone number on his cellular.

After a few rings, a sleepy voice answered. "Am I speaking to Amina Dadakne?" Lonsdale asked in English.

A cautious "Yes. Who's this?"

"My name is Kane. I am a private investigator working for Jason Moscovitch's mother. I'm sorry to call you so late, but I wanted to be sure I'd find you at home."

"Who gave you my number?" She was suspicious.

"Mrs. Moscovitch, of course."

The woman hesitated. "I have already told the police everything I know."

Lonsdale gave Frakkos a thumbs-up sign.

"I'm sure you did." Lonsdale was at his persuasive best. "But Mrs. Moscovitch is understandably worried about her son and wants to leave no stone unturned in the search for him." He watched Frakkos leave, already on the phone to his people to get them into position. "I'd really appreciate your helping me out by spending a few minutes with me. Mrs. Moscovitch said you were not only working with her son, but you became friends with him too."

"It's late and I'm tired. I'm already in bed." Probably a lie. "But call me tomorrow and I'll see what I can do."

"What time?"

"Ten o'clock." Amina hung up. Lonsdale sensed a brush-off.

Lonsdale dialed Frakkos' special cell number. "She's either going to go out to see someone or make a call from a public phone booth."

"Why not from home?"

"Because she's afraid someone may be tapping her line."

CHAPTER 11

Budapest, Sunday, October 14

By the late spring of 1945, the victorious Soviet Army had 'liberated' Hungary. The country's army had been defeated and the Germans chased out.

Two years of feverish reconstruction activity had followed, fueled by the hope that, at last, a democratically elected government would lead the country.

This was not to be.

When, in 1947, Stalin saw that the vast majority of Hungarians had voted for the Smallhoders' Party and that the government would be composed principally of Social Democrats and Small Landowners rather than Communists loyal to Moscow, he 'called' for new elections. He also decreed that the "friendly occupying forces," the Red Army, manifest its "solidarity with the people".

The 1948 elections resulted in a Communist landslide and, within a year, Hungary was absorbed into the Soviet bloc. In 1949, after the Communist government had mounted the bloody circus that it had chosen to call the Rajk Trials, individual freedoms ceased to exist in Hungary, as did any semblance of free enterprise. The economy became centrally controlled and one ambitious Five Year Plan followed the other.

Of course, few of their lofty goals were ever reached. On the contrary, corruption, waste and inefficiency became rampant as high-ranking officials tried desperately to cover up their inability to meet quotas.

One of the grandiose schemes involved the conversion of an ancient market town called *Dunapentele* into a center of heavy industry. To please Stalin, the place was renamed *Sztálinváros* (Stalin City) and hundreds of millions were spent on creating a major industrial complex there.

This included a combined steel mill and barge-building facility alongside the Danube.

Stalin City was well located for such a purpose. Access by rail and water were excellent and the Capital's airport, *Ferihegy*, was less than eighty kilometers to the northeast.

Business was brisk while the Comintern existed. Western business executives from as far away as Canada came to buy Hungarian steel at *Sztálinváros* because the quality was good and the price right. The Hungarian Forint was pegged to the Russian Ruble and the Ruble to a ridiculously priced US Dollar.

Then the Berlin Wall fell, the Soviet Empire disintegrated and the Comintern ceased to exist. Looking westward, Hungary adopted a market-style economy once again and transferred all nationally owned assets to the country's State Property Agency. The SPA then took on the responsibility of privatizing all but a few strategically important enterprises (the airline, the railway, and one TV and radio station).

The steel complex at *Dunaújváros* (the new name for Stalin City) was put up for sale, but nobody bid on it because there was just too much competition in the region. Hungary had already privatized its other steel fabricating facility at Ozd in the northern part of the country near the Slovak border.

Stuck with the plant, the SPA had no choice but to mothball it, arrange for a watchman to keep an eye on it and wait for someone to come up with a viable plan for its use. That someone turned out to be Drusza.

While planning the Moscovitch kidnapping he had hit on the idea of temporarily holding the scientist in a semi-trailer complex at the abandoned barge-fabricating facility. Exercising his authority as a Deputy Director of the SPA, and using Amina Dadakne as a go-between, he had had the watchman 'guarding' the property replaced by a low-level Al Qaida sympathizer and his wife. Illegal immigrants from Bosnia, Selim and Yovanka Dankovic were very happy to move into the semi-trailer their predecessor had occupied and to supervise the installation of the plumbing, sewage and electrical work Drusza had organized to create the facility for holding Moscovitch.

This would consist of four semi-trailers: the watchman's, and three others. The first of these would hold the scientist, the second—attached to the first—would contain a mini-lab. The third, set up in bunkhouse configuration, would accommodate up to as many as eight 'workers', some of whom would act as guards.

The facility was ready in time for Moscovitch to be installed in his temporary quarters the morning after his kidnapping. The Dankovices were appointed his jailers.

Well satisfied with this arrangement, Drusza then turned his attention to legalizing the situation. He had Hassani rent the barge-building facility through one of his Cyprus companies.

*   *   *

On Sunday, October 14, the *Maria* docked at *Dunaújváros* shortly after dark. Next morning, Juric hurried ashore and helped Dankovic, the watchman-jailer, to position the project's reach-loader in the most effective way for discharging the vessel's cargo. There was no way he wanted to rent a tractor for use in the unloading; the less attention drawn to the abandoned barge manufacturing yard, the better.

The operation was not simple. Each of the four semis had to be positioned to align precisely with the plumbing and sewage connections that had been installed prior to the *Maria*'s arrival.

It would take four days to unload, line up and connect the semis. While the work was being completed, Hassani and Al Adel would continue to occupy the two cabins at the stern of the vessel, with Juric and Delic bunking in with the security men. Naturally, everybody was required to pitch in to ensure that the installations were completed as quickly as possible.

CHAPTER 12

Budapest, Monday, October 15

Having decided not to phone Amina on Monday morning because he wanted to keep her guessing, Lonsdale called Eva at the SPA instead. "Contrary to what you said, your friend has not cancelled my appointment with Mr. Drusza. Does this mean that the appointment for two o'clock this afternoon stands?"

Eva became flustered. "I haven't any idea Mr. Kane, but let me check. I call you back in five minutes." She was back on line a short time later. "I'm surprised," she reported. "His secretary telling me her boss cancelled the cancellation. He does want to meet you this afternoon.

Lonsdale assured the woman that no harm was done. Then he took a cab to Budapest Police Headquarters a tall building of shining aluminum and glass on *Váci* Boulevard. He asked for Detective Lieutenant Zoltán Horváth, the officer in charge of the Moscovitch-Phylaxos file, or so Morton had told him.

He was in luck. The detective was free and agreed to receive Lonsdale in his surprisingly spacious office in the relatively new building.

At five feet six inches and with a beer belly of considerable proportion, Horváth, in his mid fifties and balding, looked like what he was, a veteran career cop. He had earned his promotion by working hard on the beat, keeping his nose clean (which meant avoiding politically sensitive cases) and being one of the few members of the force who had volunteered to study English, a language considered non-essential by his socialist bosses. This Lonsdale learned when he asked the man to tell him where he had mastered the language so well.

"Although they officially frowned on those who opted for English, my superiors needed people who spoke the language. There was plenty of work for English-speakers. Nevertheless, hypocritically, those who did were not promoted as fast as the rest."

"So why did you do it?"

"Because I knew that, one day, us guys would be rewarded."

"And were you?"

Horváth scratched his balding pate. "I was a uniformed policeman for twenty-two years. Then the regime changed and they promoted me to detective sergeant. Ten years later, that was two years ago, I made lieutenant. So you see, two is my lucky number."

Lonsdale laughed. "That's a healthy way of looking at it, but I suspect the twenty-two years on the beat must have been pretty tough."

"They were, and the pay was lousy too."

"But you're OK now, aren't you?" Lonsdale couldn't help noticing that the detective was very well dressed.

Horváth looked away. Lonsdale was about to continue with banalities, but the Lieutenant interrupted. "Enough about me. Tell me how I can be of help."

Lonsdale gave him the 'I'm working for Moscovitch's mother' routine. Horváth became pensive.

"Who gave you my name?"

"Mrs. Moscovitch."

"And how did *she* hear about me?"

"External Affairs I guess."

"What's that?"

"The Canadian Foreign Office. We call it External Affairs."

"You mean the people your ambassador and his staff report to?" Horváth looked at his visitor questioningly. "I assume you've signed in with your embassy?"

"Not yet, but I intend to this morning."

"Why don't you do that, then come back tomorrow with a letter from the First Secretary, asking me formally to assist you in this file. That way we'll both have our asses covered."

'Impressive' Lonsdale said to himself. 'A nice way to establish my bona fides while shifting responsibility to Canadian External Affairs in case I become an embarrassment'.

He gave Horváth a big smile. "That's a good thought. What time shall we say tomorrow?"

"How's two o'clock? While we're at it," the police officer gave Lonsdale a wink, "why don't we get going on the paperwork and fill in the standard questionnaire right now?"

"Good idea. Give me the form. You do have it in English I presume."

Horváth handed him the paper and asked for his passport.

"While you're scribbling I'll make a copy of your travel document."

'And check up on me with Interpol' Lonsdale added silently, impressed by the sophisticated and inoffensive manner in which the lieutenant had trapped him into handing over his passport.

Horváth was obviously no dummy.

*   *   *

The trip to the Canadian Embassy on *Istenhegyi* Boulevard took less than twenty minutes. The First Secretary would not receive Lonsdale. Instead, they told him to see the Consul, Mademoiselle Thérèse Lapointe, an attractive thirty-something French Canadian diplomat. She had long blond hair, strikingly green eyes and a remarkably slim, well-proportioned figure—obviously the result of regular, strenuous physical exercise. She carefully read Lonsdale's references (from the RCMP, courtesy of the Canadian Security Intelligence Service as a result of Morton's intervention). Next, she produced a convincing-sounding letter requesting Detective Lieutenant Zoltán Horváth whom, it turned out, she knew, to extend assistance to 'Mr. Kane' in the Moscovitch matter.

*   *   *

The two o'clock interview with Drusza, a small, swarthy-looking man with a full head of very black hair and a forbidding looking black mustache below a potato nose, surprised Lonsdale by its tenor. He had expected a polite, courteous reception at best. Instead, Drusza was affable to the point of being effusive.

His corner office was surprisingly large and luxurious. One set of windows faced the Danube; the other overlooked a pretty park. The pictures on the wall, all carefully chosen, were reproductions of a couple of Matisses and one Bonnard. A very expensive-looking hi-fi-phonograph-radio combination with a wide variety of knobs, fabricated of richly veneered wood, sat on top of the credenza behind his host's desk that it matched beautifully.

After urging him into a comfortable leather armchair Drusza arranged for two espressos and Perrier water then settled into a recliner across the coffee table and offered his guest a Marlborough. Lonsdale declined.

"You don't mind if I do?" His English was accented, but very good.

"Of course not." Lonsdale lied without hesitation. He hated smokers.

"Well then, how can I help?" Drusza took a deep drag on his cigarette. Lonsdale noted that, although his host seemed perfectly at ease, his fingers were trembling. Was he nervous or did he have something physically wrong with him?

He gave Drusza the standard story about working for Mrs. Moscovitch and, for good measure, mentioned that he had just presented his credentials to the Budapest Police.

"So you know as much about the case as I do." Drusza seemed pleased. "Saves us a lot of time."

"How so?"

"We can get down to the nitty-gritty." Drusza rested his cigarette on the lip of an expensive-looking ashtray tastefully engraved with the logo of Sanofi, a French drug company. He leaned back in his armchair and steepled his fingers. "There is no need to dwell on the generalities since you must have heard the details from the police. Incidentally, whom did you see there?"

"A Detective Lieutenant Horváth. Do you know him?"

Drusza shook his head. "'fraid not."

Lonsdale drank some Perrier. "Tell me about this fellow Delic, Moscovitch's working partner."

"An excellent man, technically most qualified. Trained in Germany, Delic has a Ph.D. in virology from Dresden University."

"Where did Delic get the money to invest in Phylaxos? Do you know?"

"His uncle in Turkey. He is in shipping and has lots of money."

Lonsdale picked up his cup and while sipping his coffee continued to put question after inconsequential question to Drusza who answered them all politely and with apparent total candor. After a half hour, Lonsdale thanked his host for the courtesies extended and made as if to leave.

Drusza seemed disappointed. "Won't you now give me an opportunity to put a few of my own questions to you?" His smile intended to disarm.

"Rude of me." Lonsdale, surprised, sat back in his chair. "Fire away."

"Where are you from?"

"Montreal, Quebec." Lonsdale told him and proceeded to stumble through a dozen of Drusza's questions, all probing his identity. Clearly, the man wanted to check on his Canadian visitor's *bona fides* in depth. At three, Drusza got up, signaling that the interview was over.

"I'm afraid we must finish. I have enjoyed our meeting very much," he said with deprecating charm, "but I have another meeting coming up."

They shook hands.

"Feel free to call my secretary, Ilona, if you need to speak with me again. Rest assured I'll help you in your inquiries as much as I can."

"Do you have a cell phone on which I can call you directly?" Drusza gave him the number and saw Lonsdale out.

'What a dolt,' Drusza murmured when the door had closed behind his visitor. 'Does not look like much of a threat. Still, one never knows. Better safe than sorry.' He returned to his desk and attacked the pile of paperwork in his in-basket.

At six-thirty he called it quits and drove over to the Hilton, Buda-side, for a drink at the bar with his friend and protector, Viktor Dózsa, the incumbent Minister of Health. By eight, he was having dinner at his girlfriend's apartment in the Sixth District with Detective-Lieutenant Zoltán Horváth with whom he met regularly and whom he paid a monthly 'salary' for keeping him informed about what was going on in circles that mattered in Hungary.

* * *

"When I got into position on Saturday night, your girlfriend comes rushing out of her apartment building, yes?" Frakkos, who was driving Lonsdale around aimlessly in his limousine on Monday night after dinner, sounded matter-of-fact.

"Where did she go?"

"Not far, just to the nearest public telephone as you said she would."

"Do we know whom she called?"

"I got the number from contact at telephone company, but I haven't traced owner yet."

"How come?" Lonsdale was puzzled.

"It's a cell number. Tracing takes time."

Lonsdale asked for the number then burst out laughing.

"What's funny?"

"Don't bother with tracing the owner. I know who he is."

Frakkos waited to be told, but Lonsdale just pressed on.

"What did she do next?"

"Went to bed I guess." Frakkos was miffed.

"And Sunday?"

"She fooling around in her apartment and, after lunch, going to do what she doing apparently every Wednesday and Sunday afternoon during six months March to October. She went kayaking."

"She went what?"

"Kayaking. Amina Dadakne is a well-known kayaker. Came third at the last Olympics and training regularly for next championship, yes. Keeps two kayaks on the *Duna*—the Danube—one for pleasure, other for racing."

Lonsdale nodded. The information matched with what he had seen in the file Morton had shown him in Washington.

"Did you actually see her on the river?"

"You mean rowing?"

"Yes."

It was Frakkos' turn to nod. "She good at it, yes? Does sprints, then slow, then sprints again. For an hour and a half she does. Then she take paddle inside and rest for few minutes maybe for coffee. After that, she go home."

"What happened on Monday?"

"She got up early and was at SPA eight o'clock. Went straight up to the sixth floor."

"To see whom?"

"We couldn't find out because she not check in at reception. She has pass. But the sixth floor is where all the big shots have offices—you know, big bosses, Division boss, Managing Director boss, and the Deputy bosses."

"Go on."

"From there she went to Phylaxos on *Zászló* Street, had conference with foreman in charge of rebuilding *laboratorium* then went home for lunch."

"Where is she now?"

"In apartment, cooking dinner and eating. I forgot. On her way home she went shopping for food, yes?"

Lonsdale looked at his watch: it showed a few minutes before ten. "Well done Frakkos," he conceded. "You seem to have matters well in hand. Are you satisfied with your set-up?"

"I guess so-so, under circumstances."

"Oh?" Lonsdale was about to get out of the car, but hesitated.

"We're a little bit short of power of man, yes? Including me there are four on job, yes? This means two work together on day shift for fourteen hours, seven in the morning to nine at night, and one on night shift, between nine at night and eight in the morning. Eleven hours. I do coordination and look after you. We need fifth pair of hands, even if our equipment is first class."

"How do you have it deployed?"

"We have electronic tracing equipment in three cars, including the one you gave me, yes? This makes easy to follow woman's car, but when she leave car we have difficulty following her on foot."

Lonsdale thought about the problem for a minute then made up his mind. "Here's what we'll do. Put listening equipment in the four public phones around the complex in which Dadakne lives. Do it with voice-activated tape recorders. Do you have some?"

Frakkos shook his head. "No, but I could buying some. But it will cost a lot of money."

Lonsdale peeled off two thousand dollars from the wad of money he had on him. Frakkos' eyes widened. Lonsdale cut off his thoughts. "Don't get any ideas. We're on a tight budget. I want invoices for everything you spend. And Frakkos, no tricks. I'll be checking your supplier's reputation. If it's not first class and his prices are high I'll assume he's giving you a kickback. I know my way around this part of the world."

"Don't worry. I'll play straight. I have reputation to maintain with foreign clients, yes?"

Lonsdale gave him a hard look. "Let's get on with the job and watch the way we spend our money."

"Will there be bonus at end of job? When we catch lovers making love, yes?"

Lonsdale laughed. He had his team leader where and how he wanted him, incentivized. "Definitely; if we succeed." He continued. "Program the tape recorders to pick up only long distance calls destined for outside of Hungary. There shouldn't be many because the people in the complex are not rich, not the kind to be calling all over the world. Pick up the tapes at night and have your telephone company contact prepare a printout of the numbers and the countries involved. Give them to me every morning before you start your shift at eight."

"What else?"

"Shorten the day shift to twelve hours, from seven a.m. to seven p.m. Have the night man work from seven p.m. until one a.m. and let him take five hours off to rest."

"This means no surveillance between one and seven a.m. yes?"

"Correct, but I'm betting the target won't stay out later than one in the morning, or go to work before seven. If she does, she'll probably go only as far as one of the phone booths near her apartment. And these we'll have covered with the mini recorders."

"You also betting her lover is not in Hungary, yes?"

"Not quite. I think I know who her lover is, and, obviously, at times he is in Hungary."

As he lay in bed, half asleep, mentally replaying the last sixteen hours' events, Lonsdale decided that, on balance it had been a long, but productive day.

He had managed to scare Drusza.

Why else would he change his attitude toward Lonsdale drastically overnight? Was he afraid and hiding something? Although he had acted with apparent nonchalance Lonsdale sensed that, deep down, he was rattled.

Why didn't he mention that Delic was a Bosnian-born orphan who had overcome incredible odds to graduate from Dresden University?

And why did he not mention that Delic was Iraqi trained?

Didn't Drusza say that he, too, was a Dresden graduate? Did they know each other there?

When did Delic suddenly acquire a rich Turkish uncle?

It seemed to Lonsdale that Drusza was not only withholding information, but also fabricating explanations.

A negative development: Frakkos' lament about being understaffed was justified and he'd have to see about that. Perhaps Lonsdale, himself, should be operating in the field for a couple of days to give the boys more cover power—but not just yet. He needed to interview Amina, then Delic. But the bugger was in Iraq, wasn't he?

Lonsdale fell asleep while planning the approach he'd use on Amina once he'd engineered a meeting with her.

CHAPTER 13

Budapest, Tuesday, October 16

Lonsdale was up very early; he had a full day ahead of him. First, he called Adys on his 'special' phone and caught her as she was getting ready for bed.

She was pleased and relieved to hear his voice. "How are you my darling and how is the hip holding up?"

On hearing her voice, Lonsdale felt a tremendous surge of love. He yearned for her and wanted to tell her about how he felt, but was afraid to show his feelings. He feared that doing so would weaken his resolve to complete the Moscovitch mission.

'You're getting old,' he told himself. 'Button it up. Don't analyze feelings. Either show them freely or suppress them!'

After reassuring Adys that he was fine he asked about her plans for the weekend.

"Gina needs my help; she's redecorating and wants me down in West Palm before Saturday. I'll hang around here until Friday then stay with her for a few days. I should be back by Sunday week to greet you when you get back."

Lonsdale laughed. "How come you know when I'm coming back?"

"A woman's instinct . . ." She wasn't about to tell him that the date was no more than wishful thinking on her part. She missed him terribly, worried about his well-being constantly and thanked her stars that she had a theater-related job. Most nights she got home late, exhausted after a long days' work and fell asleep as soon as her head hit the pillow.

"You might just be right," Lonsdale said with as much conviction as he could muster.

This cheered her up enormously. "You can't imagine how much I want you back here. Please hurry home."

He laughed, basking in her love for him. "You can bet on that! I adore you," he heard himself say to his own great surprise. But it felt good!

"And me you."

They hung up. Although they were doing their best to communicate their feelings, they were having a hard time. Her day had just ended while his was just beginning. 'Face it, you're still an emotional cripple' he thought wryly after he had hung up. 'Maybe, just maybe, in time, the love for you she radiates will straighten out your screwed up head.'

But that was a big 'maybe'. Time was working against him. Few, if any, women could manage for long the stress of living with a man whose life was almost constantly in danger and who had systematically trained himself not to show his emotions.

Lonsdale envied Adys for her large family. She had uncles and aunts and cousins all over Cuba and South America. And parents and a sister in the States. In contrast, Lonsdale's grandparents and parents were 'only' children. They had no siblings. Except for his older brother, Anthony whom he had idolized, Lonsdale had no relatives more or less the same age as he.

At age thirteen, Anthony was killed by a stray grenade during the Russian siege of Budapest in 1944/45. The ten-year old Lonsdale, having lost his confidant and mentor, was left to cope on his own. His father was at the Russian front, his mother a guilt-ridden wreck, forever blaming herself for not having protected Anthony.

By the time his father came home from Russian captivity six months later Lonsdale had become prematurely old, temperamental and stubborn. His parents, unwilling and unable to manage him because they lacked a role model, sent him to boarding school in England, thereby further removing him from the emotional security blanket of a loving family.

This made him even more unhappy and insecure.

Lonsdale shook his head. "Get on with it," he commanded.

He firmed up his appointment with Detective Lieutenant Horváth for two in the afternoon. Then he called Amina. To his surprise, she was in and sounded friendly, so he invited her for lunch.

He met her at the *Kis Sipos*, a well-known fish restaurant in the *Óbuda* District, around the corner from where she lived. Both ordered the fish soup 'with roe' for which the establishment was famous, and lots of delicious farmers' bread and white wine to wash the meal down.

Amina confirmed that she had worked closely with Moscovitch and had gotten to like him. It was a shame he had disappeared without a trace.

"Were you intimate?"

"Not really, but we were a small team and soon everybody became very friendly with everybody else." She sounded genuine.

"How many were you?"

"Mr. Delic, Jason, me and two lab assistants."

"Tell me about Delic."

She repeated substantially what Drusza had told Lonsdale and, like Drusza, failed to mention Delic's sojourn in Iraq.

Lonsdale sensed that this highly intelligent woman was not only beautiful and sexy but also very much capable of using her feminine wiles to reach her goals. As for not being intimate with the handsome and reputedly virile Moscovitch, who, according to his mother, was quite a ladies' man, Lonsdale was sure she had not told him the truth. Therefore, she was probably lying about other things as well.

Amina's file at Langley was sketchy. She was born in Hungary; her father was Turkish, a fact Lonsdale had noted with interest, her mother Hungarian. She was twenty-five years old, had a diploma from Budapest Secretarial College and she had been with Phylaxos for four years. She spoke Hungarian and English and, apparently, Turkish. Was she Christian or Muslim?

Lonsdale made a mental note to check.

What the file did not show was that when Amina was twenty she went on her first ever trip outside Hungary with her girlfriend, Yasmina, two years older than she. They visited Dresden where Yasmina introduced Amina to Delic, an old friend from her university days in that city.

Delic and Amina fell in love and, within a year, Amina became an enthusiastic secret Jihadist under his influence.

The interview with Horváth at two p.m. unnerved Lonsdale. Although affable, the police officer studiously avoided giving information additional to what Lonsdale had learned when he had read the initial police report in Morton's office.

"Are you keeping Moscovitch's co-workers under surveillance and are you monitoring their telephone calls?" Lonsdale asked.

"Our budget is limited and so is our manpower. We can do spot checks but only on the secretary. There's no money for anything else."

"What about Delic?"

"He has gone to Bosnia to visit his family."

"And you let him go, just like that?"

The detective kept his cool although he was visibly annoyed. "You must remember that Mr. Delic, a Bosnian citizen, and a legal resident in this country, is employed by a company that is part-owned by the Hungarian Government. Since there is no proof that Mr. Delic had anything to do with Mr. Moscovitch's disappearance or the fire at the lab, we could not stop him from coming and going as he pleased without creating an international incident."

"You say there is no proof."

Horváth held up his hand. "Mr. Kane, please don't take us for complete fools. We do realize that the most likely suspects in this case are members of some terrorist movement. But, Al Qaeda is not active in our country, nor is Hamas or Islamic Jihad, or Hezbollah for that matter. The Russian Mafia and the Chechens yes, but not the others."

"So?"

"Mr. Delic, who is neither Russian nor Chechen, has an airtight alibi. He and his boss, Mr. Abel Drusza, a Deputy Managing Director of our State Property Agency, had dinner with Amina Dadakne on the night Mr. Moscovitch disappeared. Mr. Delic then took Miss

Dadakne home around eleven o'clock and spent the rest of the night with her. He and Miss Dadakne have, as you say in America, been intimate for quite some time."

"What about the surveillance on Miss Dadakne?"

The police officer stood up. "I do appreciate that you enjoy the full confidence of your government. This confirms it," with his glasses, he tapped the letter from the Embassy Lonsdale had given him and which now lay on his desk, "but I am not at liberty to give you details of our methods, only a general outline."

Lonsdale bit his lip in disappointment. "Could you give me such an outline?"

"With pleasure." Horváth put on his spectacles and looked at his guest owlishly over them. "We check on the woman roughly three times a week, following her around during different hours of the day. We also tap her telephone from time to time, but we had to stop doing that a couple of weeks ago."

"Why?"

"Our wire tap authorization expired." Horváth sighed, smiling. "You see we, too, have our burdens to bear." The smile disappeared and the Lieutenant's voice took on a less friendly tone. "Nothing in Miss Dadakne's comportment indicates her having had anything to do with her boss' disappearance, or the bombing of the lab."

"Did you say the bombing?" Lonsdale feigned ignorance.

"I thought you knew the lab was burnt down by remote-controlled incendiary devices which were probably detonated by wireless."

"And you have no leads left to follow up?"

"Actually, there is one that I should have mentioned to you the other day. As you know, the *Zugló*, where the Phylaxos laboratory used to be located, is zoned for both residential and light industry. There are always people on the street walking their dogs or looking out of windows, that sort of a thing."

"And?"

"Well, when we questioned the people living near Phylaxos some of them mentioned that they had been woken up by the noise from a heavy truck. One eyewitness said he did see a tractor trailer towing a container in a street near the plant."

"When was that?"

"On Sunday morning around four."

"Did you follow up on the lead?" Lonsdale held his breath.

"Yes we did, and we found the container in question two weeks after we advised our people to look out for such a one. It had been abandoned on the highway near *Záhony,* not far from the Polish-Hungarian border with some of the missing Phylaxos lab equipment still in it."

"But no sign of Moscovitch?"

The police officer nodded.

"I'm afraid we're running pretty low on leads, but, with time, I'm sure we'll develop new ones. Although, as I said, we're shorthanded we're anxious to cooperate with your country. Canada has always helped us. We won't close the file just yet and will keep your consul posted on new developments as they occur." He extended his hand. "I'm certain Ms. Lapointe must have told you that she and I have a good working relationship, so keep in touch with her. She's easier to reach than me."

The message was clear; Lonsdale was being given the brush-off.

CHAPTER 14

Budapest, Wednesday, October 17

In the morning, Lonsdale took a taxi to *Zászló* Street in the *Zugló* District. He wanted to see how the construction of the "new" Phylaxos was coming along.

There was disappointingly little to see.

The property, with two very large structures on it, was huge. Building A, by far the bigger of the two, housed the coffee-brewing and decaffeinating facilities of the German beverage specialty giant Tschibo Kaffee GmBH. Two of the three floors of Building B accommodated the company's Central European sales and administrative offices. The third floor had been home to Phylaxos' laboratory and pilot plant.

Building A seemed to be undamaged, probably because it was situated some distance from the lab across the common courtyard. Nevertheless, it did bear signs of the explosion that had wiped out the veterinarian pharmaceutical company's facilities. A number of windows and their frames that had been blown out had been replaced. They looked grotesquely new in the façade of a dirty, old structure.

Building B, seriously damaged by the phosphorus fire that had followed the detonation, had been repaired quickly by the Germans and, as far as Lonsdale could see, the Tschibo offices were fully operational.

Lonsdale took the stairs to the third floor and was surprised that none of the few workers loitering about challenged his being there. He stepped into a corner and watched some men erecting brick partitions European style. Another group was applying gyproc to external walls already lined with insulation. It seemed to Lonsdale that, in contrast with what the Germans had achieved, the people employed by Phylaxos had precious little to show for their labors.

He 'walked' the space slowly to get a feel of the size of the area: fifty meters by a hundred meters; fifty thousand square feet more or less.

Too much for a modest research lab.

May be the space was needed for the pilot plant, for the feedstock tanks and the centrifuges, he supposed.

He was not clear about how the vaccine was going to be manufactured. The raw material for the product was bovine blood, that he knew. He also knew that this 'base' would be purchased in fractionated form from one of the five or six gigantic blood processing plants operating around the world.

Why, then, the need for so much space?

The visit was a disappointment. Nothing was making sense.

*   *   *

In the evening, Lonsdale took the metro to Franciscans' Square. He kept checking for pursuit as he went and, finding none, headed toward the Karpatia Restaurant. He was meeting with Frakkos and one of the latter's team members.

"Thanks for inviting us for dinner." They were in one of the fabled restaurant's private rooms named after Zrinyi, the sixteenth Century Hungarian hero who had sacrificed himself and his two thousand men in a futile effort to stop Suleiman the Magnificent and his Turkish army from advancing on Vienna.

The driver seemed genuinely grateful. "This afternoon George," he nodded toward his teammate, "picked up analysis of phone calls from phone booths near Dadakne's apartment. I paying lots and lots money to my telephone company contact. We reviewed the stuff in the surveillance car."

"Find anything?"

"Eighty per cent of calls from four phones we tapped were domestic."

"Over what period of time?"

"Two days more or less, yes?"

"How many calls in total?"

"About a hundred plus."

"That's sixty calls per day. How many families in the complex?"

"Three hundred more or less."

"Get to the point." Lonsdale was impatient.

"Of hundred and twenty-two calls twenty-two were long distance, mainly to neighboring countries." Frakkos consulted his notes. "Nine to Rumania, five to Slovakia and Czech Republic. Another three to Yugoslavia and four to Bosnia. The rest go all over the place: to Western Europe, America and Canada, even to Australia. So I ask my contact for other unusual calls—big long distance calls. He then tolding me about Turkey. Many calls come and go to Turkey."

A bell went off inside Lonsdale's head. "Where in Turkey?"

"Since you telling me Dadakne half Turkish, I ask. So I found out: Cizre."

"Where the hell is that?"

"In Southeastern Turkey right on border with Syria and within fifty kilometers from Iraqi border, yes?"

"You don't say!"

"There's more. Telephone people telling me the number in Cizre has been called every Sunday and Wednesday at eleven a.m., *pontosan*, punctually, for the last five weeks anyway."

"From the same public phone booth?"

"No. Taking turns in time—how you say in English—by luck among the four in the complex."

"You mean at random."

"Yes."

"And whose number is it?"

"The mayor's. He hate Americans, yes? It says so on Internet."

"Why, for god's sake?"

"Cizre is small rural community, about five thousand people. Is also the location of U.S. Air Force communication place with forty airmen and commander there. Power for heavy communication systems coming from combination of commercial grid in nearby town and U.S.A.F. diesel generators. Power source in Cizre not reliable so generators run long time and make lots of racket that residents don't like, yes? Noise could be made a lot less at cost of forty thousand dollars or so, but Uncle Sam not wanting to pay."

"Instead, he is content with creating five thousand enemies." Lonsdale's head was spinning. He needed to get away to analyze what he had just learned, but he was not finished with Frakkos. "What about Dadakne's movements?"

"No suspicious contacts, no break in routine. Goes to Phylaxos job in morning, and then goes home for lunch. Has gone nowhere in evening."

"Did you tap her phone in the house?"

"Yes. She got no calls from anyone recently except you."

"Does she have a cell phone?"

"She has, but we can't monitor that."

Lonsdale got up to leave. "Anything else I ought to know?"

"Yeah. Almost forgot. She calls the number you said you knew once or twice per week; just before finishing time, four thirty p.m. that is." Lonsdale was at the door, but what Frakkos said next stopped him dead in his tracks. "Funny, these calls, sir. Conversation is all Arabic and we can't understand what she saying, yes?"

* * *

Lonsdale kept tossing and turning in his bed. There was no way he could fall asleep. He had too much on his mind.

Why was Amina calling Drusza so often and talking to him in Arabic? Was Drusza not originally from Bosnia? And wasn't Delic also a Bosnian?

Why did both Amina *and* Drusza carefully avoid mentioning that Delic was Iraqi-trained? It was no secret.

How come Amina and Drusza spoke Arabic? One was of Turkish the other of Bosnian origin. Were they Muslims? Probably. The Koran was in Arabic; the *lingua franca* of Islam.

Why was Amina calling Cizre twice a week?

Was the mayor of Cizre really Amina's uncle?

Didn't Delic also have a Turkish uncle? An uncle rich enough to stake Delic to his share in Phylaxos? What was it again? Oh yeah. Twenty per cent for seventy thousand bucks. Lonsdale made a mental note to have Langley trace the seventy thousand dollar transaction.

Lonsdale finally fell asleep, wondering where Moscovitch was, alive or dead.

He dreamt that he was at his country house north of Montreal, his home before having to give up his identity to enter the CIA's Employee Protection Program to save his life.

There was a note from the cleaning lady wishing him a Merry Christmas and could he please leave her a check to cover her services for the next three months—she charged twenty-five bucks for her weekly visits, rain or shine . . . whether the house was occupied or not. It was comforting for Lonsdale to have someone look in on his home regularly, especially when he wasn't around.

He liked the arrangement with the woman whereby they would communicate without having to come face to face. He'd leave her a note and some money in a designated kitchen drawer and she'd reciprocate in kind. Months would go by without his having to speak with her.

He sighed heavily and reached for his checkbook. Then he went to sit on the porch for a while, letting the silent calm of the house soak into his tired mind and exhausted body. Idly he wondered how someone who wanted so desperately to belong would crave solitude, silence, aloneness . . . a place, a home, in the country miles from everywhere and everybody.

And the same answer as always emerged from his subconscious: only alone could he feel really free, at peace, safe . . .

He dozed for a while, then dragged some wood downstairs and built a fire in the basement library. Surrounded by his cherished books resting on solid oak shelves in a room he had designed by himself for himself he watched the fire take, then spread and roar into life in the huge Spanish-style fireplace. He gulped down some scotch—neat, no mix, no water—and felt its raw bite. Its heat spread through his body, mercifully numbing his brain.

He watched the flames, golden red tongues, flickering forever upward, reaching for the chimney-hole in their bid to escape, and his eyes slowly lost their focus. The flames seemed to meld . . . and he soon saw that what he was looking at was not a fire . . . no, not a fire, but Amina's face: a lovely, desirable, dangerous face with beautiful eyes that could not be trusted . . . lips that smiled, but not an open inviting smile, for the smile quickly turned into a grotesque grimace of betrayal . . .

And this made Lonsdale feel very sad, very vulnerable and frighteningly lonely . . .

He awoke with a start. "You don't trust her because you don't trust anybody, not even yourself, you stupid, lonely pervert . . . you miserable intellectual misfit . . . you arrogant shallow nothing . . ." he whispered into the darkness.

But if one does not trust, how can one love?

Did he trust Adys? Did he love her? He wasn't sure.

He fell asleep again while trying to answer his own questions.

CHAPTER 15

Wednesday, October 17, (cont'd)

The rasping sound of the container door's opening had snapped Moscovitch out of the lethargic reverie into which he had sunk on what he reckoned was the thirtieth afternoon of his captivity. Instead of working, he had been lying on his cot, unwashed and unshaven, depressed, unmotivated and without hope.

His spirits had been high a week earlier when his captors had shown signs of willingness to negotiate, but as time passed, he realized he had no-one but himself to rely on. There was no cavalry riding to his rescue, he had to engineer his own escape before he lost his mind.

Four weeks of being locked up without speaking to a human being had taken a heavy toll on Moscovitch's psyche. Although physically in good shape, eating well and exercising regularly, his mind was turning to mush. Even the smallest decision like changing underwear or taking a shower had become a major challenge. His will to survive was weakening, as was his resolve to escape, especially after his first and only attempt to get away. The acid he had used to burn through the hawser restraining him during his nightly walks had left him with a nasty chemical burn on his left wrist that was well on its way to becoming seriously infected.

Surprised at hearing someone at the door, he had struggled to his feet, and had run his hands through his hair to make himself look more presentable.

A glance at his watch showed that dinner was two hours earlier than usual.

A wave of incredible relief swept over him when he saw that the person in the doorway was not his jailer, but Amina, his erstwhile lover and secretary. She entered his living quarters with determination and stopped to face him as the door behind her clanged shut.

Her steps were light; she was wearing sneakers.

"I see they never arranged for your nose to be set after I broke it," she said by way of greeting.

Moscovitch stared at her, too stunned to speak. In her light blue tracksuit under a short, white, fleece jacket and a matching woolen cap that enhanced the jet-blackness of her long, lustrous hair she looked breathtakingly beautiful.

Moscovitch could not help but start lusting for her all over again.

Then the bitter disappointment of her betrayal jolted him into the present, igniting his fury. Blinded by rage he stepped forward to strike her.

She made no move to defend herself. "Hit me. I deserve it," she said, sounding matter-of-fact.

That stopped him as she had hoped it would.

"Come to gloat, have you bitch?" he spat at her.

"No Jason, I have not."

"Then what do you want?"

"To save your life and to make you rich and famous." She stepped closer to him.

"Bullshit." He backed away. No way was he going to allow her to beguile him again—ever.

Her piercing black eyes seemed to look right into his soul. "It's all right to hate me Jason, because I hate and despise you too. But my friends and I need you as much as you need us and we'd both be fools if we didn't set our personal differences aside: you, to save your life, and I, to further my cause."

"What the hell are you talking about bitch?"

"Stop calling me bitch Jewboy, and I'll stop calling you Jewboy."
Amina gave as good as she got. "Keep a civil tongue in your head and
I'll do the same. Now listen to what I have to propose."

"And if I don't?"

"I'll have you shot tomorrow morning."

"Then I'd be a fool not to listen, wouldn't I? Besides, I have
nothing else to do anyway, do I?" Moscovitch made his voice drip
with sarcasm.

"Jason, I'm not bluffing. I can deliver on what I've just said if you
are willing to do two things: work for us full time with enthusiasm
and be willing to assume a new identity."

"Who's us?"

"Islamic Jihadists."

"You're out of your fucking mind."

"Get off your high horse big boy. It's me, Amina, you're talking
to. We've been close enough and have worked together long enough
for both of us to know that we're whores: you for money and fame,
me for the cause of Islam."

"Me, a Jew, work for Islam? Me, a Jew, help the Arabs destroy
Israel? Me, a Canadian, assist in the manufacture of weapons of mass
destruction for use in North America with impunity? NEVER."

Amina dropped into his recliner, Moscovitch sat down on his
cot. "Hold on, hold on Mr. Righteous. What have the Israelis done
for you recently? Did they come over here to help look for you? You
know damn well they didn't. Did the Canadians institute a search
for you? If they did, which they didn't, believe me, they were not very
successful at it, were they? As for the Americans, I don't think they
even know that you've gone missing and if they did they couldn't
care less."

Moscovitch said nothing.

"What about your widowed mother, Jason?" Amina went on.
"She's spending the money she's saved for her old age on private
detectives she retained to find you. You're her only child. Who will
help her after her money is gone? Who will support her in her old
age?"

"She'll sell my shares in Phylaxos and get some money from
that."

Amina relaxed. Moscovitch was beginning to show signs of listening. Soon her ex-boss would come to the inevitable conclusion that he faced two alternatives: cooperate or die. It was up to him to choose how to cooperate; willingly, thereby getting a crack at making money and, perhaps, working his way out of captivity, or unwillingly, in which event he would be tortured and killed.

Amina waited patiently for the Canadian to make up his mind.

After several minutes' silence Moscovitch broke. "I'm willing to listen, but I want guarantees."

Amina let out a silent sigh of relief. "I can understand that and I'll see what can be done."

"With whom do I negotiate and when?" Moscovitch's native intelligence had kicked in.

"Three men will visit you tomorrow. I'm sure you will be most impressed by at least one of them."

"I don't want to deal with middlemen, only with people who have the authority to commit."

"Don't worry Jason. One of the men I've managed to convince to come to see you is fully authorized to make whatever deal the two of you work out tomorrow."

"Who is he?"

Amina got up to leave. Her job was done. Moscovitch was hooked.

"Don't be impatient. You'll find out tomorrow."

She rapped on the door to be let out. "In the meantime, enjoy your dinner, get some sleep and make yourself as presentable as possible under the circumstances." The door opened and she slipped out so quickly that he did not have time to ask when, if ever, he'd see her again.

CHAPTER 16

Thursday, October 18 (1)

Next day, when Moscovitch heard the door open he headed for his cot to assume the position expected of him at lunchtime.

His surprise was absolute when, instead of his jailer, he saw his partner, Esad Delic, walk through the door carrying a big bottle of Coke and three large glasses. He was in the company of a swarthy, middle-aged man with a thick mane of graying hair, bushy eyebrows and a fierce mustache . . . and a Browning automatic pointed at Moscovitch's belly in his left hand. A third man, in his late thirties, clean-shaven, short, lightly built and effeminate looking, brought up the rear.

All three were wearing modest workers' clothes and boots.

"Hello Jason," Delic said, smiling. "Meet your new partners." Moscovitch, speechless, could only gape. Delic brandished the Coke bottle. "Let's all have a pause that refreshes. The Coke is nice and cold."

Moscovitch nodded in dumb agreement.

"Please do me the honor and make room for us on your bed by moving over to your armchair." The man with the pistol, fluent in English, motioned him toward the recliner and sat down on the chair next to the scientist's cot. "That way we'll all be comfortable."

Moscovitch found his voice. "I'd be a hell of a lot more comfortable if you'd put your gun away." He sank into the recliner and watched Delic make himself at home on his bed. His third visitor remained standing.

"I'll gladly oblige if you give me your word that you won't attempt anything foolish." The man looked at Moscovitch expectantly.

The scientist shrugged. "I'd be an idiot to attempt anything. There are three of you and I'm alone. Besides, I heard the door being locked from the outside, so here goes nothing: I promise to hear you out without getting physical."

The man with the weapon, formal and polite to a fault, smiled and put his pistol under the chair. "Thank you. Now allow me to introduce myself. I am Barzan Hassani, Senior Advisor to his Excellency Ali Hassan Al-Majid, Iraq's Minister of Industry."

"Sure, and I'm the Queen of Sheba." Furious and bitterly disappointed Moscovitch turned to Delic. "What the fuck are you up to now you no good, rotten son-of-a-bitch bastard. You kidnapped me, locked me up for weeks to soften me up, then sent your whore Amina to feed me a pile of bullshit," he shouted. "What for? Just so you can put on a theatrical performance to confuse me even more?" He made as if to lunge for his visitors. They did not react.

Frustrated in the extreme, Moscovitch sank back in his chair, clenching his teeth to fight back tears. "You are a treacherous and cruel specimen of humanity; a disloyal partner and now that you've allied yourself with the devil, a menace to mankind."

"So then you do believe that this man," Delic, unfazed, nodded toward Hassani, "is who he says he is."

"Not for a moment. I do know who Barzan Hassani is. His nickname is The Butcher, and he would never risk his neck by traveling outside Iraq. He's wanted on an international war crime charge and can't afford to be caught in the West."

"Don't be an asshole Jason, and stop insulting your visitors. Ask yourself—and I can see you're already doing so—why would I come to see you with such an implausible story if it weren't true? Give yourself a chance and let me outline what we have in mind."

Moscovitch said nothing. Hassani chose to take his silence as consent. "I'm sure you're aware that Iraq has a problem with its bio-pharma industry," he began. "Everyone suspects us of manufacturing biological weapons of mass destruction, when we really don't have such a program *yet*." There was a distinct emphasis on the word "yet".

Moscovitch tried to say something, but the Iraqi held up his hand. "Please do me the courtesy of not interrupting. I assure you I'll give you ample time for questions and a rebuttal after I've finished."

"Ever since kidnapping you we've been trying hard to duplicate the vaccine the samples of which you so cleverly denied us when we captured you. Unfortunately for us and luckily for you, we have been unsuccessful in our efforts and now find ourselves in a situation in which we possess a potential biological weapon of mass destruction—your nv. Creutzfeldt-Jakob disease virus—which we dare not use. We need an anti-virus because our core leadership does not wish to kill our co-religionist brethren worldwide." Hassani's English, albeit accented, was excellent.

"As I said," he continued, "our *core* leadership does not wish to proceed, but there are significant elements inside and outside Iraq who are not so squeamish. We fear that the virus we possess may find its way into unscrupulous hands thereby causing a disaster of major proportions for which Iraq would be held unjustly responsible. So, you see, we must absolutely find a way of producing a vaccine, and soon, and we are willing to pay substantial money to those who would help us in this endeavor."

Moscovitch was flabbergasted. "Have you taken leave of your senses? Are you proposing that I assist in doing irreparable harm to the West in exchange for" Moscovitch paused, ". . . for what exactly? Money? My freedom? What?"

Hassani seemed unperturbed by the outburst. "We do not wish to harm the West provided it stands aside and allows us to deal with Israel as we see fit, and it then lets Iraq unite the Arab world. Nor do we wish to harm you personally, but you must understand that if you refuse to cooperate we will have to kill you sooner or later." Hassani's matter-of-fact way of speaking about his eventual demise almost made Moscovitch throw up.

"You leave me few options,"

Hassani nodded. "Only two. Cooperate or die."

"And if I cooperate?"

"For starters we will pay you an upfront retainer of one million dollars which, I'm sure, you'll want your mother to have because she's fast running out of money. The cost of searching for you has already consumed half of her savings and she's about to mortgage her house, her only asset, to enable her to continue."

"Bastards. Leave my mother out of this."

"But we are Jason. By the way, may I call you Jason?" Hassani smiled, polite as ever. "We have not touched a hair on her head," the smile disappeared, "though we easily could have ..."

"Call me whatever the fuck you want." Moscovitch was beside himself with rage and fear. "Just leave my mother out of this or I'll never help you ... never ... never ... never."

"Please calm down. I'm sure we can come to terms." Hassani continued as if he were negotiating a simple business deal. "We propose that in return for your full time and enthusiastic and imaginative cooperation we will deposit one million dollars in your mother's name in a Swiss bank of her choosing. We will also provide transportation to Switzerland and cover the cost of her stay there for three months at a luxury hotel of her choice. For you, we propose a salary of fifty thousand dollars per month during the same three months, credited to your account monthly in advance in a Swiss bank of your choice. In this respect, we'll allow your mother to monitor that your money is where it's supposed to be. If, during the next three months you perfect the anti-nv. C-JD vaccine, we will buy its patent from you for five million dollars and let you go free, it being understood that you will not take action against us for forcible detention."

Moscovitch's mind was racing. "What happens if, in spite of my best efforts, I am unable to produce the vaccine in the specified period?"

"Your mother goes home with her million dollars and your saved-up salary of one hundred and fifty thousand dollars ..."

"And I?"

"That depends. If we're satisfied that, in our sole informed opinion, you had really done your best, but have failed to complete your task due to unforeseeable complications or *force majeure*, we'll move you to Baghdad, give you a new identity and may even put you in charge of our entire bio-pharma effort. Of course, your salary will continue."

"And, if at the end of three months there's no vaccine and you're not satisfied with my work?"

Hassani shrugged. "We don't envisage such a possibility because we have great confidence in your professional abilities, but should our judgment be proven wrong, we shall have no choice but to terminate your employment with extreme prejudice."

So there it all was for Moscovitch to contemplate. He was being offered a sure way to save his mother and provide a decent income for her for the rest of her life, and a chance to get out of captivity after three months, or perhaps even sooner, free and rich, but tainted.

"Who would be the judge of my work?" he asked to gain time to think.

"Esad Delic, of course."

"But he hates my guts, and me his. I can't trust him again." Moscovitch protested.

Hassani looked him up and down coldly, satisfied that Moscovitch would not be negotiating unless he were interested in the deal. "I suppose the two of you will just have to find a way to mend fences."

Moscovitch glanced at his watch: it showed a quarter past two. "I need twenty-four hours to think things over."

Delic spoke up. "You've got until nine tonight to come up with a workable proposal within the parameters Colonel Hassani has just outlined. If you can do so I'm willing to bury the hatchet provided I get adequately compensated for my efforts." He got off the bed. After retrieving his weapon, Hassani followed.

Moscovitch stood up. Surprisingly, Delic held out his hand for the Canadian to shake. "As the Sicilians say 'Nothing personal, just business.'" He winked at Moscovitch then fished a piece of paper, a photograph, out of his jacket pocket.

"I told you earlier that your mother was spending her money—lots of money—on trying to find you," he said. "She even went so far as to hire a private detective to come to Budapest to help the authorities in their search for you."

"As you can see," Delic handed the sheet over to his 'host': it was a very good copy of a Canadian passport's information page, showing the owner's name, place of birth and picture, "your compatriot's name is Bernard Kane. He says he's a private investigator, hired by your mother to search for you. I was wondering if you've heard of him before or, perhaps even knew him."

Moscovitch pretended to examine the picture carefully even though he had recognized the face immediately. He shook his head. "Never saw the guy before."

"Come on, Jason," the Bosnian insisted, "I repeat my offer. Let's bury the hatchet and cooperate. You could start by telling me about Mr. Kane. He says he is a good friend of your mother's."

"As I said, I never met him. I know nothing about him."

"No matter." Delic gave up, headed for the door and rapped on it. "See you at nine tonight. I'm sure we'll be able to come up with something that'll work for you provided you cooperate, so don't worry."

Moscovitch held up his hand. "Just a minute, Esad. I want to know who this person is and what he's doing here." He nodded toward his third visitor.

"Forgive me." Hassani, polite as ever, gave Moscovitch a fleeting smile. "Under the circumstances I believe it would be premature to effect formal introductions. Let me just say that my friend here will have a financial as well as an emotional interest in the transaction we are contemplating."

Before Moscovitch could protest, Hassani and his companions were exiting through the door that had just been unlocked.

Moscovitch forced himself not to show the relief and elation he was feeling. Mr. Kane was none other than his old acquaintance of Plasmalab days, Robert Lonsdale, the man who had tracked down the fugitive Chief Executive Officer of the Canadian surgical glue manufacturing company and who had been instrumental in bringing him to justice.

CHAPTER 17

Thursday, October 18 (2)

The pressure on Moscovitch was intense. He had less than six hours to come up with a foolproof method through which to monitor that The Butcher was not fucking him over, that he was regularly depositing Moscovitch's money in Switzerland.

He was not going to settle for a lousy million bucks—that was for sure. Familiar with the Semitic mentality, being a Semite himself, he knew that the bargaining had only just begun. He would ask for three million for his mother, a monthly salary of one hundred thousand for himself and ten million for his patent. Then he'd sit back and watch how quickly Hassani would scale up. That would give him an indication whether the deal was real or not. The Arab would give in quickly if the intent was to make Moscovitch work then get rid of him and repossess the money.

Step one—relatively easy—was to get his mother over to Switzerland and somehow give her control over at least two million dollars. The rest would follow. How to ensure that Hassani could not suck his money back once the vaccine was in Iraqi hands was the challenge.

Then it came to Moscovitch: Kane/Lonsdale!

By showing the Canadian the picture, Delic had put the private investigator in play, enabling the scientist to use him as his representative in what was rapidly becoming a kidnap-for-ransom situation.

Relieved, Moscovitch wolfed down the lunch that his keeper had brought him after his visitors had left. Next, he took a nap to the astonishment and annoyance of Delic and Hassani who were monitoring his moves by remote TV.

Well refreshed after his sleep, Moscovitch dawdled over his dinner at the usual time then jotted down a few more notes while waiting for The Butcher, Delic and the Third Man to show. This they did at nine on the dot, with Delic carrying a large thermos and three mugs. "There's excellent espresso in here." He held up the thermos. "I hope you have milk and sugar."

Moscovitch watched his visitors serve themselves then got down to business.

"I thought long and hard about your proposal," he led off, "but I can't go along with it. Its terms are just not generous enough."

Hassani was surprised. "You want more money?"

"Yes—up front and lots more of it. Once I agree to work for you, I'm finished. My chances of being allowed to continue in my chosen field will be severely limited."

"Not if you stay in Baghdad. You will have a very rewarding, high profile position and an enviably comfortable existence."

"As a virtual prisoner, subject to dismissal or worse at the whim of your President." Moscovitch shook his head. "No, my best shot is my first shot. I want enough money up front for my mother and me to be able to live comfortably in some quiet country like Costa Rica, where the climate is good and the natives friendly."

Delic laughed. "And how much will that take?"

"Five million US."

"No way."

It took an hour and a half of wrangling to agree on two million dollars up front and a monthly salary of sixty thousand dollars for three months.

"What about the patent?" a weary Delic finally asked.

"I want ten million bucks."

"Out of the question." Hassani was adamant.

Another hour of arguing back and forth passed, but Hassani would not budge and Moscovitch gave in. He accepted the figure of five million dollars.

"So much for the easy part," Moscovitch said after they shook hands on the financial part of the deal. Although the hour was late, he felt rested and refreshed by his afternoon's nap. His visitors, on the other hand, were showing clear signs of wear and tear.

"What does that mean?" Hassani became suspicious.

"You don't really expect me to simply take your word that you'll live up to your agreement, do you?" Moscovitch made himself sound incredulous.

"What do you have in mind?"

"Kane." Moscovitch replied without hesitation.

"Come again?" His visitors did not understand.

'I said 'Kane'. He'll be my intermediary."

"Elaborate."

Moscovitch went through the routine he had carefully thought out while eating his dinner.

"After you've deposited two million dollars in one of your Swiss bank accounts, get in touch with Kane and tell him to arrange for my mother to come to Zurich. She'll make the trip if he tells her he needs her help there to arrange for my release. Once she's settled in a decent hotel and her stay for three months paid in advance, again, through Kane, he is to take my mother to one of the banks chosen from this list." Moscovitch handed Delic a sheet of paper with five names on it. "Have her open an account in her own name. Provide a code word and the address of your bank to Kane so he can get my mother's bank to request the transfer of the money from your bank to my mother's bank account." Moscovitch took a sip of his Coke. "Everything clear so far?"

Delic nodded.

"Once the money is safely in my mother's bank account arrange for Kane and me to meet to confirm face to face that the transaction was completed."

"What about your monthly pay?"

"Deposit eighty per cent of it in a bank account I will have Kane open for me in Zurich and give me the rest in cash. Kane is to contact me every month to confirm that my salary has been paid."

"And the sale of the patent?" The question pleased Moscovitch immensely. It showed that perhaps, just perhaps, the Iraqis intended to honor their side of the bargain.

"The entire series of transactions, including the conditions under which I'm to be set free, my rights and remuneration as a future employee, as well as proper provisions to protect your position, will have to be written up in contract form and signed by your representatives before a Notary Public in Switzerland. I'll sign here."

"That's unacceptable. By signing, Iraq would be confessing to kidnapping, attempted murder, robbery, destruction of property and blackmail and God knows what else, and would leave itself open to a massive civil lawsuit by you for compensatory damages."

"Not if the contract were cleverly written."

The Butcher cut in impatiently. "I know of no lawyer I could entrust with writing up such a document."

"Don't worry; I have a solution to that problem," Moscovitch reposted. "I'll write a draft of the document myself. Kane and your lawyer can then refine it to suit all parties concerned."

"I need a couple of nights to think about all this." Hassani stood up, as did Delic and the Third Man who had not uttered a word during the entire meeting. "Let's meet again for lunch or dinner on Saturday. In the meantime Doctor," the Iraqi fixed Moscovitch with an impersonal stare, "why don't you start on an outline of the document you propose we all sign."

Shortly after his visitors left, the lights in the container went out. Lying on his cot in the dark Moscovitch reviewed what he had accomplished and concluded that he had made significant progress toward ensuring the survival and financial well-being of his mother and his own eventual salvation as a rich man. He was not concerned with the problem of having to reinvent the vaccine. There were six vials of the stuff hidden in the furnace room of the building in which he lived.

Before going to sleep, Moscovitch thanked Providence for bringing Kane/Lonsdale into the picture. 'Let's face it, my whole scheme hinges on his skills as a negotiator and his special talents and contacts that I suspect he has as a private investigator'.

Neither he nor Delic nor Hassani, or the Third Man for that matter, were, at that moment in time, aware that Kane, alias Robert Lonsdale, was a tough and experienced senior operative of the Central Intelligence Agency.

CHAPTER 18

Budapest, Friday, October 19

Lonsdale met Frakkos in the Cafeteria of the Aquincum Hotel for an early lunch.

"I need an English transcript of all Dadakne calls to Turkey urgently. Do we have the translation capability here?"

Frakkos shook his head.

Lonsdale held out his hand. "Give me the tapes. I'll get them translated at my office. My partner speaks Arabic."

"What's the rush?"

Lonsdale did not answer. He had begun to suspect that Amina Dadakne, besides working for the SPA, was also moonlighting in some sort of a job involving Abel Drusza, her daytime boss, to whom she must be transmitting information from Turkey.

But why Turkey?

May be Iraq as well. And Iran, for good measure.

Moreover, what kind of information?

It had been the word 'Arabic' that had triggered Lonsdale's inner voice—the voice to which he *always* listened. Its insidious whispering had begun a couple of days earlier and had continued relentlessly. 'Might it be that Amina is Drusza's local Control and Drusza the head of a clandestine Islamic cell operating in Budapest?'

Lonsdale's felt sick to his stomach as he had continued to speculate about this possibility.

May be the mayor of Cizre and his bosses were the ones who had conceived the Moscovitch kidnapping, a Jihadist plot, dreamt up by the Al Qaeda leadership, orchestrated by Drusza and executed by Dadakne and Delic. His speculations went in every direction, searching for a pattern that made sense.

What about Juric? How did he fit into the scheme of things? Was Moscovitch being held prisoner in one of the Bosnian's containers on the *Háros* property where Amina visited him every time she went kayaking?

Lonsdale made up his mind.

He needed to get the Cizre phone bugged immediately so that those in contact with the mayor—probably people from all over the Middle East—were identified before Amina discovered that the game was up and warned the mayor.

He needed to talk to Morton, and fast.

To Frakkos he said, "Tell me about the target's activities."

"Same old shit. Goes to job site, reports to number you know, yes?"

"Abel Drusza's at the SPA."

"Correct."

"Is she kayaking regularly?"

"Wednesdays and Sundays."

"Any unusual activity on the kayaking site?"

"None, but George hearing in the *kocsma,* how you say in English—the pub, yes, that Juric coming home soon with barge."

*   *   *

"We can't be of much assistance with regard to the barge people." Horváth was at his most charming in his comfortable office. "You see, the barge people are supervised by the River Police on the waterways and by the Border Patrol at the frontiers."

"But I'm not talking about what they're doing on the river, "Lonsdale protested, "I'm concerned about what's happening on shore."

"Such as?"

"Look Lieutenant, let's stop playing games. I told you I've spent time following Amina Dadadkne around. She goes kayaking on the Danube every Wednesday and Sunday, rain or shine, even in the kind of weather we've been having. Stops by where she keeps her boat, ostensibly for a cup of coffee."

"So?"

"The people she visits, a couple, are Bosnian Muslims. The husband is expected to come home on board his barge any day now, yet there is no sign of any unloading equipment on the property."

"Maybe they are doing the unloading *en route*."

"Maybe, but consider this. The Bosnians acquired a new, a third, container about six weeks ago, right around the time Moscovitch disappeared."

While appearing to be listening intently to what Lonsdale was saying Horváth bent down and fished a file out of one of his desk-drawers. He adjusted his tie that looked like an original Ferragamo to Lonsdale's trained eye, put on his reading glasses, Silhouettes no less, opened the file and began to read.

After politely hearing Lonsdale out, he reluctantly closed the dossier, took off his glasses, sighed and called his assistant. "Csaba, come in here for a few minutes and bring three coffees with you." He looked at Lonsdale. "How do you take your coffee Mr. Kane, regular or black?"

"Regular."

The police officer relayed this information then hung up. Carefully polishing his glasses, he turned to his visitor. "Csaba is a very popular given name in Hungary. Legend has it that it was the name of the son of Attila the Hun. It may also derive from the name of a town called Csaba."

Lonsdale decided to be helpful and friendly. "I know that name. Isn't there a sausage they call Csabai?"

Horváth ignored the remark. "Detective Sergeant Csaba Vas is the field commander in charge of the Moscovitch file. Listen to what he has to say about the people you suspect of having kidnapped and now holding Mr. Moscovitch prisoner."

Vas, a thin, mustachioed man in his late twenties with piercing gray-blue eyes, military-style blond hair and a stubborn chin, appeared almost instantly with three steaming mugs of coffee. His clothing, compared to Horváth's elegant attire, in spite of being spotless and neatly pressed, looked shabby.

Lonsdale made a mental note. Vas was evidently not in on the take that was making Horváth affluent.

While his subordinate was looking for coasters, Horváth told Vas in Hungarian that he should briefly outline, for 'this foreign simpleton in my office', meaning Lonsdale, the contents of the Moscovitch file.

With exaggerated care, Vas placed the mugs on his boss's desk and began in surprisingly good English. "Amina Dadakne was our first suspect, then Esad Delic. But they provided alibis for each other. We also had the alibi provided for Dadakne by Mr. Drusza, a senior SPA official, so we couldn't charge anyone. We followed them around for about a week with no results. We got even more suspicious when we saw Dadakne kayaking at the Juric property twice a week. We raided the place one week after Moscovitch's how do you say . . ." he looked at Horváth for help.

"Abduction."

"That's it, abduction, and found a new container next to the Juric's office which is fitted out so people could sleep in it."

"And what did you find?" Lonsdale asked.

"Nothing. We interviewed the Jurices and found out that Mrs. Juric, who was born in Turkey, is Amina Dadakne's cousin."

"About the container, had it been used? Why was it there?" Lonsdale wouldn't let go.

"Milan Juric told us he had contacts in Turkey who manufactured agricultural machinery which they wanted to sell in Hungary. The cheapest transport is by river barge, but the trip would be long so they'd need more help. The container would be a place where the extra deckhands could sleep for a few nights."

"Why not on the barge?"

Coffee cup in hand, Horváth interrupted. "It's called rest and recreation Mr. Kane. Don't you think even deckhands would want a couple of days off after being on a stinking barge for ten days?"

"A final point Mr. Kane." Vas added and stood up. "I can understand that to you it would look like the Jurices were working with the kidnappers, but I'm sure you know that many people live in containers, like the guest workers in Saudi Arabia for example. Containers are cheap and easily movable."

Horváth stood up as well, signaling that he, too, had had enough. "Besides" he remarked, "we found the container near *Záhony* in which Moscovitch must have been kept captive and transported towards the east, remember?"

* * *

With his bulky frame squashed into his maroon-colored Fiat *Cinquecento*, Horváth pointed his minuscule car toward the downtown area. He cursed everything and everyone in sight: the bumper-to-bumper Friday afternoon traffic, the stupid cops on point duty that made it worse, the idiotic layout of Budapest, his native city and—especially—the foreign visitors who, like this asshole, Kane, were making his life more miserable than it needed to be.

Oh yes, he knew all about Mr. Kane and suspected that the Canadian was planning to raid the Juric's establishment near *Csepel*, probably with help from the Bulgarian Embassy. That's where Frakkos always went for extra muscle. The Bulgarians had made a cottage industry of providing manpower for strong-arm tactics in Hungary. Their security guards, enjoying diplomatic immunity, were encouraged by their boss, the Consul, to make themselves available to whoever needed them. The Consul would take a cut of the men's earnings and, in return, see to it that when they were caught, they were shipped home with little fuss and without getting a negative fitness report.

Of course, they seldom got caught. They had an uncanny ability to fade into the night. The Consul was protecting his own as well as *their* backs by keeping Detective-Lieutenant Horváth informed of impending strong-arm activities well before they were scheduled to take place.

Horváth was aware of it all because it was his business to know: the antics of the Bulgarians, Frakkos' 'extra-curricular' activities on behalf of adulterous foreigners living in Hungary, the roughshod behavior of the enforcers imported by the Russian mafia, the misdeeds of wandering groups of gipsy children trained to pick pockets . . .

Yup, he knew it all because he maintained a widespread and efficient informants' network based in part on what the Russians called '*blatt*', or bribes, and part on the principle of tit-for-tat, give and take. He not only listened to information, he also disseminated it. Of course, for him, the nicest part of this operation was that some of the '*blatt*' stuck to his hands as well.

Quite a bit of it, actually.

He was always careful not to flash money and never lived beyond the means appropriate to his salary, hence the modest Fiat. A confirmed bachelor, he spent a lot on fashionable clothing, his only weakness, because he had no need to save any part of his salary. Assured of a reasonable pension at age sixty, *and* a 'supplement' from interest and dividends in Switzerland where he stashed all the bribes he earned, he was comfortably off.

He swore roundly and expressively, only as a Hungarian can, invoking the act of sexual intercourse in connection with his mother as a practitioner of the world's oldest profession. Then, having negotiated *Andrássy* Boulevard and *József Attilla* Street, he reached Roosevelt Square and saw that traffic up ahead had come to a screeching halt at the entrance to the Chain Bridge roundabout.

To get to the Canadian Embassy, he had to cross the Danube.

There was only one way out. With great reluctance, he retrieved the flasher-blue-light-siren combo from under the seat next to his and slapped it on his tiny car's roof then plugged the contraption into the cigarette lighter. All eyes turned toward the little Fiat when the siren began to wail.

He knew his vehicle hardly looked like a police car and that the drivers around him found the spectacle of a matchbox with a flashing blue light on top of it comical, but he couldn't have cared less. The move had the desired effect. He was across the bridge and at the Embassy ten minutes later.

Canada's representatives in Budapest labor in palatial surroundings on the grounds of an estate that once belonged to a rich banker. There are three buildings in the compound. One houses the political section and the offices of the Ambassador, and of the First and the Second Secretaries. Another, the Annex, is home to the Consular Section and Security, while the so-called Garden House accommodates 'non-diplomatic' activities such as the meetings of the Hungarian-Canadian Businessmen's Association, for example.

Thérèse Lapointe, the Consul, alerted by telephone in advance of his visit, was waiting for Horváth in her office at the Annex. The detective wasted no time in coming to the point. "You remember the letter of introduction you prepared for a Mr. Bernard Kane, a private investigator?" The Consul noted with surprise that her visitor was upset.

"In the Moscovitch file, yes."

"Exactly." Horváth went on. "I believe he's planning to assemble a private army to raid the premises of a tugboat owner near *Csepel* because he thinks Moscovitch is a prisoner there."

The Consul was dumbfounded. "Is he?" she finally managed to stammer.

This infuriated Horváth even more. 'Who the devil do these people think they are?' he asked himself, fuming. 'They come here and act as if they owned the place and to hell with our country's sovereign rights and laws.' Out loud, he said firmly, carefully enunciating every word. "You and I enjoy a pleasant working relationship in which we constantly help each-other out. I don't want to see this relationship change. That's why I'm here today."

Bewildered and getting out of her depth, Mademoiselle Lapointe reacted with what she considered to be the appropriate response. "I appreciate your frankness. How can I be of help?"

"I don't want a diplomatic incident involving Canada on my watch." The detective sounded mildly threatening. "I want you to have a word with this fellow Kane and tell him that if he breaks the law, he and his friends will be arrested and held pending trial, no matter that he is a Canadian citizen." For good measure, he added, "and we will hold up extradition proceedings as long as possible."

"I'm sure it won't come to that." Mademoiselle Lapointe assured the Hungarian. "I will try to contact Mr. Kane immediately and warn him. By the way, do you have any idea when he is planning to stage the raid?"

"No, because I understand that he has not picked a date yet."

"Where is he staying?"

"At the Hotel *Béke*."

After an icily polite 'goodbye', Horváth left. From his car, he called Drusza on his cellular and asked that the head of the SPA's Medico-Pharmaceutical Division meet him at six at their usual place of assignation—the apartment of Drusza's girlfriend in the Sixth District.

He wanted to make sure that Kane's raid, if ever it did take place, would yield no clue as to Moscovitch's whereabouts. Nor did he want Kane to find out that Horváth was on Drusza's payroll. Horváth considered himself a *hazafi*, a patriot. He had no desire to see his country become involved in a pissing contest between Iraq, Canada and God knows whom else.

That's why he decided to give orders not only for Kane's sporadic surveillance, but also for "having him slowed down" if the circumstances so warranted.

CHAPTER 19

Budapest, Friday Evening, October 19

From police headquarters, Lonsdale doubled back to the Intercontinental Hotel to collect his car.

He drove to the Parliament building where, on the Duna-side of the structure, he stopped on *Széchenyi* Quai. At six p.m. sharp, Budapest time, he called Morton using his encrypting telephone, which looked exactly like a Nokia Model 9300 World Communicator. The guts of the instrument were another matter. It contained circuitry that scrambled and unscrambled voice communication at enormous speeds.

His Control answered on the second ring. Lonsdale wasted no time. He summarized his activities in a few sentences. "All those involved in this Moscovitch affair seem to be communicating in Arabic, which is very strange. I'm getting the distinct feeling that I have stumbled on a Jihadist conspiracy. What's more, I think the local cops know about it, but are turning a blind eye."

Morton cut him off in mid-flight. "What concrete proof do you have?"

"None yet, but I intend to develop some."

"How?'

"Tomorrow night I plan on reconnoitering the Juric property in *Háros*. While I'm busy with that I want you to arrange for the translation of the Amina tapes."

"How do you propose to get them to me?"

"I'll drop them off within the hour at the designated alternate Cutout. Get one of the Embassy people to pick them up and flash them over to you. Have a specialist stand by to start translating at . . ." Lonsdale glanced at his watch. "Let's say fifteen hundred hours, your time. Can do?"

"No problem."

"He should be able to provide you with a transcript by Sunday noon. Flash it back to the Embassy for typing overnight and have your people here leave it for me at Cutout number three where I'll pick it up between eight and eight fifteen on Monday morning."

"Consider it done. Where do we go from there?"

"If the tapes and my visit to the Jurices bear out what I suspect, place taps on the Cizre phone and keep me in the loop."

"When do we speak again?"

"Noon Monday, my time."

"What do you want me to do about Detective Lieutenant Horváth?"

"Nothing under the circumstances. The Cizre thing has priority over everything. We must not spook the prey."

They hung up.

Lonsdale drove back to the hotel and parked his car. Then he took the elevator up to Reception, got an envelope, addressed it to 'HNERIETTA', making sure to misspell the name, placed the tapes into the envelope and asked the clerk for some Scotch Tape. He sealed the envelope and, for good measure, secured the flap with some tape to ensure that no one could get to the contents without leaving behind signs of tampering.

He hopped onto a stool in the lobby bar and ordered a Chivas on the rocks. When his drink arrived, he asked the bartender what his name was.

"Zoltán, sir," came the polite reply.

"Is Henrietta in tonight?"

The man nodded toward a woman sitting behind the cash register at the end of the bar. "She's at her station, as always on Fridays, sir."

Lonsdale took his time to finish his drink. He needed time to make sure that none of the customers around him looked out-of-place. When he was satisfied, he emptied his glass, picked up the bill Zoltán had placed in front of him and walked over to the cashier. Shielding his gestures from those around him with his body, he handed her the bill, the envelope and some money. "Thank you for your help," he said.

She opened the cash register and gave him his change. "You are quite welcome."

Lonsdale left the bar and headed for the parking elevator. Just before entering it, he looked back and saw that the cashier was on the phone.

Their eyes met and she gave him an almost imperceptible nod.

*   *   *

For a change, Klara Moscovitch was looking forward to her evening out on the town. Friday nights had been difficult for her as a widow because, it seemed to her for reasons she could not fathom, that men became animals on weekends—at least the men whom she had had the misfortune to date on weekends in the past.

The only explanation she could come up with was that they all labored under the 'lonely widow' misconception: once you got used to 'it', you continued needing 'it', they thought.

Unfortunately, in her case, they were right. She was a passionate woman, susceptible to succumbing to a handsome male physique, especially when the said physique contained an intelligent, educated, elegant and witty brain.

Roger Sanders had all of that.

She had met him a week earlier at the P&A Supermarket on Montreal's Park Avenue, an establishment just around the corner from her home, where she shopped on Tuesdays and Fridays. She liked to buy fresh produce for her weekend meals and the store had excellent meat and vegetables.

"Can I help you with that?" he had asked from behind when he saw her struggling to place her purchases on the cashier's conveyor belt. Without waiting for an answer he leaned over to help.

She got a close look at him as he eased back and was struck by his good looks. In his late forties, tall and slim, suntanned and seemingly fit, with a ready smile on his lips framing gleaming white teeth beneath a finely chiseled nose, he was the answer to a widow's prayer, at least physically.

"Thank you." She reached for her purse to pay. "Do you live around here?" She immediately regretted the corny line, but felt distracted and could think of nothing else to say.

"Actually, I just moved in. I'm originally from South Africa. Lived in Toronto for five years." He was watching her intently, his eyes liquid pools of thick oil. With his full head of wavy jet-black hair and bushy mustache to match, he looked incredibly virile—and Jewish.

She blushed, ashamed of thinking that way and felt herself becoming aroused and wet.

After walking her home, he had asked her out to dinner the next day, which was Saturday. They had a great time, laughed a lot, drank quite a bit and had even visited a Salsateca briefly. Roger turned out to be a terrific dancer.

Obviously well off, he wore beautifully tailored, expensive clothes. He told her his family was in metals trading in Cape Town and that he had come to Canada to open a branch of the business. He explained that, albeit his business contacts were mainly in Toronto, he preferred to live in Montreal. The bohemian atmosphere of the Plateau suited him particularly well.

Klara Moscovitch was in heaven. She had found a kindred spirit: a companion really to her liking, an obviously high-spirited man capable of great passion.

She could see it in his eyes when he looked at her.

Moreover, she added to herself, if Roger wanted to become a little animalistic with her, she would resist his advances only a bit, just enough so that he should not think that she was 'easy'.

CHAPTER 20

Saturday Lunchtime, October 20,

On Saturday, Moscovitch could hardly wait for lunchtime to roll around.

He had gotten up early and had made an extra effort to make himself look as presentable as possible by washing his hair and beard with the shampoo his jailer had provided the day before. He could not shave because he had no razor, but he did manage, using a blunt pair of scissors rounded at the tips, to trim his beard that had grown out quite nicely during his weeks of captivity. He had also cleaned up his living quarters to the best of his ability and had squared away the mess on top of his worktable.

By eleven thirty, he was ready for the big meeting: the closing of the deal that would define his future.

His 'guests' did not show until three in the afternoon by which time Moscovitch was a nervous wreck. After agonizing for hours over whether the Iraqis had changed their minds, or his having overplayed his hand the last time they had met, Moscovitch could not stop his mind from starting to play 'what if'.

What if someone had found a way to replicate his vaccine thereby making him redundant? What if Kane was not willing to take on the assignment? What if his captors did not trust Kane, or were afraid of him? What if. What if. What if; and here his heart missed a beat, what if the bastards were to kidnap his mother and hold her hostage?

There and then Moscovitch resolved that the first thing he would want from Delic's new masters when they showed was proof that his mother was safe, and he would insist that they involve Kane in validating such proof.

Jason Moscovitch had always been a happy-go-lucky person. He was intellectually gifted and very quick on the uptake. There had been no need for him to work very hard at his studies. He had an exceptional memory. As for the rest . . . well, his loving mother and doting father had provided everything for him.

Moscovitch's parents had been well-respected educators whose combined income had allowed them to live a comfortable life in Westmount, a district of Montreal populated by professionals and intellectuals and middle-management types. In spite of his mother's Israeli background and his father's definitely left-wing political beliefs, Jason grew up with no particular interest in either Zionism or social justice. He was not passionate about anything except his freedom to have as good a time as possible. There had not been enough traumas in his life to make him reflect about the meaning of his existence.

He had gone to an exclusive elementary school, St. George's, round the corner from the house where he lived, so he walked to school and back home daily, no fuss, no muss, no bother—no complicated car-pooling. He and his classmates then progressed *en masse* to attend LCC (Lower Canada College), a high-school for the privileged where Moscovitch found out that he was very good at playing basketball. He obtained his B.Sc. at McGill and his Ph.D at the University of Toronto at no cost to his parents—there were no tuition fees involved; he was coasting on a basketball scholarship.

And there were always plenty of girls around for college athletes, especially for one whose nickname was 'Stud', so life was easy, uncomplicated and great fun.

His father had died when Moscovitch was twenty-one. By then, the son's character was fully formed – a constant compromiser, a man always looking for the easiest way out of a painful situation no matter what principles were involved.

Although he had vehemently objected to working for the Arabs, his opposition to The Butcher's proposal a couple of days earlier had been more of a bravado-induced reaction than the result of a carefully thought-out process. Having reflected on his situation under pressure he now felt that the initial position he had taken had not been the only acceptable one. No, sir. Why not work for the Arabs as long as they paid the freight and provided ironclad guarantees for his eventual liberation and some professional recognition of the importance of his work.

By the time his visitors arrived—there were only two this time, The Butcher and the Third Man—Moscovitch was ready to give in on every aspect of his deal because he knew that if he didn't get away from his container he would lose his sanity.

"Sorry we kept you waiting," was the first thing the always-urbane Hassani said after they had sat down, "but we wanted to be sure we had the go-ahead from the highest level to proceed with your proposed deal. You will, I'm sure, understand that getting such authorization often takes longer than expected."

Moscovitch was hugely relieved. Could it be that they were going to accept his conditions?

"Do we have a deal then?" he asked.

The answer came from the Third Man who had not uttered a single word during any of their earlier meetings. "We think so." He spoke softly, his voice unusually high for a man.

"What does that mean?"

"We need to work out safeguards so that you don't do a quick bolt once you're out of here." The man's English was faultlessly colloquial.

"I'm listening . . ."

"We want you to include in the contract you are preparing an undertaking to put up some sort of an acceptable guarantee that would ensure your wholehearted cooperation for at least a year."

"I suppose I can live with that. What do you have in mind?"

"That depends on you. What kind of collateral can you provide?"

"Collateral?"

"Yes, something of real value to you, something you wouldn't want to lose under any circumstances."

"Like what?"

The Third Man gave Moscovitch a hard look. "If you want to get out of here you had better come up with something meaningful, otherwise we cannot guarantee your physical safety for very much longer." He sounded matter-of-fact, impartial, remote, which made his implied threat even more sinister.

"Listen carefully to what my colleague is saying," Hassani chimed in. "I must emphasize that without such meaningful collateral we cannot make a deal!"

Moscovitch became seriously concerned. Negotiations were not going the way he had expected. This was a new twist, and he was at a loss to understand what the two men were driving at.

"Let me give your request some thought," he temporized. "In the meantime" he added," allow *me* to make a request."

"And what would that be?" Hassani sounded impatient.

"I want to be sure my mother is safe and sound. I want to talk to her."

To his surprise, the Iraqi gave him a dazzling smile. "Now you're talking." He turned to the Third Man, "I told you our friend is no fool. Let us now leave him to work out the problem."

They got up to leave. "Thank you for your cooperation," the Third Man said politely on his way out. "We'll try to arrange for you to speak with your mother some time during the next couple of days."

His visitors then withdrew quickly, leaving Moscovitch with a multitude of unanswered questions.

Were his captors looking for monetary collateral, such as a mortgage?

Could a lien on his shares in his Hungarian company satisfy their requirements?

Would it suffice if he assigned them his patent to the new vaccine he had developed?

What did Hassani mean by the scientist not being a fool after Moscovitch had asked to speak with his mother?

Did he mean that they wanted his mother to guarantee his performance—perhaps by mortgaging her home?

No, that couldn't be it. Such an arrangement could easily be cancelled once they'd let him out.

Moscovitch fretted and worried . . . and waited for sleep to claim him, hoping that his subconscious would provide the answers to at least some of his questions.

CHAPTER 21

Budapest, Saturday Afternoon, October 20

Thérèse Lapointe found herself in a quandary. What to do about Mr. Kane.

Having reread the confidential memo she had received about him from her bosses in Ottawa and his excellent references from the RCMP, she concluded that Kane was working for Canada's Department of External Affairs *sub rosa*, trying to resolve the Moscovitch problem in an informal way. She was surprised to hear that he was planning something as risky as a raid on private property. 'That would be taking the law into one's own hands' she reasoned, 'and put Canada into a very difficult position.'

Could it be that Horváth was misinformed, or, worse, bluffing? But why?

Overworked and under-qualified she did not know where to turn for help.

Originally from Granby, a small town in the Eastern Townships in Quebec, she had won a scholarship to the Université de Sherbrooke from where she graduated *magna cum laude* in Political Science and Economics. Perfectly at ease in English and French (her mother was Irish, her father French Canadian) she had aced the Civil Service exams leading to a career in the Canadian Foreign Service and, after stints in junior postings in France and Morocco, was appointed Canadian Consul in Hungary, her first senior position.

Aged thirty-four and single, she was proud of her achievements, outgoing and somewhat promiscuous.

Her present boyfriend was Rezzah Khamani, an unmarried Iranian businessman and Hungarian resident who owned a successful vehicle rental agency in Budapest, and a knack for discreetly bedding female diplomats.

Serially of course. That went without saying.

And the ladies did not mind. What was good for the goose was good for the gander. The only strict rule was "discretion".

Thérèse's affair with Rezzah was discrete, superficial, entertaining, and sexually very satisfying. During the week they ran into each-other every now and then at diplomatic receptions that they both liked to frequent. At these, they were careful not to betray any signs of intimacy. They saw each other only once a week in bed, usually on Saturday afternoons near Heroes' Square at the *Beatrix Panzio,* a quiet B&B on *Széher* Boulevard, where Khamani lived in a luxurious suite that occupied the entire top floor of the building.

Of course, everybody knew anyway. Budapest's diplomatic community was small and its members made sport of gossip.

This particular Saturday, Thérèse's lover was in a bad mood. He had had two of his cars stolen overnight and was expecting a hefty insurance premium increase as a consequence. This cooled his usual ardor considerably. Since she, too, was preoccupied—she couldn't put the Kane problem out of her mind—their lovemaking had been desultory and had ended in a lengthy post-coital conversation about the vicissitude of life for non-Hungarians in the Capital.

After listening to Rezzah's insurance problems, she felt compelled to reciprocate. "You, at least, can look for tangible rewards for your efforts." She was speaking in English, the *lingua franca* of ex-pats in Budapest, a language in which both were highly proficient. "I, on the other hand, get little satisfaction from my job, which is very bureaucratic in nature. You know what I mean, lots of silly formalities, lots of paper . . . Plus, there is the additional irritant of the idiotic behavior of my visiting compatriots who lose their passports, run out of money, get into fights in bars, and insult policemen."

"Insult policemen?" Rezzah, his right arm under her neck on the pillow, was stroking her breast absentmindedly with his left hand, only half listening.

"One of them is planning to break into a business establishment. Can you imagine?"

"Break in? For money? And why would he insult a policeman?"

"He didn't. The policeman found out and told me to tell him not to."

"Did you?"

"Haven't had time yet."

"But where is the insult?" The Iranian wasn't that interested in the story, but he played along.

"The policeman doesn't think it's right for visitors to take matters into their own hands and ignore the host country's laws."

Rezzah tried to focus. He had more than a nodding acquaintance with the Budapest police because of his car business. "Are you talking about a specific cop or in general?"

"I'm talking about my liaison policeman, Detective-Lieutenant Horváth."

The left hand suddenly stopped caressing the right breast. "I know Horváth. He's a bulldog. What's he up to?"

So she told him about Kane's impertinence and the Moscovitch story. After all, what harm could it do? Everyone in Budapest had read about the Moscovitch disappearance after the fire in his lab, or had the fire been before the disappearance? She couldn't remember. Besides, it didn't matter anyway because the break-in would not happen. She had just made up her mind that she would, for sure, see to that.

Thérèse reached for Rezzah's hand and put it gently between her thighs.

To her surprise, he reached for her hungrily and took her with a forceful passion that left her quite breathless.

CHAPTER 22

Budapest, Saturday Afternoon and Evening, October 20

After a leisurely lunch, Lonsdale headed for the shopping mall at the Western Railway Terminal and wandered around in search of cheap workmen's clothing. In an army surplus store he picked up a couple of steel-toed construction boots, a pair of waterproof, olive-green hunting pants, a thick, green flannel shirt and a matching green cap popular with Hungary's more modest classes.

At another establishment, a few meters away, he found a suitably rough woolen sweater and a modestly priced, heavily lined, waterproof windjammer with hood attached.

A pair of thick socks completed his outfit.

He dropped his parcels at his hotel then crossed the street to a sporting goods store catering to hunters and anglers that he had spotted earlier and bought a small inflatable rubber dinghy, complete with paddles and a tiny electric compressor. He dragged the package to a cab and told the driver to take him to the Intercontinental. He loaded the dinghy into the trunk of his car and crossed the Chain Bridge to the Castle District where he spent an hour sightseeing and verifying that nobody was following him.

Next, he drove to the *Béke*, found a parking spot in a nearby street and, by six, was back in his room where he took stock of the contents of his special kit. He found everything in order. A call to room service got him a snack with lots of coffee. After eating, he lay down to rest for a while.

He donned his new garb a few minutes past midnight, took the elevator all the way down, crossed the staff-room, nodded to a couple of employees polishing silverware in the basement and let himself out into the street behind the hotel. He sprinted to the nearest corner, turned right, stopped dead and waited.

Nobody followed.

He walked to his car, got in and took the quay along the Danube to the *Petőfi* Bridge. He crossed the river—he could almost feel the dirty water rushing by underneath him—and swung onto *Budafoki* Boulevard, then onto the avenue that would bring him near to the *Háros* peninsula.

Traffic was light. It took him less than forty minutes to get to the little fishermen's camp on the side of the peninsula opposite to where the Jurices lived. Forty minutes is a short time, but an eternity when one's brain is crowded with unpleasant thoughts. He missed Adys and this made him unhappy about doing what he was about to do. Yet he knew that he no longer had a choice; he had to follow through.

'Here you go again' he admonished himself, 'risking your life once more, going into action at your age'. Then he laughed aloud. 'You know damned well why you're doing it. Certainly not for the money, or for lofty ideals. Admit it, you're doing it for the thrill—for the rush of adrenalin you crave, you addicted, fucking freak'.

He pulled in between two shacks, killed the engine, opened the window and spent ten minutes waiting quietly in the dark.

Not a sound.

He got out and sniffed the wind. It was blowing cold and from the north. There was no moon and it felt as if rain were imminent. He walked to the end of the rickety old dock and looked along the riverbank.

Sure enough, he could easily spot the nearby glow of the two crime lights illuminating the Jurices' riverfront property.

'Just as Frakkos described it,' he reflected. 'Got to find a way to hug the coast and then sneak ashore.'

He got his kit from the trunk, brought it to the front seat and, without turning on the light, opened it. He strapped his dagger to his left forearm, placed his night-vision goggles on his forehead and tightened the straps. Then he screwed the silencer into the barrel of the automatic and stuck the weapon in his belt.

He stopped to listen. All he heard was silence.

He activated the portable GPS Unit, left it and his kit on the front seat, clipped his special phone to his belt and started the car. He drove—very slowly and in low gear—to the base of the dock and contemplated driving onto it.

'Better not; too risky,' he observed. 'The damned thing might give way under the weight of the car.' He went to the trunk and opened it again then looked at his watch: one-fifty-three a.m.

He dragged the paddles, the rubber dinghy and the compressor to the dock, inserted the compressor hose into the dinghy's air intake valve and plugged the compressor into the cigarette lighter. The motor began to chug away merrily and, within seconds, the small boat began to take shape. When inflation was complete, he pocketed the keys and pulled the night vision glasses over his eyes.

Then he turned around.

Two men were racing toward him and reached him before Lonsdale could get his weapon out. The short one charged from the left and bowled him over. The fat one, a mountain of a man, kicked him in the ribs. Lonsdale immediately assumed the fetal position and reached for his dagger, but could not extract it. His arms and elbows were too busy fending off his assailants' kicks.

He tried to roll away, but they had him cornered and were taking turns at pummeling him. He had to chose—protect his face or go for the dagger. He went for the dagger and paid for it dearly. A well-aimed kick from a panting and wheezing Fatso caught him on the cheekbone and almost knocked him out.

Almost, but not quite.

By the time it was Shorty's turn to do the kicking, Lonsdale had his dagger out. He rolled away from Fatso toward Shorty who, surprised, tried to redirect his foot. Lonsdale plunged the dagger into the man's thigh and felt it grate against bone.

His assailant collapsed on top of him and began to bleed profusely, splattering blood over Lonsdale's face and clothing and soaking his hand still holding the dagger. Lonsdale couldn't move. The man's weight pinned him to the ground.

Fatso slapped the dagger out of Lonsdale's hand and kicked him in the gut. Then he slung Shorty over his shoulder and headed for Lonsdale's car. He groped for the key in the ignition and, finding none, was about to leave when he spotted the kit on the front seat. He grabbed it and trudged away, his colleague's now limp body draped around his neck.

Lonsdale was in bad shape. His ribs, face, head and arms were screaming with pain, his hip aflame with ache. He rested on the ground for a while then willed himself to sit up.

He almost fainted from the effort.

Patting himself down, he found that the beating had resulted in no broken bones because his thick woolen shirt and heavily lined windjammer had cushioned the kicks and blows somewhat. An exception: his right cheek that throbbed dully, but more than the other parts of his body.

He knew he was supposed to do something urgently, but for the life of him, he couldn't remember what it was.

Then it came to him. 'Grab the fucking automatic, you asshole' he whispered. 'The bad guys may come back before you can get away.' He tried to laugh, but even smiling hurt. 'And more may come back, not just the original two,' he added.

He shook his head, trying to clear the cobwebs then tested his teeth with his tongue. He was gratified to discover that, although some were loose, none had broken or cracked.

On his hands and knees, gun in hand, Lonsdale felt for his goggles and found them a few yards away. He held them over his eyes gingerly, got to his feet with great difficulty and spotted the dagger. It lay right next to his feet.

He sheathed it, hobbled over to the dinghy, unplugged the compressor hose and connecting wire and dumped the motor into the river. Then he tried to get into his car.

'The keys, where did you leave the keys, you idiot?'

In his jacket pocket, thank God.

Getting behind the wheel was a symphony of agony, but he managed it somehow.

In excruciating pain, he drove back to the Intercontinental with exaggerated caution, torturing himself with dozens of questions.

How come he did not spot that people were following him?

Were his assailants Hungarians? (He seemed to recall that, after he had stabbed Shorty, the man had cried out "*a combom, a combom*", 'my thigh, my thigh' in Hungarian).

If they were Hungarian, who had sent them? Surely not the Jurices!

How come they did not try to rob him, or steal his car? They also left the GPS behind, but had taken his kit.

Lonsdale could think of no answers.

He drove into the garage and began a meticulous examination of his vehicle.

It took him twenty minutes to find what he was looking for, a small, sophisticated transponder, almost identical to the one he had fastened to Amina's car, magnetically attached to the spare wheel in the trunk.

Question: who could have gained access to the inside of his trunk?

Answer: the car rental agency, or the police.

Too sore and tired to think constructively any longer, Lonsdale took the elevator to the hotel lobby. He spun a tale of having been robbed to the horrified front desk manager who contacted the hotel doctor on duty whose apartment-surgery was just around the corner. The physician agreed to see Mr. Kane immediately, provided, of course, Mr. Kane was willing to shell out five hundred US dollars for a thorough examination and an X-Ray.

Medication would be extra.

CHAPTER 23

Montreal, Sunday Noon, October 21

Montrealers are not blessed with temperate weather overall. The winters can be very cold, especially in January and February. Snowstorms are frequent in April, and spring seems never to come. By the time the short summer arrives in late June, people are fed up with complaining about the cold, but there is no respite: the warm weather turns hot and humid in August and the bitching starts all over again, this time about the unbearable heat.

Every now and then Montrealers get a break from Mother Nature. In mid-October the weather turns unseasonably warm for a week or so during the Indian Summer, *l'été des indiens*, and the sun is warm enough for shirt-sleeve excursions. The period usually coincides with the time of year when the maple trees change color. Hordes of tourists, some from as far as Japan, then descend on the Laurentian hills north of Montreal and on the Thousand Islands in the middle of the Saint Lawrence River. They come to marvel at the beauty of a countryside covered with a carpet of maple trees stretching as far as the eye can see, shimmering in the brilliant Fall sunshine in striking shades of red and yellow and green under a vivid, clear blue sky.

To Klara Moscovitch's great delight it was just that kind of a week that the forecasters were predicting.

She had plans!

Although it was Sunday, she knew that her favorite Hungarian delicatessen on St. Lawrence Boulevard would be open 'till noon, so she got up early, took a quick shower and picked up four slices of very thin veal and a medium sized plastic container of cucumber salad. Next, on to the fishmonger for some shrimp.

For desert, she bought a small praline cake at the Patisserie Gascogne on Laurier Boulevard. She didn't bother with wine; Roger would be bringing that.

Ah, Roger . . .

Their dinner date the previous evening had been a smashing success.

He had taken her to Milos, an excellent, but very expensive Greek restaurant on Park Avenue. They ate fish and drank lots of white wine. The ambiance was great, the meal inspiring, and the conversation scintillating. Roger spoke with authority about South Africa and the plight of the poor in that country. He also discussed the difficulties that Arab immigrants to France faced. From the way he spoke Klara judged him to be a left-of-center intellectual, a rare animal indeed for a businessman, but definitely *her* cup of tea.

After dinner they had gone dancing to the Salsateca again, where Roger managed to arouse her sexually to the point where she was not sure she would be able to resist his advances later that night.

But she had done so—with Roger's help.

"I don't want a slam-bang-thank-you-ma'am kind of relationship with you," he had said while parking his car, a spanking new Jaguar, in front of her condo.

He had leaned over to kiss her lightly on the lips and she had thrilled to his touch. Sensing her yearning, he had pulled away. "I want you as much as you want me," he had added gently, "but I don't want to rush, I want you to be completely mine."

"What do you mean?" She could hardly speak; she was burning with desire.

"Here is what I propose we do." He had kissed her lightly again and she had felt her wetness soak her panties. "If you're game, I'd like to take you away for a few days so we can thrill to each-other without having to worry about anything else but us."

"Where would we go?"

"I have a friend who owns a house on one of the Thousand Islands. Do you know where that is?"

She had nodded and, taking his hand, had kissed it, then had held it to her cheek. She had felt genuinely touched by his delicate concern.

"He's on vacation, so we could be alone at his place for as long as we want. He won't be back for a couple more weeks."

She had nodded assent.

"Good. Then pack a few things, and I'll pick you up tomorrow morning."

"Be here at noon and don't have breakfast," she had managed to say, finding her voice. "I'll prepare an early lunch and we could be on our way by two. Kingston and the Thousand Islands Bridge are only a couple of hours away. We could be across it by four-thirty, well before sunset."

He had seemed to hesitate for a moment then had kissed her for the third time. "Done deal—and I'll bring the wine. Now get out of the car before I change my mind and rape you right here and now."

And here she was at eleven thirty in the morning of the day after, rushing to get lunch ready for her soon-to-be lover.

Earlier, she had called her brother, Joe, to say that she'd be away for a few days. She and her brother, five years younger, were very close. He immediately sensed that something important had happened in her life.

"So who's the lucky man?" he had inquired. She had told him. "And may be, just maybe, he's Jewish," she had added as an afterthought.

Although secular Jews, religious tradition was important to Klara and her brother. Their father, the late Henry Goldstein, the only member of his family to survive the Holocaust, had managed to get to Israel shortly after World War II ended. There he had married a liberal-minded Sabra whose Hungarian parents had emigrated to Palestine in the mid 1930's. Klara, born in Haifa, had gone to school there. She had been ten when she, her parents, brother and grandmother left Israel for Canada, fleeing once more, this time from Arab terrorism. She had no difficulty adjusting to Montreal as a child; by the time she got there she could read, write and speak Hebrew, Arabic and English, had a working knowledge of 'kitchen' German and a nodding acquaintance with Hungarian, thanks to her grandmother.

For Klara, to learn French had been child's play. She had an ear for languages.

Exceptionally bright, she graduated from high school at sixteen and gained immediate admission to McGill University where she obtained first a B.Sc., then a Master's Degree in Education. After four years as a teacher, she met and married Simon Moscovitch, a professor of biochemistry. Their only child, Jason, was born a year later.

Her son had been twenty, and she forty-seven, when Simon Moscovitch was diagnosed with advanced melanoma. He died within twelve months.

That had been seven years ago.

*   *   *

Roger arrived a few minutes past noon and, from that moment onward, things began to develop in a totally unplanned, but, in retrospect, perfectly predictable, way.

They started with a *schluck,* a gulp, of ice-cold Slivovic (Yugoslav plum brandy), then another *schluck.* This highly alcoholic drink set the stage for the drinking to follow: lots of champagne with the shrimp cocktail and a bottle of excellent German white wine to accompany the Wiener schnitzel and home fried potatoes and cucumber salad.

He rose to help her fetch the dessert, but, by that time, they were both tipsy and very horny. When she bent down to reach for the cake in the frig he sneaked up on her and grabbed her breasts from behind. She turned around and gave him a French kiss that made his head spin.

He lost control and dragged her into the bedroom where he literally tore her clothes off. He began to kiss her breasts then worked his way down to her navel, constantly probing for her clitoris with his finger. Tremendously aroused, she pushed him against the bed. He fell on his back. She ripped down his zipper, freed his manhood, straddled him and, with a swift movement of her hand, guided him into her body. He pushed against her and she began to ride him, then screamed with pleasure as all the pent up sexual frustrations of her last few years dissolved into one gigantic, ecstatic flow of pleasure that shook her body with repeated orgasms.

Panting, she got off him and saw that he, too, had climaxed. She ran to the bathroom for a wet washcloth. By the time she returned he had all his clothes off and was already getting hard again.

He made her kneel on the bed and, for a final climax, took her from behind with a ferocity that gave them both such intense pleasure that they were left breathless to the point where, when they finally rolled apart, she lay gasping for air, with her loins still twitching with post-orgasmic contractions, totally exhausted sexually.

They fell asleep in each other's arms and, after an hour's nap, left her house at five in the afternoon. At eight they crossed into the US on the Thousand Islands Bridge, drove to Clayton, a small town at the bend of the St. Lawrence River, found a place to crash, the Bertrand Motel on James Street, and were fast asleep by ten.

CHAPTER 24

Budapest, Monday Morning, October 22 (1)

Having slept for twenty-six hours straight and dazed by the double dose of extra-strength painkiller that he had taken after getting up, Lonsdale drove to the Thermal Hotel on St. Margaret Island in his jogging outfit. Every muscle, every bone in his body, especially his hipbone, ached dully.

Lonsdale put on his running shoes in the car park and painfully limped over to the exercise track that rings the island, timing his arrival to hit the track a few minutes after eight. He soon identified his contact, a shapely woman running in a stylish sports outfit made of lycra depicting the red Maple Leaf, Canada's national emblem.

The late October weather was brisk, but not cold, though the sun was barely above the horizon. He took deep breaths of the fresh air that smelled lightly of wood smoke. This made him feel better because he could pretend that he was back in North America in the Fall. He decided to allow himself the luxury of gently jogging a lap before taking a seat on a bench alongside the track on which the woman had left her sweater that matched what she was wearing.

"I thought maple leaves were green," he said laughing when she sat down beside him, sweating. He kept pointing to her outfit.

She laughed back. "Not in the Fall."

He stopped pointing. Contact had been established.

They chatted for a while about this and that. He told her he was from Montreal, she said she was from Iowa, additional recognition signals. Then they walked to the main parking lot.

She started her post-exercise stretches and Lonsdale joined her. He was decidedly feeling better; the workout had loosened up his aching muscles.

"I'm parked over there," she pointed at a non-descript Volvo. "And you?"

"At the Thermal."

"I'll give you a lift." They walked over to her car.

The sheets the woman gave him numbered in the dozens. It took Lonsdale an hour and a half to sift through them, only to find that they contained no conclusive evidence about anything other than that the mayor of Cizre seemed to be a caring uncle and Amina a dutiful niece.

As for Drusza, he and Amina appeared to be very good friends, perhaps even lovers, who enjoyed working together. The transcript contained pages and pages of references to invoices, equipment specs and cost estimates. Evidently, Drusza was relying heavily on his employee to keep the cost of reconstructing the Phylaxos lab within the limits of a tight budget.

Unless, of course, the conversations was a charade, intended to deceive the enemy. Or, maybe, the two were using some sort of a verbal code. Why else such urgency about the mundane matter of invoices? Didn't the two see each other twice a week anyway?

He reread the sheets more carefully this time and suddenly felt the nagging tug of his subconscious mind. Something did not make sense, but he was damned if he could figure out what it was. The exchanges contained a hidden message, but he just did not have the key.

*   *   *

At noon, Lonsdale called Morton again. His Control picked up right away.

"Good morning ace. You did well! We're in business." He sounded uncharacteristically excited. "Although the evidence is inconclusive, there are traces of something going on, but we need more information. Did the mayor call Amina yesterday? If so, can you provide us with a tape?"

"Yes I can, but no earlier than this afternoon."

"How come?"

Lonsdale told him about the beating.

"Any idea who's behind it?"

"Not really. It was dark and they got behind me somehow."

"So what do you propose to do next?"

Lonsdale shrugged. "I don't know yet. You say the transcript reveals nothing conclusive—just a lot of bull about construction invoices."

"That's what I thought too, initially, but my guys think otherwise, so get us that tape a.s.a.p. so we can come up with something positive." Morton stopped talking.

"All right, all right, I'll get on it right-away," Lonsdale snapped irritably. Time to take a couple more Motrins. The pain was coming back big-time. "First, I'm meeting Frakkos to find out if someone, perhaps one of Juric' people, had gotten wounded the night before last."

"Our next contact?'

"Noon tomorrow my time, six am yours."

* * *

Like so much about the Iranian state, the Qods Force, which conducts overseas operations for Iran's Islamic Revolutionary Guard Corps (the I.R.G.C.), remains remarkably mysterious even to those who closely study the country.

The I.R.G.C. was created after the ouster of the Shah because the Ayatollah Khomeini did not trust the army. To protect himself and his government, it formed the Guard as a parallel military force, a section of which became the Qods Force, considered today as the long arm of the Islamic Revolution abroad.

The Force, El Qods in Arabic means Jerusalem, has in the past participated in overt and covert operations in Lebanon and Bosnia and maintains 'sleeper' agents throughout the Middle East and the Balkans. Their job is to watch and wait, and to act only when they see an outstanding opportunity to advance the cause of Islamic Revolution worldwide.

Members of the Force, always Shia, are the handpicked elite of an already elite ideological army who generally mistrust the Sunnis, though they do cooperate with them when it is to Iran's advantage to do so. For example, the Qods supported the Sunni Bosnian Muslims against Serbian forces.

Rezzah Khamani was a dedicated senior officer in the Force, a thirty-eight year old Lieutenant Colonel, who had served with distinction in the Balkans before establishing himself in Hungary to observe, report and act as ordered.

Being on the fringes of Budapest's diplomatic community where gossip was a daily sport he had become aware of the Moscovitch kidnapping almost immediately after it had taken place. After reading his report on the incident, his superiors ordered him to forward all new relevant information to Teheran immediately. When he related his conversation with the Canadian Consul to his Control in Teheran, he was told that 'an operative in the field' would contact him in due course with further instructions.

His Control also told him that it was not in Iran's interest to allow Moscovitch to fall into Iraqi hands alive. The ayatollahs remembered only too well what had happened during the 1980-88 war with Iraq when Saddam Hussein's army had killed many thousands of Iranians with chemical weapons.

The vicious Iraqi dictator, who was already stockpiling the nv.C-JD Biological Weapon of Mass Destruction, was not to end up being the only one in the world to posses the antidote against it as well!

* * *

At one o'clock Lonsdale and Frakkos had lunch at the *Bagolyvár*, the Owl's Nest, close to the Zoo. The food was the same as that served next door at Gundel's, one of Central Europe's best restaurants, but the presentation was less elaborate, the service less elegant and cheaper.

The two eateries were owned by the same people, George Lang and his partner and financier, Ronald Lauder, former US Ambassador to Hungary and son of Estee Lauder.

Frakkos watched Lonsdale limp into the establishment, took one look at his face and became very concerned. "What happened to you?" he blurted.

"Pulled a muscle jogging and fell. Probably strained my Achilles tendon," Lonsdale lied. He had spoken to Frakkos earlier in the day by phone and had said nothing about the attack, too interested in the information the driver was providing.

"Sunday, after supper, owner's barge came home," Frakkos had reported. "His wife pleased. He and she and the deckhands went into the house to have celebration."

Lonsdale's antennae had begun to twitch.

"Was Amina still there?"

"No. She go home earlier."

"How many deckhands?"

"We couldn't get close to be sure. Half a dozen maybe . . ."

"How come you couldn't get close?"

"No trees. The complex is on riverbank, on side of dead branch of river Duna, Danube to you. The Jurices have cleared land of trees as far as about fifty meters back from the water, yes? By day, they seeing everything going on around three containers. Between containers, there is high, wooden garden wall with gate. So, we cannot see from across river Duna people going in and out on other side, yes?"

"What about approaching the property from the land side?"

"Fenced in with gate locked. There's no way to get close without being seen, yes?"

"Is the barge still there?"

"I guess so."

"Have they unloaded it?"

"I don't know. Cargo consists of lumber."

"Where did the barge come from?"

"No idea, sir. We too busy watching the target and servicing you. We have no manpower to do extra work, yes?"

Lonsdale was quick to apologize. "I did not mean to sound critical." He shook his head to clear his mind. "It's just that I'm a suspicious kind of guy." 'Keep calm', he admonished himself silently.

'You need this asshole so don't let him see how pissed off you're at him. You can give him shit once the mission is finished for delaying to report what may be the most crucial bit of information we've stumbled across to date.'

He then told the man that he should hire more people to watch the Juric property—and to be on the lookout for a deckhand who limped and another who resembled a man-mountain.

"So, what have you found out?" Lonsdale now wanted answers to his earlier questions.

"Nothing new. Amina kayaking yesterday as usual, her uncle called from Cizre. All routine."

"You got the latest tapes?"

Frakkos handed them over.

"What about the deckhands?"

"We've verified there are five in total: two younger ones, two medium and an older guy. None of them wore bandages, none of them limping. All of them big, but not that much."

Lonsdale was very surprised. "You sure?"

"Absolutely." Frakkos couldn't help wondering why his client paid so much attention to the hired help. Weren't they supposed to be looking for Amina's lover?

Lonsdale read his mind and dropped the subject.

They finished their meal in silence and went their respective ways.

*   *   *

At three thirteen in the afternoon Lonsdale emerged from the Zoo he had gone to visit briefly. It was next to the restaurant. He intended to take a couple more Motrins after delivering the tape, and then lie down. His entire body was just one dull ache.

A few minutes later, a cab drove by slowly. "Taxi?" the driver yelled through the open window. Lonsdale glanced at the car's serial number; it matched the one they had given him when he had called the US Embassy from a public phone inside the Zoo.

He got in and had himself driven to the *Béke*.

En route, he handed the driver the tapes Frakkos had given him at lunch.

CHAPTER 25

New York State, Monday Morning, October 22 (2)

Klara Moscovitch woke early and stole a glance at her lover snoring ever so lightly beside her. He was even more handsome asleep than awake.

'Life would be perfect,' she said to herself, 'if only this man Kane could find my son Jason.'

She sighed deeply. He awoke instantly with a start—just like an animal, she thought—and reached for her. She snuggled into his arms and he held her. They remained motionless for a while; then he began to caress her breasts and she felt the familiar wetness starting to flow out of her again. He put his hand between her thighs and her clitoris erected as soon as he touched it.

They made love again, gently and lovingly this time. After showering, they breakfasted at the nearby Riverside Café at a table by the window with an impressive view. She dawdled over her second cup of coffee while Roger picked up some groceries at the supermarket behind the marina.

"We'll leave the car in the parking lot here," he told her as they were walking down towards the water. "I gave the clerk in the store ten bucks to keep an eye on it for a few days." He gave her a friendly nudge. "Grab a couple of bags and help me load up the boat."

"What boat?"

Roger laughed and pointed at a small blue-hulled runabout moored between two sizeable sailboats alongside the quay jutting into the river. "I forgot to tell you, the romantic adventure starts right here. We'll go by boat to our secret island. See, it over there? It's the nearest landmass out there." He pointed and Klara looked upstream across the water glittering in the bright autumn sunshine. "Put on your windbreaker; it's warm here on land, but it can get a bit cold on the water."

Roger knew exactly where to look for the boat's ignition keys. Within seconds, he had the engine running and after transferring the food into the hold, he cast off and they were underway.

"Do you know which way to go?" she asked anxiously as he headed across the wide river. There seemed to be an awful lot of open water around them and she was an unwilling sailor.

He laughed. "It's no sweat as long as you know the compass bearing you're supposed to steer." They were sitting side by side in the sheltered part of the boat, he steering, she, to his left, hanging onto him for comfort.

"And do you?"

He gave her a dazzling smile. "Of course, I do, silly."

Since he didn't elaborate she stopped asking questions, noting idly that the little black compass on the dashboard showed the number 333. She smiled; three was her lucky number.

After a twelve-minute crossing on a windless day with hardly a ripple on the water they landed on their 'secret' island a few minutes after noon.

Klara was more than delighted, she was ecstatic. The area seemed unbelievably idyllic, preordained for a lovers' autumn tryst.

Roger had obviously visited the place before because he knew his way around. After tying up at the dock in a small bay, he led her up a gently rising path to the main house, an imposing stone building set near the edge of a bluff overlooking the St. Lawrence.

The covered verandah that ran along two sides of the house faced the river, but Roger gave her no time to admire the breathtaking view. "There will be plenty of time later for gawking. Come on," he called to her as he opened the massive front door. "Give me a hand with the groceries. The kitchen is to the right as you go in."

While she put the food away Roger got the fire going in the immense, grey fieldstone fireplace that dominated the living room, but she didn't want to stay indoors. He sensed her fidgeting and disappeared into the kitchen, so she put on her overcoat again and went outside.

Sometime later, Roger found her in one of the two immense wooden armchairs on the verandah, looking south over the river. "I don't want you to catch cold so come in darling and have something to eat. I made us some lunch."

She began to cry and this surprised him. He frowned.

"What's wrong?"

"Nothing. Just tears of joy," she assured him. "You cannot imagine how happy I feel being here with you. I feel so at peace, so safe." Then a shadow crossed her face. 'If I could just get word from somebody about my Jason' she said to herself. 'I don't even know if he's still alive . . .' Aloud she said nothing, not wanting to break the spell of the moment.

She was helping Roger with the dishes after lunch when her cellular phone rang. "Mrs. Moscovitch?" A heavily accented, male voice, perhaps Russian.

"Speaking."

"Hold on, your son Jason would like to speak with you."

Klara Moscovitch's heart rate went through the roof and she almost fainted. She grabbed the counter to steady herself.

"Hello Mom, it's Jason." The oh-so-well-known voice was strong and sounded confident. "How are you?"

"I'm fine my darling," she forced herself to calm down. "But never mind that. How are *you?*"

"I'm just fine, in good health and good spirits."

"Where are you?"

"I can't tell you because I don't know, but don't worry. I'm in the process of working things out with my new . . ." a pause ". . . associates. If all goes well, I'll be seeing you sooner than you think." His voice caught. He was close to tears.

"Oh Jason, Jason, it's so good to hear your voice." She was going to lose control and he sensed it.

He took a deep breath and forced himself to set a good example. "Pull yourself together Mom and please don't cry. I need to ask you a few questions."

"Questions? What questions?" She couldn't understand.

"Mom, are you all right? I mean physically."

"Just fine my darling son, never better, now that I've heard your voice." Her heart was singing. Jason was alive and well.

"And where are you now?"

"I'm visiting friends for a few days in the Thousand Islands."

"Would I know them?"

"I don't think so Jason, they're from South Africa."

'Oh." Silence, then: "Are you alone in the room Mom?" What a strange question at a time like this. She made a mental note to remember it.

"Now I am, son. My friend—he's very discreet—has just left the kitchen."

"What are you doing in the kitchen?"

"Washing up after lunch, what else?"

He laughed. "I forgot about the time difference. When are you going back to Montreal?"

"In a few days. Why?"

"I might want to call you again."

"I promise to keep my cell phone open for you at all times Jason, you can be sure of that."

"I guess I knew you would, Mom, but I just wanted to be sure. Do me a favor Mom, and don't tell anybody except your brother that I called."

This alarmed her. "Why not?"

"My negotiations have reached a delicate stage and I don't want anybody upsetting the apple cart."

"How much longer . . . ?" Then she caught herself; she was no fool. The men who held him captive must be listening in. "I mean . . . when are you going to call again?"

"Hopefully, before the end of the week." There was a noise, as if somebody were saying something to her son. "I must hang up now Mom, so please, please look after yourself, and don't worry; everything will work out all right in the end, you'll see. And Mom, I love you."

He hung up before she could tell him that she loved him too . . . very much.

When Roger returned a few minutes later, he found her sitting with her elbows on the kitchen table, her head in her hands, sobbing uncontrollably.

Alarmed, he knelt down and put his arms around her. "What happened? Did somebody die?"

She shook her head, laughing now, and, through her tears, told him the story of her son's disappearance. "Nobody could tell me anything. Nobody knew whether he was dead or alive. Imagine. Two months of agony, of absolute silence, and then he calls as if nothing happened!"

Roger clapped his hands together. "Splendid news. This definitely calls for a celebration. Let me get you a drink, a good stiff one."

He was back in seconds with two double Scotches. He lifted his glass. "To Jason," he said. "May his troubles be over soon. Now go call your brother Joe while I finish tidying up here."

Her brother was elated and wanted to hear every detail of their conversation. She obliged and, with Roger sitting at her feet in front of the fire, spent half an hour, happily speculating about how soon she'd see Jason again.

"You had better call External Affairs in Ottawa tomorrow," her brother counseled her. "They'd want to know what's going on, that Jason is alive and well and negotiating his release. And also call that investigator fellow you hired. What's his name again?"

"Kane, his name is Kane, and he is in Budapest."

"The more reason to call. Do you have a number where you can reach him?"

"Yes I do. He left me his world phone number, a cellular he said rings everywhere in the world."

"Do you really think I should call all these people? Jason said I shouldn't tell anybody that he called, except you."

"The government and Kane have the right to know that Jason is alive and well," he argued and she gave in.

After hanging up she turned to Roger. "I can't sit still. I'm too happy and excited. Come on, let's go for a walk."

"Let's, and you can then tell me about Jason and his problems while we walk."

The island was larger than she thought and during the hour it took to crisscross it Roger told her that the property belonged to a very wealthy public company CEO, a friend, who used it as his summer hideaway. "He has a big boat he keeps near where he lives and comes upriver whenever he has time."

"Where does the house get its water from?"

"From an excellent artesian well."

"And its electricity?"

"By underwater cable from the mainland grid."

"I suppose there's also a telephone cable . . ."

"Actually, there isn't. Everybody uses cell phones."

"So we're totally isolated . . ."

". . . and happily self-contained. We have food and wine and a fireplace . . ."

". . . and each-other."

She could not remember when she had last been so happy.

For dinner, they ate the cold roast chicken they had bought in Clayton and washed it down with a bottle of excellent Chilean wine that Roger had procured, an Erazuriz, no less. They had their coffee and cognac of course, sitting in front of the roaring fire.

Stimulated and excited, Klara was eager to yield to Roger's sexual advances that evening. She had lots of nervous energy to burn before she could fall asleep.

She was having a very bad dream and awoke with a start. How did Roger know her brother's name? She had never mentioned Joe's name to him. Or had she? She wasn't sure. Where was Roger anyway; he was not in bed beside her.

She needed him!

It was pitch dark in the house, but she had no difficulty finding her way to the balustrade at the head of the stairs. She could hear faint sounds from downstairs and occasional laughter. Her immediate reaction was that Roger was married and had snuck away to call his wife. Jealous and a little upset, she decided to investigate, but she was barefoot and wearing only a flannel nightgown.

Never mind!

She started to work her way noiselessly toward the muffled sounds emanating from the kitchen and began to discern what was being said just before reaching the bottom of the stairs. The words she was hearing shook her so profoundly that it took her several seconds to realize their terrible implication.

Roger, her supposedly South African lover, was speaking in Arabic, Palestinian Arabic to boot; a language she understood perfectly.

"...just a fucking machine *habibi*, I'm telling you, an incredible Yehuda nympho who can't get enough of it."

Pause.

"No, no, don't worry, you'll get your turn on the boat, I promise."

Pause.

"Around ten-thirty will be good. It'll give me time to have a go at her once more before we leave here. It will make her more submissive."

Pause.

"Don't worry, she's snoring away merrily upstairs. All fucked out I suppose."

Pause.

"You mean the call from the son? Perfectly timed. Tell Selim he couldn't have done better."

Klara, terrified almost to the point of paralysis, had heard enough to realize that she was in mortal danger.

CHAPTER 26

New York State, Tuesday, Dawn, October 23

Klara Moscovitch steeled herself to give the greatest theatrical performance of her life.

She had tiptoed away from the kitchen without a sound, and had hurried upstairs to flush the toilet after which she had headed for the bedroom. She had switched on the light for just long enough to see where everything was: her cell phone and the car and boat keys on Roger's night table, the socks she had worn and her dressing gown thrown over an armchair.

She had made it under the covers seconds before Roger had come hurrying into the room.

Now she lay, stretched out, willing herself not to tremble with fear, pretending that she was wiggling to get comfortable, having just returned to bed after relieving herself.

He bent down and kissed her on the forehead. "I went to get a drink of water," he murmured, "and brought some for you too." He placed the glass on the night table beside her.

She reached up and pulled him to her. Surprised, he yielded. She began to stroke his manhood then took it into her mouth. Soon he was wanting to penetrate her, but she would not let him. Instead, she kept playing with him, always stopping just before he was ready to climax, until he could resist no more. She pushed him on his back, straddled him and began to ride him with a merciless, furiously rough insistence of which she had never thought herself capable.

Revenge!

She remained on top of him even after his orgasm, forcing him to get hard again and to climax once more. Then she rolled off him, making sure she landed on the side of the bed next to the keys and her phone.

She curled up, and pretended to fall asleep.

After what seemed an eternity, he began to snore in his accustomed, light manner. The luminous bedside clock radio showed seventeen minutes past five. She waited for another ten minutes before carefully rotating out of bed and lifting the keys and their two cell phones off the night table.

He stirred and she froze.

Mercifully, he did not wake and started snoring again.

Getting to her dressing gown and socks was more difficult. There were a couple of chairs and a coffee table to circumnavigate. She couldn't take the risk of bumping into them in the dark, so her progress across the room, feeling her way first with her right foot and then her hands, was painfully slow.

Her luck held. He had left the door open and she slid through the opening and tiptoed down the stairs the way she had earlier, by stepping on the boards as close to the wall as possible, minimizing the possibility of creaking.

The kitchen door seemed the best way to the outside. It was furthest from the bedroom and closest to the path leading to the little inlet where they had moored the boat. She slipped into her dressing gown and socks and thanked her guardian angel for making Roger insist that they keep as much of the dirt out of the house as possible. Her overcoat and boots were next to the door where she had left them the previous night.

This made her think of the bastard and she froze. Had she just heard a noise from upstairs?

No, thank God. All was quiet.

She put on her dressing gown, struggled into her overcoat, stuffed the keys and the phones into her pocket, left the house and felt the cold wind bite into her face.

It was still pitch dark.

Her first stab at finding the path leading to the boat was a miss. She fell into a thicket of low brush. Scrambling away from the house on all fours she somehow managed to stumble onto the trail and ran toward the water as fast as she dared.

At the dock, she hesitated. Would the noise of her footsteps on the wood carry as far as the slightly open bedroom window? No choice; a graying of the horizon over the water meant dawn was about to break.

Her watch said six-thirty-three. She figured she had an hour at the most before the son-of-a-bitch stirred and started groping for her.

She clattered toward the boat, untied it and hopped in. Using the oar she found lying alongside the starboard gunwale she pushed away from the dock. The wind immediately began to propel the little craft toward the opposite shore of the small inlet. She raced to the throttle and pushed it all the way forward then turned the key in the ignition. The engine coughed and died.

Damn! She must have flooded the motor.

She crossed over to port and began paddling furiously, trying to direct her craft into the main stream before it hit the shore.

Her strength was no match for the wind.

The bow hit a tree sticking into the water and the vessel became entangled in its branches about a hundred feet from the point where the shore rounded off toward the north. She climbed onto the foredeck and grabbed at the branches to pull the vessel along the tree to free it. One broke. She fell backward and felt something whistle past her head.

She rolled into the boat.

She heard a series of small, firecracker-like explosions preceded by whistling sounds and a loud ping from the side of the boat.

Roger was shooting at her!

Keeping behind the gunwale, she crawled forward into the small shelter that served as pilothouse. With her head down, she centered the throttle and turned the key again. This time the engine caught. She yanked the gear lever into reverse and the boat shot into the middle of the inlet. She corrected by slamming it the other way. There was a grinding noise as the gears protested and the vessel began to make headway, accelerating nicely just as Roger started firing again.

His aim was improving rapidly and his bullets began to find their target. There was another loud ping and in a little while the engine began to screech, then smoke and it finally quit.

By that time, she saw she was out of pistol range and she hoped that her craft might even clear the point and make it into the main stream of the St. Lawrence River.

But it didn't, quite.

As the boat rounded the point, it ran aground on an underwater rock and stuck fast.

No way to get it free, however hard she tried.

What next?

For Roger to reach her overland would take at least an hour, she estimated, if she stayed put. He was unlikely to bother trying though. He'd wait for his friends to arrive by boat which would happen within a couple of hours, and they would then help him capture her with ease.

The adrenaline was wearing off and she was beginning to feel tired and chilled. Could she last another three or four hours without getting pneumonia?

Doubtful.

She needed help, and quick. What to do?

She could never explain afterwards why she had done what she did do.

She called Bernard Kane, probably because it was the easiest thing for an exhausted brain. His telephone number was on her cell's speed dialer.

CHAPTER 27

Budapest, Tuesday Morning, October 23

A veteran of many terrorist campaigns, Saif Al Adel, the Third Man, had a nose for trouble. How else would he have survived for almost forty years?

Born in Egypt, he had started his terrorist's career in that country's Islamic Jihad. After finishing his apprenticeship as a bomb maker in Lebanon, he went to serve in Afghanistan, Pakistan and the Sudan, and from there to the Balkans, to act as coordinator of Al Qaeda's efforts there. By then, he had become one of Osama Bin Laden's most trusted operatives, in charge of planning the bombings of the US embassies in East Africa. After that, he led the attack on the USS Cole. As a reward for completing this mission with outstanding success, he was named Al Qaeda's Security Chief and a member of the organization's Military Council.

Al Adel had awoken on edge after a restless night. He had been greatly disturbed the previous evening by what Juric had reported hearing on the radio. There had been some sort of an explosion at Budapest Police Headquarters; the work of terrorists.

Once more, as so often in the past, his nose was telling him that the mission in which he was participating was derailing and that, as a result, his life was in danger. Since his nose was never wrong, he was anxious to start his day as early as possible. He needed time to develop an alternative plan for dealing with Moscovitch in case things went wrong.

Al Adel was a secretive person who trusted nobody. He decided not to share his concerns during breakfast with his bunkmate, Colonel Barzan Hassani, another early riser, in spite of having become friendly with him during the time they had spent in close contact on board Juric's barge.

Where Moscovitch was concerned, he and the Iraqi had differing agendas.

*   *   *

A week earlier, on Wednesday, Amina had slipped away from her police 'minder' to *Dunaújváros* to confer with Delic, The Butcher, and Al Adel. Losing her 'tail' had not been difficult. She had kayaked downriver for five kilometers, just far enough to get out of sight of the man who was trying to follow her by car on shore. She had then been picked up by Juric at a prearranged spot and driven to her conference with Delic and his colleagues; a half-hour drive.

Her meeting with Moscovitch to soften him up for his visitors the next day had taken an hour, after which she had hurried back to the Jurices the way she had come.

Total elapsed time while 'black', (out of sight of surveillance), including the trip and her two meetings: two hundred and twenty-five minutes.

The tenor of the meeting with Amina present had not sat well with Al Adel.

Too much Iraq, too little Al Qaeda.

Hassani had emphasized to Moscovitch that he would be accomodated in Baghdad, that the facilities in which he would be required to work would be in the Iraqi Capital and that Delic, whom Al Adel considered to be decidedly Saddam's man, would supervise his work.

Neither Hassani nor Delic, and certainly not Amina, had paid even so much as lip service to the need for Al Qaeda to be provided with access to the results of the Canadian's work.

Hassani had not remedied this unfortunate oversight after the meeting with Moscovitch, even though he had had ample opportunity to do so during the trio's trip on board the *Maria* from *Dunaújváros* to *Háros*.

This had made Al Adel more suspicious than ever about Iraq's true intentions.

*   *   *

After shaving very carefully, Al Adel produced a long, lustrous, jet-black wig from his duffle bag and put on the clothes he had borrowed from Rada Juric the previous night. He spent an hour painstakingly applying makeup to transform himself into an attractive female with a mysterious, Middle Eastern look. He pulled the wig over his short-cropped hair and was, by half past eight, ready for Juric to drive him to *Érd*, a suburb of Greater Budapest. He spent a half hour pretending to be one of the many homemakers who rose early to shop in the village's market, well known for its bargain priced fresh produce.

When he was sure no one was tailing him, he took the bus to the foot of the *Szabadság* Bridge, Pest-side. Since he spoke English fluently and almost without an accent, he was not worried about getting lost, secure in the knowledge that he could always find an English-speaker pleased to assist an attractive foreigner.

*   *   *

The headlines screaming at Losdale from the front pages of the Hungarian language papers on the hotel cafeteria table gave him a nasty turn.

"MYSTERIOUS EXPLOSION AT POLICE HEADQUARTERS" wrote the *Magyar Nemzet*, the most conservative of the dailies. "TERRORISTS BOMB POLICE BUILDING ON VÁCI BOULEVARD" roared the *Népszava* in typically sensationalistic style. The tabloid *BLIKK* showed graphic photographs of the tall, concrete skyscraper's façade with a large hole at the sixth floor level.

All the articles contained essentially the same information. Monday, late in the afternoon, while attempting to open a box that had come into the possession of detectives during the weekend, the package had exploded, killing two officers and blowing a hole about two meters in diameter in the building's wall facing *Váci* Boulevard. Several passers-by had suffered light injuries by the falling debris. The officers' names were being withheld for security reasons.

There was, of course, widespread speculation about the package's origin.

Lonsdale was feeling better after ten hours of painkiller-induced sleep, and a subsequent short workout in the hotel's gym. As he studied the papers while having his breakfast, he arrived at a conclusion that he found difficult to accept.

Horváth must have had the transponder in his car installed shortly after Lonsdale had begun to use the Intercontinental's underground parking garage.

'Betrayed again,' Lonsdale thought.

Betrayal was nothing new to Lonsdale. Compared with the treacherous situations he had survived in the past, Horváth's duplicity was small beer.

There had been the agent sent by Langley to work with him in the Cayman Islands who had turned out to be a double—an operative working for the Soviets.

And the case of the DDCI? Unbelievably, the Cubans succeeded in blackmailing the Deputy Director of the Central Intelligence Agency into working for the Cuban G2, Castro's secret police.

That had almost cost Lonsdale his life.

His assailants the other night had obviously been Horváth's goons, police officers in mufti, sent to 'discourage' him from pursuing his investigations. When he had turned on them, they had panicked and had fled, grabbing his 'kit' as they went.

He felt no pity for the two fools who had gotten killed while trying to get into the metal case. Its handle, laced with four ounces of C2 plastic explosive, was connected to a detonator programmed to fire after three consecutive attempts were made to open the box using the wrong code. Why was Horváth so determined to slow Lonsdale down? Was he in cahoots with Moscovitch's kidnappers? Had he somehow tumbled onto Lonsdale's real identity? Had the Canadian Consul? Had it been she who had encouraged the police Lieutenant to take drastic action?

But why?

Wasn't everybody anxious to solve the Moscovitch kidnapping case?

A few minutes after ten Lonsdale called Horváth from his room. The phone rang for a long time. Finally, someone answered.

"*Halló, ki beszél?*"

"May I speak to Lieutenant Horváth?" Lonsdale inquired in English.

"Moment."

Then a new voice that Lonsdale didn't recognize. "Vat do you vant?"

"I would like to speak with Lieutenant Horváth."

"Not here."

"How about Detective Vas?"

"He not here too. Vat's your name?"

"Bernard Kane from Canada."

"Vere you calling from in Kanada?"

"Actually, I'm in Budapest."

Silence. Then a hesitant "Vere in Budapest?"

"In the *Béke* Hotel."

"Ve vill call back to you in half hour. Vat's your room number?"

Lonsdale provided the information then, frowning, hung up. Where were Horváth and Vas? If the man who had answered the phone was working for them, he'd know who Bernard Kane was and where he was staying.

Something was wrong.

Lonsdale gulped. Could it be that Horváth and his sidekick had been foolish enough to attempt to open his kit themselves, only to be killed in the process?

Probably yes, if they were conducting an unauthorized operation.

In which case there was big trouble ahead.

The Hungarian cops, like cops all over the world, would want to cover up their mistake—probably by trying to implicate Lonsdale in some sinister terrorist plot.

Time to move on!

Lonsdale grabbed his hat, coat and cell-phone and headed for the door.

The phone near his bed rang. After hesitating for a moment, he picked it up.

"Mr. Kane?" A soft, educated voice.

"Yes." Lonsdale's tone was brusque.

"Am I calling at an inopportune time?" The language and accent were vaguely British.

"Somewhat."

"Then I shall be brief." The voice was polite, but insistent. "You and I share a common interest in the well-being of your recently vanished scientific compatriot. I would appreciate an opportunity to speak with you about this matter at length."

"Who are you?"

"All in good time," the voice sounded matter-of-fact. "Let's meet this afternoon at three for tea at the Central Coffeehouse. Do you know where it is?"

Lonsdale thought fast. This was a trick question. He was not supposed to be familiar with eateries not generally known to tourists. "I'm afraid I don't, but I'll ask the concierge," he answered, but he knew damn well that the Cafe was near Franciscans' Square in the inner city and famous for its desert, the *flódni*, a Jewish apple, wallnut and poppy seed layer cake.

"I take it then that you won't have any difficulty finding it." More of a statement of fact than a question.

"How will I know you?"

A chuckle. "I'll know *you*." The line went dead.

Lonsdale took the stairs down at the double and exited the hotel through the back entrance he had used Saturday night. He sprinted to the corner and hailed a cab. He gave the driver a thousand forints, told him to drive around to the front of the building and park across the street from the *Béke's* entrance.

Sure enough, a few minutes before eleven a police car screeched to a halt in front of the door. A uniformed police officer and two men whom Lonsdale took to be detectives, rushed into the hotel.

Obviously, they were there to arrest him—probably on suspicion of murder and terrorism.

Lonsdale sighed and told the driver to take him to the US Embassy.

'Time to start playing hardball,' he resolved, and sat back for the short ride.

CHAPTER 28

Tuesday, October 23 (3),

Before agreeing to participate in the Moscovitch kidnapping as Al Qaeda's representative, Saif Al Adel had carefully researched the opportunity and had interviewed Esad Delic at length. He had found the ingenuity and simplicity of the proposed form of delivery of the lethal nv. C-JD contaminated surgical glue very much to his liking. Packages made to look like harmless medico-surgical items, were to be distributed by unsuspecting hospital supply firms to their clients around the world.

Brilliant!

He was sympathetic to Delic's argument that Iraq should be allowed to mass-produce the packages, but he was seriously concerned about surrendering Al Qaeda's discovery to the ruthless Iraqi dictator without Al Qaeda having access to a vaccine against it. Saddam's solemn promise to use the contaminated glue to kill only non-believers was worth nothing because this new form of Creuzfeldt-Jacobs disease was transmissible by the very air that people breathed. Containing it would be almost impossible without an anti-virus.

Since Moscovitch was most probably *the* person able to create a vaccine in the shortest time, he was the *sine qua non* player in the game, because, as far as Al Adel could judge, Delic, Moscovitch's partner, who also had strong credentials in the field, was far less of a scientist than the Canadian was.

Without Moscovitch there would be no ready defense against the disease in the near future. Handing over the Canadian to Saddam would be tantamount to suicide, especially since the Baghdad-trained Delic had already shipped contaminated glue feedstock to Iraq to start mass production.

Al Adel had not been aware of this before the Cizre meeting and had fought tooth and nail against any plan that called for the kidnapped Moscovitch's transfer to Iraq.

As a result, the Cizre participants had finally agreed, after wrangling for most part of a day, to keep Moscovitch in Hungary and had charged Drusza with setting up a mini-lab for Moscovitch to work in. Hassani and Al Adel had then volunteered to find ways of motivating the virologist to work on the vaccine with enthusiasm.

All had gone as planned. Even the arrival of that bumbling private investigator, Kane, had not been enough to derail the operation, principally because of the protection extended to Drusza and his team by the eminently bribable Police Lieutenant Horváth who hated North Americans with a passion.

When Moscovitch turned out to be more difficult than expected, The Butcher and Al Adel acquiesced to Drusza's suggestion, inspired by Saddam, to kidnap the scientist's mother thereby leveraging their advantage over him.

No sooner had they put this plan in motion than things began to unravel in Budapest, although the pathetic bumbling oafs hired by Kane to spy on the Jurices had not caused problems. They were incredibly incompetent. This very morning, he had waved at one of them from the Bosnian's car as they headed for *Érd,* and the idiot had waved back.

He must have mistaken Al Adel for Mrs. Juric!

No. Thanks to the Horváth connection, Kane's people had not worried the team. Now, Al Adel thought, this protection was likely to be withdrawn due to the bombing at Police Headquarters.

This had put Al Adel's nose out of joint, or at least, had caused it to twitch.

At a quarter to eleven, he made a call to the *Béke* from a public telephone in the *Centrál Kávéház* (Central Coffeehouse) near Franciscan's Square.

After hanging up, he made another call to a number he had memorized.

"May I speak to Frank Lloyd Wright, the famous architect?" he enquired in English.

A pause, then "Which one?"

"The Second, of course."

"Who wants him?"

"Frank Lloyd Wright the Third, of course."

The line went dead.

Al Adel waited for exactly one minute then called back.

The phone was answered after the first ring. "Meet me at the Gerbeaud Pastry Shop at eleven fifteen sharp. It's on *Vörösmarty* Square."

"I'll be there, but make sure you bring your girlfriend Bridget with you. I've heard a lot about her and I am dying to meet her." Al Adel hung up.

The reference to Bridget had meant that Khamani should bring a silencer-equipped pistol with him.

At the *Centrál* Al Adel asked the cashier for an Inner City map and found he was within six blocks of his next meeting place. He figured he had enough time to get there and reconnoiter and, on his way, to visit the phone boutique the cashier had told him was just down the street.

He ended up buying two identical, unlocked inexpensive, quad band instruments, complete with high-speed chargers. He also bought two SIM Cards.

Near the Gerbeaud a few minutes before noon, he spent time pretending to be admiring the statue in the nearby square while checking for unusual activity.

He could spot none.

Entering the pastry shop he readily spotted his contact—the man's appearance had hardly changed since Al Adel had said goodbye to him in Bosnia some years ago.

Khamani, the supposed car dealer, knew he was taking a chance when he had suggested that his caller should meet him at the Gerbeaud, but he had little choice. The call had interrupted an important business meeting, and since the operative had said he was Frank Lloyd Wright *the Third*, which had meant maximum urgency, the Iranian had to pick a venue public enough to allow checking for surveillance and near enough for the Qods Officer to reach on time.

Khamani was a well-known personage about town. Therefore, he could always claim, should the need arise, that he had no control over who came to speak with him while he was having a cup of coffee in a public location.

Sure enough, at three on the dot, a woman who looked like a high class call girl approached his table and sat down opposite him without being asked to do so not an uncommon occurrence at one of the world's most well-known *patisseries*, frequented by wealthy tourists.

He began to protest when, to his amazement, his uninvited guest said softly in Arabic, "Rezzah, don't behave like the bastard son of a stinky female camel and buy your old friend a cup of coffee."

The Iranian, momentarily rattled and at a total loss, couldn't think of anything to say. He raised his hand and asked the waiter for two espressos. Then he turned to the woman. "Who the fuck are you?" he asked, also in Arabic, a language he had forced himself to master for two reasons. He had wanted to read the Koran in its original version and he had wanted to be able to communicate in the Jihadists' *lingua franca*, Arabic.

Al Adel permitted himself a discreet, lady-like laugh. "I guess my disguise must be nearly perfect. So, may be, you'd like to make love to me?"

The Iranian looked at the person sitting opposite him with great care—and the penny dropped. "May Allah be praised. My eyes, if they do not deceive me, are beholding my friend of Bosnian days. Welcome to Budapest, Sheikh Saif Al Adel. How can I be of assistance?"

""I am told you are familiar with the Moscovitch file, are you not?"

"That I am."

"And you are under orders to follow my instructions, are you not?"

"Indeed I am."

"Then listen carefully. By midnight at the latest Moscovitch will be moved by barge from the location where he is now being held."

"Where is that?"

"*Dunaújváros,* at the southern tip of *Csepel* island. After that, an attempt will be made to transport him to *Constanza,* in Rumania, and thence to Iraq. It is not in Iran's interest for him to reach Iraq alive, nor is it in Iran's interest that he fall into American hands. You must, therefore, make arrangements to kill Moscovitch if you see that either of these two scenarios is about to take place."

"Where can I pick up his trail and when?"

"I brought you a present that will enable you to do so." Al Adel handed Khamani one of the telephones. "Here is the SIM Card that goes with it. I have its number. I have an identical phone with a SIM Card, so make a note of *its* number."

The Iranian scribbled it down.

"You must be in position to follow the barge by ten tonight at the latest."

Al Adel then spent the next half hour briefing Khamani about what he needed to know to accomplish his mission.

At one p.m., Al Adel rose to leave. Khamani grabbed his arm.

"I almost forgot. Allow me to reciprocate your kindness by giving you this box of chocolates." He produced a package from under the table. "They are the best chocolates in the world, from Belgium, with a 'B'."

In other words, the weapon in the box was a silencer equipped Beretta. Al Adel understood perfectly.

"One last question. Why is this man so important?" The Iranian asked.

"Soon the world will be divided into two camps. Those who have the vaccine against nv. C-JD and those who don't. Those who don't, will be killed by those who do. Since we cannot get the vaccine, we must make sure nobody else does before we do. Moscovitch might discover the vaccine any minute now. So, if we don't have him in our power, we must make sure nobody else does!"

CHAPTER 29

Budapest, Tuesday Noon, October 23

The Marine at the main door of the US Embassy on *Szabadság* Square was polite, but unyielding.

"Sir, I'm sorry, but there's no way I can let you in to see Mr. Jenkins unless he confirms that you have an appointment with him."

"You've told me that already and I asked you to call him."

"And I did, Sir, and his secretary told me you have no appointment with Mr. Jenkins today."

"So you spoke to Mr. Jenkins' secretary and not to Mr. Jenkins himself."

"That is correct, sir. Mr. Jenkins is not taking calls."

'Fuck that noise.' Lonsdale was boiling mad. He'd been calling Jenkins and been getting the runaround for the last ten minutes, first from the man's voice mail, then his secretary's.

Who the hell knew where they were.

What if his life depended on being able to speak with the CIA Duty Officer right away?

So much for emergency procedures, reflected Lonsdale and walked over to a park bench to call Morton, ten minutes past the appointed time. His Control answered on the first ring. "You're late. Where have you been?"

"Running away from the cops and getting screwed by State Department bureaucrats."

"What do you mean?"

Lonsdale told him in no uncertain terms.

Morton chuckled. "Give me a few minutes and I'll fix your problem, then walk back to the Embassy and call me from there. I've got lots to tell you."

"And me you." They rang off.

The Marine at the door was all smiles and apologies when Lonsdale returned. "Sorry for the mix-up, sir. It seems Miss Espinosa, she's Mr. Jenkins' secretary, seems to have misread her agenda." He gave Lonsdale a wink.

"Ain't that a bitch," said Lonsdale and winked back.

Jenkins, tall, solidly built, blue-eyed, with a jutting jaw, looked surprisingly young for his posting: Acting Deputy Chief of Station. He apologized profusely for the mix-up in the contacting procedure then spent a few minutes with Lonsdale to explain how the sophisticated scrambler-communications system on his desk worked. Lonsdale asked him to leave the room, which he did—definitely not a happy man, presumably after having been at the receiving end of a rocket administered by Big Boss Morton.

Lonsdale would have liked to make nice, but was pressed for time; Morton was waiting for his call.

". . . and the tapes bear it out," his Control was now saying and Lonsdale cut him off.

"For Christ's sake, get on with it."

Morton laughed, a full-throated guffaw, something Lonsdale hadn't heard him do since 9/11. "You've hit the jackpot ace! You've probably uncovered Al Qaeda's most important Central European sleeper cell." Morton then went on to explain how the mayor of Cizre, Amina's Turkish 'uncle', Drusza and Amina herself had attempted to avoid detection.

"Secure, reliable and fast communication was their main problem, which they solved in an imaginative way. They would have gotten away with everything had you not intervened."

The Mayor of Cizre was the hub of a simple radio communication system with Amina acting as both messenger and code setter.

"Elaborate."

"She'd talk to her 'uncle' twice a week. Either he'd call her or she'd call him. They'd chat about this and that. Then Amina would say 'I'm seeing so-and-so on Tuesday the 13th' and the 'uncle' would correct her: ' . . . but Tuesday is the 14th'. Amina would apologize for the error and continue the conversation."

Lonsdale interrupted. "And then someone would send a grouped coded message by high-speed burp transmission in which only every thirteenth word would mean anything."

"You've got the gist of it. Of course they complicated the thing a bit by appending the burp to the end of a legit transmission of the USAF station in town and by doing everything in Arabic."

"The *lingua franca* of Islamic extremists." Lonsdale paused. Then: "Who is doing the radio work in Budapest?"

"Abel Drusza, who else? He's the cell's head honcho and Al Qaeda's big man in the Balkans."

Of course. This explained the man's long working hours and the elaborate hi-fi set in his office. But Lonsdale was surprised. His money had been on Juric. "Did the transmissions and conversations indicate where they're holding Moscovitch?"

"No, but it follows that . . ."

A loud screeching sound—cell phone special alarm.

"What the hell's that?" Morton wanted to know.

A glance at his phone's monitor told Lonsdale there was big trouble ahead.

"Mrs. Moscovitch is calling me on the emergency number I gave her, so hold on. I'll be right back."

He punched the HOLD button. "It's Bernard Kane, Mrs. Moscovitch. How can I be of help?" Cool.

"Thank God you're there," she stammered, sounding very frightened. "I'm being kidnapped."

"What?"

"Listen carefully Mr. Kane. I'm not joking . . ."

Lonsdale punched CONFERENCE. "Repeat that again Mrs. Moscovitch. Jim, do you copy?"

"I do."

"Who's Jim?"

Lonsdale said sharply. "A friend who can help." Then: "Why do you think you're being kidnapped?"

Klara Moscovitch took a deep breath and began to speak through teeth chattering with cold. When she finished ten minutes later, Lonsdale asked, "Do you know the name of the island where you are now?"

"No."

"But I do," Morton cut in with authority. "While you were speaking, my people traced your call from Mr. Kane's phone to yours, and the telephone company helped us locate you position. You're on Bluff Island opposite to Clayton in New York State near the north shore of the St. Lawrence River."

"Oh my God." She began to cry.

"Mrs. Moscovitch . . ." Lonsdale's voice was firm, but friendly.

"Please, Klara," she sobbed.

"Klara, then. Pull yourself together. We'll send help, but it will take time to get it to you."

"How long? I'm freezing to death. I'm only wearing a nightgown and a dressing gown over it, and my overcoat over that. My boots and socks are soaked and I have no scarf or gloves. And it's very windy."

"Is the sun up yet?"

"No it's not eight o'clock yet."

"Are you in the boat?"

"Yes."

"If you can, wade ashore and seek shelter in the bush. It'll be less windy there. Can you do that?"

"Yes, but for God's sake, tell me how long before help gets here?"

Lonsdale would not budge. "Where is Roger now?"

"I think he went back into the house."

"Then wade ashore NOW, and hide. MOVE!"

The call disconnected.

"Jim, are you still there?"

"Affirmative."

"What's the score? And thanks for acting so decisively so quickly."

"We're in the process of scrambling two SWAT helicopters from Syracuse, each with a pilot, a sharpshooter and four specially trained officers on board. ETA is oh nine thirty hours, give or take fifteen minutes."

"That leaves forty-five minutes for meaningful action. Presumably one team will try to find the woman and snatch her, and the other will neutralize Roger so we can prepare a nice welcoming committee for his friends when they get there by boat."

"That's the plan."

The cell phone started screeching again and Lonsdale connected the three of them.

"What happened?"

"I lost my balance while wading ashore. I dropped the phone in the water."

"It's still working." Lonsdale.

"I don't know. I'm calling on Roger's phone."

Morton was flabbergasted. "You mean you have his phone?"

"Yes. I stole it. Sorry, I forgot to mention that."

Lonsdale laughed. What incredible luck. "Well," he said, "please be careful and don't drop it for a while. It's worth its weight in gold!"

"Oh my God, Oh my God, Oh my God!" Klara was screaming. "He's raking the boat with gunfire and turning it into firewood." They could clearly hear the sound of automatic weapons fire.

"Are you hit?" Lonsdale.

"I'm in the woods, hiding as you said I should."

"Klara, listen. Get away from the boat and the house as far and as fast as you can. Don't raise your head. CRAWL. Stay in the woods and follow the shoreline. Don't lose sight of the water. We're sending a helicopter to pick you up on the beach."

"When?"

"In about an hour and a half. And Klara, whatever you do, DON'T switch off the phone. It might lock."

Morton: "Call us every twenty minutes if you must, but keep the conversation brief. You need to preserve battery power."

CHAPTER 30

New York State, Tuesday Morning, October 23

Kane had been right Klara Moscovitch had to admit, as she crawled away from the water. It was less cold in the woods.

Her challenge now was to stay warm and watch Roger without him seeing her.

Keeping her head down she began to work her way into a position from which she could not only observe the water, but also the little dock that Roger's so-called friends would have to use to tie up their boat. She stumbled on a pile of wood stacked chest high at the base of a large boulder on a hillock overlooking the water. She knelt down behind the stack and, by knocking out a couple of half-rotten logs, managed to create a clear view of both the dock and the house overlooking it.

Next, she went hunting for pine boughs, low tree branches that she could break off. She intended to weave them together into a sort of rough blanket to shelter her from the cold somewhat. She laughed, remembering where and how she had learned the rudimentary survival skills she was now putting to good use.

Her closest friends in high school had not been Jewish, so when they joined the Girl Guides she joined too. Her parents did not like the idea, but said nothing. When she announced on her thirteenth birthday that she wanted to go to Girl Guide Camp they strongly remonstrated. Why could she not go to a nice Jewish summer camp? There were so many around.

She would not budge, challenging their hypocrisy by demanding to know how they could reconcile their claim of being 'liberal minded' with trying to prevent her from living like a *goy* for a while.

Her parents finally gave in.

The two summers she had spent at the Guides' Lac Bouchette camp near Morin Heights, sixty miles north of Montreal had been the happiest of her teen years. That her stubbornness would save her life one day was an added bonus.

She knew she had to keep moving to keep warm and to keep herself from falling asleep at all costs for at least another hour. Her watch now showed ten minutes past nine.

God, was she tired and cold. Though the sun was shining, it gave no warmth; it was too early in the autumn day. All this misery, all this danger, caused by her stupidity; falling in lust with a stranger because . . . because the bastard had set out to seduce her and she had fallen for his charm and good looks, and the bullshit line he had fed her about caring.

How could she have been so stupid as to let down her guard and throw caution to the wind when she knew she was in a precarious and emotionally very vulnerable position?

Had Kane not warned her? Had he not said: "Be careful with new acquaintances that materialize out of nowhere."

Sitting behind the woodpile on the log she was using as a chair was causing her legs to cramp up. She kept staring at the dock and the house across the inlet, watching and waiting for that miserable, treacherous and highly dangerous son-of-a-bitch bastard to come out and then get his come-uppance when the helicopter arrived.

She was glad she was angry: angry enough to the point of wanting to see him beg for mercy before he died.

Besides, being angry seemed to help her keep warm.

She had to leave her post: had to walk around to restore circulation to her lower limbs, and she had to find a sheltered place to relieve herself. Her bladder was so full it was ready to burst.

Goddam it, where *was* that bloody helicopter anyway? Her watch said ten a.m. on the dot.

By the time she got back to her observation post she was crying, from the cold, from the stress and from fear that, by allowing herself to be duped, she had somehow harmed her son's chances of being freed.

"Jason, Jason, forgive me," she sobbed, "forgive me for not thinking, for being weak, for forgetting about your troubles, for acting irresponsibly." She made an effort to calm down and gritted her teeth to stop herself from crying. "Pull yourself together," she commanded. "It won't be long now, so be strong. All is not lost yet!"

A throbbing in the air, a pulsating feeling signaling the approach of a high compression engine, that of a helicopter perhaps, made her sit up.

She glanced at the sky. Nothing.

Roger must have heard something too, for he came running down to the dock carrying a rifle and a heavy looking duffel bag. The fullness of the sound she was feeling finally reached her. It was the rumbling of a marine engine on a sizeable boat making for the dock in the inlet at reduced speed.

Her heart constricted. Roger's friends had arrived ahead of Morton's helicopter.

With a hand trembling from cold and fear, she reached for the phone to call Kane. She had trouble flipping it open because her fingers were stiff. It took her time to find the 'Select' button and then to press 'Recent'. Before she could press 'Outgoing', the phone in her hand began to chirp.

"Hello."

"Klara Moscovitch?"

"Yes, speaking. Who's this?"

She watched as the boat, a cabin cruiser about forty feet long approached the jetty. Roger slung his rifle across his chest, threw the duffle bag on board and yelled something to the man on deck closest to him. Although she could not hear what he was saying, she guessed from his gestures and pointing that he wanted to get on board and have the boat head in her direction.

"It's Jim, Bernard Kane's friend. We identified your assailant's cell number. What's the situation?"

An immense wave of relief swept over her. "Thank God it's you. I thought it was a stranger calling."

"No, you're talking to the right person. What's happening?"

"The boat has arrived, but your helicopter hasn't."

"Where is it now and how many men on board?"

"Three men, I think, one up front, one in the back and the third is driving. Roger is climbing on board now. They're going to turn the boat around and head my way."

"Are they armed?"

"Roger has his rifle and he has just given two of the men pistols. He is now removing a second rifle from the bag he has brought along and is handing it to the man steering the boat. They're approaching the shore this side of the inlet."

Morton made up his mind in a flash. "Klara, listen. The 'copter was delayed because it had to refuel, but it's on the way now and will be there in less than five minutes. Get into the woods, go around the bay and circle back to the house. It will never occur to them that you'd do such a thing. I'm sure they're convinced you'd try to get as far away from them *and* the house as possible."

"I'm on my way."

"Klara, Klara wait! Memorize Kane's telephone number: I'll be here to answer it. Don't forget to dial 011." Morton made her repeat the number and hung up.

Throwing caution to the wind, Klara ran into the brush as far as she dared without losing sight of the water. Then she turned left and, following the shoreline around the inlet from afar, began to fight her way through the undergrowth toward the house. The going was heavy and she was glad to have thought of putting her boots on.

She heard gunfire behind her, but as far as she could judge, the shots were not coming her way. Morton had been right: the way to safety was toward the house. Then she heard the typical sound of a helicopter approaching. As the *whoomp-whoomp* increased in volume so did her heart rate.

Help had finally arrived.

Again, there was gunfire, but the burst was longer and sounded as if it were coming from a different direction, from the inlet itself. She got down on her hands and knees and began to crawl towards the water as fast as she could. When she judged the distance to be about right she straightened up behind a thick tree and peeked around it.

The helicopter was hovering at the entrance of the inlet, seemingly afraid to come near the boat, fearing gunfire from it, she suspected. Then, it rose suddenly and, in an arc, swooped down toward the boat. She saw the sharpshooter standing on one of the aircraft's pontoons and taking aim. He squeezed the trigger and a short burst shattered the windows and windshield of the pilothouse.

The 'copter completed the arc and came in for a landing. But little blue lights, muzzle flashes she thought, began winking among the trees and the helicopter started trailing what looked like a fine kind of misty smoke. A lucky pistol shot must have found its target and severed a hydraulic line. The pilot pulled on the yoke and the craft rose, clearing the boat, then banked steeply to the right, and landed hard with a tremendous splash some distance from the shore.

The marksman was thrown clear, into the water.

Klara Moscovitch needed to resume her flight, but first she wanted to call Jim to tell him what was happening. An impersonal voice answered: "Please purchase additional long distance minutes."

Damn and damn and damn! Roger's cell phone could no longer be used for overseas long distance calls. What incompetence on Jim's part. Why had he not foreseen this? How was she to communicate with Kane? What was she to do now? Lie down and die?

She looked back at the inlet as she ran. The marksman was climbing onto one of the pontoons with another man's help. The helicopter was drifting towards the dock. She continued fighting her way through the brush, but the going was getting heavy and she was getting tired.

Where was Roger and where were his friends?

She stopped to catch her breath as she rounded the end of the inlet and saw that the helicopter had reached the dock. Men dressed in black, with FBI written in glaring yellow on their chests and backs, were spilling out of the craft. She started to run again and was about to reach the kitchen side of the house when the door burst open and Roger came charging at her, pistol in hand. "Give me my phone bitch. Give me my phone," he screamed at her and raised his weapon. She saw death in the grimace on his face and closed her eyes.

She felt something warm and sticky spray onto her cheek and before she could open her eyes heard a shot that seemed to come from far, far away. Then she beheld the most awful sight she had ever seen in her life.

Roger, her terrorist lover, was lying at her feet with half his head blown away and blood still squirting out of his carotid artery, soaking her boots.

She began to scream and could not stop even after one of the FBI men, his weapon still smoking, came scrambling out of the bush to put his arms around her.

CHAPTER 31

Budapest, Tuesday Early afternoon, October 23

In Central Europe, coffee houses are respected institutions dating back to the days of the Ottomans who had warred with the Austrians and the Hungarians for centuries. When the Turks were chased away for good they left behind indelible imprints on the habits and tastes of the people they had subjugated: filo pastry, hence the strudel; croissants, crescent-shaped pastries emulating the flag symbol of the Ottomans; and coffee, a deeply satisfying and stimulating drink for men of letters and of strong opinions.

The *Centrál Kávéház* (Central Coffee House), in Budapest's Fifth District on *Károlyi Mihály* Street near Franciscans' Square has a venerable history. Opened for business in 1887, it has always been a home away from home to well-known writers, actors, politicians and busybodies.

All this flashed through Lonsdale's mind as he looked around the premises, trying to avoid thinking about Klara Moscovitch's ongoing ordeal.

The appearance of the coffeehouse surprised him. Only recently remodeled, the eatery nevertheless retained an art deco look: huge windows, big mirrors and an exquisitely decorated ceiling. The antique clock on the wall showed ten to three. He picked up the menu and ordered a *flódni*. He hadn't had time for lunch and was starving, his appetite stimulated by the aroma of expensive coffee mixed with the smell of sweet pastry.

In spite of being intent on his food, Lonsdale did notice the exceptionally handsome woman who had entered the café at three on the dot. Her eyes met his and she came straight over.

"Mr. Kane?"

He nodded, speechless.

"May I sit down?"

Recovering quickly, Lonsdale pushed his plate away and stood up. "Of course. Please do."

"I did not mean to disturb your meal . . ." Her smile was dazzling. Gleaming white teeth surrounded by full, carefully made up lips under a slightly beaked nose in an oval face, the color of fine milk chocolate.

"It's all right, just some pastry. May I offer you something to eat or drink?"

"I'll have an espresso if you promise to finish your food."

Lonsdale signaled the elegant waiter who, like all the staff, was dressed formally in black tie.

"My name is Fara," the woman said, "and I want you to think of me as an envoy of the Iranian Embassy. I'm a secretary." Her English was excellent.

And I'm the Queen of Sheba, Lonsdale said to himself while carefully appraising the person across the table from him. Dressed in a simple, flowing robe, over which she wore a stylish leather coat with a silk scarf around her lovely face, she exuded intelligence and self-assurance. 'Must be about thirty-five,' Lonsdale estimated, 'and probably an undeclared.'

Which meant she had no diplomatic status, and was working for the Iranian secret police, or, perhaps, for the Qods Force, otherwise known as the Iranian Revolutionary Guard, a new creation of the Iranian Government.

When the waiter left, she adjusted her scarf and began. "My boss is connected to the Embassy in a sort of unofficial capacity and could not risk meeting you personally in a public place."

Lonsdale decided to be helpful. "So he sent you instead because he did not want people to see me and him together."

"That's right, and because he wanted to convey an urgent, but very confidential message."

"Go on."

"He says the mother of the man you are looking for is not where she is supposed to be. Nobody seems to know where she is."

Lonsdale went rigid. The Iranians were suspecting that Mrs. Moscovitch had been kidnapped. How had they found out so quickly?

She anticipated his question.

"My boss thinks you will start asking me how we know these things and I am instructed to tell you that we have a very close, but uneasy relationship with certain Islamic factions so our information is sporadic." She adjusted her scarf again and seemed to be listening to something. Lonsdale began to suspect that she was wearing a two-way mini-transmitter in her ear and that her boss was prompting her from nearby.

"Your boss is right."

"We cannot help you any more with this. We do not know any more."

"Why would you want to help me anyway?"

"Because it is not in Iran's interest to have the Canadian scientist operate within the sphere of influence of these people." Obviously a pre-rehearsed speech, thought Lonsdale. Aloud he said. "So you want me to find him and free him."

"Yes, but we cannot help. We don't know where he is being held."

"What, then, do you know?"

"That he is going to be moved soon. Maybe even tonight."

"And the mother?"

The woman adjusted her scarf again and finished her espresso. "Our friends in Montreal say she went away for a week-end with a man we believe is an undercover Jihadist. That's all we know." She got up, and before Lonsdale could say anything, she was gone.

CHAPTER 32

Budapest, Tuesday, Late afternoon, October 23

Al Adel walked toward the other end of *Váci* Street, ducking in and out of chichi ladies' dress shops as he went, pretending to be examining the merchandise, but, in reality, looking to see if he was being followed.

He had accomplished what he had come to do—to suck the Americans into chasing Moscovitch's mother thereby preventing the Iraqis from taking her to Teheran, a ploy that would have allowed Saddam to blackmail the scientist into working for him.

Two blocks before getting to the Gerbeaud again, he turned left toward the river and took a taxi from the Forum Hotel to the square near the famous Hotel *Gellért*.

Meeting Kane and Khamani had been a huge, but unavoidable, risk since it was likely that they were both prime targets for police surveillance, especially the Iranian, who had spent over two years in Hungary already. Hence the probability of everyone coming in contact with either of them being tarred with the same brush was very high.

It was essential that, before returning to the Juric property, Al Adel make quite sure to lose any tail he may have grown during the meeting.

The *Gellért* Square ploy was something Al Adel had used on previous visits to Budapest.

To get to the hotel from the square it was necessary to cross the very wide, divided Béla Bartok Boulevard which was always teeming with high speed traffic, a veritable racetrack. A woman running across the boulevard was not an uncommon sight, even if she continued to jog towards the hotel. Of course, once through the main entrance, one could easily spot pursuit sprinting to catch up.

Al Adel had elevated the ploy to a higher plane by adding a new twist. He'd only stop long enough inside to glance toward the street, after which he'd turn abruptly toward the ladies' room and, when safely ensconced in one of the cubicles, step up onto the toilet seat and squat down. For as long as he could, anywhere from three to five minutes, he'd remain stock still, then emerge quickly and be on his way, which is what he did that afternoon.

He left the hotel by a side entrance, hailed a cab and told the driver to take him to the *Budai* Boulevard *Csárda* in Érd, where Juric picked him up at five o'clock.

* * *

Over the secure communications setup in Jenkin's office Lonsdale heard Morton describe how it took a couple of agents the better part of an hour to clean Klara Moscovitch up and calm her down. "She kept cursing them all the way to Clayton."

"What happened to the rest of the terrorists?"

"The one steering the boat was killed by the marksman in the 'copter. The other two tried to get away by disappearing into the bush. We let them thrash about until the second 'copter arrived and then we literally smoked them out with tear gas. They gave up because they had nowhere to go. We had their boat."

"And Roger's telephone?"

"A veritable treasure trove. We have a preliminary analysis that connects Roger, alias Ahmed Al Zawarri, a Jordanian, with the mayor in Cizre, who called him regularly. The mayor's number is listed in the phone's directory under 'Amu', which in Arabic means 'uncle.'"

"Similar to the Amina situation."

"Right."

"Where is Mrs. Moscovitch now?"

"The agents are still debriefing her in Clayton at a motel where we have her in more-or-less protective custody. They'll give her a sedative after dinner which will make her sleep soundly until tomorrow morning. Then another debriefing session and, after lunch, we'll drive her back to Montreal."

"So soon?"

"She will have told us just about everything she knows by then. Besides, she'll be insisting on going home and we won't be able to hold her against her will. She's a Canadian citizen, legally in the US, not suspected of any crime and free to come and go as she pleases. She's also a very ballsy lady who will not stand for being pushed around. Crossing her will create all kinds of trouble. She's already plenty pissed off about us."

"What's she so worked up about?"

"Come on ace, think. She's in shock, having just survived a very harrowing experience. Although she is grateful to us for saving her life, she thinks we're a bunch of bumbling amateurs. She blames me for the delay in getting the chopper to her in time. Also about my suggesting that she should flee toward the house and not away from it, plus my not foreseeing that Roger's phone would not work for unlimited overseas calls."

"What else?"

"She's pissed at you too. Thinks you're an incompetent who couldn't find a black bear in a white field of daisies, let alone her son in captivity. Anything else you want to know? I'm running out of time."

"I have another urgent problem."

Morton sighed. "So what else is new?"

Lonsdale ignored the sarcasm and told Morton about his conversation with Fara, the Iranian woman. "I've got Frakkos and his men watching both Amina's and Juric's place 24/7, but if Juric starts moving his barge and Moscovitch with it I have no back-up force to effect an extraction. I can't call on the Hungarian police for a favor. My bridges are burnt here. They suspect me of being a terrorist, a murderer and a fugitive from justice."

"Because of Horváth's death?"

"Among others."

"What do you suggest we do?"

Lonsdale was getting upset. Why was Morton not being more pro-active?

"Jim, I need help. If the shit hits the fan, Amina will bolt and so will Drusza. We can't afford to lose them. Give me direction. Where do my priorities lie?"

"Drusza is number one, Amina number two."

"And Moscovitch?"

"Last on the list. Don't forget we also have Cizre to worry about."

Morton was being callous, but Lonsdale understood and sympathized. Like he, his Control was also under great pressure. The foiling of the Klara Moscovitch kidnapping and the neutralizing of the perpetrators meant that Morton had to implement an immediate snatch of Cizre's mayor and his collaborators and the seizure of the equipment the mayor was using to run the Central European Al Qaeda network.

The operation had to take place before word got out about the failed kidnapping and those involved disappeared after destroying valuable information and equipment.

"OK, Jim. I'll take care of Drusza and Amina. You take care of Cizre."

"It's got to be tonight ace!" Morton was emphatic.

"I know. I'm on my way." Lonsdale hung up and turned to Jenkins who had been assisting him in handling the communications equipment. "I need a weapon, preferably a handgun with a magazine holding at least six rounds. If you have one with a silencer, so much the better."

Jenkins nodded. "I'll lend you my 9 mm SIG-SAUER 220. It has the latest safety features for 'Cocked and Locked Carry'. Be careful about how you handle it. There's a round up the spout and nine more in the grip. Release the safety and then fire away."

"Give it to me." Jenkins obliged. Lonsdale took the pistol. He was familiar with the slim weapon, a favorite with diplomats who were, at times, forced to arm themselves even when attired in formal wear. He practiced releasing the safety with a flick of his thumb a couple of times then, satisfied, slipped the unholstered weapon and an extra magazine into his overcoat pocket.

"Nice balance," he ventured, and was gone.

CHAPTER 33

Budapest, Tuesday Evening, October 23

The State Property Agency on *Pozsonyi* Boulevard is not far from the US Embassy on *Szabadság* Square. Unfortunately, it took Lonsdale fifteen full minutes in the pouring rain to get there because he could not find a cab as fast as needed in the mess that was Budapest during rush hour.

Which was twelve minutes too long.

The SPA is a large bureaucracy whose employees are ponderous civil servants, except at quitting time when they resemble a herd of gazelles. It is widely believed that if one were foolhardy enough to stand at the front door at four thirty in the afternoon one could get killed in the rush.

Lonsdale's taxi drew up in front of the building at four forty two. By then, there were only six vehicles left in the lot adjacent to the front entrance: five imposing looking Mercedes, and a modest Suzuki Swift 1000 in one of the spots reserved for visitors.

Amina's car.

Lonsdale rushed to the front door. A burly security guard barred his entry. Behind him, luck was with Lonsdale that day, stood Eva Illman, trying to leave for home.

"Eva, Eva," he pleaded in English over the guard's shoulder. "I must speak with you. It's urgent; it's about your friend." He pushed past the startled man who spun around and looked questioningly at the receptionist.

Taken aback, but mindful of having to set a good example by being helpful to foreign visitors at all times, she nodded to the guard and, with visible reluctance, led Lonsdale to her work station.

"You surprised me Mr. Kane," she said haltingly. "We are closed now and I have to go home. Tomorrow morning is better time for talking."

He ignored the obvious tone of annoyance in her voice. "Is Mr. Drusza still in the building? I must see him."

"He is, I think so, with Amina and Mr. Delic and cannot be disturbed. Tomorrow I will make an appointment for you, but now you must go."

'So Delic is back, no doubt to whisk Moscovitch away,' Lonsdale thought, and pulled out all the stops. He had no choice but to switch to Hungarian. "Eva, I must see Mr. Drusza this very minute. The lives of many people hang in the balance."

Her eyes grew large with surprise. "You speak Hungarian like a native." She immediately became suspicious. "What's all this about? Are you trying to fool me?"

"Sit down Eva and listen carefully. I work for the American Government's Drug Enforcement Agency. Your boss is an international drug dealer and so are Amina and Delic. I'm here to arrest them because they are accomplices in the kidnapping of Jason Moscovitch and his mother in Montreal."

The woman turned white. It was clear she thought she was dealing with a lunatic. She looked around for help from the guard who was still at the door, locking up.

Lonsdale took out his pistol and laid it on her desk. "I mean you no harm; that's why I put my gun down. If you don't believe me, pick it up and use it to make me your prisoner. Just be careful. The gun is loaded." He waited for a few seconds and when the undecided and overwhelmed receptionist made no move, he pocketed his weapon again.

"I know it is against regulations, but take me upstairs to Mr. Drusza's office. If they try to blame you tomorrow for helping me today, you can say that I forced you at gunpoint to do so."

Petrified, Eva led the way to a bank of elevators at the centre of the lobby.

They got off on the sixth floor and turned towards the corner office that Lonsdale knew belonged to Drusza. He'd been there before. They found the door of the antechamber leading to the office itself closed, but unlocked.

"Eva," Lonsdale whispered, "I have no choice but to trust you. I'm going in. Stay out in the corridor and take cover." He removed his pistol from the pocket of his overcoat, opened the door noiselessly and went in.

The door to Drusza's office, Lonsdale recalled, was made of thick wood and lined with insulating material on the side facing the room to prevent people in the antechamber from hearing what was being said inside. As Lonsdale approached, the door, it suddenly clicked open and he heard Amina call out *"Gyertek már"*—"Come on already," in Hungarian. Lonsdale kicked the door wide open, sending Amina flying backwards.

He stepped inside. Amina was sprawled on the floor to his immediate left. She had tripped over a coffee table and was scrambling for her handbag under it. Drusza, who had been facing away from the door when Lonsdale had burst in, had whipped around to see the cause of the disturbance and was now turning back toward the hi-fi set behind him. Delic was standing next to him his back to Lonsdale. He seemed unarmed.

From the corner of his left eye, Lonsdale saw Amina reach her handbag. "Freeze, the three of you," he yelled in English at the top of his voice and flicked off the safety on his pistol. Arms extended, he pointed the weapon at Drusza who stopped his turn. Peripherally, Lonsdale saw Amina extract a pistol from her handbag. He pivoted to his left and shot her in the head twice, Mossad style.

She dropped her gun and fell back on the floor.

Lonsdale then pivoted toward Delic who had turned toward him. He froze.

Lonsdale completed his sweep, but by the time he had Drusza in his sights the man was bent over the hi-fi set. Lonsdale had to hurry his shot at Drusza, and missed. Before he could correct his aim and fire again, Drusza pressed the destruct button on the equipment. The explosion annihilated the set, blew out both windows, killed Drusza and Delic, and hurled Lonsdale backward through the open door, past the antechamber. He ended up on the floor of the corridor, disoriented, with yet another severely bruised rib and a nosebleed, but otherwise unhurt because the two jihadists had partially shielded him.

A dazed Eva survived the blast without injury in the corridor.

She started screaming for help. Lonsdale crawled over to her. "Pull yourself together Eva. You're not hurt. You're all right. Don't worry about anything. Help is on the way. If anybody asks you about what happened tell them you have no idea what caused the explosion."

"What about you?" she managed to stammer.

"Forget about me. Just tell them I forced you at gunpoint to bring me up here."

He left her sitting behind the remnants of the secretary's desk and staggered out of the room. Breathing was becoming very painful. "Little wonder," he said to himself as he struggled toward the stairwell leading to the lobby, "after the shit kicking I took over the weekend it's a wonder my ribs aren't sticking into my lungs."

He reached the stairs before the arrival of the first responders and stumbled down to the lobby quickly. Within three minutes, he was out the door.

CHAPTER 34

Budapest, Tuesday Evening, October 23

Khamani was in a quandary.

Although ordered to follow blindly the instructions of the 'field operative' who would make contact with him, he could not get over the fact that the person had not been an Iranian, but a highly placed Al Qaeda leader.

How come the connection? By way of Hamas? Were the ayatollahs finally beginning to embrace extreme Jihadism? Was Iran beginning to flex its muscles on the international scene?

His chest swelled with pride at the thought.

But what about Moscovitch? Was he really as important as Al Adel seemed to think? Did Iran not have scientists capable of rising to the challenge of inventing the vaccine?

*   *   *

Sitting in his employee's, George's, car, strategically parked to allow for simultaneous surveillance of the SPA building and the front parking lot, Frakkos was debriefing George about Amina's movements when there was a tremendous bang, followed by a shower of glass.

George stayed put. Frakkos hurried over to the main entrance. As he mingled with the people evacuating the building, he spotted Lonsdale coming through the front door, disheveled and groggy. They made eye contact. Lonsdale staggered over and Frakkos put his arms around him to stop the man from keeling over.

"What happened? What's going on?"

Lonsdale made an extraordinary effort to protect his 'legend', his cover story. "I don't really know," he said. "I had a meeting scheduled with Amina and Drusza and I went up to see them. Before I could reach Drusza's office there was this explosion. It bowled me over and I fell hard on my ribs. I think I broke one of them," he wheezed.

"Do you need a doctor, yes?" Frakkos did not like the way Lonsdale looked, pale, weak, unfocused.

Lonsdale ignored the question. "Where is your car?" he asked.

"A block away."

"Help me walk there then drive me back to my hotel. They have a doctor."

"You sure you can walk?"

"Let's try, slowly."

While driving to the *Béke,* Lonsdale told Frakkos that Amina was probably seriously wounded and that there was no need to follow her around any longer. "You and George go out to the Juric property to see what's going on there. Report back to me by phone as soon as you can."

"You have your phone, yes?"

"Inside my coat pocket. I felt it when I fell on it. That's what hurt my ribs."

Frakkos was no fool. "Are you going now to tell what is happening really or do you want to go on making a showing that we are chasing Amina's lover who does not exist?"

"OK, Frakkos, you're right. The game's up." Lonsdale improvised rapidly. "I am an undercover agent of the Royal Canadian Mounted Police, the RCMP. We're chasing drug dealers here in Hungary, in Rumania and in Turkey. We suspect Amina and the Juric family are involved somehow."

"I knew it!" Frakkos was beaming. "Something like this I was suspecting from beginning." Lonsdale was pleased, his spontaneous fabrication sounded plausible enough.

"How come? Am I so bad at my job?"

"No, no, it's because of the—how do you say in English—the *fuvar*, the . . . the . . . transportation, that's it. The barge of Juric. And Turkey and the Turkish connection."

"You are one mother of a smart guy," Lonsdale managed to croak.

"Mother? I do not understand, yes?"

"Figure of speech." Lonsdale said by way of saying goodbye. He gritted his teeth and got out of the car. The pain had eased a little. "Call as soon as you know something."

In the hotel lobby, Lonsdale kept as far from Reception as possible. He watched Frakkos drive off then hailed a cab and directed the driver to take him to the US Embassy. En route, he called Jenkins and told him to get a doctor to meet him at the office.

The pain in his chest was becoming almost unbearable. He could hardly breathe.

He reached the embassy at a quarter to six and passed out in the arms of the Marine who had opened the gate for him.

When he opened his eyes again, he was lying on Jenkins' couch. The doctor bending over him was smiling. "Welcome back to the world," he said in English as he put down the stick of smelling salts in his hand. "You have badly bruised ribs, probably a result of a number of falls, maybe down some stairs; am I right?" He winked, and Lonsdale nodded gratefully. The man was obviously with the program.

"Anything broken?" Lonsdale asked.

"I don't think so, but I can't tell without an X-Ray. For that you'll have to come to my surgery."

A light blinked on in Lonsdale's addled brain. "Aren't you the one . . . ?

". . . who patched you up after you were robbed a few nights ago? The answer is, yes. Now let me help you sit up and allow me to examine you properly. It'll be painful, but it can't be helped, so grit your teeth. In the meantime," the doctor said, "hold this icepack to where it hurts most."

After fifteen minutes of pure agony, the doctor addressed Lonsdale again.

"As I said, your ribs are badly bruised, may be even cracked, but your lungs do not seem to be punctured. There are old and new contusions, bruises, all over your body and you are suffering from a mild concussion. I recommend that you spend a couple of days in a private clinic under observation."

He gave Lonsdale a questioning look.

"What's the time?" Lonsdale wanted to know.

"Seven o'clock." This from Jenkins.

Lonsdale shook his head as if to rid his brain of cobwebs. "Doc, I have a vitally important conference call scheduled for midnight that I can't miss. That's about five hours from now. Give me some painkillers and let me sleep here for as long as possible."

He turned to Jenkins. "Get me a pillow and a blanket and wake me up at five to midnight."

*   *   *

Juric knew the game was up when, Tuesday evening, while listening to the radio, he heard about the explosion at the SPA—the second terrorist bombing in twenty-four hours.

The best laid plans of mice and men . . .

Furious, he felt like laughing and crying at the same time. Perhaps the most active member of Al Qaeda's Balkan cell, he spent a great deal of time traveling up and down the Danube, and had a fair idea of what his organization's plans were for the region. Bombings were not on their agenda—yet. How ironic then that their elaborate kidnapping plans should have to be abandoned because of acts of apparent terrorism by people who were probably not terrorists at all.

His first reaction to the news had been to call Amina for information, but he had resisted it because he knew that the police were tapping her phone periodically and now was not the time to draw attention to oneself.

Damn whoever was responsible for the blasts. Everybody was becoming afraid of terrorists, which meant that a witch-hunt would soon follow. It was time for Juric to lighten load, so to speak, just in case.

He was glad that, as soon as he had heard about the first explosion, the one at Police Headquarters, he had had the foresight to activate his plan for getting Barzan Hassani out of the country with the help of the Iraqi ambassador. He had suggested that Al Adel, too, avail himself of the opportunity, but the man had stubbornly declined, claiming that Juric's plan, involving an ambulance in which he and Hassani were to be transported from *Háros* to the Iraqui embassy in Budapest, was too risky.

Juric, who was no fool, saw through the objections because he sensed that a parting of the ways between Saddam and Osama was imminent. They were rivals and nobody could foretell which of the two would come out on top in the end. As far as he, Juric, was concerned his loyalty was, above all, to The Cause, the creation of a secular pan-Islamic European region that would ultimately destroy the West.

A lot of work and planning had gone into the Moscovitch kidnapping. The scientist was an important prize, and Juric felt responsible for keeping him safe and well and at the disposal of those who would best further The Cause. In his opinion, as matters now stood, Iraq was the player most likely to succeed in the game that was being played with Moscovitch' life.

Juric watched his wife as she laid out their evening meal. She looked tired. No wonder; she had been cooking and caring for a lot of people during the past week. Including Hassani, Delic, and Al Adel, plus the deckhand/bodyguards, they numbered close to a dozen.

"Rada, we must leave this place," he said to her quietly. "The bomb at the SPA will lead the police to Amina and from her to us. You, yourself, have said that you have noticed strange people hanging around here recently."

"I did, but it didn't seem to worry you a week ago."

"That was then, when we still had police protection through our leader's contacts. But this is now, and I fear we may have lost our contact and our leader too."

Her hand flew to her mouth in a gesture of fear. "When must we leave?" She had been dreading this moment ever since Moscovitch had come into their lives.

Juric made up his mind. "I'll tell the men to transfer to the *Maria* quietly by midnight. They will have to help you pack enough food for all of us to last three days. We'll go downriver." He never told her too much; it was safer that way for them both.

"What about Amina?" She was a second cousin on her father's side.

He shook his head. "She's beyond our help my dear. We can't risk waiting for her."

"What about the dogs?" He knew she loved them. They had, at times, been her only companions for days on end. "Can we bring them?"

He looked away. "Put them to sleep. Forever."

CHAPTER 35

Budapest, Tuesday Night, October 23

Moscovitch could sense that something was wrong.

Monday night just after dinner, a man, whom he had never seen before, had come to see him holding a pistol in one hand and a cell phone in the other. "Jason," he had said in accented, but fluent English, pronouncing his name as Yason, "it's time you spoke with your mother."

"Who the hell are you?" Moscovitch had stammered, trying to recover from his surprise.

"Never mind that!" The man had seemed impatient and had waved his pistol at the Canadian menacingly. "Where do I call her?"

Disoriented, it had taken Moscovitch three tries before he could come up with the right number.

This had seemed to amuse his visitor, a swarthy-looking, bearded man with coal black eyes, who had looked at him with undisguised contempt. "Here's what we're going to do," he had said. "I'll dial the number and if it's your mother that answers I'll pass you the phone." He had plugged in a set of earphones to allow him to hear both sides of the conversation then held the telephone up for Moscovitch

185

to see. "Your mother will ask how you are and you will tell her that you're well. Then she'll ask where you are. You'll tell her the truth."

"But I don't know where I am."

"That's right. That's what I want you to tell her." The man had cocked his pistol. "You can ask your mother some questions, but I want you to keep the conversation very positive and very short and I don't want you to ask her anything stupid."

He had pointed the weapon at Moscovitch's head. "If I don't like what you say I'll shoot you down like the dog that you are."

Moscovitch blanched. "But, but . . ."

The man had cut him off. "There is no if and there is no but. The final decision is mine, so be a good Jewish boy and don't upset me any more than I already am."

"What do you mean by that?"

"I don't like your race, but I have to put up with you because my partners want me to. You're lucky that they are the ones who are driving the bus for the time being. But not for long my friend, not for long . . ."

Moscovitch had become so upset that had almost lost it while talking to his mother. Without meaning to, he had begun to antagonize his 'visitor' with his innuendo about 'associates' and then with his inquiry about South Africans. He had come to his senses only after the man had pointed his pistol at his head again.

When he had asked his mother if she were alone, Moscovitch had seen his captor's finger tighten around the weapon's trigger. He had thought he was about to die, but no. The man had let him go on talking for a short while. Then he had started making cutting motions across his throat with his hand and Moscovitch had thought that his life's end was near again. It had taken him a few seconds to understand the true meaning of the gesture. He was to hang up immediately.

Which Moscovitch had done, trembling, and with the cold sweat of fear on his brow.

Shaking his head in disapproval his visitor had extended his hand. "Do you have the paper you are supposed to be preparing?"

With clammy fingers, Moscovitch had handed him the pages he had been working on so hard.

Without uttering another word his captor had then left.

Moscovitch knew he was running out of time, but he didn't care. He had been faking the work; he wasn't really focusing on what he was supposed to be doing, relying entirely on the six vials of the serum he had secreted above his apartment in the boiler room attic of the building on *Széchenyi* Street where he lived.

What a joke. He had discovered the vaccine quite by accident, and however hard he had tried during the past month, he had been unable to recreate the catalyst essential for replicating it.

Exhausted, he had finally fallen asleep again around four a.m., happy with the thought that his mother was safe; at least that is what he chose to believe at that moment in time.

On Tuesday morning, he had awoken tired, grouchy and out-of-sorts. His mood did not improve as the day dragged on. He had hoped, he had been certain, that someone would return after lunch to comment on the document he had given his captors.

But nobody came.

Six weeks' virtual solitary confinement had made him susceptible to frequent periods of depression that he knew he had to fight at all costs. He felt one of these bouts coming on which he usually fought off with a brisk half hour workout on the treadmill, something he had done that morning.

Apparently, that had not been enough.

Therefore, instead of continuing to work after lunch he treated himself to viewing a video cassette his woman guardian had brought him the previous week.

He figured he'd watch TV until dinner then, after eating, exercise again in the fresh autumn air by running back and forth at the end of his chain.

Unfortunately, his dinner was served late, and not by the woman who usually brought him his food, but by the man who had helped him speak to his mother.

Again, the man was contemptuous, even antagonistic. He waved his gun at Moscovitch impatiently when he deemed the scientist was not quick enough to follow orders. The food was different too, only a sort of club sandwich and a mug of hot chocolate.

Instead of leaving the Canadian to eat his meal alone, the man stayed at the door and motioned for Moscovitch to start his meal.

When he finished his chocolate drink, the man picked up the dishes and left.

Moscovitch became disconcerted. Like all prisoners, he had become accustomed to an unvarying routine and change made him nervous. "Guess the bitch has been given a day off," he grumbled, "and forgot to leave instructions for me to be let out after dinner. I sure as shit hope she'll be back by tomorrow evening,"

Though upset, he didn't sweat the point much. He was too tired.

CHAPTER 36

Budapest, Tuesday, October 23,
Midnight

"I have good news!" Morton sounded positively buoyant. "We were able to solve the Cizre problem without creating a diplomatic incident."

"How so?" Lonsdale was only half listening to the words emanating from the speaker phone on Jenkins' desk. He was putting on his clothes after the doctor, who had come back shortly before midnight to minister to him, had gently taped up his bruised ribs.

Officially, Edward Jenkins was Secretary and Consul at the US Embassy. *Sub rosa*, he was also the CIA's Deputy Head of Station in Budapest, taking his orders from the Head of Station for the Balkans who lived and worked in Vienna.

Jenkins was often required to work late, or even through the night. To rest on such occasions, he had a hide-a-bed in his office that looked like a comfortable sofa.

Lucky for Lonsdale!

It had meant five hours' more or less comfortable sleep, thanks to the bed and the painkillers the doctor had given him earlier in the evening.

But his waking moments had been pure hell.

Stiff and in pain, his head fuzzy from the drugs and the stress he was under, he found it very difficult to concentrate.

". . . that problem is solved," Morton was saying and Lonsdale felt obliged to ask "How?" He wasn't sure he had heard everything Morton had said.

"Pay attention." His boss's tone became testy; he too was under pressure. "As I said, we were lucky. The commander of the USAF communications unit in Cizre, remember, the listening post, a NATO thing, had previously made an appointment with the mayor to discuss the perennial problem of the noise caused by the base's generators. The appointment involved an inspection of the generators and was scheduled for late this afternoon . . ."

"So he kidnapped the mayor . . ." Lonsdale interrupted.

"Not quite. During the inspection, Cizre's Police Chief came around and placed the Mayor under protective custody based on a warrant from the Turkish Interior Ministry invoking emergency anti-terrorist laws."

"Another NATO thing, I presume," Lonsdale chuckled. "Where is the mayor now?"

"You're right. Without the NATO arrangement, we would never have gotten our hands on the mayor in time. The Turks are holding him while evidence against him is being collected at his home under the provisions of the same warrant."

"Who is doing the collecting?"

"We are, of course. A team from our Ankara office flew down there this afternoon. It has instructions to make it look as if the Turkish police were in charge, but that's only cosmetic."

"Any chance of rendition?"

"Very much so."

"Where to?"

"That depends on what will happen in your neck of the woods."

After Lonsdale finished his report on the Budapest situation, there was an awkward silence.

"That's not such good news." Lonsdale didn't like Morton's tone. Too hesitant. "I'm getting complaints about you from the Canadians. They say you're a loose cannon, have no respect for the local laws and the cops want to arrest you. You've now caused the death of three Hungarian citizens and are suspected of having caused the death of two police officers. This is growing into a major diplomatic incident."

Lonsdale became very upset "Don't give me this crap, Jim. I shot one in self-defense; the other four blew themselves up. We're not dealing with starry eyed idealists here. These are cold-blooded terrorists, conspiring to destroy our way of life." He was going to continue, but his cell phone rang.

It was Frakkos.

"There's only normal action here at Juric, yes? People going into house and coming out to and from the barge. George, near the entrance by main road saw just now an ambulance drive in. I'm watching from the other side, the *Duna* side."

Lonsdale reacted quickly "Tell George to follow the ambulance when it comes out and report to you about where it goes. Then call me."

"OK. What I should do?"

"Stay where you are and watch. If the barge moves, call me." Lonsdale returned to his conversation with Morton and updated his boss. "Jim, what am I to do if the barge leaves? I have no manpower."

"Do nothing. The barge will probably go downriver. We'll intercept it when it crosses the border into Croatia."

"But what if they download Moscovitch before the barge gets that far?"

"Don't jump to conclusions. You're assuming Moscovitch is being held by the Jurices and will be moved by barge. Have you considered that may be he's in the ambulance as we speak? Leave the barge to me and concentrate on the ambulance."

"But . . ."

"No buts." Morton was firm. "I've got to go. Call me at noon your time." He hung up.

Morton had a point. There was no way the Hungarian authorities would react on short notice. The barge was likely to depart within the hour. Without the police, Lonsdale had no legal right to stop the vessel from leaving. It would take at least twelve hours to organize any action, even if the US State Department pulled out all the stops and the Hungarian Ministry of the Interior cooperated fully.

After all, it was one o'clock in the morning in Budapest. People in Washington were on their way home from work and the bureaucrats in Hungary were asleep!

Lonsdale had no car, no passport, no charger for the telephone he absolutely needed to keep on top of things, no change of clothing, or anywhere to wash up or sleep.

He was down to his last few hundred dollars, had no credit cards he could use, and had not been in touch with the love of his life, Adys, for the last week except for a few moments of light, meaningless banter.

His inner voice began to whisper. 'Time to look after number one!' This, and Morton's seemingly sudden lack of interest in helping Lonsdale find Moscovitch quickly, made him feel abandoned and insecure.

Was it possible that The Agency did not realize the scientist's supreme importance to the West? Or was it that someone else had succeeded where Moscovitch had so far failed? Even worse. Were they beginning to play politics at Langley again, looking for a fall guy to blame for bungling the mission and screwing up Washington's relationship with its NATO Allies, Turkey, and Hungary?

Of course, the designated fall guy would be Lonsdale, an outsider, a rogue agent, acting without authority, entirely deniable.

Lonsdale needed to set up his defenses against 'friendly fire' pretty damned quick, and there was only one person through whom he could forestall and counter any action against him by his superiors.

Jenkins.

With his help, Lonsdale could 'legitimize' himself publicly and undeniably and obtain the assistance he needed to reorganize his position. For this, the man had the right to know what was going on.

"Do you know who I really am?' Lonsdale asked the Deputy Chief of Station.

"No, sir. Mr. Morton only told me what I absolutely needed to know. He did mention that you were a very senior officer and outranked me by several grades."

Lonsdale nodded. "That is correct. As you've heard from our conversation, we are conducting a very complex anti-terrorist operation, international in scope. You know me as Bernard Kane, a Canadian private investigator. I'm neither and I cannot continue using this legend. I need US State Department Diplomatic Grade documents including a passport in the name of Philip Johnston, driver's license, credit card, social security documentation, the works."

"For when?"

"By tomorrow eleven a.m. For authorization and details, call the duty officer at Langley, quoting code Victor UDR Triple A 9. I also need you to make a reservation for me at the Kempinsky Hotel right away. Tell the clerk that I have lost my passport and luggage, that the Embassy is going to pay my bill and that you'll be bringing me over within fifteen minutes. Do you know anyone working at that hotel?"

"Yes, sir, the night manager, George Medgyesi."

"So much the better. Also ask him to lay on a powerful car for me, Mercedes or BMW or Audi, for eleven-thirty tomorrow. Is there anyone reliable on duty here tonight beside yourself?'

"Only the cipher clerks and the Marine security detail."

"Then I'll have to ask you for one more thing."

"Fire away."

"Once you've deposited me at the Kempinsky, call the Canadian Embassy and find out how to locate Miss Thérèse Lapointe, the Consul. Do you know her by any chance?"

Jenkins' face turned red. "As a matter of fact, I do, and very well. I was posted here as Acting Deputy Chief of Station two years ago, at the age of thirty-five and a bachelor. A year or so ago Thérèse and I had a very discrete 'thing', a casual affair. It was safe and convenient for both of us because we were more or less on the same team, though at different embassies."

"What do you mean by that?"

"You know, don't you that she's CSIS?"

"No, but I suspected it, I suppose."

"Thérèse was very discrete, and so was I. We stopped seeing each other months ago, around the time I was confirmed as Deputy Chief of Station. I still have her home phone number, but I almost never call her there anymore. She has a new boyfriend, an Iranian, also very discrete." Lonsdale's tiny inner voice began to chant again 'too much coincidence, too many Iranians, too much coincidence, too many Iranians'. It knew Lonsdale did not believe in coincidences.

He pretended to be amused although he was anything but, and Jenkins grinned. He seemed relieved.

"Then we're in luck. Tell her that she needs to go to my hotel, the *Béke*, immediately, to claim the stuff in my room there."

"Room number?"

"Suite B on the top floor. Make sure she does not overlook the phone charger. It's plugged into one of the sockets beside my bed. She also needs to fish my pistol out of the toilet cistern in the bathroom near my bed. I hung it on a string on the flushing mechanism inside a sealed zip lock bag and didn't have time to retrieve it when I fled." Lonsdale scribbled a quick note and handed it to Jenkins. "Here's a letter of authorization for her. The signature will match what's on my registration card at the *Béke*."

"Have you met Miss Lapointe?"

"Once."

"Not a very forceful personality, is she?"

"Are you implying she might have difficulty getting my stuff out of my room?"

"Do I have your permission to suggest that she bring one of the security men at her embassy with her? I know there's one who acts as a sort of liaison with the hotels when Canadian tourists get into trouble."

"You do whatever you want as long as it gets me my things before nine thirty. By the way, don't worry about you and the lovely Miss Lapointe. Your secret is safe with me. And stop calling me 'sir'."

"Thank you for your understanding. I'll have your things brought here and I'll personally ferry them over to you first thing tomorrow morning."

"That will be much appreciated. As far as the blast you must have gotten from Uncle Jim, I'll see what I can do to make him forget about your sins."

"You realize then how badly stretched we are personnel-wise?"

"Don't sweat it Jenkins. Remember the Hungarian proverb: *Kéz kezet mos.*"

"One hand washes the other."

"Well done, Jenkins. In other words, you scratch my back and I'll scratch yours. Makes the world function better, don't you think?"

CHAPTER 37

Budapest, Wednesday, October 24
Dawn

Al Adel knew exactly what he had to do, stick close to Moscovitch. No way was he going to allow Juric to whisk the Canadian away to Iraq.

But he had to tread carefully.

Although all members of the Drusza cell were Al Qaeda, it was not clear what would happen if they had to choose between loyalty to Saddam and loyalty to Osama Bin Laden. For instance, the pragmatic Delic would likely opt for Iraq because he wanted fast action on the scientific front, something Al Qaeda was not in a position to offer. Drusza would probably follow Delic's lead and Dadakne would side with the two of them.

As for Juric, Al Adel felt that the Bosnian could go either way and this was a problem. Juric not only controlled the group's means of safe transportation—the barge—but, with Hassani absent, also the loyalty of the guards who were bound to follow the barge owner's orders.

In the event, Al Adel had declined The Butcher's offer of safe haven at the Iraqi Embassy and had volunteered to help Juric implement his plan for keeping Moscovitch in captivity at a safe location. The Jordanian had tried to pump him for details, but Juric had stonewalled him, pleading extreme business, which was true.

So the *Maria* had five souls on board when she slipped her moorings shortly after midnight: Juric, his wife, two deckhand/bodyguards and Al Adel.

They had headed downriver in absolute silence and total darkness, the *Maria* completely blacked out, no navigation lights showing, her engines ticking over only enough to propel the vessel forward at the minimum speed needed to steer her. In the pilothouse, Juric, who knew the river like the back of his hand, was at the wheel, with his wife standing beside him. The two guards posted up front on the bow to port and starboard were holding gaffing poles, ready to ward off any obstacle that might suddenly appear out of the inky darkness.

Al Adel had remained in his own little cabin, just below the pilothouse in the rear, still wearing his wig, his shawl and women's clothing,

About four hours into the trip, Al Adel felt the barge slow down then turn toward starboard. He went on deck. They were coming up to the huge hangar that was home to Moscovitch and his future biological weapons laboratory. Al Adel had made certain there was nobody within earshot when he depressed the SEND button on his newly-acquired mobile phone, programmed to redial Khamani's number automatically.

The Iranian had answered on the first ring.

"After passing the southern tip of *Csepel* Island we turned into the inlet leading to the abandoned shipyard on our right that I told you about. Did you buy a map of *Dunaújváros* as I suggested?" Al Adele was at the guardrail.

"Yes I did."

"Identify the *Révi* Street Bridge and pass under it. You'll see a long peninsula to your right. Don't follow us into the inlet. Go across the river and tie up from where you can watch the inlet's entrance without being spotted. I'll call you again in an hour." Al Adel pressed the DISCONNECT button.

By the time Juric finished docking his vessel in the hangar it was six o'clock in the morning and Mrs. Juric began to prepare breakfast in the galley.

Juric signaled for Al Adel to join him in the pilothouse.

"So what do we do now?" Al Adel asked in Arabic. He was not at ease. His nose was twitching again.

Juric smiled. "We'll start by having breakfast, then we'll change the *Maria*'s name and then we'll see." He led the way back into the galley.

After eating, the security men headed for their dormitory in the hold of the vessel. Al Adel called Khamani and told him to get some rest because the Maria was not going anywhere for the time being. After a last cup of coffee he and the Jurices retired to their respective cabins.

Exhausted, Al Adel undressed, crawled into bed and crashed.

*   *   *

Lonsdale's conversation with Adys, essentially a twenty-minute 'please-come-home-soon-and-don't-leave-me-alone-for-such-a-long-time-again' session at one o'clock in the morning, had unsettled him profoundly.

In his heart of hearts, he agreed with everything that Adys had said. No relationship can last in which one of the partners is frequently absent for weeks, especially when the partner left behind has not had time to develop a support circle in her new city of residence.

Lonsdale profoundly believed in the central thrust of his job—to fight an enemy bent on destroying his way of life in a tolerant, and pluralistic society where a man was innocent until found guilty by his peers. He could not fathom how others would not see that such a fight demanded unavoidable and, at times very painful, sacrifices.

"In the past the struggles were between nation states. Today's confrontation is between two different *eras*. On one side," he would repeatedly point out to Adys, "we have the western democracies with their advanced twentieth century civilization. On the other, there are the concepts of those who still live as if they were in the Middle Ages."

"What do you mean?"

"Islam is a religion that is seven hundred years 'younger' than Christianity. Just think back to what we Christians were doing from the twelfth to the fifteenth centuries: fighting Crusades to 'liberate' the Holy Land that belonged to the Arabs, burning so-called 'witches' on the stakes, and so on."

"Are you saying it's pay-back time?"

"In a way, yes."

"And how do we stop this insane vicious circle of tit-for-tat?"

"By not acting surprised that our opponents are using the religion of Islam as a false pretense, that they reject the idea that life is sacred and propose that the Mosque be the State, which, of course, would deprive the people, through Sharia Law, of the right to freedom of choice under democracy."

"Make your point."

"I'm saying that we must not only make an effort to understand why our opponents act the way they do, but we must also help them accelerate their intellectual, economic and social development so that they reach our level."

"At the point of a gun?"

"If we want our civilization, our way of life, to survive, yes. And we do, don't we? None of us wants to regress into the darkness of the Middle Ages and then have to start seeking enlightenment again."

Only after he had hung up had he realized that Adys was trying to make him define precisely the sacrifices they would both have to make, and were willing to make, if he continued working for The Agency. Were they willing to endanger their relationship? Was he willing to endanger his health, even his life?

The answer, as far as she was concerned, was 'no' to both questions. Her implied threat, it had been a threat, Lonsdale was sure of that now, had been that she would leave him if he persisted in what he was doing.

And he certainly did not want that!

But what *did* he want?

Did he want to save the world, a world in which Man was deliberately mocking his God?

No, that was not it.

"Finish the job on hand, asshole, then go home and quit. You've done enough, asshole," he mumbled and willed himself into falling asleep.

CHAPTER 38

Budapest, Wednesday, October 24
Morning

Lonsdale woke with a start and looked at the alarm clock. It showed a quarter to six a.m. He hurt, especially his rib cage. The pain was, however, less sharp than the previous night. Four additional hours' sleep had helped.

Or was it the painkillers still in his blood from the night before? He took two extra-strength Tylenols. He suspected that the day ahead would be trying, to say the least.

No sooner had he moved into his room at the Kempinsky the previous night than his cell phone had begun to chirp. Frakkos was reporting that the barge was in the process of leaving with the entire Juric entourage on board.

"What about the ambulance?" Lonsdale had asked.

George had followed it to the residence of the Iraqi ambassador on *Eszter* Street in the *Rózsadomb* district.

"Are you sure?" Lonsdale had been furious. He was losing Moscovitch's scent. The scientist was getting away from him.

"Iraqi ambassador's house, yes. George, he waits around. Ambulance comes out after five minutes and driver drives home with it."

This did not compute. "Please explain, if you can."

"Sure." Frakkos had been glad to oblige. "George follows the ambulance to home of driver at *Ecser*, a village near airport. Driver goes home to sleep. George, he goes home to sleep too." Useless information.

Be patient, Lonsdale had admonished himself. 'Everybody is tired and stressed out. Sort things out in the morning.'

After a careful sponge bath, Lonsdale ordered breakfast from room service.

He was starving. No wonder. During the last twenty-four hours, all he had eaten had been a *flódni* at the Central Coffeehouse.

The copy of *Magyar Nemzet* on his food tray featured a huge front page headline: SECOND TERRORIST BOMB IN 24 HOURS. The accompanying article was ambiguous, but did refer to two, possibly three, victims. It ended with the statement that the police were being unusually tight-lipped. "We have very strong leads, but cannot comment further because of national security considerations," their spokes person had said.

No mention of Mr. Bernard Kane or of any North American involvement. Obviously, Morton had initiated formidable damage control.

Frakkos was not to be fooled. He had phoned at six-thirty. "Interesting articles in papers. Should I go on working with you, yes? Is safe for me?"

Lonsdale decided to take the man's question as a joke. "Don't worry," he laughed, "just tell me what's happening."

"My night man following the barge downriver by car for a while, yes? Very difficult because of darkness. We don't know where barge is now. What do you want to do?"

"Where are you now?"

"At home, dressing."

"Can you find out something about the ambulance George followed last night?"

"Give me a few hours."

At nine-thirty on the dot, a visibly impressed Jenkins turned up with Lonsdale's possessions, including his charger.

"I got a SIM on you and so did the Ambassador."

"SIM?"

"Secret Information Memo." He handed Lonsdale a sheet of paper. "Of course, the Ambassador's is suitably sanitized."

The document outlined the Drusza-Dadakne-Delic-Juric situation, alluded to the Cizre seizures and confirmed that The Agency had an agent *in situ* in full charge of the ongoing operation, who was to be afforded maximum assistance.

"As we speak," Jenkins went on, "the Ambassador is briefing the Minister of the Interior."

The Deputy Chief of Station then told Lonsdale that the police, who had gotten to the *Béke* before her, would not give Thérèse Lapointe Lonsdale's belongings. The situation changed when the detective in charge received a telephone call instructing him to hand over everything without further ado.

"Good old Uncle Jim," murmured Lonsdale.

Jenkins ignored the remark. "My informant tells me the police found the woman who led you to Drusza in deep shock. She began to remember things only a couple of hours later."

'Such as my name.' Lonsdale silently thanked Eva Illman for trying to give him time to get away.

"And it was Drusza's secretary—they made her come back to the office—who finally told them that you were staying at the *Béke*."

According to Jenkins, the police had then called the Canadian Embassy looking for the Consul who was not immediately available. The terrorist connection came to light when, much later, Ms. Illman finally 'recalled' what Lonsdale had told her about Amina and Drusza. The Hungarian anti-drug and terrorist squads had then been called in, but by the time they had sorted themselves out it had been too late to stop Juric's barge from leaving. They contacted the river police who told them they only took orders directly from the Ministry of the Interior.

"An unbelievable screw up of monumental proportions." Lonsdale would have laughed had he been less upset.

"True," said Jenkins. "Finally, this morning at six, coordination among the various Hungarian law-enforcement agencies was established and a helicopter search for the barge initiated a half-hour after first light."

"What time was that?"

"Around eight."

"Did they locate the barge?"

"No. They flew over the river as far down as *Tolna*, which is about a hundred miles to the south of here. They figured that the barge's speed downriver would not exceed ten knots and that it could not have covered more than that distance during the seven hours it's been gone."

Jenkins got up to leave. "Your identity papers will be delivered by messenger at eleven. Your car, an Audi A6, will be here a half hour later. Is there anything else I can help you with?"

Lonsdale shook his head. "No, nothing, but rest assured I'll stay in touch and let you know if the situation changes."

Just before Jenkins reached the door, Lonsdale asked as casually as he could: "Do you know this Iranian fellow Thérèse Lapointe is seeing?"

"His friends call him Rezzah, but his full name is Rezzah Khamani. Owns a successful Audi dealership and an Avis car rental franchise on *Galamb* Street. Does business with many ex-pats and diplomats. Actually, we rented your Audi from him. He's well-liked and popular with the ladies."

"Have you tossed him?"

"Thoroughly. He's squeaky clean."

Lonsdale didn't believe him. Nobody was squeaky clean.

CHAPTER 39

Budapest, Wednesday, October 24
Morning (cont'd)

After breakfast, Lonsdale called Frakkos to plan their day together. Then he called Morton. Let the bastard taste some of his own medicine.

"We need to find that damned barge for two reasons," he said without preamble. "One, to see if Moscovitch is on board, which I now doubt, and two, to make the people who *are* on board tell us where he is."

Morton was furious. "You're calling me at three a.m. to tell me something both of us already know. Are you out of your mind or are you just trying to piss me off, in which case you're succeeding."

Lonsdale ignored the outburst. "The river police have no idea what the *Maria* looks like. Unbelievably, the only photograph that exists of her is in Frakkos' camera, taken when he started working for me. This morning, we're making copies for distribution to the police so that they can start looking for the vessel in earnest."

"Why didn't you do this yesterday?"

"Because I just found out that the police had no idea of what the barge looked like. Besides, Frakkos only told me about the photo this morning." Lonsdale paused and tried to control his frustration.

"It's amateur hour around here, Jim. I need you to get the Minister of the Interior to receive me so that I can outline what needs to be done and then make sure it *does* get done. At present, the cops are floundering."

"What do you want them to do?"

"I believe the barge is trapped in Hungary, hidden somewhere along the Danube, either south or north of Budapest."

"You're not convinced that it has gone downriver?"

"Probably, but I can't be sure. I can't even be sure that the barge hasn't already slipped into Croatia to the South, or Slovakia to the north." Lonsdale plunged ahead. "I'm betting that Juric, who is hiding somewhere, has used the night to repaint the barge's name. I'm also betting that he'll stay hidden all day long and wait for the paint to dry so he can dirty it to make it look old. Of course, by now he may have unloaded Moscovitch and other passengers of interest to us."

"Such as?"

"Some of the deckhands, but I'm guessing."

"Go on."

"I'm going to send Frakkos south to *Mohács* near the border between Hungary and Croatia and his man, George, north to *Esztergom* near the border between Hungary and Slovakia with instructions to have the river police stop and inspect every barge passing through that bears even the slightest resemblance to the *Maria.*"

"That will create a fair-sized traffic jam on the river."

"True, but it can't be helped. We can't let the barge slip through our fingers."

"The countries involved won't like that. They will protest."

"That's where you come in. The Hungarian cops will not want to cooperate because they know they'll have to go on living with these barge people after the emergency is over. You and State must coerce the minister by using threats, bribes, reason and whatever else it takes to order the police to follow my guys' instructions."

"You're not asking much, are you?" Morton asked, his voice dripping with sarcasm. He was getting pretty tired of Lonsdale's unreasonable requests.

Again, Lonsdale chose to ignore his boss's comment. "I will also ask the minister to order the river police's motor launches and its 'copter, and the Army's helicopters, to search the river for possible hiding places for the *Maria*."

"What will *you* be doing during that time?"

"Once I've finished with the minister I'll go to the Counterterrorism Control Center and keep tab on the progress of the search."

"What's your best guess as to what will happen?"

"A disguised *Maria* will try to cross into Croatia tomorrow morning between two and six a.m. I will be there to greet her, hopefully with a platoon of SAS men from their base at Banja Luka."

"Which you want me to arrange for you."

"You've got it, Jim. After all, what are friends for?' It was Lonsdale's turn to sound sarcastic.

CHAPTER 40

Budapest, Wednesday, October 24
Noon

Lonsdale's problems were multiplying and becoming more and more acute.

First, there was Morton.

His boss had not considered the barge's disappearance significant when Lonsdale had reported it to him earlier. "I told you, don't sweat the barge. It's my responsibility," he had said with finality. "Get after the ambulance".

Following his orders, Lonsdale and Frakkos had gone to interview the driver at the *Rokus,* the hospital to which Frakkos had traced the ambulance. Very suspicious at first, he began to open up a little after a fifty-dollar '*borravaló*', or tip, from Lonsdale.

Apparently, his supervisor had instructed him to have the ambulance's oil changed. As a reward for undertaking the task during his day off, he was given permission to take the ambulance home for twenty-four hours.

"This they do all the time, yes?" Frakkos had chimed in. "So ambulance driver can make extra money with private patients." The 'dispatcher' for such arrangements was the mechanic at the garage the *Rokus* used to service its vehicles.

206

"Driver collects money from patient then pays off supervisor and mechanic. Normal business in Hungary. Hospital pays for gas and oil and maintenance of ambulance."

"Charming." Lonsdale had been totally disgusted. Some things never changed.

The mechanic had told the driver to pick up an envelope at a nearby café in which he would find money and instructions. The driver had followed the instructions, had picked up the 'patient' at the Juric property and had driven him to the Iraqi ambassador's residence.

"Was the patient this man?" Lonsdale had asked through Frakkos and had shown the driver Moscovitch's picture.

No, the patient was much older with a bushy black moustache and graying hair. He looked like an Arab, the driver had added.

"Was there only one 'patient'?

"Yes," the driver had said "and he rode up front with me, pretending to be my assistant, but not saying a word."

"What happened at the ambassador's residence?"

"I was told to drive to the front of the villa. A security guard opened the gate. We drove in, the patient got out and I went home."

There was no sense in trying to find out more. Lonsdale recognized a dead-end lead when he saw one.

But one never knew.

As an afterthought, he instructed Frakkos to give the driver his cell number in case the man subsequently remembered something pertinent. "Tell him," Lonsdale said, "that if he helps us find the man we're looking for, we'll give him a really big '*borravaló*'."

It was clear to Lonsdale that Morton had been wrong not to have recognized the ambulance for what it was: a red herring, a ruse, to divert attention from the barge.

Or so Lonsdale had thought at the time.

Moscovitch was gone and his scent was rapidly dissipating. Whoever had spirited the scientist away had an eighteen-hour lead on Lonsdale now.

He wondered fleetingly about the identity of the 'patient'. 'Probably one of the deckhands,' he thought and dismissed the matter from his mind. He had been mortified when, much later, at his disciplinary hearing, he had found out that the 'patient' had been none other than The Butcher, Colonel Barzan Hassani, Chemical Ali's right hand man.

The next problem Lonsdale had to solve was his relationship with the Hungarian police's anti-terrorist unit.

Since Horváth and Vas were dead, he thought that presenting himself to Police Colonel Imre Nagy, the Center's international coordinator, as Phillip Johnston, a State Department diplomat, would not create a problem. He was sure Nagy would have no difficulty in reading between the lines and interpreting 'State Department' as being what it really was: CIA.

He found Nagy, an angular sort of man in a rumpled suit with a bespectacled, bookish-looking face and thinning blond hair, in his office at the *Főkapitányság*, the Police HQ. It took the Colonel, who spoke fluent English and German, and was not too keen to cooperate, a couple of hours to process Lonsdale's request to speak with the helicopter crew that had flown the search mission for the *Maria*.

It was four in the afternoon by the time he finally got to interview the flyers. They were tired after a busy day and anxious to go off duty.

"The order to look for the barge you're talking about came through this morning just as we came on duty," the pilot was saying. Thin, and well into middle age, with a cadaverous face, bad teeth and the bad breath that went with it, he was clearly annoyed about having to hang around to answer stupid questions from self-important foreign diplomats.

"What time was that?" Lonsdale needed to know every detail.

"At eight, but we couldn't start searching for another hour because it was still fairly dark and too foggy over the water."

"There was another reason," the copilot, a short chubby man with very little hair above a round, cherubic face, interrupted. "Nobody knew what the barge looked like." Both aviators spoke good, though strongly accented, English.

Lonsdale had to restrain himself from laughing. He couldn't help thinking that he was interviewing Don Quixote and his sidekick, Sancho Panza.

"How did you solve that problem?"

"We had been told that the barge left Budapest around two in the morning and that its approximate speed downriver was about ten knots or fourteen kilometers. We took off at around nine thirty and flew south above the river as far as *Tolna*. We refueled there and at eleven began to work our way upriver." The pilot was warming to his subject. He was obviously a conscientious man who took pride in doing a good job.

Sancho Panza picked up the tale. "The total elapsed time between the vessel's departure and the commencement of our search was seven hours, so we felt safe about starting to work our way back from *Tolna*, because the town is one hundred and twenty kilometers south of Budapest."

"It had taken us three quarters of an hour to fly down there. It took us three hours to fly back, during which we inspected forty-two vessels of which four were questionable, but none of them bore the name *Maria*." The pilot was getting ready to leave.

"What do you mean by 'questionable'?"

"A freshly painted or obliterated name. All vessels are required to have their names displayed on both sides of the bow, and on the stern, so changing a barge's name takes time; about four hours. They are easy to spot for at least forty-eight hours after the job is finished, because most of these barges are old and dirty, with their paint peeling, so a fresh paint job stands out."

The pilots stood up. They looked exactly like their ancient *alter egos*.

Lonsdale squeezed in one last question. "How did you deal with the 'questionables'?"

"We raised them on the Mayday Channel. They all have radiotelephones. We asked them for their particulars which we forwarded to the river police to sort out at the border."

And that was that. Juric was sure to know exactly how the river police operated. He had had the benefit of at least five hours of darkness during which to find a safe hiding place where, away from prying eyes, he could repaint his boat's name.

As he pondered over what the pilots had said, Lonsdale began to wonder about the correctness of the assumption that the barge was heading toward Croatia. Although Frakkos had been sure that the *Maria* had disappeared from view going downstream when leaving the Juric property, nothing would impede her owner from turning her around once she had reached the main branch of the river.

Had Morton not ordered him to worry about the ambulance and not the barge, had he been able to speak with the pilots earlier he could have, perhaps, persuaded them to fly upstream first, and then downstream. Now, it was too late. Another night was approaching, and with it the darkness that would allow the wily Juric to outwit him.

Discouraged, Lonsdale returned to the Kempinsky to deal with his third pressing problem, Adys. He was beginning to feel that his relationship with her was in the process of seriously deteriorating.

He called her during her lunch break, six thirty p.m. Budapest time.

"My darling," she said in Spanish, "it's not that I don't understand, it's just that I'm not sure I can handle the solitude. I know very few people in Washington and you've been so busy since we've met that we haven't developed much of a social life."

"You've got to give me more time Adys," he pleaded. "I'm just about finished with my job here." He knew he was lying, but he had to save their relationship somehow. "I'm pretty sure I'll be home within a week."

"You mean well, Roberto, I know, but you're not in control of your life. The Agency is."

"What you're telling me, then, is that I should quit."

"After you've finished this job, yes."

"But they need me. There's a war on, a religious war. Our enemies want to force us into fundamentally changing our way of life. They want to limit our right to chose." Lonsdale's central theme, his *raison d'être*, was to fight for freedom.

"You've done your bit Roberto, even Jim admits that. Unfortunately, this does not stop him from pressuring you over and over again."

"He saved my life in September."

"And you saved *his* neck on many occasions, I'm sure. No, Roberto, it's time you stopped letting him use you."

"But he's a friend."

"That's where you're wrong, *Querido*," she told him with uncharacteristic vehemence. "He's just a consummate manipulator." Her voice caught. Lonsdale sensed she was close to crying.

There was a pause. "I've got to get back to work," she told him brusquely. "Call me at midnight my time and we'll talk more about all this." She hung up without telling him that she loved him.

Lonsdale was devastated.

He called Morton in Washington to summarize the day's events.

Morton, quite shaken, would not admit he had been wrong, and Lonsdale lost his temper. "God dammit, Jim, who's running the show in Hungary, you or me?"

The outburst got Morton's hackles up. He was about to give Lonsdale a dressing down, but then he remembered. The man, although at times very likeable, was bothersome. Impossible to control, he had a tendency to usurp power and to make decisions beyond the ambit of his mandate. He was always snidely confident of being right. He seemed to consider himself superior to everyone and made sure that everybody knew it.

The maddening thing was that Lonsdale turned out to be more often right than wrong. He was also very brave, unquestionably loyal, had charisma and achieved results. Morton hated to admit it, but Lonsdale was one of The Agency's better deep-cover assets.

He sighed with resignation. He would have to continue pretending that Lonsdale was calling the shots and that Morton and his people were there only to offer backup, infrastructure support, and money.

Especially money. Lonsdale loved money and spent it with relish.

"Both of us," he finally said.

"No fucking way Jim. Such an arrangement never works because there is no unified command. Everybody gets confused and communications break down."

"How do you want to run the file then?"

Lonsdale was taken aback by the question. Morton and he had been working as a team for years. Why this sudden questioning of the old, accepted and proven routine?

"As we have always done in the past," he replied. "I'll run the operation in Hungary and you run the rest of the world. Support me when I ask for support and guide me when I ask for guidance, but don't order me to do things with which I, as the Agent *in situ*, do not agree."

There followed a painful silence. Morton didn't like to be told off, but then who does?

"OK, sport we'll do it your way, but bear in mind that if you screw up it's your ass on the line, not mine. I'll hold you responsible."

This meant, Lonsdale suddenly realized, that Morton had just managed to wiggle out from under any responsibility for the mistakes he had already made, or had caused to be made. If the mission failed, Lonsdale would get the blame. If, however, Lonsdale secured Moscovitch's release, he and Morton would share the glory.

Adys had called it right. Morton was no longer a friend. He had demoted himself to being just a colleague playing it safe, probably because he was too close to retirement to be able to take yet another hit, after already having taken a big one on September 11.

What Lonsdale did not know was that his Control was terminally ill. He had an inoperable brain tumor, malignant glioma. The prognosis was very bad; he had less than a year left to live.

Morton had kept his illness a strict secret, but knew he would be found out soon. His compulsory annual physical was coming up in January and he wanted no blemish on his record during his last few months of service.

To leave The Agency in a blaze of glory after four decades of faithful and effective service was his fervent desire.

CHAPTER 41

Budapest, Wednesday, October 24 (cont'd)

The Iraqi ambassador's residence in Budapest is a three-storey villa in one of the most elegant districts of the Hungarian Capital, the *Rózsadomb*, (Rosehill).

The ambassador and his family live on the two upper floors, which include the 'Mansard', or attic, apartment. The ground floor accommodates the 'salon', the formal dining room and the kitchen. In the finished semi-basement, there is a guest suite combination designed for important visitors to use overnight in an emergency.

In the large garden, the stand-alone garage to the left of the villa can accommodate three cars. The small apartment on top of it is home for the security guard/chauffeur whose wife acts as maid-housekeeper.

The Butcher had arrived at the Residence in the middle of the night and the first thing he had done was to run himself a bath, scented with a large quantity of aromatic oils. He had then luxuriated for an hour in the fragrant hot water to remove the stench oozing from his pores. 'That's what happens when you live in close proximity with peasants,' he thought with disdain. 'You end up stinking like they do.'

Next, he had left word that he was not to be disturbed before ten in the morning then went to sleep in the Residence's comfortable bed. Consequently, he learned about what had happened in Cizre only around noon on Wednesday and had to spend the afternoon in damage control mode.

The mayor's arrest had destroyed the key element of the communications network set up for the 'Moscovitch snatch', so The Butcher was flying blind. When he discovered through the media that Amina, Delic and Drusza were dead and that Drusza's police contacts had also been eliminated, he concluded that the best course to take was to abandon the operation.

But first, he'd have to find a way of either killing or freeing as many of the remaining participants as quickly as possible, because they knew too much. This meant that, instead of disposing of Moscovitch, a possibility he had discussed with Juric before they had parted, he had to find a way to trade the scientist somehow for his own people, and for Al Adel, of course.

Or, ex-filtrate as many of them as possible.

Third Man indeed! 'How aptly named' The Butcher thought, 'and how ironical that the Jew, Moscovitch, had hit the nail right on the head when he began referring to Saif Al Adel as The Third Man. Al Adel, master of a thousand disguises, was exactly that. He was the number three person in the Al Qaeda chain of command, a member of its Consultation Council and Military Committee.

Nothing but trouble, ever since he had come on board.

Hassani had told both Chemical Ali and his cousin, Saddam Hussein, that getting involved with Al Qaeda would lead to trouble, but neither would listen. "Sooner or later the Americans will find out that we have no Weapons of Mass Destruction," Saddam had argued, "and they will no longer fear us. We must have at least one WMD, and this one that Al Qaeda has identified is a very good one."

Delic and Drusza and the Jurices were Al Qaida too, but manageable. But Al Adel was very much his own man, insisting that the Moscovitch kidnapping be a joint venture. Understandably, he did not want Saddam to have exclusive control over both the virus and the vaccine.

Iraq possessed feed stock for manufacturing nv. C-JD contaminated glue, and so did Al Qaeda, through Delic, but what nobody had was the vaccine against the virus, and it seemed that the person most likely to produce one quickly was Moscovitch.

Hassani had offered Al Adel the opportunity to get out of Hungary via the Iraqi Embassy, but the man had declined at the last moment. He seemed to prefer taking his chances with Juric and the rest of them on the barge, rather than getting into the ambulance with him. Al Adel did not know it, but Hassani was fully aware of the Al Qaeda leader's real motive: he wanted to stay close to Moscovitch. He, like everybody else, knew that Saddam, the ruthless killer, would not hesitate to release the virus without waiting for a cure against it, even if it did kill thousands of Muslims.

So far, so good. The Butcher was protected at the ambassador's residence by diplomatic immunity, and Al Adel was safe for the time being on board Juric's barge that had yet to be found by the police.

It seemed to Hassani that the moment for action was not at hand yet, so he decided to accept the invitation to dine with the ambassador and his family.

*   *   *

Lonsdale's meeting with the Minister of the Interior had not gone well.

Although the US ambassador had pleaded with the man to receive Lonsdale as soon as possible, the request had gone unheeded until noon. By that time, total confusion was reigning on the river. The river police, detailed to check barges traveling along the Danube, complained that it lacked manpower and decided to work to rule in protest. To boot, it refused to cooperate with the helicopter because it was under the command of the Budapest land-based police.

The Counterterrorism Unit, charged with the coordination of the search for the *Maria*, had overlooked providing guidance to the Border Patrol at the points of entry into and exit out of the country via the Danube, which meant that these vital checkpoints had been rendered useless through oversight during the crucial early hours of the search. Had it not been for the presence of Lonsdale's people at

215

these crossings, George to the north and Frakkos to the south, the *Maria* could have slipped out of the country unnoticed.

Those attending the meeting with Ernő Kupa, the Minister of the Interior, included Lonsdale, Police Colonel Nagy, and the US ambassador, Herbert Goodman, whose two major qualification for the job were his ability to contribute handsomely to the Republican Party and his marriage to a Hungarian woman.

Nagy had made it clear from the start that he resented Lonsdale's intrusion on his turf. He changed his tune when he learned that the man he had been ordered to work with for the second day in a row was a senior US State Department envoy specialized in counter-terrorism who also had considerable say in shaping US support for Hungary's admission to NATO.

Lonsdale was embarrassed, but grateful to the ambassador for having exaggerated his importance because he could see that the search would have been seriously compromised had permission to assist in it been refused.

In the event, Lonsdale quickly won the Colonel over when he began to speak with him in fluent and colloquial Hungarian.

"You son-of-a-gun, you sure had me fooled earlier," Nagy said, laughing. "I could have sworn you were pure Yankee. Have a seat." He swept a bunch of magazines off the chair beside him. "Where do we start?"

Lonsdale was pleased. "With a few questions."

"Fire away."

"Did the photos of the *Maria* get distributed?"

"They did, but only at noon."

Lonsdale looked at his watch. "So no meaningful searching took place this morning."

"I wouldn't say that. The helicopter kept flying up and down the Danube and the river police kept checking barges for new paint jobs. I'm pretty sure the *Maria* is still in Hungary and holed up somewhere along the Danube. Personally, I don't think she'll emerge from hiding before dark."

"Funny you should say that. I feel the same way, you see." Lonsdale gave Nagy a hard look. "But where?"

"That's the sixty-four thousand dollar question, as they say in America. I'm betting that it'll be at *Mohács,* tomorrow at dawn."

CHAPTER 42

Dunaújváros, Wednesday, October 24
Afternoon/evening

At noon, Juric woke up and set to work.

He roused the deckhands sleeping in one of the two specially outfitted containers on board and ordered them to change the names that appeared on his vessel's stern and bow from *Maria* to *Karlovac*. He also had them paint *Komárno* under the name on the stern, which would indicate that the barge's home port was in Slovakia. Then he broke out the Slovak flag and ran it up the mast at the barge's stern.

There was method to his madness. Juric had foreseen that the time would come when he would have to flee with all his worldly possessions loaded onto his ship. As a precaution, he had procured false papers supporting the claim that his was a Slovakian barge owned by Karel and Yulia Velan.

He even had passports for his wife and himself bearing the Velan name.

By mid-afternoon Juric was ready to put the next phase of his plan into operation.

He went ashore, conferred with the Dankovices, the couple in charge of guarding Moscovitch and, using their telephone, called the ambulance driver whose cell number he had obtained when the man had picked up Hassani the previous evening. Juric knew he was taking a risk, but the situation in which he found himself left him no other alternative.

When he got back on board, he outlined his plan for getting Moscovitch out of Hungary to Al Adel.

"I have spoken with the ambulance driver who took the Colonel to safety the other night. He will help me take you and the prisoner to Croatia through a border crossing point where he is known and where we won't need papers except those already in the ambulance."

Al Adel did not believe him. "How did you manage to arrange such a thing so easily?"

"In Hungary almost everything can be arranged with money."

"Do you know this ambulance driver?"

"I've known him for years," He realized Al Adel was watching him like a hawk, so Juric lied without blinking.

"And do you trust him?"

"We've done deals like this many times in the past."

The Jordanian thought things over for a while. "How much is the man charging for this service?" He finally asked.

"Five thousand US dollars. Half up front, half when we're safely across."

"Do you have the money?"

Relieved, Juric permitted himself a small smile. "Yes, I do." Al Adel was hooked.

But the Jordanian would not give in that easily. "Isn't he worried about the border police being extra vigilant? By now, half the population must be looking for us."

"Yes he is and he said so."

"What did you tell him?"

"That there would be a diversion near our crossing point at the same time we'd be going through."

"A diversion? What diversion?"

Juric looked at Al Adel straight in the eyes, ready to outstare him.

"The barge *Maria*, of course."

In spite of himself, the Third Man could not help laughing out loud.

After dinner, Juric waited for everybody to go to bed then told his wife to have coffee with him in the pilothouse. He poured himself a shot of Slivovic something he only did during moments of great stress, and gulped it down.

"We've been together for over five years," his voice was soft and low, "and during this time you've been a very good wife to me Rada."

"Since the Genocide." she whispered.

"You have never complained, and you have been steadfast and loyal . . ."

"Yes. To you and The Cause." It was dark in the room and he had difficulty seeing her face in the dim light shed by the tiny bulb above the stove in the galley.

Was it tears that he saw glistening on her cheeks? He could not tell.

"Life has treated us unfairly and has tested us terribly, but somehow we have persevered in our work, praise be to Allah, and have advanced the goals of The Cause. I tell you, without your support I would never have been able to carry on and I thank you for it."

"What troubles you my husband?"

"I have to make a very difficult decision tonight and I do not know how."

She put her cup down, rose to stand behind the captain's chair in which he was sitting and leaned forward. Resting her chin on his left shoulder, she put her arms around his chest. "Tell me about this decision," she whispered into his ear. "Maybe telling me will make it easier for you to decide, maybe you will see clearer, maybe the path you are to follow will be revealed to you that way."

He stared out through the window and watched one of the guards emerge from the container on shore for a smoke and to catch a breath of fresh air. He was sure the man was as fed up and as anxious to move on as he was.

Without turning his head, he began to speak.

"As you know, Moscovitch is a very important Canadian scientist, imprisoned in one of the semis you saw lining the dock. He knows things that could help The Cause, but he does not want to cooperate. We waited, hoping he would change his mind, but he is stubborn and

we have run out of time. Amina, your cousin, has been shot dead."
He heard her gasp and felt her stiffen, but she did not interrupt.

She was a seasoned fighter and a stoic woman.

"Our superiors in this country have also been killed and I am
now responsible for running this operation."

"What about the stranger, the Jordanian, sleeping in the cabin."
He felt her nod toward the deck below. "Is he not higher up than
you?"

"He is, but he does not have the same ideas about The Cause as
I have."

"How so?"

"He is not a European. He is a Jordanian, a tribal Arab, who
trusts only members of his own tribe and no other. He does not trust
the Iraqis, or us Bosniaks. As long as he and Colonel Hassani were
working together he felt comfortable. But with the Colonel gone,
and me being in charge, he fears I will take the scientist to Iraq.
The Jordanian does not want that. He does not trust Saddam and is
afraid of him."

"Then what does *he* want to do with the scientist?"

"He wants to kill him if he cannot have him for himself."

"And why do you not want to give the man to the Jordanian?"

"Because I am afraid that the Jordanian's organization will take
too long to make the scientist work for The Cause. They will lose
patience and kill him, especially because the Canadian is also of
Israeli origin and Jordanians hate Israelis."

"Then your duty is clear. You must do whatever is best for The
Cause."

"Which is?"

"You must not allow anybody to kill the scientist. Play along with
the Jordanian as long as possible and after that becomes impossible
you must take the scientist away and hide him somewhere and keep
him safe for The Cause,"

"Even if it means losing all of this?" He made a sweeping motion
with his arm toward the bow of his barge, "and perhaps losing you
too?"

His wife's arms tightened around his chest. "We are star-crossed
lovers, you and I, who have been granted a second chance for a while.
Maybe we'll be granted a third, maybe not. Let us be grateful for

having had a second one and let us not be greedy. Let you and I do our duty as we see it to be."

* * *

Even though things seemed to have returned to normal, with the woman bringing him his meals regularly and being allowed to exercise outside in the evenings, Moscovitch had the impression that something was up.

During his last outing, he had heard the rattle of heavy equipment and human voices!

Although he had been expecting news from his captors, neither Delic nor Al Adel had come to see him. This did not discourage him. Having listened carefully to the noises around him, he convinced himself that Delic and company were in the process of arranging to move him in anticipation of an agreement being reached.

His impression was re-enforced when, Wednesday night, his dinner was served late again and once more by the same man who had arranged the call to his mother. The menu was similar too: a tuna salad sandwich, but this time with strong hot tea sweetened with honey. Although the tea had tasted a little bitter Moscovitch did not realize he was being drugged until he began to feel dizzy.

By then it was too late. He fell asleep on his cot, dressed in his jogging outfit and wearing slippers.

* * *

Al Adel called Rezzah Khamani in mid-afternoon and told him to stand by 'at the ready' because the situation was turning critical.

Instead of returning to his office after meeting Al Adel at Gerbeaud Tuesday, the Qods officer had hurried to a public telephone booth. Before dialing, he had inserted pieces of bread he had brought with him between his teeth and his cheeks and covered the mouthpiece with his scarf to disguise his voice as much as possible. He had then called the Iranian Consul's secret cell number.

Pitching his voice high to disguise his identity further he provided the official with his code designation. This allowed the man to confirm Khamani's *bona fides* instantly via computer.

"How can I help?"

"I need to borrow one of your security men for forty-eight hours."

The Consul was not surprised. He saw from the code that he was speaking with a Qods officer who not only outranked him, but who was working under deep cover. Since he, himself, was Qods, he was ready to cooperate to the fullest.

"Any particular talents?"

"A basic knowledge of Hungarian, a driver's permit valid in this country, relatively athletic, discrete and reliable."

"I have just the man for you. Where do you want to meet him?"

"Along the section of the *Korzo* in front of the *Dunasörözö.*"

"When?"

"At 18:35 hours."

"Would you like him to bring you some dessert or anything else to eat?"

"Two Bridget cakes with that delicious filling only Iranians know how to make, six little chocolate bombs, six pieces of baklava, two special walking canes and two special sunglasses."

"Are you going camping?"

"Sort of."

"So he had better bring some warm clothes."

"Good idea."

"Recognition signal?"

"Salmon Rushdi—response in *farsi;* he writes forbidden books."

They hung up.

Khamani had then dashed off to buy groceries for a few days, and to assemble his warm clothes and kit for the journey he was about to make. He got back to the office just before closing time and found out from his secretary that he had completely forgotten about his promise to be the guest speaker at the Hungarian-American Business People's monthly luncheon.

"What did Jenkins say?" The US Consul was the *ex officio* president of the Association.

"He tried to be polite, but I could hear from his tone of voice that he was none too pleased."

Khamani bit his lip. He could not afford such a *gaffe* and made a mental note to apologize profusely as soon as possible. "What excuse did you finally give him?"

"That you were in bed with high fever."

Next, Khamani asked the night watchman to help him attach his motor boat's trailer to the hitch of his SUV. Everybody in Budapest knew that the Iranian was an avid angler who often ventured out on the river in his little cabin cruiser, *Valliant,* in passionate pursuit of two hard to find fish: the *Roach* in the Danube and the even more elusive *Fogas* (pike-perch) in Lake Balaton.

The meeting with the guard, Ahmad, had gone off without incident, and the transfer of the 'dessert' from the Embassy car to Khamani's Range Rover had been easy. Everything had been packed into two large suitcases: two Berettas with silencers, and twelve spare clips of ammo, two rifles with sniper scopes, six standard US Army hand grenades, six stun grenades, two Scorpio submachine guns with lots of ammo, and two night vision goggles. For good measure, the guard had also brought along two flak jackets, just in case.

By nine that night, they had loaded their gear into the cabin cruiser and had launched the little vessel from the *Alsó Rakpart,* the so-called Lower Loading Wharf.

It had been bitterly cold on the water, but being busy and well clad had kept them warm. By ten, they had been in position off *Háros* and that is when the crushing boredom and discomfort of waiting in the dark for the *Maria* had begun.

They had had to concentrate hard to keep awake.

The vessel's sudden silent appearance on the main branch of the river shortly after midnight had galvanized them into action. Taking turns at the wheel as they followed her had kept them on their toes and by six in the morning they were pretty well exhausted. Shadowing a blacked out vessel in the pitch dark on a moonless, starless night was not child's play, even with night vision goggles and two men navigating.

They got a scare at *Dunaújváros.* On their first pass, they had missed the entrance to the shipyard towards which the *Maria* was headed, but they had scored on their second try.

They found a suitable mooring for *Valliant,* as instructed, and then drew lots for who would keep the first watch.

Khamani made sure that he lost.

Noblesse oblige. An officer is by definition a gentleman, and has to act like one.

The guard curled up in the cabin and was asleep in seconds.

At around eight, Al Adel called. The Iranian set the alarm on his watch for noon, bundled up and went to sleep on deck.

Ahmad made tea on the little Primus in the cabin at noon. They ate some sandwiches and took turns—four hours on, four off—watching for the *Maria*. At dusk, Khamani moved *Valliant* into the inlet, approached the false quay shielding the entrance to the Moscovitch compound and scanned the area with his binoculars. The *Maria* was at the quay near the compound and there was another vessel—a little tugboat—tied up near her.

The Iranian piloted *Valliant* back across the Danube to her previous night's mooring, made fast, and told Ahmad to bundle up for some more 'four on, four off' work during the night.

*   *   *

At two a.m., Juric slipped noiselessly into Al Adel's cabin. The Jordanian was in a deep slumber, knocked out cold by the sleeping potion Juric's wife had sprinkled into his tea at dinner.

Using a powerful flashlight, Juric searched the cabin and found what he was looking for under the Al Qaeda leader's pillow: a forty-five caliber Beretta. He gingerly extracted the weapon from under the sleeping man's head, removed the bullets and then replaced the gun.

He hoped the terrorist would not notice when he awoke that the Beretta was lighter than usual.

Then Juric went ashore and helped Dankovic pull Moscovitch's coat over his jogging outfit and to carry him on board the little tugboat tied up near the *Maria*.

CHAPTER 43

Dunaújváros, Thursday, October 25
Morning

Al Adel awoke feeling wonderfully rested. He realized that for the first time in days, he had been able to enjoy nine consecutive hours of deep, uninterrupted sleep.

He had surely needed it, as the stress under which he was operating was beginning to get to him.

Lately, things had started to go his way. Khamani was proving to be a solid ally, so he was no longer alone. The reliable Iranian, in possession of a considerable amount of much welcome artillery, was at his post, accompanied by a trained security guard from his embassy, another plus. The only negative was the Qods officer's report that conditions on board his little craft were uncomfortable; unfortunate, but unavoidable for the time being, but not for long, hopefully.

Al Adel liked Juric's plan, especially the part where the barge would provide the diversion that would almost guarantee their crossing into Croatia without difficulty.

Once there, another Al Qaeda cell would take over and the balance of power would shift away from The Butcher who was definitely Saddam's man.

So too, it seemed, was Juric. He didn't fool Al Adel—not for a second. As soon as he had felt the lightness of his weapon when he retrieved it from under his pillow in the morning, he knew that the Jurices had drugged him the previous night. Otherwise, he would have sensed someone trying to remove an object from under his head while he slept.

Experience had taught him that to know something without your enemy knowing that you knew gave you a tremendous advantage. He was, therefore, careful not to show that he was aware of Juric's act of disloyalty.

The missing bullets caused him little concern. He had hidden a spare clip for his Beretta under his mattress that he now gleefully snapped into his weapon.

The transfer of Moscovitch to the tugboat had been further proof that Juric, like Al Adel himself, was playing a double game and that he was planning to hand the scientist over to Saddam ultimately. The handover was likely to happen in one of two ways: with the extraction of the Canadian from Hungary by boat, or via ambulance. What mattered to the Jordanian was not how the scientist would get to his final destination, but how and by whom his talents would be used when he got there.

Al Adel guessed that Juric himself did not yet know which way he would jump.

'He's playing an intriguing and dangerous end-game' Al Adel said to himself 'in which my best defense is to do nothing, but observe and cooperate as long as possible.' He sighed and added 'At the end, I shall have to strike with lightning speed and make sure to destroy all evidence of my ever having participated in the game.'

He reminded himself not to forget about the Dankovices.

And Khamani.

The Jordanian was a careful, thorough professional and a ruthless, cold-blooded killer.

He called the Qods officer and told him to follow the tugboat and not the *Maria.*

*   *   *

Moscovitch kept telling his mother that he did not want to go back into the dark little room without the windows. "Mummy, it stinks in there, like when they repair the roads," he kept repeating. "It smells of tar and it's making me sick." His mother would not let go of his hand and pulled him down into the hole with her.

"What a crazy dream," Moscovitch muttered when he woke up with a splitting headache and suddenly realized that the dream had not really been a dream.

He was lying on a cot in total darkness, wearing his jogging outfit minus his shoes, and the air enveloping him was heavy with the smell of tar. Groping for his watch, he realized two things: his timepiece was no longer on his wrist, and his cot was gently rocking back and forth.

The swine must have drugged him and then, while he slept, had imprisoned him in a windowless room on some sort of a vessel.

Gone were his privileges as a much needed scientist, gone his hopes for making a lucrative deal for his freedom. Clearly, the reasons that had led to his being kidnapped were no longer valid. His captors were preparing to get rid of him, to terminate him with extreme prejudice, as Lonsdale would say.

Ah, Lonsdale! He had placed so much faith in the man's ability to find him, such high hopes of using him as an intermediary.

All in vain. The end was near.

"Don't panic," he commanded as claustrophobia threatened to engulf him. "Get up and take a look around."

He was in a space measuring approximately six feet by ten, roughly trapezoidal in shape as far as he could tell, with a heap of rusty chain in a corner.

He was in the chain locker of a boat!

'There must be a way in and out of here,' he reasoned and began to search for an opening. He found a door and turned the little handle. To his amazement, it gave way.

The opening led into the pilothouse of a tugboat behind which, in the galley, a bearded man he had never seen before was frying eggs.

"Sorry to have had to put you to sleep last night, but we had some traveling to do," the man said in accented English, his demeanor towards Moscovitch friendly. "How is your head?"

"Fine." Not surprisingly, knowing that he was not about to die just yet, Moscovitch's headache had evaporated.

"You hungry?"

"I sure am. What's the time, by the way? I seem to have lost my watch."

"Don't worry, I have your watch. It fell off when I put you to bed." He laughed. "Nice watch."

The Canadian looked around. The table in the small galley was set for two.

"The food will be ready in a few minutes. How do you like your eggs Jason?" He also pronounced it "Yason".

"Sunny side up." Moscovitch answered automatically. He was in shock. What was going on?

"The time is noon. You have slept about thirteen hours."

"But, but . . . where am I? And who are you?"

"I am, your jailer." The man let out a sort of grunt and added, ". . . as for where you are, go on deck while I finish up here and have a look around. Don't be too long. I don't want your eggs to get cold."

Moscovitch did as he was told.

The tugboat was anchored in the middle of a large, rectangular, covered basin, a gigantic hangar really. On the surrounding quays, rusty derricks, and abandoned cranes and old locomotives looked out over the oily, slimy brown water. The air was cold and fetid.

One side of the hangar was open to a sort of river and, on the side furthest from the water he could make out three semi-trailers on cinder blocks and connected by high walls, so he figured that the one in which they had been keeping him was one of them.

In one corner of the basin, tied up about a hundred yards away, he spotted another vessel: a large, dirty barge that seemed vaguely familiar. He could not tell whether there was anyone on board, though he did notice smoke curling from its stack.

Nothing is more desolate than an abandoned shipyard.

Moscovitch went back inside.

He got the message. It was suicide trying to escape.

CHAPTER 44

Budapest, Thursday, October 25
Noon

Lonsdale was tired, frustrated and worried. Police Colonel Nagy's prediction that a renamed *Maria* would suddenly materialize at *Mohács* on Thursday at dawn had not come true and everyone involved had been made to look ridiculous.

Morton had arranged for a platoon of SAS men to drive up from their base in Banja Luka, Croatia, to assist the Hungarians with taking over the barge by force if necessary, but their trip had been in vain.

When Lonsdale, who had motored down from Budapest the night before, had called him at six in the morning (midnight in Washington) to report total failure, he got an earful from his boss.

"What am I going to tell the Brits about this?"

"That we guessed wrong and that we need their men for another thirty-six hours."

"That's out of the question." Morton was adamant.

"Jim, that damned barge is still in Hungary and sooner or later it will come through here."

"But will Moscovitch be on it?"

Lonsdale was stumped. "I can't give you any guarantees."

There had been tension in the long silence that followed. Finally, Morton made up his mind. "I'll try to convince the Brits to give us another day, but I don't think I can ask for more." Lonsdale would have the help of the world's best anti-terrorist team until Friday morning. After that, he was on his own.

"With Delic, Drusza and Dadakne dead, Moscovitch's fate is becoming of less and less significance to us," Morton added in diplomatic jargon that Lonsdale understood only too well. "We are keeping the Opposition distracted with what we've learned from the Cizre raid and the information we are continuing to gain from the Klara Moscovitch fallout."

"Meaning?"

"Our friend Roger, the leader of her kidnap gang, was fairly high up in their organization. The content of his telephone's memory, coupled with the information his two captured colleagues are providing."

"Who, I presume, are already in Guantanamo." Lonsdale permitted himself this indiscretion because he was using his special scrambler phone and he was alone in his car.

"You presume correctly." Morton went on. "The information we are developing is leading us toward the region where the Taliban are active and where the brains of this entire enterprise seem to be residing."

"But Iraq is still involved?"

"Definitely, and we are keeping Saddam, busy trying to cover up."

Lonsdale drove back to Budapest. He had a luncheon scheduled with Jenkins and a conference with Frakkos in the afternoon.

The Deputy Chief of Station met Lonsdale at the Clark *Söröző* or beer-hall, a misnomer if there ever was one. The tavern is a pleasant, inner city restaurant that offers remarkably good Wiener Schnitzel a stone's throw from Roosevelt Square near the Chain Bridge.

Lonsdale briefed the DCS on where the search for Moscovitch stood and asked him for his impressions on fall out relating to the explosions and the hunt for terrorists.

"People are skittish, but not overly worried," Jenkins reported. "As far as we are concerned, what we're having trouble with is the attitude of the government and, more specifically with the lack of cooperation among the country's law enforcement agencies."

Lonsdale nodded vigorously. "Don't I know! I've spent three days watching Police Colonel Nagy tearing his hair out trying to coordinate the activities of the river and regular police, the border patrol and the counterterrorist service. He's struggling away in this small office, using an antiquated communications system that greatly delays inter service communication and the dissemination of vital, real-time information."

"Is he making any headway?" Jenkins swallowed a mouthful of schnitzel and mashed potatoes, and took a gulp of his beer.

Lonsdale shook his head. "Whose fault is it, do you think?" he asked.

"Kupa's, the Minister of the Interior's. He's too weak." The consul pushed his plate away. "What you had to say about the mystery of the *Maria* reminded me of an incident I think you should know about. It may be nothing, but one never knows." He shrugged his shoulders deprecatingly.

"Fire away, I'm all ears."

"Remember the Iranian I told you about?"

Lonsdale grinned and gave him a wink. "You mean your rival?"

Jenkins was not amused. "The guy is a chartered and active member of the US-Hungary Business People's Association. He does good work for the group and is usually very reliable."

"Go on."

"He was scheduled to be the guest speaker at our weekly lunch Tuesday, but he didn't show."

"He must have forgotten."

"No, not him. He is always very reliable and punctual, so I called his office after lunch. Frankly, I was quite peeved. He had left me holding the bag in front of a bunch of important people and I had to make an improvised speech that was far from my best."

"What did you do?"

"I sort of intimated to his secretary that I was pissed. She told me he was in bed with the flu, that he had a high fever and must have forgotten."

"So?"

"I live in an apartment on *Belgrád Rakpart,* Belgrade Quay."

"If your apartment faces the Danube you must have a beautiful view of the river, the Castle and the Fishermen's Bastion, Buda-side."

"It does and I do and I love walking home in the fall at dusk. Wednesday night, I did just that. Because it was on my way, I decided to stop by Khamani's car rental agency on *Galamb* Street to see how he was doing."

Lonsdale held his breath. He thought he knew what was coming.

Jenkins went on. "I got there just after six and they were already closed, but the night watchman who knows me was still there and he came out to say hello. I asked him how his boss was doing. Fine, he said, after giving me a funny look. He said Khamani had gone fishing. I looked over to where Khamani parks his little fishing runabout. It was not there."

Lonsdale's inner voice exploded in his brain. 'Too many coincidences involving Iranians' it screamed.

"Describe the vessel and tell me its name," he snapped at Jenkins and picked up his phone.

He was dialing Colonel Nagy before Jenkins had stopped talking.

CHAPTER 45

Budapest, Thursday, October 25
Afternoon/evening

Klara Moscovitch's plane arrived in Budapest shortly after eleven Thursday morning. She cleared Customs and Immigration quickly and, on her way to her hotel, the Kempinsky, called the Canadian Embassy, gave her name and demanded to speak with the Consul.

"This is Thérèse Lapointe." The voice was unfriendly, the tone cold.

"Are you the Consul?"

"Yes I am."

"Do you know who *I* am?"

"Yes I do. You are Jason Moscovitch's mother. How can I be of help?"

"I would like to make an appointment to see you."

"Where are you at present?"

"In a taxi on my way to the hotel."

The Consul could not believe her ears. "Here in Budapest?"

"Where else?"

A very long pause. Then, finally: "Would two-thirty o'clock suit you?"

"That would be fine. I'll see you then."

Ms. Lapointe suddenly remembered her manners. "Do you know where we are located?"

"I don't, but I'm sure my driver does." Klara Moscovitch hung up.

At the Kempinsky she had a spot of luck. Her room was ready. She ordered a sandwich and coffee from Room Service and then had a bath, luxuriating in the foamy, perfumed, hot water as long as time would allow. After all that she had been through since Sunday, her nerves were frayed and she needed every moment of rest and relaxation she could get.

She was out the door, sandwich in hand, by two pm.

At precisely half past two, Klara Moscovitch marched into Thérèse Lapointe's office in a killer mood, ready to take on the world.

After a perfunctory 'How do you do' and having refused the offer of coffee, Klara Moscovitch got down to business. "Where is my son?" was her opening salvo.

The Consul did not know what to say. She finally managed a very tentative "I'm afraid I have no idea."

This inane reply enraged her visitor to a point where she could barely control her fury. "This is all you have to say after you've had six weeks to find him?"

She tried not to shout, knowing that in her present state of fatigue, she was barely in control of her emotions. "You sit behind your desk in your snug little office in these palatial surroundings, for which I, a taxpayer, foot the bill. For the last six weeks, you have done nothing for my son except arrange for a bumbling, half-baked private detective to come to my house to soft-talk me. Shame on you," she hissed and threw some sheets from her briefcase on the Consul's desk. "Where is he anyway?"

"Who?"

"Don't get cute with me! You know damned well I'm talking about Bernard Kane."

Thérèse Lapointe decided to call for help. She rang her secretary. "Bring me the Kane file please, Evelyn. Make sure it contains the latest address we have for him." She hung up and picked up the papers on her desk. "What are these?" She had been taught that in crisis situations it was best to keep your opponent talking while you waited for help to arrive.

"Copies of the press releases about my son and the way he and I have been treated by the Canadian and US governments. They will be sent out first thing tomorrow unless I hear from Mr. Kane personally before then."

Lapointe then made a big mistake. She said, "You have his phone number. Why don't you call his cell?"

She bit her lip, but it was too late. Mrs. Moscovitch pounced.

"How do you know that?"

"When he visited me here some weeks ago he told me you had his coordinates."

"I've called him repeatedly, but all I get is his voice mail."

The secretary entered, file in hand, and the Consul began to feel braver. "You should leave him a message then," she said smiling primly and turned to her assistant. "Well?"

"We have him living at the *Béke* Hotel." She announced.

"Where is that?"

The woman looked at the file and read out the address.

Without another word, Klara Moscovitch stormed out of the room. Seething, she swore that, one day, she would exact revenge on these incompetent, insensitive bureaucrats who did nothing but spend the public's money and pass their time thinking up ways of improving their own lot and not that of those whom they were being paid to serve.

She was still very upset when she got back to her hotel after an interminable cab ride exacerbated by an excruciatingly long wait at the western end of the tunnel leading to the Chain Bridge.

She found Thursday evening traffic in Budapest not at all to her liking.

"A nice, hot cup of tea and some pastries is what I need. It would calm my nerves," she murmured as she strode into the lobby and selected a comfortable armchair to rest in.

The waiter took her order almost immediately, and when her tea and scones arrived, she sat back with a sigh to observe the passing scene. It pleased her that she could see what was going on around her through the foliage of a chyferella plant while she, herself, remained half-hidden.

That was the reason why Lonsdale did not spot her when he returned to the Kempinsky, bone weary and hurting, after a day of pointless and needless arguments with the authorities that had accentuated his sense of frustration.

Of course, the soreness of his ribs and the dull, pulsating pain in his bruised cheekbone had not helped matters either. The entire world seemed to have conspired against him and he was beginning to feel that he was losing his edge.

Even Morton appeared to have lost confidence in him and was in the process of pirouetting away. Police Colonel Nagy was finding him too demanding, and the SAS people, twirling their thumbs in *Mohács,* had been openly hostile when he had spoken with them earlier.

The meeting with Frakkos at the *Pilvax* Coffee Shop had not gone well either.

"George sitting in *Esztergom* watching for *Maria,* yes?" the driver had said. "So I send less experienced man to follow ambulance."

"What ambulance?"

"You remember I giving ambulance driver at *Rókus* hospital my telephone number, yes?"

Lonsdale had nodded.

"He calling me to tell he has same client as for Arab last time to meet him in *Dunaújváros* for new job." When Frakkos became excited, his sentence construction became almost unintelligible. "I sending Imre, less experienced man, to follow the ambulance."

"When was this?"

"Just after three o'clock."

Lonsdale had looked at his watch. "That was an hour ago. Have you heard from him since?"

"No, but I keeping you posted if I hear."

Lonsdale had strolled back to the Kempinsky. 'Dunaújváros' he had kept repeating as he trudged along *Váci* Street. 'It rings a bell. Was it something the late lamented Amina had said?'

He was tired and cold and old and for the life of him, he could not remember.

CHAPTER 46

Dunaújváros, Thursday, October 25
Late afternoon

Dankovic's Trabant was a rickety old thing, ready to give up the ghost, but Juric had no trouble driving it. He was good with old machinery.

Gazing out of window, Al Adel sat beside him surveying the dreary countryside. There was not much to see. Just as well, dusk was closing in fast.

After leaving the compound, they had turned onto the peninsula's main road the continuation of which, *Magyar* Boulevard, ran into the M6, the Highway to Budapest.

Juric had chosen the spot where he was to meet the ambulance well. The M6 *Csárda* was a glorified tavern, catering to truckers hungry for a bite and a pint in one room, and to wayfarers and locals wanting something more sophisticated in another. There was ample parking behind the building and, on some weekends, itinerant gypsy musicians provided local color.

After a twenty-minute drive during which neither Al Adel, nor Juric spoke, they pulled in behind the restaurant and stopped at a spot from where they could see the traffic coming into the lot. The ambulance arrived a few minutes before five and the driver went in to slake the thirst he had worked up during the fifty-minute drive from Budapest.

Juric made no move to go in after him.

Sure enough, thirty seconds later a black Volkswagen Jetta appeared, drove by the ambulance and then backed up to park two rows behind it.

The driver did not get out.

Al Adel looked at Juric who nodded several times in rapid succession, his lips twisted into a bitter, derisory smile.

"Police?" Al Adel whispered.

Juric shook his head. "No. Free enterprisers, but it makes no difference. I'll deal with it."

He went into the tavern and sought out the ambulance driver at the bar.

"Thanks for being punctual."

The man was pleased. "Don't mention it." He downed his beer. "Where do we go from here?"

"I'm waiting for a colleague who knows the way." Juric paid for the driver's beer. "When you're ready, just drive out of the lot, turn right and wait for a few minutes. I'm sure my guy will be here soon. He has a red Trabant. Just follow him when he shows. I'll be in the car."

The driver got off his stool and hitched up his pants. "On my way. Just give me time to have a pee." He headed for the washrooms.

Juric returned to the Trabant to consult with his cohort, but before he could say anything Al Adel staggered out of the little car, faking the gait of someone who was slightly under the weather. As he stumbled past the Jetta without glancing at it his peripheral vision picked out the driver in his seat clearly. The man was pretending to be searching his pockets, presumably for a cigarette.

The Jordanian shuffled by. He kept going until he reached a row of cars that hid him from the Jetta driver's view.

He put on his gloves.

The ambulance man appeared and climbed into his vehicle. The Jetta's tail-lights winked white as the driver turned on the ignition and then shifted gears, past REVERSE. Al Adel stepped toward the Jetta and reached the vehicle's side just as the ambulance was beginning to move forward.

He knocked on the Jetta's left front window. The window came down and the driver turned toward the Jordanian. "What do you want?" he snarled.

Al Adel shot him through the forehead with his silencer-equipped Beretta 42. The dying driver fell away from behind the steering wheel. Al Adel opened the door, reached inside the vehicle and pushed the man's body under the dashboard. He closed the window, turned off the ignition, and withdrew the key.

He walked away slowly, stumbling every now and then, keeping up the pretence that he was drunk. Before getting into the Trabant, he locked the Jetta by pressing the appropriate button on the car's remote.

Juric felt sick to his stomach. Al Adel had just sent him a deadly message that went something like this. "I know what you did to me and my weapon during the night. Fuck with me again and I'll kill you."

They got back to the compound a few minutes past six.

Juric had the driver park his ambulance behind Moscovitch's erstwhile semi. He did not want those on board the *Maria* to see the vehicle nor did he want the driver to see his two vessels.

He climbed in beside the man and offered him a cigarette.

"I don't smoke."

Juric smiled. "Good for you. Nor do I. Now tell me, what do we do next?"

The driver looked at his watch. "Everywhere, the border guards change shifts at eleven, so we can cross any time after that."

"And when does their shift end?"

"It's an eight hour shift with a half hour food break that the guards take in turn in the middle of their shifts. That way, there is at least one guard on duty at all times."

"So, to be safe and to make sure we get to deal with the guards you know, we shouldn't try to cross between two and four."

"That's right."

"Where do you want to cross?"

"At a small town called *Udvar*, about ten kilometers south of *Mohács*. I know just about every border guard who works at the *Udvar* crossing."

Juric pretended to be pleased, though he couldn't have cared less. His plans had drastically changed as soon as he had discovered that the ambulance was being followed. "Great. Do you have the necessary papers?"

The driver produced them. "You told me the patient is in his early thirties, so I had them made up that way. Do you see?"

Juric nodded.

"What about you and me and the ambulance? Do we need passports?"

"The two of us do. The ambulance's papers are in the glove compartment."

Juric was happy. He now had two ways of getting Moscovitch out of Hungary: by boat and via ambulance, albeit the ambulance route seemed to be compromised.

Decision time.

He looked his watch. "It's seven o'clock. We need a couple of hours at the most to reach the border, so we have lots of time to eat something. Come and have dinner with us."

He told the man to drive ahead and stop at the end of the line of semis. When the unsuspecting driver bent down to pull up the handbrake, Juric shot him through the right temple.

Not too messy.

The Bosnian emptied the glove compartment of all documents, searched the dead driver's pockets and confiscated his identity papers, dragged the corpse over to the passenger seat, fastened the seat belt around it and opened all the windows, including the ones in the rear doors.

He then drove the ambulance onto the quay of the lot next to the shipyard, accelerated and jumped free at the last moment.

The vehicle plunged into the river and sank within minutes.

Juric picked himself up, took off his gloves and slapped them against his trousers and pea jacket to get as much of the dirt off his clothes as possible.

By the time he got back to the *Maria*, dinner was over. However, his wife had kept a generous helping of food for him and Moscovitch that she was reheating when Al Adel came in, looking anxious.

"What's the plan now?" he inquired.

"First I'm going to grab a quick bite to eat, then I'll take some food to Dankovic so he can feed Moscovitch."

"His wife not here?"

"Gone back home to Bosnia for good yesterday."

"When are you planning to get underway with the *Maria*?"

Juric glanced at the galley clock. "Within the hour."

"What about our little problem?"

"It has been resolved."

"And Dankovic? He knows too much."

Juric nodded. "I know, but leave him be. He can't hurt us once we're gone."

Al Adel said nothing.

*   *   *

The Butcher had carefully handpicked the young and athletic lab technician/bodyguard, Omar Al Malaki, for membership in the team that had boarded the *Maria* in Novi Sad two weeks earlier.

He was family; he hailed from Tikrit.

Al Malaki had special talents. He was an expert shooter who, in addition to Arabic, spoke English and Hungarian, a language he had picked up while working in Budapest for some years. This made him an efficient information-gatherer.

His cell phone was special too. It could not ring, only vibrate; it could receive calls from everywhere, but could dial only one number: The Butcher's.

The technician had two identical overalls. When one got dirty, he switched to the other while the first one was in the wash. He was dressed in overalls day and night, always sleeping in one of the garments or the other.

He kept the cell phone on his thigh in the pocket of his garment. This enabled him to 'feel' calls to his cell 24/7 without those around him becoming aware of them.

The reason why the wily Hassani had put these complex arrangements in place was that he did not trust either Juric or Al Adel. He wanted to have the means by which to know what was happening to Moscovitch at all times, especially when he, Hassani, was not present.

241

Whenever the technician felt a 'vibe', he'd pretend he had stomach cramps and would go to the washroom. From there he would call Hassani back, and report.

Hassani would not call more often than twice a day and only when he was away from the Moscovitch compound.

Friday evening, Al Malaki did not wait to be 'vibed'.

He called The Butcher shortly after eight with an update on events.

"We're abandoning the compound. We've been ordered to board the *Maria*. We're moving out."

"Where is Moscovitch?"

"Moscovitch, Juric and Al Adel are on board a tugboat that also belongs to Juric. He asked me to go with them. The rest of the group is on board the barge. Mrs. Juric will be steering, and Youssouf."

"Who's Youssouf?"

"The guard who has papers that say he is a mate."

"Oh yes. I remember him now. Where are you all headed?"

"To a town called *Mohács* where we hope to cross into Croatia."

Hassani instantly grasped what was going on.

He explained to Al Malaki that the barge was a diversion to draw the authorities' attention away from the tugboat. Al Adel would help Juric spirit Moscovitch out of Hungary. He would then kill the Bosnian and Al Qaeda would end up with Moscovitch.

Checkmate. Iraq would lose the game.

Unless, of course Juric killed Al Adel first.

Or if someone would come to Moscovitch's rescue at the last minute.

"Like me," said Omar Al Malaki.

"That's right. Don't let Moscovitch out of your sight my son and help Iraq in its quest for glory. I will personally reward you with ten thousand US dollars and a big promotion if you succeed."

CHAPTER 47

Budapest, Thursday, October 25 (cont'd)
Evening

Klara Moscovitch sighed as the desired effects of the hot tea spread through her tired body and her muscles relaxed. She looked around the lobby. It was certainly an elegant place, but cold and somewhat overwhelming. 'Typically *Kempinsky*, typically German' she said to herself. A plant was partially blocking her line of sight and she shifted in her armchair to improve her view of the entrance.

Her eyes were slightly unfocused as she stared straight ahead and watched as a smartly dressed, familiar-looking man came through the revolving door and was greeted with obvious respect. He said something to the bellhop, they both laughed, and the man shook his head. He then quickly disappeared from view.

It took her sleepy brain a few seconds to digest this visual information. By the time she reached the reception desk after extricating herself from her armchair and circumnavigating the coffee table in front of it, all she could see was the man's back as he stepped into one of the elevators as its doors were closing.

She turned to the clerk on duty. "Can you give me Mr. Kane's room number please?"

"I'm afraid we don't give out room numbers, but you can ring him." The clerk tried to be helpful. "Feel free to use the house telephones. They're over there, on the ledge by the wall." He pointed across the space behind her.

She walked over and picked up one of the instruments.

"We have no-one registered under the name of Bernard Kane," the operator informed her.

"Bernard Kane, from Montreal. Please check again." Klara insisted.

The operator was back on line a few seconds later. "I'm sorry madam, I checked again, but there's no-one registered here by that name."

"But I just saw the man in the lobby." Klara's voice began to rise.

"Perhaps he was just passing through the lobby or visiting,"

"Nonsense," Klara snapped. "I saw him take the elevator up."

The operator's voice turned icy cold. "May I suggest you check at Reception and have them verify recent arrivals. It always takes some time for us to receive check-in information."

Mrs. Moscovitch slammed down the receiver.

What now?

She spied the bellhop with whom the man had been talking.

'Calm down,' she commanded herself. 'You catch more flies with honey than with vinegar.'

"Peter," she called out after glancing at his name tag.

"Yes, madam."

"I need your help." She held out a five-dollar bill. "I saw you joking with Mr. Kane in the lobby a few moments ago. I want to send him a bottle of champagne because it's his birthday today. Can you find out his room number for me? They can't seem to locate it at Reception."

"That's because the guest I was joking with is not Mr. Kane." The bellhop took the five dollars. "He is Mr. Philip Johnston, an important guest. High up in the US State Department."

"Johnston? Are you sure?"

"Absolutely, madam. We all know about Mr. Johnston, a very good friend of the American ambassador." The boy was bursting with pride. It sure paid to listen to gossip.

Klara Moscovitch hesitated. Could it be that she was mistaken? There was only one way to find out.

*   *   *

Lonsdale was undressing, painfully and slowly. He hung up his coat, took off his tie, shirt, and jacket and then went to the bathroom for a couple of painkillers.

His ribs were killing him, his cheekbone was aflame and fatigue was making him feel nauseous.

Colonel Nagy had told him not to expect much from the river blockade at *Mohács*. The town was an important port, traffic was heavy, customs and border police facilities, housed in an obsolete building that had been slated for demolition ages ago, totally inadequate for the volume they were required to handle.

Communications with Budapest and Central Terrorist Command? When the Internet worked, good.

"And when it is down?" Lonsdale asked.

"Via cell phone."

Christ Almighty, Lonsdale had said to himself, here we are, fighting terrorists who have tremendously sophisticated communications expertise, and we are using means straight out of the Dark Ages, or almost.

To complicate matters, Nagy had gone on to say, the Danube was exceptionally wide at *Mohács* so that erecting an effective temporary physical barrier across the river was out of the question.

"What the hell are we doing then? Why are we working so hard at pissing up a rope?" Lonsdale said in English.

Nagy had guffawed. He loved to learn colorful slang expressions that had no equivalents in Hungarian. "Let's summarize the situation, shall we?"

"Go ahead."

"The men you captured in Cizre and in the States can't help you find Moscovitch, even if they wanted to, because they are too far removed from the field. The people who knew where he was being kept are dead—at least those about whom we know."

"Except the Jurices."

"Bravo. That's my point. It no longer matters whether Moscovitch is on that damned barge or not, and he probably is not any more, because all we want now is to capture someone alive who knows where he's gone."

"What are you saying?"

"Sooner or later the *Maria* will reappear either with the Jurices on board or not. Even if they're not on board, there will be people on board who will be able to tell us where the Jurices have gone."

"I agree."

"Then stop worrying about not finding Moscovitch because I can guarantee you that we *will* find the *Maria*."

"Oh?"

"You just can't hide a vessel that size on the Danube for long." Nagy took a deep breath. "When we do find her let's not attack openly. Let's just identify her when she gets near *Mohács* and let's let her pass through. We can then ambush her quietly south of the town where the river narrows. For this, you will have to redeploy your SAS people and change their instructions.

"And take everybody prisoner."

"Alive."

Lonsdale was mulling over Nagy's idea while trying to remove the large bandage covering most of his left rib cage. He was wondering about how to take a much-needed bath because he could smell that he stank to high heaven. Problem was that if he got into the bathtub alone he would never be able to climb out of it solo in his present condition.

A shower, perhaps?

There was a knock on his door.

May be the maid with the turn down service.

"Who is it?"

"Mr. Philip Johnston, I need to talk to you. I am Klara Moscovitch."

Lonsdale reacted swiftly. He grabbed the Sig Sauer off the night table, cocked it and sidled over to the wall next to the door away from the knob. Pistol at the ready, he crouched low, right knee down, reached over and tore the door open with his left hand.

Klara Moscovitch stepped into the room and turned to face Lonsdale. What she saw made her gasp and cover her mouth in shock. "Oh my God, oh my God, what have they done to you," she finally blurted.

Lonsdale uncocked his weapon, lowered it, and closed and locked the door. "Do I look that bad?" He forced a grin. It hurt plenty.

"You need a doctor, you should see a doctor," was all that Klara could manage.

The face and chest of the half-naked man facing her was covered with black, blue and yellow bruises just about everywhere. His right cheek was swollen, his red eyes rimmed with fatigue. Although he made an effort to pull himself together when he sat down on his bed, she saw that his hand was trembling when he laid his weapon on the night table.

"You're just in time to help me take a bath," he joked. "I stink."

Involuntarily, her eyes welled with tears. He looked so helpless.

"Stand up," she commanded gently, "and let me help you off with your clothes."

Lonsdale obeyed. He was far too tired to resist. She ran his bath for him while he brushed his teeth then let him tell her about how he got hurt and where he thought her son might be. She helped him stand up, gently washed his whole body and let him lean on her as he struggled to step out of the tub.

She patted him dry ever so carefully, led him to his bed and lay down beside him with her back to him. He put his arms around her and she snuggled into him—spooning.

"Thank you," he whispered softly into her ear.

"Don't mention it."

Within minutes, they were both fast asleep.

The phone rang a few minutes before one a.m. It was Frakkos.

"They found Imre, yes? Dead. Shot in head. Customers from *Csárda* found him in parking lot when tavern closing."

"What parking lot? What Csárda?"

"Near *Dunaújváros* by the highway, yes?"

"Where are you?"

"At home, getting dressed. Imre's wife called me after police called her. I driving her there."

247

"Where is 'there' exactly? I'm coming too. I'll drive myself."

"Take autoroute M6 Budaside. Just before getting to *Dunaújváros* watch for sign *Magyar utca*. Tavern is at intersection, left hand side. Big sign says *Csárda*."

"How far is it from here to there?"

"From your hotel, sixty kilometers."

"I'll be there within the hour." Lonsdale looked at Klara. She was up and wide awake.

She met his gaze. "I'm going with you. You owe me at least that."

He couldn't argue.

CHAPTER 48

Dunaújváros, Thursday, October 25 (cont'd)
Night

Klara Moscovitch marveled at her companion's recuperative powers. Six hours' sleep had made a new man out of him: clear-eyed, vigorous, and decisive. Even the swelling of his cheek seemed to have subsided somewhat.

Before getting into his Audi in the hotel garage, Lonsdale had handed her his phone.

"When we get cell coverage outside dial this number." He rattled it off while he maneuvered out of the building.

"It's ringing."

"Ask for Mr. Jenkins and when he comes on line say 'I am scrambling' and press the little red button in the middle at the top. Then give me the phone."

She did so. He saw the scrambler light glowing so he cut to the chase.

"You know who this is."

"Yes, sir."

"We got a break in the kidnap case and I need a secure multiple communications facility in *Dunaújváros* immediately. Drive down

249

there in the Battle Wagon and bring your communications guy with you."

"Full Metal Jacket?"

"Affirmative, Full Metal Jacket."

'Where do I meet you?"

Lonsdale told him about the *Csárda* and hung up. He handed Klara the phone without taking his eyes off the road. They were on the open highway with not a vehicle in sight and he was driving at a speed of one hundred and eighty kilometers per hour.

The Audi rocketed along, hugging the road, steady as a rock.

'Who is this man sitting beside me?' Klara Moscovitch asked herself. 'What is his real name? Where is he from? Whom does he work for?' Out loud, she asked: "What is a Battle Wagon?"

He gave her a quick sideways glance. "I'm sure you've seen them. All our embassies have at least one. They are big black SUV-looking panel truck kind of vehicles with tinted windows and a flashing blue light on top. They are equipped with secure and rapid multiple communications facilities and other toys that are nice to have when one finds oneself having problems."

She wanted to ask what 'Full Metal Jacket' meant, but the phone rang.

"Answer it and say 'Mr. Johnston's phone' then ask who is calling."

It was Colonel Nagy.

"The river police has located *Valliant,* Khamani's boat. She was tied up on the left, or west, bank of the Duna near the town of *Dunaújváros.*"

"Did you say *Dunaújváros?*" Lonsdale wanted to be sure he had heard right. This was the second time that someone had mentioned the town's name within the hour.

Was this a coincidence, or did it mean something?

And then there was also this constant, nagging feeling whenever he heard the name that he had seen it in writing.

For Lonsdale there was no such thing as coincidence.

"Yes, *Dunaújváros.* A patrol boat spotted her at nine last night."

Lonsdale exploded. "God dammit! That was six hours ago."

"Yes, yes, I know, but they only told me about it ten minutes ago."

"How come?" Lonsdale could barely control his anger.

"The usual communications fuckup." Nagy tried to sound apologetic. "I'm afraid there is some more bad news. As instructed, the patrol boat did not approach; it sailed by the target and then kept it under discreet passive surveillance from a distance."

"And?"

"The men's shift in the patrol boat ended at eleven. They radioed for instructions."

Lonsdale finished the sentence for him. "But nobody wanted to make a decision because the matter was being handled by you, and you were not available."

"I was available all right. It's just that nobody called me."

'So *Valliant* sailed away and nobody bothered to follow it." Lonsdale could barely keep the sarcasm out of his voice. "One last question Colonel. Did your brave patrollers perchance notice any other vessels in the vicinity of the target?"

"I'm afraid not."

'What monumental incompetence' was what Lonsdale was bursting to scream for all to hear. Instead, he said "Thank you for calling me so promptly Colonel. I am sure you are trying to do your best under very difficult circumstances."

A long silence. Then: "Shall I send a police car around to your hotel to help you get to *Dunaújváros* quickly?"

"Thank you, but that won't be necessary. You see, I'm in *Dunaújváros* already. Just find someone who can show me the spot where *Valliant* was tied up when last seen."

CHAPTER 49

Dunaújváros, Friday, October 26,
Dawn

The crew on board the police launch, a sergeant-helmsman, a corporal and a constable, were surly and uncooperative.

Lonsdale did not blame them.

They, and six of their colleagues, had the impossible task of patrolling a sixty kilometer long stretch of river along which there were several very busy locks. Their shift was not long enough to do their job properly. Eight hours on board a vessel capable of a sustained cruising speed of only fifteen knots gave them sufficient time to run up and down 'their' entire stretch of water, but only once a day.

Provided, of course, they did not have to attend to extra tasks, such as sorting out foul-ups and quarrels at locks or searching for vessels such as the *Valliant* and the *Maria*.

Lonsdale started by explaining why he was looking for the boats and mollified the crew by speaking in Hungarian. When they discovered that Klara Moscovitch, whose son was the target of the search, also spoke Hungarian a little, as did the US consul, Jenkins, who was accompanying them, they became friendlier.

"Stupid people, those officers at headquarters," the sergeant said. "It's easier to do a good job when you're told why it has to be done."

Then he explained that although they had spotted *Valliant* on their way up river around noon, they had paid no attention to it until the order to look for her had reached them at five in the afternoon on their way back down.

"But you didn't report the sighting until nine. Why?"

"I wanted to be sure that the boat was still where we had seen it first. We only sighted it again from upriver at nine."

"What happened then?"

"We kept watching her for an hour and a half. Then our shift ended. We asked for instructions, but got none."

"So you went home."

"After our shift finished at eleven, yes."

"And here you are again, three hours later, because of us. I'm truly sorry."

The sergeant shrugged. "Orders is orders. We don't live far from here." He started the engine and swung the wheel. "You've seen where *Valliant* was tied up. Now let me tell you what I think."

"About what?"

"Although they had a couple of fishing lines in the water, we saw nobody come out of the cabin to check them. If you ask me, the the people in that boat were watching the inlet opposite to where *Valliant* was moored. We should have a look at what's in there. You interested?"

Lonsdale nodded emphatically.

The sergeant deftly maneuvered his craft across the Danube and entered the inlet. Lonsdale was surprised by how much reflected starlight there was on the water by which to steer.

Cautiously, they started moving up the inlet.

"Most of the buildings on your right are abandoned factories and warehouses belonging to the State Property Agency." The sergeant was at ease in his role as tour guide. It was obvious that he knew the area well. "One of the few factories that were still operating in this area was a sort of textile mill, but I heard the SPA closed down that one too. That was a month ago."

"What's next to it?"

"An abandoned shipyard."

"Doesn't look abandoned to me." Lonsdale observed as they chugged by it. "Look. There are crime lights on."

"The SPA must have installed them recently. They also own the shipyard."

Lonsdale felt as if somebody had tapped him on the head sharply with a ruler—like his elementary school teacher used to when he failed to see the obvious. He suddenly realized what it was that had been bothering his subconscious about *Dunaújváros*.

The Amina transcripts!

In one of their discussion about invoices, Drusza and Dadakne had had a lengthy verbal exchange about a price quotation from a company called DVV, *Dunaújvárosi Villanyszerelő Vállalat*. This local electrical contractor had been bidding on the job of installing three powerful crime light units mounted on six meter high poles.

"Slow down, but don't stop." Barely able to contain his excitement, Lonsdale forced himself to speak to the helmsman with calm, but with emphasis. "I think we have just found what we are looking for. Go further up the inlet while I call for reinforcements."

He took a map from his pocket and studied it for a few seconds by the light of the dashboard lamp. Then he turned to Jenkins." Where is the Battle Wagon?"

"Standing by at the *Csárda*, manned by my communications guy."

"Call him. I want to tell him how to get here fast."

* * *

The plan Lonsdale and Colonel Nagy developed to capture the shipyard and its occupants was simple.

The Battle Wagon would be used as a communications center.

The police would seal off the compound's exit to *Ruhagyár* Street and would then advance on the buildings. Lonsdale, Jenkins, the sergeant and the constable would do the same, but from the Danube side.

The corporal and Klara Moscovitch would remain on board the launch that would anchor in the middle of the inlet and watch for escapees who might try to swim for it.

The two teams took half an hour to get into position and to establish reliable communications with each other.

It took another thirty minutes to penetrate the compound and to comb through the semi trailers on the lot.

To no avail.

All the birds had flown, including the Jurices and the deckhands and, presumably, Moscovitch.

His mother was allowed to inspect her son's 'prison' where she confirmed that the few sheets of paper that had been left behind were, indeed, in her son's handwriting.

She was also shown through the four semi trailers on the lot that were lined up parallel to the water. She was not allowed to enter the semi-trailer in which the watchman/caretaker's body was found, shot through the head from behind while eating his evening meal and studying a road map of southern Hungary. A closer examination revealed that the village of *Udvar*, a border-crossing point between Hungary and Croatia, was circled in pencil on the map.

There was no sign of any ambulance or of the *Maria*, or any indication that she had ever been there.

CHAPTER 50

Dunaújváros, Friday, October 26
Dawn (cont'd)

Before getting underway, Juric had gone to say goodbye to Dankovic and to pay the couple for their services. The deal was for the caretaker to leave for Bosnia to join his wife there as soon as the *Maria* left.

Unfortunately, Al Adel had seen to it that that would never happen.

Juric was neither a complicated nor a sophisticated man, but he was worldly, shrewd and determined. Although The Cause to him was everything, he had set certain parameters within which to operate and senseless, wanton killings were definitely not within them.

Yes, it had been necessary to kill the ambulance driver and the man who had followed him, because if found alive, they would have been able to lead the authorities to Moscovitch.

Now that the Dankovices. Drusza, Delic and Dadakne were dead, Hassani was safe. Since the rest of those involved would leave within the hour and disappear soon thereafter there had definitely been no need for Dankovic to die.

On the other hand, one never knew, did one? Better safe than sorry.

Juric had to admire Al Adel's professional, thorough, ruthlessness in eradicating all clues that might help the police.

A ruthless thoroughness he, Juric, might have to deal with sooner than later!

That is why he decided to bring along young Omar Al Malaki. Although the The Butcher and the technician had shown no indication that they had a special relationship, the crafty Juric, well aware of the Arab way of doing things, had correctly deduced that the technician's inclusion in the *Maria*'s crew had not been a random choice.

As Master of his ship, the Bosnian had had no difficulty finding out that the young man, like Saddam Hussein Al Tikriti and Barzan Hassani Al Tikriti, was also from Tikrit—his full name on his papers had said so: Omar Al Malaki Al Tikriti.

Logically, the young man was not only The Butcher's spy but, probably, also his distant relative.

*   *   *

When Al Adel realized that the tugboat had turned north rather than south after emerging from the inlet into the main stream of the Danube, he was surprised, but not particularly concerned.

He had confidence in Juric as a tactician and this confidence was well-placed. The Bosnian had an uncanny sense of timing and purpose.

He was also lucky.

His instincts had made him order the *Maria* to leave the Moscovitch compound earlier than necessary for the vessel to reach *Mohács* around seven in the morning. As a result, she was not spotted because she was gone by the time the police launch discovered *Valliant*.

As for the tugboat, Juric had temporized, postponing its departure for as long as possible because he needed time to ascertain that there were adequate provisions and fuel on board.

There was also the problem of gathering up Moscovitch's working papers, of providing adequate 'street clothes' for him and of making sure that he could not free himself. Juric had left him locked in the crew's cabin, but he had not been happy with the arrangement.

Too loosey-goosey.

Once underway, he had asked Omar Al Malaki to see to it that Moscovitch could cause no trouble during their forthcoming journey. The Iraqi, a pragmatist, made short shrift of the assignment. In addition to locking the scientist in the crew's cabin, he handcuffed him to the lower bunk bed.

Al Adel had surprised Juric by insisting on helping, and would not leave his side for a moment. This had meant that Juric did not get a chance to review his plans in peace and had to improvise as he went along.

His luck was still holding when the tugboat, called *Bulldog*, finally cast off around midnight, by which time the river police watching *Valliant* had gone.

The tugboat was not spotted.

The Bosnian's plan was brilliant in its simplicity.

It called for his wife to get the *Maria* to *Mohács* around seven a.m., just as the day's traffic would start picking up. With the boat made fast, she would go to the border police office like any other Master and leave her papers with the inspector on duty. Then, claiming that nature was calling, she would ask to be excused.

She would cross to the other side of the building using the corridor leading to the washrooms, exit and take a cab or a bus to *Udvar*, a border crossing about ten kilometers south of *Mohács*.

Once there, she would walk across to Croatia and either hitch a ride or take a bus to Osijek, the fourth largest city in the country, about sixty kilometers south of the Hungarian border, where she knew people who would help her disappear.

The *Maria* and all those on board would be left behind to fend for themselves.

Juric had replayed this scenario in his mind's eye a dozen times.

He could see the riot police and SWAT team positioning themselves for an attack as soon as word reached them that a vessel resembling the *Maria* was approaching the docks. The name on her bow would confuse them and they would not act before verifying her *bona fide* with the Slovak authorities, but, as a precautionary measure, they would not allow anyone other than its Master to leave the boat.

Because the Slovak registration was genuine, the name would check out.

More confusion, hesitation and feverish consultation would follow during which his wife, Rada, would get away.

By half past eight, the authorities would realize that something was seriously amiss, start searching the ship and commence interrogating those on board. It would probably take them until nine or even ten to learn about the existence of the tugboat and the location of the Moscovitch compound.

A contingent would be dispatched post haste to search it and the discovery of Dankovic' body would prompt the authorities to charge the detainees with being accessories to murder.

The accused would deny their guilt and shift the blame onto the Jurices, Hassani and Al Adel.

'What information could the deckhands divulge?' Juric asked himself as he reviewed his plan for the umpteenth time.

Nothing much that would be useful to the authorities searching for Moscovitch.

None of those detained, including his wife, knew the real identity of Al Adel or Hassani. They would have seen the tugboat last in the compound and would have no way of knowing whether Moscovitch had remained on board after the *Maria* had sailed. Nor would they know which way the tugboat would have headed after it had exited the inlet.

As for the ambulance, about which the police would have found out by then, they would say that they had, indeed, seen an ambulance arrive, but that, as far as they knew, it had still been at the compound when the *Maria* had cast off.

The scenario would differ only slightly in the event that his wife failed to get away because Juric had never given her details about what he intended to do with Moscovitch.

She did know about Delic, Drusza and Amina, but then, they were dead weren't they? She would confess knowing about the group's struggle for The Cause and for this, she would go to prison.

Juric called the ambulance ploy his 'master touch', a piece of disinformation designed to waste the time of the police and diffuse the intensity of the search for the tugboat. He could just see the authorities frantically looking for the vehicle in the area stretching from *Dunaújváros* to *Mohács* and beyond, into Croatia, past *Udvar* even.

Regardless of which scenario would play out, Juric felt sure that the search for the tugboat would not start before ten in the morning. Hopefully, by then he would have reached the *rendez-vous* point he intended to arrange with The Butcher and would have 'hidden' the tugboat.

He glanced at the dials on the dashboard. *Bulldog* was at her cruising speed, fifteen knots. Deduct the flow rate of the river, about five knots, so he was travelling upriver at the rate of ten. Within five hours, six at the most, he'd reach the very busy commercial port at the northern tip of *Csepel* Island, just south of the Capital.

Juric chuckled. 'Where else can one best hide a fair-sized boat than among many other such boats?'

'Plenty of time to look for a hiding place once we get there' he reassured himself and turned to Al Adel who was standing beside him. "We have about six hours of navigating ahead of us. If you want, I can ask Omar to move Moscovitch out of the cabin so that you can sleep in one of the bunks for a few hours."

The Jordanian yawned. "I would appreciate that. Omar can keep you company for a while. Wake me in three hours and I'll help you stay awake on the last leg of our journey."

Al Adel helped Al Malaki to bring Moscovitch to the bridge and to shackle him to the stove in the galley behind it.

Then he went below and called Khamani. "We're on our way to our final destination which is the port at the northern tip of *Csepel* Island. I expect that some Iraquis will meet us there. I don't know when and how many. They will probably try to abduct the Canadian and leave me behind. This must not happen."

"What are your orders?"

"First, tell me where you are."

"Moving upstream about half a kilometer behind you. We're running low on food, water and fuel."

Al Adel bit his lip. "How much longer can you manage?"

"We can make it as far as *Csepel* no sweat, but not much further."

Al Adel had to react quickly. "There are four of us on board: Juric, Moscovitch, an Iraqi technician and me. At dawn, the Iraqi will be asleep in the cabin, Moscovitch will be shackled to the stove in the galley and I will be on the bridge beside Juric who will be at the helm. At five a.m., I will call you. Let the phone ring. If the coast is clear, I will let it ring twice and then hang up. Bring your boat alongside ours on the port side as quickly as possible and come on board. I will be there to help you."

"What if the coast is not clear?"

"I will let the phone ring longer, you'll answer it and we'll talk."

*   *   *

"The Jordanian is probably calling for reinforcements as we speak," Juric remarked to Omar on the bridge. "He is a dangerous man and very suspicious. I tried to disarm him, but he found me out and no longer trusts me. We must be very vigilant."

"What do you want me to do?"

"Call Colonel Hassani and tell him about the situation. Then let me speak with him."

"Why do you think I know how to reach the Colonel?"

Juric was impressed. The young man was trying to maintain his cover to the very last moment.

"Because I have been around for a long time and know how to read people," he said, laughing. "Don't worry," he added, "we're on the same side."

CHAPTER 51

Dunaújváros, Friday, October 26
Dawn (cont'd)

The mindset of a person in solitary confinement is difficult to fathom. The prisoner himself does not understand it.

Strictly speaking, the nearly six weeks Moscovitch had spent in his semi trailer did not qualify as solitary confinement because he had had repeated meetings with his captors, had been allowed to watch movies, exercise outdoors regularly, and had been provided copies of his hometown newspaper on a daily basis.

Moreover, he had been permitted to pursue his research in a well-equipped laboratory.

What he *did* have in common with prisoners in solitary was a forced daily routine that varied little, and the total lack of control over his freedom and his fate. He depended on the whims of his captors for even the smallest privilege, and had to live with the constant, all invasive and debilitating fear of his life ending at a moment's notice.

During his captivity, Moscovitch had alternated between emotional highs and lows, between moments of great well-being and sheer terror, between despair and hope.

His panic at finding himself in the chain locker of a tugboat moments away from death had been followed by an incredible emotional high when, moments later, his jailer had invited him to a breakfast of bacon and eggs and conversation.

When they had made him get dressed in the clothes in which they had kidnapped him six weeks earlier, his mind had filled with hope because he felt that his liberation was imminent. Then they had locked him in a small, dark cabin for hours without telling him anything and his despair and disappointment had been almost more than his heart could bear.

He began to torture himself with negative arguments, reasoning, for example, that they had dressed him up nicely because they wanted him to look smart when they shot him. This thought had made him hyper-ventilate and he had almost passed out.

A fragment of Milton's *Paradise Lost,* a literary work he had been required to study in his first year at the university, had suddenly emerged from his subconscious. Why he had remembered it, he could not say:

> *The mind is its own place, and in itself can make a heaven*
> *of hell, a hell of heaven.*

An isolated, abandoned man's imagination can drive him insane.

* * *

Moscovitch had no idea what time after dark the tugboat had finally gotten underway because he had still been without his watch. He did notice that the other boat he had spotted, the bigger one, had left before them.

Just before their departure, a man he had never seen before had entered the cabin, pistol in his hand. He was young, moved with the fluidity of an athlete and had the look of intelligence about him. Without much ado, he shackled Moscovitch to the railing of the lower bunk and told him in English that he'd return in the morning with an early breakfast.

After suggesting that the scientist get some sleep, his new jailer left, locking the door behind him.

Moscovitch groped about in the little cabin and discovered that by lying down he could reach the switch of the reading light above the lower bunk. He turned the light on, but found that this prevented him from seeing through the porthole, so he switched it off.

The ability to control the light, the chug-chugging of the engines and the prospect of a breakfast next day reassured Moscovitch to the point where he could start thinking rationally again.

He noted that although the engines seemed to be straining, the boat's progress was slow judging by the odd light they passed on their way.

'Must be going upriver and working against a strong current, probably the Danube's,' he mused, 'and there must be at least two, maybe three, people on board beside myself.'

He had no idea about where they were headed: Budapest, Czechoslovakia, Rumania, the Black Sea . . .?

Just as he was getting settled, his young jailer returned, undid his handcuff and, with a wave of his weapon, ushered Moscovitch outside. On his way to the bridge, the scientist passed a woman who looked vaguely familiar.

She did not acknowledge him.

'The bitch is having me turned out so she can sleep alone,' Moscovitch fumed as he looked about him. In addition to his young guard, there was yet another man on the bridge: his jailer.

"I'm afraid you will be far less comfortable here than you would have been in the cabin" the young man said, "but it can't be helped." He led the Canadian to the galley and clipped his handcuff to the stove's oven bar.

"There," he added. "You'll be able to move about a bit, perhaps even lie down on the floor." He slid the oven door lock to the open position.

Moscovitch was furious. God, he hated that goddamned woman, that bitch-of-a-cabin-usurper. In his rage, he gave his handcuff a sharp, angry jerk. The oven door flew open. Moscovitch lay down on the floor.

The noise made Juric turn his back to the wheel and Omar looked up at him.

The Bosnian shook his head. "Leave him be. Let him get some rest," he told the Iraqi in Arabic.

Moscovitch did not understand what they were saying, but he recognized the language. He realized that he was in the hands of Islamic terrorists who were taking him away from Hungary to where, only the Good Lord knew, probably to his place of execution.

No one was coming to his rescue, and he was beginning to think that no one had even tried, except perhaps Lonsdale, and only because he had been hired by his mother.

'Get a hold of yourself and face facts. Your fate is sealed unless you, yourself, do something about saving your sorry ass. Take advantage of your improved circumstances. Start by freeing your hand and then wait for the right opportunity to act!'

Easier said than done.

Perhaps not so.

When, in his rage, he had viciously tugged on his handcuffs, he had gotten the impression that the bar on the stove was loose.

He looked over to the bridge. His young jailer and the helmsman were focused on steering the boat. Nobody was paying attention to him.

He sat up, making as little noise as possible, and bent over the oven door to examine it more closely. The stove was old enough to qualify as an antique, a wood burner, no less. Made of cast iron, it had been designed with no frills, and without insulation on the back of the door he was examining.

He could see by the feeble light of the lamp over the stove that the bar to which he was handcuffed was attached to the door with two bolts, one near the left edge, and one near the right.

He groped at the bolts, testing—and found that the one on the left *was* loose.

* * *

When the cell phone on The Butcher's night table rang at two in the morning it took him a few seconds to realize that he was not in his own bed in Baghdad, but still in the Iraqi ambassador's residence in Budapest.

He recognized his caller's voice immediately.

"Where are you?"

"On board the tugboat Colonel, about four hours' sailing south of the Capital," Omar reported. "The Master wishes to speak with you."

"Plan A failed Colonel. The vehicle became compromised and had to be destroyed completely," Juric reported.

Hassani understood. The ambulance and its driver were no more. "Do you want me to activate Plan B?"

"That is in the affirmative Colonel."

"I have done some preliminary work, but, for obvious reasons, I won't be able to finalize arrangements before you tell me how many packages there are."

"Four in all."

The Butcher was not happy with the number. "That's too heavy a cargo. I don't think we can manage more than half of that."

Juric was shocked. The Iraqi was telling him that he could arrange for the extraction of only one other person beside Moscovitch. He took a deep breath. "I know you like cod fish, but what would you like in the second package?"

"I leave the choice to you."

"I will have to think very carefully about this and take into consideration many factors."

Silence. Then: "I know," said The Butcher. "I rely entirely on your good judgment and experience, and your loyalty."

"Thank you for your confidence in me." Juric felt trapped. The Butcher was at his most dangerous when he was being accommodating and complimentary.

Hassani continued. "I think I can have everything ready by the afternoon. Is that convenient?"

Juric had anticipated the delay and was prepared for it. "Let's set up a meeting as soon after dusk as possible."

Hassani was pleased, "Shall we say between seven and seven thirty?"

That worked for Juric. "I'll let you know by five where and how."

"That's too late. The people involved need time to square the paperwork."

"All right. I'll call you around noon."

"Good. Then I'll proceed on that basis. By the way, say hello to my nephew. He seems to be doing a good job for you." The Butcher hung up.

Juric gagged.

He had just been told who should accompany Moscovitch to Iraq.

If young Omar Al Malaki was a nephew, however distant, of Hassani, he was probably also related to Saddam Hussein.

The Bosnian suddenly found himself in a lose-lose situation.

On the one hand, Al Adel would never agree to Moscovitch being left in the sole custody of a relative of Saddam Hussein because doing so would not serve Al Qaeda's best interest.

On the other, sending the scientist on his way accompanied by Al Adel would infuriate the Iraqi dictator for two reasons: first, the loss of control over the vaccine against nv.C-JD; and second, the probable death or capture of Omar Al Malaki, a member of his—the Al-Bu Nasir—tribe.

'When in doubt, do nothing. Let time help you to solve your problems,' was what his mother used to say when cornered by the inevitable vicissitudes of life.

The Bosnian concentrated on steering his vessel and put the Moscovitch problem on the back burner.

Before going back to sleep in the Ambassador's guest bedroom, Hassani reviewed where he stood with Plan B.

On Wednesday morning he and his host had discussed the possibility of having to ex-filtrate one or more persons from Hungary.

The ambassador was not receptive. "You must understand Colonel that I cannot have any part in, or knowledge of, such a matter."

Hassani had laughed. "Of course I understand. You want to be able to lie with conviction, and you have a reputation for being a bad liar."

The ambassador had not found the remark in any way funny, but had kept his counsel. Being mindful of his guest's exalted position, he tried to be helpful. "May I suggest that you speak with our consul about this matter? Perhaps you will allow me to invite both of you for lunch here today. Of course, I myself shan't be able to attend because I have a previous engagement."

Hassani had given the pompous little man a wink. "Most gracious of you."

The consul had been very helpful. He had explained that the diplomatic community in Budapest left the kind of heavy lifting Hassani had in mind to the Bulgarians who had the properly qualified manpower and equipment: big, brutish men and fast, reliable cars.

"Mind you they're not inexpensive, but very dependable."

Hassani had then given permission for arrangements to be made for the extraction of four people from Hungary.

The consul had come back to report at breakfast the next day. "The plan is for two Bulgarian Embassy Mercedes with diplomatic plates to escort four distinguished Bulgarian visitors from Budapest to tour the city of Arad in Rumania, where, after a tour of the city which is one of the most prosperous and historically significant in Rumania, they will be flown to Iraq by private plane."

"Why two Mercedes?"

"Each car will be manned by a chauffeur and a bodyguard and accommodate two distinguished visitors."

"How far is Arad from Budapest?"

"Less than three hundred kilometers, about three hours drive."

"How much?"

"Including four diplomatic passports, forty thousand US dollars."

"You are out of your mind!" Hassani was furious. "This is blackmail."

The consul explained that the price was high because the four guards had to be paid, and that, if anything went wrong, the cars would be confiscated and the Bulgarian consul would have to pay for replacing them. Furthermore, the man wanted ten thousand dollars for himself to arrange the trip.

"What happens if all goes well and the cars are not confiscated? Do we get a rebate?" The Butcher was an old hand at such negotiations.

The Iraqi consul said he didn't know and would have to ask.

After haggling back and forth all day the parties agreed on fifteen thousand dollars for one car, two guards and only two passengers with diplomatic passports.

The car and the men would be ready to go at any time after Friday noon on six hours' notice.

Of course, the reduced fee affected all parties concerned. The Bulgarian consul wanted not a penny less than the ten thousand dollars that he had demanded to start with, of which he was willing to kick back two thousand to the Iraqi consul. The secretaries, who would be physically preparing the two passports and on whom all the blame would fall if something were to go wrong, wanted a couple of thousand each. This left a thousand dollars for the two guards from which they were required to pay for all incidental expenses such as food and the required fuel.

They were not happy because the way they saw it, they were doing all the work and taking the biggest risk.

CHAPTER 52

Dunaújváros, Friday, October 26

Accompanied by Colonel Nagy's men, Klara Moscovitch and Lonsdale spent three hours combing through the Moscovitch compound. When she saw the piles of Toronto Globe & Mails that her son had accumulated and the number of issues in which he had completed the crossword puzzle, she realized how terrible his isolation must have been and she began to cry.

Lonsdale did his best to comfort her. He even went so far as to say that the authorities would find Jason soon, though he knew better. With the departure of the *Maria* the chances of success for finding her son had diminished considerably.

The trail was growing cold.

He figured that by now Moscovitch could be anywhere: on board the barge, off-loaded to another boat, whisked away in the ambulance . . . All leads would dry up soon unless the police found the vessel or its owner, or the ambulance Imre had followed.

The involvement of the ambulance was something that really puzzled Lonsdale. Why would the scientist's captors arrange for two trips with the same driver when combining the voyages would have left less of a trail? What about that business with *Udvar* being lightly circled on the map? What was that all about?

Yet another red herring?

Nagy had checked with the border people and had found that no ambulance had crossed into Croatia there that night.

What did give Lonsdale a glimmer of hope was the realization that the people who had taken the Canadian away had also taken all his samples and his working notes with them.

Presumably, this meant that they were transferring him to a facility where he could continue working on the vaccine.

A preliminary analysis indicated that, before departing, the Jurices had sanitized their place in *Dunaújváros* with great care. It seemed they were paying for everything by cash and communicated with the outside world via cell phones without permanent numbers. Lonsdale figured that, like all well-trained subversives, they were using prepaid calling cards that they would purchase in bulk and distribute at random amongst themselves.

There were no hard-wired telephones in the Moscovitch compound, no documents indicating the existence of bank accounts, no meaningful pieces of paper.

Very professionally done, Lonsdale had to admit.

He suspected that when the police started tearing the Jurices' home near Budapest apart, they would find the same frustrating state of affairs there too.

Of course, a more thorough look at what had been left behind was likely to develop additional valuable information, but Lonsdale did not have that luxury. He was very pressed for time.

*   *   *

By five a.m., the adrenaline rush that had kept everybody going during the night had pretty well worn off. Londdale and Klara were tired and very hungry. Colonel Nagy suggested they adjourn to a greasy spoon he knew about, open 24/7, to accommodate people who worked at night.

Lonsdale sat down to eat with a motley group: Nagy, his driver, Jenkins and his communications man, and Klara. The driver spoke some English, so conversation was not a problem. Everyone was relaxed, even Klara Moscovitch.

Frakkos had returned to Budapest earlier with the late Imre's widow.

Lonsdale was on his second cup of coffee and ready to go back to the Kempinsky when Nagy's cell rang. He listened intently, got up and threw some money on the table.

"Let's go," he ordered. "A barge resembling the *Maria* is heading for the *Mohács* harbor. She's still quite far upriver, about an hour's sailing. The name on her bow says she is the *Karlovac* and she hails from *Komárno* in Slovakia."

Lonsdale was dubious. "Another false alarm?" He looked at his watch: five-thirty.

"Not necessarily. My people are trying to check her out, but our friendly neighbors in *Komárno* are still asleep."

Lonsdale took over. "With your permission, Colonel, I would like to suggest the following. The six of us drive down to *Mohács* as fast as we can in a convoy of three cars. I'll ride in the Battle Wagon which has a blue rotating light on its rooftop so it should go first. Jenkins will drive. You," Lonsdale pointed to the US consul's technician, ". . . will help me with the communications equipment."

Lonsdale turned to Nagy. "Perhaps your driver could take Mrs. Moscovitch to *Mohács* in my car."

"Of course."

"That means that you will have to drive your car yourself, Colonel."

"Won't be the first time."

"We'll set up multiplex communications from the Battle Wagon. You, Colonel, order your people in *Mohács* to observe, but to take no action other than to the extent necessary to stop people from disembarking."

"Except for the Master, right?"

"Right. Let's make things look as normal as possible, with no fuss, especially because the vessel may not be the one we're chasing . . ."

". . . and we don't want to create an international incident." Nagy completed the sentence for Lonsdale.

"That's right." Lonsdale continued. "I will tell the SAS people to deploy in two places: at the quay where the *Karlovac* will be directed to dock, and further downstream where the Duna narrows."

"How come?" This from Jenkins.

"If the boat is not the *Maria* we'll just let her go. End of story. If she *is* the *Maria*, we'll pretend to let her go and jump her further downstream. Our attack will be a bigger surprise there, conducted in a less public place. Isn't this how you want us to conduct the operation, Colonel?"

"Absolutely. We'll take more people alive this way, people who are bound to have information that we desperately need."

Lonsdale put on his coat. "In other words, easy does it. Above all, no sirens please!"

CHAPTER 53

Mohács, Friday, October 26
Early morning

The operation in *Mohács* turned into a major fiasco.

The Border Police, following Colonel Nagy's orders to the letter, allowed the *Maria* to dock a few minutes before seven without interference.

Three SAS men were in the Customs building, camouflaged as Customs Officers. They sauntered out nonchalantly and took up position at the *Maria*'s gangplank, ready to stop anyone other than the Master from leaving the ship.

The convoy of three cars arrived twenty minutes after the *Maria* had docked.

By then, the Master had gone ashore, had presented her papers to the border police, and had gone to the washroom.

The border police, backed by the SAS, moved in at seven-thirty and arrested the five crewmen on board. The vessel was searched from stem to stern and nothing of interest was found, certainly not Moscovitch.

With the aid of one of the SAS men who spoke passable Arabic, Lonsdale began interrogating the crew at eight thirty. They all had valid Lebanese passports and visas allowing them multiple entries and exits into and out of Hungary, to work as transient marine deckhands, on condition that they did not stay in the country for longer than a maximum of ninety days.

The entry stamps in their passports showed that they had entered Hungary at the beginning of October. So they were in the country legally.

All but one said, in Arabic, of course, that they had been hired by the *Maria's* Master, Juric, in *Constanza* as deckhands and odd job construction workers. The exception was the oldest of the lot, Youssouf, who had papers showing that he was a qualified riverboat first mate.

He spoke broken English and German.

When asked what happened with the Jurices, all confessed total ignorance. They had last seen Juric a couple of days earlier when he told them he had another big cargo coming up from *Constanza* and that he wanted the whole crew there as soon as possible. Mrs. Juric then took over as Master of the *Maria* and he, Youssouf, acted as Mate. Youssuf assumed that Juric and the others were following in a tugboat.

"What tugboat?"

Youssuf had shrugged. "It's called the *Bulldog*, that's all I know."

Where was Mrs. Juric now? She had gone ashore to talk to customs and the border police.

Yes, they did help assemble machinery at *Dunaújváros*. Yes, they had help from a technician who was now on board the tugboat.

"What about Moscovitch?" Lonsdale had asked. "Never heard of him." Youssouf replied.

"Did he not live on the compound with all of you?"

"Oh, you mean the mysterious crazy scientist who had to be kept locked up because otherwise he would run away?"

"That's the one." Lonsdale then asked the key question. "What happened to him?"

"He went with Juric on the tugboat."

So there it all was, neatly laid out for Lonsdale to see. Juric had outfoxed him big time.

With the disappearance of Rada Juric, there was no-one left on board the *Maria* who was familiar with the big picture.

As for the tugboat and its passengers, only God knew where they were.

Lonsdale did not question the deckhands about Hassani and Al Adel because, at that point in time, he had not been aware of their presence in Hungary. He discovered their role in the affair only after the professional Arabist interrogator, flown in from Langley, stumbled onto it three days later.

By that time, the matter was academic.

Colonel Nagy had the detainees transferred to Budapest under guard and took his leave. Lonsdale sent Jenkins and his assistant back to Budapest in the Battle Wagon, and, disappointed, disgusted and exhausted, drove Klara Moscovitch back to the Capital in his Audi.

CHAPTER 54

Budapest, Friday, October 26
Morning

Five hours into his trip, Juric realized that he was out of time.

Having just passed the M0 Bridge, a structure with which he was very familiar because he and his wife had lived in its shadow during the past few years, he knew exactly where he was.

Less than one hours' sailing from the general area of his intended destination.

It was time to decide which of several alternatives to choose and there was nobody to whom he could turn for advice.

Omar was in the cabin, resting. Moscovitch was bent over the stove door in the galley, trying to sleep. Al Adel, still in his disguise as a woman, was standing next to Juric, watching their progress. He had decided earlier not to activate the plan to have Khamani board *Bulldog* because he had been unable to find out what the Bosnian's end-game plan was, what the arrangements were to whisk Moscovitch out of Hungary.

There was nothing much to see in the darkness of the false dawn.

"How far to go?" Al Adel inquired.

"About three quarters of an hour. We've got to get off the river by eight thirty at the latest."

"Why?"

"The border police will know by then that the *Maria* was only a diversion.

"How?"

"One of the crew members will tell them about the tugboat."

"Not your wife?"

"Hopefully not." Juric then told him about how his wife was planning to get away.

Al Adel was impressed. "When will you know?"

Juric looked at his watch. It was six o'clock.

"In a couple of hours."

"What do we do now?"

"First we change the name of the boat, then we find a convenient place to hide, then we dock and have breakfast."

"How do you expect to accomplish all of this in ninety minutes?"

"Wake up Omar. The two of you have work to do."

The registered name of the tugboat, chosen with great foresight and care, was *Bulldog*. At least, that's what was painted on her bows and stern. Since she had often to flit back and forth across borders, it was useful, for purposes of providing bribable border guards with plausible cover stories, to be able to change her name at a moment's notice.

To achieve this, Juric had installed hooks above and below the painted text on which he could fasten tightly fitting boards displaying a variety of words that would cover up "*Bulldog*", such as *Levente* and *Katynka*.

He decided on *Katynka*, fished the appropriate boards out of the locker below the chart table and handed them to Omar.

"Our guest," he pointed at the Jordanian, "will help you affix these covers over the bows and stern the way I explained earlier. You have an hour to complete the job."

Omar took the boards and went outside. The sliding door leading to the deck slammed shut and woke up Moscovitch who began to swear and curse and rattle his shackles.

Juric had no choice, but to ignore him. He dared not leave the wheel unattended. They were approaching a section of the river where the current was tricky to navigate.

This seemed to infuriate the scientist, who continued to bang on the stove door with increasing ferocity for almost an hour and only quit when Omar and Al Adel returned.

Both were worse for the wear; wet, cold and smudged with dirt.

"What's next?" the Al Adel inquired.

Juric turned to Omar and pointed out the window to starboard. "Traffic is picking up because we are approaching the duty free port at *Csepel*. See the channel we're just passing?"

Omar nodded. He could see the opening, but barely; it was still dark and raining lightly.

"I'm going up the next channel to the right."Juric throttled back." It leads to the grain elevator known as the MAHART building near the container terminal. With luck, we'll find a small hole into which we can disappear. Are the boards in place?"

The men said they were.

"Be ready to go forward when I give the word. As you can see, the port is busy and space will be at a premium, so I'll need your help to squeeze into a tight berth when I find one."

Then he proceeded to explain in detail what he wanted his helpers to do when the time came.

Al Adel excused himself, went to the head, flushed the toilette to create a noise cover and called Khamani. "Where are you?"

"We are just passing the Budapest Gas Works on our right. We're very low on fuel."

"Not to worry, we're almost there. I saw the Gas Works too, about fifteen minutes ago. We're now heading into a dead-end channel to our right—the second one for you—which apparently leads into a container port near the MAHART building. Have you heard of it?"

"Yes I have. That's where I bring in my cars from Japan."

"Excellent. Tie up somewhere near us, but out of sight. I'll call within two hours. Be prepared for action."

Al Adel hung up.

CHAPTER 55

Budapest, Friday, October 26
Morning (cont'd)

By the time Al Adel emerged from the head, Juric had sailed *Bulldog* (now called *Katynka)* into the MAHART bay, a rectangular body of water roughly a kilometer long and two hundred meters wide, surrounded by an assortment of buildings on three sides.

The port was very much a 24/7 operation, with powerful overhead lights ensuring that work could go on night and day, except in extreme weather. Cranes running along rails circling the bay were working flat out although it was only six in the morning.

Juric circumnavigated the basin at low speed and found what he was looking for after half an hours' searching: a berth just long enough to accommodate his tugboat.

Located along the quay in front of the south wall of the grain elevator and parallel to it, the berth stretched from a barge loading wheat at one end to a river ship taking on general cargo at the other. The cargo ship lay along an abutment jutting into the bay perpendicularly, thereby forming a corner, which meant that if Juric could position his vessel with its bow pointing east, the names appearing on her could only be seen from the landward side.

Not by a police launch passing on the other.

The perfect corner, as far as Juric was concerned.

But there was a hitch, as always.

The space was very tight and Juric could get his vessel berthed only if his amateur deckhands, Omar and Al Adel, performed their assigned tasks perfectly.

He nudged *Bulldog*'s nose toward the corner and sent Omar forward. The Iraqi was to leap ashore as soon as the tugboat was within jumping distance of the quay. Al Adel was then to throw two ropes to Omar. The end of the shorter one Omar would make fast on an appropriately placed bollard, (they were spaced along the wharf at ten-meter intervals), the end of the longer one he would 'walk' along the quay to the next bollard.

Then, having given the rope a half-turn around the second bollard, he was to keep it taut while Al Adel carried his end of the rope from the boat's bow to its stern and, to complete this part of the operation, attach it to a stanchion there.

Omar would go on pulling on the rope until the bumpers attached to *Bulldog*'s stern touched the quay.

Juric supervised the work from the pilothouse because he wanted to be near the controls in case something went wrong. Fortunately the maneuver went off without a hitch.

While Omar adjusted the tension of the stern rope, Al Adel did likewise at the bow.

To 'cradle' the vessel, the two men ran a rope attached at the bow to a bollard at the stern, and one attached to the stern to a bollard at the bow.

Sounds easy, but far from being so in practice, without gloves in a downpour of freezing rain on a slippery deck and a muddy quay.

Meanwhile, Moscovitch had watched and waited.

He had found that, with the oven door closed, he could stand up. He had done so on several occasions during the night when the pain from lying on a hard floor had gotten to be too much.

Then he'd sit down and, bending over the door, he'd work away at undoing the nut on the loose bolt that held the oven bar in place. Once the nut was off, he had started to work on the bolt itself. Freeing it had taken a long time; it had rusted into place. When it had finally fallen free after considerable jiggling and poking, the Canadian was able to bend the bar far enough away from the door to allow him to slide the handcuff out from under.

Luck had been with him during the night. The chugging of the engine had muffled the noises caused by his exertions and they had gone unnoticed.

But conditions were changing.

He had stood up again when he had seen the overhead lights of the port heave into sight as *Bulldog* sailed up the channel. Soon she would dock, the engine would stop and he would find himself back in the cabin, chained to the bunk.

Moscovitch had watched the docking process unfold, and had decided to make his move when he saw that the operation was about to end.

Omar and the woman were still outside; Juric was alone in the pilot house.

He slid the handcuff free and rushed at Juric who, having stepped away from the wheel to peer out to port, had his back to him. He hit the Bosnian in the left kidney with his right shoulder and drove him into the instrument console.

With a groan, Juric, a big man, buckled and fell to his right knee. Moscovitch tried to kick him in the face, but Juric, sensing what was coming, got his hands up and absorbed the impact with his forearms. Moscovitch stumbled on top of him and both men went down.

Juric rolled away and Moscovitch scrambled toward the port sliding door. His plan had called not for fighting, but for fleeing—jumping ashore and then running away.

The handle was within his reach. He grabbed it and tore the door aside . . . and found himself face to face with Omar who, quick as a cat, punched him in the nose.

It broke for the second time in less than two months. Moscovitch went down screaming with pain.

Juric picked himself up off the floor and, in a gesture of rage and revenge, kicked the Canadian in the ribs. Moscovitch stayed down.

Cursing and swearing, and enraged by his own carelessness, Juric ordered Omar to manacle Moscovitch and lock him in the cabin.

Al Adel objected. "We need that place to dry out and to rest. Omar and I are soaked and bone tired."

"So what do you think I am?" Juric snarled at him, holding his hand to his bruised kidney. He then went to the galley to find out how Moscovitch had managed to get free.

His phone rang. It was his wife. When she told him she was safe and in Croatia, Juric felt better.

Omar looked at Al Adel. "What's next?"

Juric provided the answer. "We'll leave the prisoner lying where he is. He's no threat with his hands tied behind his back and his nose broken and bleeding." He looked over to where the Canadian lay, softly moaning. "You two get dried out and warm while I make breakfast. After breakfast we'll call the Colonel."

"Why not now?" Al Adel's voice was sharp. He was not happy.

Juric looked at his watch. It showed a few minutes past eight. "Too early. Besides, why not let him sleep? I needn't tell him about our whereabouts before noon."

Al Adel was relieved because he thought he understood. It seemed, Juric wanted to deny Hassani the opportunity to grab Moscovitch for the Iraqi side until the Bosnian figured out how to protect everybody's interests.

Perhaps he had not forgotten his pledge of loyalty to Osama Bin Laden after all.

Al Adel turned to Omar. "Go ahead and use the cabin. I'm going to relieve myself first. I'm bursting."

Juric started the generator and began preparing the morning meal. Al Adel flushed the toilette and called Khamani.

"Where are you?" He whispered.

"On the other side of MAHART bay, between you and the entrance channel. I have you visual a couple of hundred meters away."

"Listen carefully. My guess is that extraction will not take place before dusk. I give you four hours to resupply, refuel and have a quick shower. Be back here by one and bunk down in your boat for a few hours' sleep."

"Are you sure?" The Qods officer did not like the plan. "We can hold out a little longer if we have to."

"Your dedication is noted and appreciated, but I need you rested. Do what I told you, but stay near your telephone."

Al Adel hung up.

*   *   *

Busy with their own thoughts neither Lonsdale nor Klara Moscovitch said much during the two-hour drive back to their hotel from *Mohács*.

They were too tired, physically and emotionally.

Halfway into the trip Klara had noticed that her companion was on the verge of nodding off and had volunteered to drive the rest of the way. At the Kempinsky, they got their respective room keys and headed for the elevators. When the doors opened they stepped forward in unison and Lonsdale couldn't help bumping into the woman.

She began to weep and he put his arms around her for comfort. When the door opened at his floor she was still sobbing and would not let go.

"Please, please," she begged, "could I come in for a moment? I must talk things over with you . . ."

He let her enter the room ahead of him then closed the door.

"We've lost him, haven't we?" she whispered, her lips trembling.

He used his handkerchief to wipe away her tears. "Not necessarily. It'll just take a bit longer to track him down, but we'll find him in the end."

"Dead or alive?" Her lips were very close to his.

"Alive, of course."

She drew him to her and kissed him gently on the lips.

He lost control. The fatigue, the tension, the pain and loneliness, coupled with the frustrations and disappointments of the past few days had been just too much.

He could not stop himself from kissing her back.

She led him to the foot of the bed and began to undress him the way she had done on Thursday evening, less than twenty-four hours earlier: gently, knowingly, lovingly, for by now she had realized how much of himself he had poured into the search for her son.

They kissed again and he lay down on the bed.

She undressed and knelt between his legs and made love to him, first orally, then by straddling and riding his manhood until they climaxed in unison.

"I'm so sorry," she whispered in his ear after it was over. "I know I shouldn't have, but I had to. I have wanted to ever since I met you."

He was too exhausted to answer and fell asleep while she was pulling the bedcovers over them.

CHAPTER 56

Budapest, Friday, October 26
Afternoon

Everybody was in a bad mood during the morning meal, Juric because he had not slept during the night and his kidney was hurting, Omar and Al Adel because they were tired and their hands were raw from the ropes, and Moscovitch because his nose hurt and his face was swelling up.

They had picked him up off the pilothouse floor after they had eaten by which time he was a mess and looked it. He had two black eyes. He could barely see through the folds of his swollen cheeks and his shoulders felt on fire from having had his arms handcuffed behind his back.

While Omar Al Adel cleaned him up somewhat and then fed him, Juric went outside for a breath of fresh air, called Hassani and told him their location.

"Very well. The Bulgarian consul will come by and take photographs for the passports."

"When?" The Bosnian wanted the information for his own plan.

"Around two-thirty. He needs about four hours to complete the documentation."

"Make sure he takes pictures of all four of us."

Hassani was surprised. "Why?"

"Because I want to wait until the last minute before telling the Jordanian that he is not going with Moscovitch."

Omar and Al Adel crashed for a couple of hours in the cabin while Juric stood guard over Moscovitch.

A few minutes after two, Al Adel fetched his makeup kit to touch up the Canadian's facial bruises as best as he could. The Bulgarian consul arrived and took two pictures of everyone, departing as quickly as he could, but not before telling Juric that the extraction was scheduled for seven-thirty.

Al Adel went to the head again and called Khamani. He told the Iranian that the action would start at half past seven.

"Will the boat be moved?" Khamani asked.

"No. Why do you ask?"

"From where we are located there is no clear shot possible at the people emerging from the tugboat. We need elevation. Let me take *Valliant* back to where I usually store her—my dealership showroom. We will then redeploy on land. We have plenty of time."

"What do you have in mind?"

"We checked the area and have found two places from where we could operate. Ahmad will shoot from on top of a shed attached to a warehouse that is less than forty meters from you, at the corner dead ahead of you."

"I know where you mean. What about you?"

"There is an overhead two-columned derrick crane on the quay about twenty meters astern of you. It supports a conveyor belt for loading grain into barges. If you look back, you'll see that it is presently pouring stuff into a barge berthed behind *Bulldog*. The machine is operated from inside the building so there's nobody on top. I will climb the ladder in the column closest to the water, and will shoot from the first maintenance platform, about eight meters above ground."

"So you'll have the tugboat in a cross-fire situation, right?"

"Correct. Since I will be closer to *Bulldog* than Ahmad, I will shoot first."

"Where are you now?"

"In my boat, across the bay from you."

Al Adel was pleased. "Good plan. But understand this. The idea is for all of us to be taken to Rumania in two cars. From there, we'll be flown to Iraq. Such a procedure is acceptable to me. Do not shoot the Canadian until you are sure I'm no longer accompanying him. In other words, allow things to unfold until the very last moment"

"How will I recognize him?"

"He'll be wearing a light, tan-colored coat."

Omar took Moscovitch to the cabin, handcuffed him once more to the lower bunk's bar and told him to get some rest. The scientist fell asleep almost immediately.

Juric fetched some mats, and he and Al Adel, tired beyond belief from lack of sleep and tension, stretched out on the pilothouse floor.

Mercifully, they had four hours to rest.

*   *   *

Frakkos was in a quandary.

After running around most of the night, he had dropped off Imre's widow at her house and had headed back home for a well-deserved hot shower and a few hours' sleep.

His Bulgarian contact, Medved, the heavy who was always playing practical jokes on his buddies had called him at half past four with a story that sounded so unlikely that it was bound to be true. Frakkos was sure Medved did not have the brains to invent such a complicated scenario.

Apparently, his boss, the Bulgarian Consul, wanted Medved and his colleague, Azimov, the ambassador's driver, to "borrow" the ambassador's DeLuxe Mercedes Coupe for a quick run to *Arad* in Rumania.

"Two hours there, two hours back and a free hour to do what you want. You leave at seven and you're back by midnight at the latest. The ambassador and his wife won't be back from Paris before Sunday night."

"How much?" Medved had asked.

"A thousand US for the two of you, but you have to pay for the gas."

That wasn't bad for driving up and down a highway in an empty vehicle on a Friday night, but it turned out that there would be two bigshots in the back seat with legitimate Bulgarian diplomatic passports, so the scene had to look authentic: big car, uniformed driver, bodyguard, ambassadorial, diplomatic plates, no stopping, lots of saluting . . . the works.

Medved was not very intelligent, but remarkably shrewd. He immediately realized that the consul was engaging in a spot of people smuggling with his and Azimov's help and that the deal also included the sale of a couple of diplomatic passports.

Azimov knew that there was a lot of money in selling such documents and he began to suspect that the consul was holding out on him and his friend, the driver.

"What has all this got to do with me?" Frakkos had asked.

"Maybe we could all make a little more money out of this."

"How?"

"Maybe your Canadian detective will pay some money to know about these two big shots."

"Why would he?"

"You told me some time back that he and you might have a job for me and my friends to help you raid a barge. Remember?"

"I do."

"Well, we are to pick up these two from a barge at seven tonight."

Suddenly, Frakkos was wide-awake and all ears. "How much?" he asked.

"Five thousand. You can have ten per cent of it."

"Twenty."

"Fifteen."

"It's a deal. I'll call you back."

"It better be before six because at six thirty we roll."

Frakkos spent the next five minutes agonizing about what to do.

Was this one of Medved's practical jokes to get him out of the house so they could go drinking and raising hell on a Friday night, with Frakkos paying?

Was the information worth five thousand bucks?

Could Kane, the cheapskate drug policeman, raise five thousand in cash on a Friday night?

In less than two hours?

Was it worth the bother for Frakkos to get the answers to all these questions for a lousy seven hundred and fifty?

Yes!

He'd give the money to Imre's widow and ask Kane to reimburse him a thousand.

He reached for the phone.

It was five minutes to five.

CHAPTER 57

Budapest, Friday Night, October 26

It took Lonsdale less than half an hour after hearing out Frakkos to organize an assault on the presumptive target: a barge berthed somewhere near Budapest along the Danube river.

"The deal is a 'go'," he told Frakkos. "Ask the Bulgarians to show good faith by meeting you and me at six-fifteen sharp by the statue on *Petőfi* Square near the Elizabeth Bridge."

Next, he ordered Jenkins to withdraw five thousand dollars from the CIA emergency cash stash kept in the consul's safe.

Jenkins and his communications assistant were then to drive the Battle Wagon with the money to the Danube side of *Petőfi* Square, and park there. On their way, they were to power up the computers and get a real time aerial view of Budapest on the screen by six forty-five the latest.

The drill was still Code Full Metal Jacket, meaning maximum armament.

By the time Lonsdale had completed his instructions over the telephone Klara Moscovitch was completely dressed.

"You are staying here." Lonsdale was putting on his pants.

"I'm not. I'm going with you." Klara Moscovitch was adamant.

"You'll get in the way and get hurt." He was out the door. She followed him.

"We're talking about my son's rescue here. *My* son's. I have a right to be present."

The elevator doors opened and he could not stop her from getting in too.

She grabbed his arm. "I won't let you leave me behind."

In the lobby, he headed toward his car, parked in front. She crowded into the revolving door with him. He couldn't shake her.

As he slid behind the wheel, she got into the back seat.

There was no time left for arguing. With a sigh, he gave in. He would let her come along as long as she stayed out of the way.

It was a decision that he would come to regret bitterly for the rest of his life.

*   *   *

The two Bulgarians showed up exactly on time, their teeth chattering from the cold rain—and from nerves. They relaxed a little when they saw Frakkos who invited Azimov into his car with him. Lonsdale took Medved over to the Battle Wagon. The Bulgarian was wearing an obviously new, tan raincoat.

"Do you speak English or Hungarian better?"

"Hungarian a little, English more better."

"English it is." Lonsdale plunged on; they were getting soaked. "My partner in the vehicle has your money. We will now get in, you will show us on the map where the barge is and he will give you the money. Any bullshit, and my partner will kill you."

Medved shook his head. "I know this vehicle. Belongs to US Embassy. You and your partner stole it. I go away now."

He turned away.

Lonsdale grabbed him by the arm and spun him around. "Listen asshole. If you know this vehicle, you also know the US consul. He's sitting inside, waiting for you to get in and show us where the barge is. You either cooperate and earn five thousand bucks, less what you've promised to give Frakkos for helping you with this deal or . . ."

Medved interrupted. "Or what? You going to kill us?"

"No, worse. We'll see to it that you, your friend and your boss, the Bulgarian consul, get thrown out of this country for human trafficking, an offense punishable under international law by imprisonment."

Without a word, Medved got into the back of the Battle Wagon and Lonsdale followed.

The screen inside showed a bird's eye view of the Hungarian Capital from a height of ten thousand feet. Medved gave Jenkins' assistant the coordinates who quickly zoomed in on the meeting area.

"See the roof where it says MAHART? That's the grain storage building".

"Where is the barge supposed to be?"

"Not barge. Tugboat called *Katynka.*"

Jenkins pointed to the corner. "There she is."

"Print the screen," Lonsdale said to Dave, the communications man. "Make three copies: one for you, one for me and one for Frakkos."

They studied the screen for a while. The port was busy. Two barges were lining up to berth at the grain storage depot, and the general cargo ship next to *Katynka* was making ready to sail. A tugboat was nudging her away from the promontory.

There was a railway siding between the MAHART building and the water. Lonsdale could see that an engine was shunting freight cars along it.

Cars and trucks were everywhere.

Lonsdale pointed to two parallel rows of buildings stretching away from the abutment corner. They looked like warehouses. "See where *Katynka* is? I'll drive in first, and park in front of the building next to the corner with my car's nose pointing east, just ahead of this shed." Lonsdale touched the map again. "I'll have a clear view of the gangplank leading to the boat through my rear view mirror, but those on board won't be able to see me."

Jenkins nodded.

"I'll tell Frakkos to lead a convoy around the back of the MAHART building consisting of his car, followed by the Bulgarian Mercedes and with the Battle Wagon in the rear. This will allow them to approach *Katynka* from the west."

"Won't those on board smell a rat?" asked Dave.

Lonsdale shook his head. "It will all look very official. The convoy, with the Battle Wagon's blue light flashing, will stop alongside the tugboat. Azimov will get out of Frakkos' car and you," Lonsdale pointed at Medved, "will leave the Battle Wagon. Frakkos will drive away. You will board *Katynka*, give each passenger his respective passport and escort them to the Mercedes."

Medved became impatient. "When do we get our money?"

Lonsdale reached for the envelope that Jenkins was tendering to him. "I will give it to Frakkos to give to Azimov before Azimov boards the boat."

"What will happen next?" Jenkins was getting anxious too.

"The Mercedes and the Battle Wagon will drive off in convoy and leave the port area. I will follow in the Audi and overtake it."

"And?"

"Exactly one kilometer from the gate here," Lonsdale tapped the map, "I will suddenly stop. So will the Mercedes and the Battle Wagon, driven by Dave. Jenkins will rush over to the right rear of the Mercedes and I, to the left. One of us will disarm Moscovitch's guard the other will free Moscovitch."

"And us? What will happen to us?" Medved was very upset. "Our boss will kill us."

"No he won't. You and Azimov will drive the Mercedes back to its garage and will tell your boss that some gangsters—you don't know who they are—ambushed you on the road to Budapest and kidnapped your passengers."

"He'll never believe us."

"Oh yes he will. Besides, he won't care. The car will be safe, you two will be safe, he will be safe and everybody will have been paid."

"But the other side will be mad."

Lonsdale looked at Medved with a pitying smile on his face. "Will anybody ever find out who the other side is?"

Lonsdale's diplomatic passport got him through the free port's entrance gate without difficulty. By seven twenty-five he was in position, about forty meters from *Katynka's* gangplank. He called the Battle Wagon. Dave told him that the convoy of cars was just rounding the grain storage building.

He tensed as the convoy reached the target and the two Bulgarians went aboard. He began to count the seconds. When he got to one hundred and eighty-seven the first Bulgarian, Medved, appeared on the gangplank and began to walk toward the Mercedes. He was followed by Moscovitch, unsteady on his feet and needing the help of the young person behind him.

Next came Azimov. His huge bulk was easily recognizable, even at thirty meters.

When Medved got to the end of the gangplank, he stumbled and fell.

And all hell broke loose.

CHAPTER 58

Budapest, Friday night, October 26

Juric and Al Adel were watching the convoy of three cars driving toward *Katynka* along the quay with concern, but not with alarm. Veterans of innumerable skirmishes, they saw nothing that would indicate imminent police action. The quay was teeming with activity and there were no suspicious-looking vehicles or pedestrians in sight.

"Real professionals," Juric murmured and Al Adel nodded. They were both nervous. Still dressed as a woman, the Jordanian had his pistol out.

"Yeah, they have even gotten hold of a chase car, just in case."

The two huge Bulgarians stepped into the pilothouse. They were dripping wet from the rain. The smaller one turned to Juric. "Are you the Master?" He asked in English.

"Yes."

He handed Juric a manila envelope. "The passports," he said.

Juric called out to Omar who was standing at the cabin door. "Bring out Moscovitch."

Omar did so. The Canadian, who had just awoken, was struggling to put on his overcoat. He still had one handcuff on and was having difficulty getting into the garment.

Juric opened the envelope, extracted two passports and threw the envelope on the instrument console.

"Let me see them." Al Adel commanded in his funny falsetto. He examined them carefully, checking the names and pictures. "Where are the others?"

"What others?" Juric was playing for time. The moment of truth that he had been talking about with Omar had arrived. "There are no others. Only two people are going: Moscovitch and Omar."

Al Adel pivoted away from Juirc and raised his pistol to shoot Omar. The Iraqi was quicker. He shot the Jordanian in the shoulder at point blank range with a short burst from his Uzzi, shredding the man's upper left arm.

Al Adel dropped his weapon and sank to the floor. The shock was more than he could bear standing up.

Juric picked up the weapon and waved it at the terrified Bulgarians. "Get going," he yelled.

Medved opened the door. Omar grabbed Moscovitch's arm and pushed him outside. Azimov followed Omar. The Canadian was wobbly and Omar tried to steady him as they walked toward the Mercedes.

First, Omar heard the thud of the high velocity bullet slam into Medved's left chest cavity destroying his heart, then the phfutt of a sharpshooter's silencer-equipped rifle. He looked to his left and thought he saw a man under the bright overhead lights, hurrying away from the crane about twenty feet away.

Moscovitch stumbled over Medved's fallen body and went down.

Lonsdale was out of the car in a flash, sprinting toward the gangplank with his pistol drawn, his hip aflame with pain. He knew from bitter experience that there were usually two shooters in every well-planned assassination attempt, firing from different directions.

He, too, had seen the fleeing man and his instincts told him that the next shot would come from the east; from behind him. He could feel the marksman's bead on the back of his neck.

He didn't give it a thought.

Lonsdale was a man of courage who believed in what Churchill had said. 'Courage is rightly esteemed the first of human qualities because it is the quality which guarantees all others.'

Having betrayed his beloved Adys by sleeping with Klara Moscovitch, Lonsdale was determined to remain true to the only virtue he had not sullied—his courage.

Klara Moscovitch was also running as fast as she could. She was trying, like Lonsdale, to reach her son before more harm could come to him.

Ahmad, the Iranian sharpshooter, sopping wet on top of the shed, was watching the scene through the sniper scope mounted on his very fine Husquarna rifle. It took him a few seconds to figure out what had happened.

He had seen one of the two big men fall and knew from the way he had toppled that he had been killed by a bullet. Then the man behind the first man had stumbled and fallen, but he was now picking himself up, trying to struggle into his tan overcoat in the pouring rain.

Lieutenant Colonel Khamani had hit the wrong target—or perhaps two men were dressed in tan overcoats.

Ahmad's orders had been clear.' Do not fire first.' Only after the colonel had fired and missed was he to fire and kill the man in the tan coat.

One of the men was down, but the other was very much alive and two people were running toward him—a man and a woman.

The man was almost there.

Ahmad made a split second decision. He would take out the running man to have a clear field of fire, and then shoot the second man in the tan coat.

He adjusted his aim, squeezed the trigger . . . and hit Klara Moscovitch in the heart.

She died within seconds.

Omar let loose with a burst of sub-machine gun fire in Ahmad's direction that Lonsdale's brain interpreted as being aimed at him.

Ahmad fled.

Jenkins jumped out of the Battle Wagon and dragged Moscovitch into the relative safety of the big vehicle.

Lonsdale shot Omar dead.

Juiric, watching the carnage unfolding around him through the port window of the pilothouse, completely forgot about Al Adel who was slowly bleeding to death on the floor behind him.

He was appalled to see the loss of Moscovitch to The Cause and blamed Hassani and Al Adel in equal parts for it.

"Fucking Arabs," he muttered, and spat in Al Adel's direction. "Always fighting and conniving against each other instead of making common cause to defeat the enemy."

That was his last conscious thought as the grenade that the Jordanian had managed to fish out from under his skirt, and arm by pulling the pin out with his teeth, exploded, killing them both and severely wounding Azimov who was still standing on the gangplank.

He later died of his wounds.

CHAPTER 59

After the ambulance had taken Klara Moscovitch's body to the morgue, Lonsdale and Jenkins had driven her heartbroken son to his apartment on *Széchenyi* Street.

Moscovitch was in deep shock.

The US Embassy doctor, Lonsdale's 'old' friend, came by to administer a sedative and Jenkins arranged for a nurse to stay at the apartment overnight.

Lonsdale contacted Morton to report on the events and to obtain the phone number of the scientist's nearest living relative, uncle Joe, his mother's brother.

On the Wednesday following, having retrieved his secret ingredient from the attic, and whatever research notes he could find, Moscovitch flew to Montreal to an uncertain future. In addition to Moscovitch the El Al flight also carried the mortal remains of his mother, Klara.

The same day, Barzan Hassani discretely left Budapest on one of Saddam's private planes.

The Bulgarian ambassador called his consul on the carpet to explain what *his* car was doing on the quay near *Bulldog* when the vessel blew up. The consul informed him that the car had been "borrowed" by *his* chauffeur and another member of the security staff for use in an operation involving illegal human trafficking.

There was nobody to contradict him. The men involved were dead.

Omar's and Moscovitch's fake diplomatic passports took a great deal more explaining because they bore the consul's signature. In his defense, he stated that the 'incident' had been a simple administrative error caused by his over-reliance on the secretarial staff's ability to check on 'facts' in depth.

He added that the dead guards might have duped the women. After all, they *had* been their colleagues, so to speak.

The consul was quietly transferred. He resigned after a decent period, and went to live in Switzerland with a rich aunt. The women were also transferred, but did not resign.

They did not have rich aunts in Switzerland.

Frakkos was in the clear. Moreover, he received a commendation and a five hundred dollar bonus from Colonel Nagy's organization for having assisted the anti terrorism authorities in their search for the *Maria*.

He took the money, added it to the thousand bucks he had made off the Bulgarians and gave the fifteen hundred to Imre's widow.

Lonsdale went home to Adys and told her everything. She said she understood, but things were never the same between them again. Eventually, Adys proposed that they separate, with the understanding that, if he managed to avoid any association with the CIA for a full year, she would be willing to try again, on a trial basis.

Lonsdale's relationship with The Agency was also on shaky grounds.

His masters decided to hold an internal inquiry into the Moscovitch Affair, a disciplinary hearing, just before Christmas.

The Deputy Director of Central Intelligence (DDCI) chaired the hearing assisted by the Director of Plans (DP) and Morton. The CIA's General Counsel was also present in a 'friendly' capacity.

Lonsdale was told that the hearing was an informal affair, held only 'for purposes of edification'. He was not convinced, but did note with relief that nobody was taking notes.

Trying for some levity the DDCI started proceedings by enumerating what he called Lonsdale's 'sins':

Causing the death of two Hungarian policemen and three Hungarian citizens, disobeying a superior officer's direct order, causing the death, through negligence, of a Canadian citizen, dereliction of duty (failure to capture Al Adel and Hassani when the opportunity to do so had presented itself).

It soon became apparent that the only 'charge' the panel considered as being 'serious' was 'disobeying a superior officer's (Morton's) direct order'.

That's what upset Lonsdale the most, his friend Morton turning against him.

He kept his cool, and refused to speak, except for repeating over and over: "As Agent *in situ*, I steadfastly strove to the best of my abilities to make decisions that, in my opinion and under the circumstances, would result in action enabling The Agency to reach its operating objectives in the present case in the shortest possible time."

He was proud of this piece of meaningless bureaucratic doublespeak and kept reading it out loud from a card every time he was asked a question. Because they knew that they would need his very special talents again, and soon, they decided to let him off with a light slap on the wrist.

There would be no reprimand.

Instead, they cancelled his contract retroactively, which meant that Bernard Kane and Philip Johnston ceased to exist and had never existed. It also meant that Lonsdale's firm would be out its fee.

However, at a nod from Morton, the DDCI agreed to approve the expenses incurred during the life of this non-existent operation.

Lonsdale was elated. Having foreseen the outcome of the hearing, he had begun to withdraw cash from the Kane and Johnston credit card accounts at the daily rate of one thousand dollars each.

He was about a hundred thousand dollars ahead of the game when they cancelled the cards.

*   *   *

During the six months following the carnage in front of the MAHART building the Hungarian authorities gradually made public a series of disturbing pieces of information.

These included an admission that an Al Qaida cell had been operating within the State Property Agency and had erected a facility on the SPA's *Dunaújváros* property to manufacture Biological Weapons of Mass Destruction.

The public was likewise told that those responsible had all been killed by valiant elements of the Hungarian Anti-Terrorist Squad during the incident, dubbed by the Press as "Mayhem on the Danube."

The spokesperson for the government confirmed that the facility had been razed after removal of all 'active' chemicals found on the site.

* * *

In Montreal, Moscovitch could find no peace of mind. Everything in the city reminded him of his mother and, wracked by guilt, he slowly became suicidal.

On New Year's Eve he went to a party and got blind drunk. The following day, he woke up in bed next to a stunningly beautiful Italian woman, unable to remember how he had gotten there. She insisted on dragging him off to church in the afternoon, claiming that, after what he had told her the previous night, he was sorely in need of confessing his sins. Too stunned and exhausted—and amused by the idea that she thought he was a Catholic—he played along and went with her to confession.

What started off as a joke in bad taste turned out to be an event that would save his sanity. The priest, a young Jesuit, got him to reflect more positively on his mother's death, his indirect contribution to that death, and his amoral values up to that event then suggested he stop feeling sorry for what could not be changed and, instead, do something constructive to redeem himself.

The next day, without telling anyone, Moscovitch presented himself at the Israeli Consulate, asked for Aliyah (the right to become an Israeli citizen) and was, with his precious samples, on the next El Al plane to Israel.

EPILOGUE

However hard they tried, the Hungarian authorities could never prove that Iran had had a hand in the Moscovitch kidnapping. Though they did have a prime suspect—courtesy of secret information supplied by Jenkins and Lonsdale—they were unable to secure a guilty verdict against Rezzah Khamani, a respected Iranian businessman of long-established standing, who had an absolutely airtight alibi.

In dismissing the case against him, the Examining Magistrate, himself an avid angler, wrote:

> *It is clear from the evidence before me that the Accused is an avid fisherman who, year after year, regularly went in search of the elusive pike perch during the late autumn because he wanted to take advantage of the opportunity to fish until the very last moment before the onset of winter.*
>
> *On October 26, he did not go fishing alone. He was accompanied by an acquaintance who is also known for his passion for fishing, and who is a respected member of the diplomatic community. He is the Head of Security at the Iranian embassy and has what is known as a Service Passport that gives him diplomatic immunity.*
>
> *He testified that he and the Accused had spent the entire time between approximately six pm on Wednesday, October 24,*

and four pm Friday, on October 26, either loading or launching or sailing or unloading and storing Valliant, *the boat of the Accused.*

His testimony was corroborated in part by the river police whose members had observed Valliant *on the water during the above-mentioned period.*

At no time did they see the vessel engage in any form of illegal activity.

Between four pm and five pm the Accused and his friend were seen having tea at the cafeteria of the Forum Hotel. Between five pm and eight pm, according to the sworn testimony of the watchman at the Accused's place of business, they were having a Chinese take-out meal in the upstairs office of the Accused's place of business that they had brought with them.

How, then, could the Accused have committed the shooting at the MAHART building at seven pm which is situated about four kilometers from the Accused's place of business on Galamb *Street?*

The trial and the attendant publicity made of Rezzah Khamani a figure of notoriety, with public opinion sharply divided between his guilt and innocence.

Khamani felt obliged to stay on in Hungary for at least six months after his acquittal because he felt that running away would be seen as an admission of guilt. There was also his 'blown' cover to consider. His Control in Teheran told him that, for the time being, he was finished in Europe as a Qods 'sleeper'. He was ordered to keep a low profile for a while and carry on as if nothing had happened. The general wisdom held that he should not put his business up for sale in preparation of pulling out until the storm blew over.

So he continued to frequent diplomatic receptions, but he did notice that the invitations were becoming less and less frequent and had entirely ceased to come from the embassies and consulates closely tied to the US, the UK and Canada.

Surprisingly, there was a rather pleasant compensating factor for this loss of face. His reputation as a suspected terrorist killer had made him even more attractive to the ladies.

*   *   *

One year to the day, after the Mayhem on the Danube incident, Rezzah Khamani received an intriguing letter from Hans Hofman, an international car dealer operating out of Pfeffikon near Zurich. Hofman explained that his specialty was buying "remainders" from vehicle manufacturers and reselling them to independent car rental agencies on extremely favorable terms.

His bank manager had recently visited Budapest, had leased a car from Khamani's agency and had met Khamani fleetingly at the office.

He had come away with the impression that the dealership may be for sale.

The Iranian remembered the conversation. The man had given him his card; he was the manager of Focobank's branch in Pfeffikon.

Khamani contacted Hofman who said he was thinking of buying an agency in the Balkans because he wanted to take advantage of vertical integration. Acquiring an agency in Hungary would be much cheaper than anything he could buy in Western Europe.

Would Mr. Khamani be interested in talking with him during his trip to Budapest, scheduled for Thursday next?

The Iranian was overjoyed. This was exactly what he needed for an exit, an unsolicited offer to buy his business.

After writing to the bank manager, who gave Hofman an excellent reference, the Iranian agreed to meet the car dealer.

Hofman seemed delighted. He was flying in early, and would be taking a day room at the Forum. Could they meet at eleven, have a leisurely lunch and then go their respective ways? Hofman had another appointment in mid-afternoon and hoped to be able to catch the last Swiss flight to Zurich at eight.

He asked for a favor. He was over eighty and needing crutches to get around. Would it be acceptable to Mr. Khamani for them to have their lunch catered by Room Service in Hofman's day room?

The meal would, of course, be on the Swiss.

The Iranian said yes, by all means.

Hofman turned out to be a bent old man with a bald pate and a bushy white beard. "Have a seat," he told Khamani in the hoarse voice of a senior citizen. "Will you have some coffee or a glass of mineral water?"

Rezzah was embarrassed. A lame old man was about to serve him drinks.

"Perhaps a glass of mineral water, but I'll get it myself."

"Good. There is a bottle there already open." Hofman, who seemed to speak English quite well, but with a horrible German accent, hobbled over to an armchair and sat down with difficulty. He laid his crutches down beside him.

"Come over here and sit on the sofa," he said to his guest and picked up his glass. "It's Evian, you know. Much better for the liver and the kidneys than coffee." He raised his glass. "Prosit," he called out and, slurping, gulped his drink down noisily.

Khamani did likewise.

Hofman put down his glass, looked at his watch and turned to the Iranian. "I see we have plenty of time. You know," he remarked conversationally, "that it is amazing how small the world is. We have two friends in common, not just one."

"Oh?" Khamani was puzzled.

"Well, there is my bank manager, you know, the fellow from Foco Bank . . ."

"And who else?"

"There is another fellow," the old man was watching his guest intently, ". . . a Canadian . . ."

"I know many Canadians." Khamani was beginning to sweat and his stomach was feeling squeaky. "What's his name and where is he from?"

"He tells people he is from Montreal and that his name is Kane." The Iranian let out a discrete groan. He was experiencing intense stomach cramps and needed to go to the bathroom badly.

Hofman didn't seem to notice. "But he lives in Washington really, and his name is not Kane."

Khamani was doubled up with pain. "His real name is Lonsdale." The old man bent over the dying Iranian. "He works for The Agency at Langley and he will never forgive you for having participated in the murder of Klara Moscovitch."

"It was an accident." The Qods officer whispered. "Ahmad was shooting at Lonsdale. He aimed too low." He was barely able to focus. "Who are you anyway?"

The old man straightened out and stepped away. He no longer looked old or crippled. "My name is Robert Lonsdale."

"Kane!" the Qods officer groaned and keeled over dead.

Lonsdale dragged his body into the bathroom, dumped it into the tub and drew the curtain.

He shortened his false beard substantially with scissors and trimmed it with an electric shaver. Next, he used a creamy gel to dye it a chestnut color. He fished a matching wig out of his satchel and put it on.

He took the crutches apart and stashed them in his satchel.

After putting on gloves, he used a fine chamois cloth to wipe the cups, bottles and glasses and every surface he remembered touching. He repeated the procedure again, being even more thorough and careful the second time around.

By the time he finished it was close to three o'clock.

He opened the door and peeked out. When the coast was clear, he affixed the Do Not Disturb sign on the handle and, with satchel slung over the shoulder, walked away.

He estimated that the body would not be discovered much before six-thirty because he had rented the room for a day and a half,

Of course, he had paid with cash.

He had about four hours to cross over to Austria by car . . . and the rest of his life to find and kill his next target, the man who had fired the shot that had killed Klara: Ahmad Bumedinejad.

CPSIA information can be obtained at www.ICGtesting.com
Printed in the USA
LVOW060017050612

284621LV00002B/1/P

9 781468 549133